I0650719

THE CRIMINAL WORLD

OF SHERLOCK HOLMES

By Kelvin I. Jones

VOLUME THREE

Crime Investigation in Late Victorian Britain; of the Immortal Sherlock Holmes; of His real-[ife and Literary Origins; about His Scientific Methods; and of Why His Creator, Arthur Conan Doyle, Kept Secret His Knowledge of the True Identity of Jack The Ripper.

MX BOOKS

First edition published in 2022
© Copyright 2022 Kelvin Jones

The right of Kelvin Jones to be identified as the author of this work has been asserted by him in accordance with the Copyright, Designs and Patents Act 1998.

All rights reserved. No reproduction, copy or transmission of this publication may be made without express prior written permission. No paragraph of this publication may be reproduced, copied or transmitted except with express prior written permission or in accordance with the provisions of the Copyright Act 1956 (as amended). Any person who commits any unauthorised act in relation to this publication may be liable to criminal prosecution and civil claims for damage.

All characters appearing in this work are fictitious. Any resemblance to real persons, living or dead, is purely coincidental. The opinions expressed herein are those of the author and not of MX Publishing.

Hard cover ISBN 978-1-78705-872-9
Paperback ISBN 978-1-78705-873-6
e Pub ISBN 978-1-78705-874-3
PDF ISBN 978-1-78705-875-0

Published by MX Publishing
335 Princess Park Manor, Royal Drive, London, N11 3GX www.mxpublishing.co.uk

Cover design by Brian Belanger

ACKNOWLEDGEMENTS
My thanks, as always, to all those good, kind and resourceful folk, both among my friends here on the UK but also in Canada and America, who helped me in my search among the forgotten corners of Victorian murder, crime and mayhem and have thus, I hope, as a result of this series, advanced our knowledge of the subterranean roots of that remarkable literary innovator, Sir Arthur Conan Doyle.

NOTE by the author

Many followers of the chronicles of Sherlock Holmes believe that Edgar Allan Poe was not only the originator of the fantasy and supernatural horror story - a fact acknowledged by the 'King of Horror,' Steven King - but that he also created and defined the modern crime story. Define? Maybe, but not invent.

Poe was certainly highly inventive and set the benchmark high for future writers of the crime genre, but none of his successors have quite achieved the apparent fluidity of style that Conan Doyle mastered in those 56 short stories and four novels; nor does Poe possess Conan Doyle's facility with dialogue. Doyle was THE master of the form of the detective story. His characters are entirely credible; his stories are nearly all highly convincing, and they carry within them the disturbing darkness and characters of the Gothic genre. The darkness of each crime solved is dispelled by the ratiocination of Holmes, who is a less imposing and far less loquacious form of Poe's Dupin, but a detective who frequently shares his *fin de siecle* despair regarding the world of crime and criminals. And Conan Doyle was no dilettante when it came to the reinvention of the ideas he purloined from Poe. He had studied both the previous forms of the genre and - this was perhaps the most significant fact of all - he had accumulated a vast library of works relating to crime and criminology. Conan Doyle had learned much about the psychology and modus operandi of the dark and often brutal Victorian world of crime. He had a degree in medicine. He knew what a profile of a killer would be like; he had studied the methods of master poisoners like Palmer and Pritchard; and the burgling antics of Charlie Peace; and in his stories he would put all this data to good use. He was about to conquer the world with his fictional detective. And the name of that detective was Mr. Sherlock Holmes.

- Kelvin I. Jones.

Fig 2. Arthur Conan Doyle, who took the genre of crime to an
unparalleled level of literary sophistication, with his creation of
the world's best known and most successful fictional detective
of all generations: - Sherlock Holmes.

Fig. 3. Edgar Allan Poe, the American literary genius who, with his 'ratiocinative' detective, Frenchman Auguste Dupin, set the scene for the appearance of literature's most famous detective - Mr Sherlock Holmes.

THE CRIMINAL WORLD OF SHERLOCK HOLMES: CONTENTS OF VOLUME THREE

PREFACE by Dr Alan Kent.

As a youngster I remember being told to read Arthur Conan Doyle by Mr James, my pipe-smoking English teacher - a man who resembled Sherlock Holmes, and, my goodness, how right he was. For a couple of years, I indulged myself in many of Doyle's core works. Inadvertently, it was his skill as a novelist that encouraged me to pursue a career in Literature. Holmes' world was mad, bad and dangerous – and I loved it. Years later, on a family holiday to London, my father took me to fictional 221B Baker Street, and there showed me Holmes' house. Even now, when I am in that area of London, I think of that moment, and the criminal world of all his stories and novels. I was next to encounter Doyle (and Holmes) in my study 'Pulp Methodism' (2002), regarding the work of Silas Kitto Hocking (1850-1935). Hocking met Doyle on the famous Findelan Glacier in the Aps, when Doyle explained to him that he had grown tired of his creation. Hocking told Doyle that this was rather a sad thing to feel about an 'old friend' but Doyle said he was determined to 'put an end to him somehow'. Hocking considered his comment and then said, 'why not drop him down a crevasse?' – and this was precisely what Doyle did, causing Holmes to disappear over the Rechenbach Falls. As Holmes fans know, this was not the end of their hero. Indeed, a few months later, he was to return in 1902's 'The Hound of the Baskervilles'. Whenever I think of Sherlock Holmes now, I always think of the conversation these two writers had over the fate of the 'Great Detective'. It is to the crimes and criminal investigations of Holmes to which this guide is devoted. It is a fine work and I can think of a better scholar to lead us through the texts than Kelvin I. Jones. An expert on both Doyle and Holmes, Jones offers the reader a comprehensive guide to all the criminal investigations completed by the Great Detective; much of which fascinated me as a child.. Jones is meticulous and erudite in his observations, noting much that other observers fail to comment on, and realising the complexity and intrigue created by Doyle. For the Holmes fanatic, like Volumes 1 and 2 in the series, this will provide many hours of happy reading.

'DOWN AT THE YARD'

By 1881 Holmes had established a rapport with the official detective force. Although Gregson and Lestrade wouldn't admit it, they frequently had recourse to call on his expertise for, as we've seen, Holmes had made a name for himself in Europe and America. Indeed, prior to events detailed in 'A Study in Scarlet', he had been of assistance to Lestrade in an important forgery case.

In the Lauriston Gardens murder inquiry this reputation paid him dividends. The crime in question was brought to Holmes' attention by Tobias Gregson whom he described as "the smartest of the Scotland Yarders."

A young American, Enoch Drebber, had been found in a deserted house off the Brixton Road at 2 a.m. on Friday, 4th March 1881. Gregson and Lestrade, the investigating officers, were unable to establish the cause or motive for the man's murder and therefore sent for Holmes to solicit his opinion about the case.

Holmes, accompanied by a sceptical Watson, proceeded to Lauriston Gardens, where a thorough examination was made of the grounds, the house and the body of the mysterious stranger. Several deductions were arrived at, much to the astonishment of the good doctor: that the murderer was tall and red-faced; that he also was an American, a stranger in London, who had been working as a cabdriver.

Knowing that the murderer could probably change his name and quit the country, Holmes acted quickly, using his own personal contacts to aid him. At 1 p.m. he sent an international telegram to the Superintendent of Police for the City of Cleveland - a man called Jacob W. Schmitt - asking about the events connected to Drebber's marriage. Seven hours later he had the information he required. Back came a telegram stating that Drebber had formerly asked for protection from an old rival known as Jefferson Hope, "at present in Europe." By the following day the murderer was in the hands of the police and the case concluded. The evidence provided by Schmitt was certainly vital for, if it had not been forthcoming, Holmes' reputation would never have received the filip it justly deserved. In a city the size of London, and with the limited data at his disposal, what chance of success would he have had? At the conclusion of the case, Watson advises Holmes, "Your merits should be publicly recognized. You should publish an account of the case." However, Holmes is less enthusiastic. After all, to him the Lauriston Gardens murder and its solution proved to be a simple matter of communicating through the right channels with police in the USA..

Later, other cases were to bring him the challenges which made his career so memorable.

Regarding the criminal investigation department of the Yard, we should bear in mind that the CID, like Special Branch, had no jurisdiction that was above or beyond that of the Met. Police.

But on certain occasions, it would be asked by the Chief Constable of certain forces throughout Britain to intervene if that could facilitate the solving of crime. At that time, they were able to use the resources of the department for their own investigations.

They did so in a total of five cases, which formed the basis for the Sherlock Holmes stories. Those were 'The Blanched Soldier,' 'The Dancing Men,' 'The Valley of Fear.' The case of Silver Blaze, the racehorse, and also, for the Nihilist story, which is entitled, 'The Golden Pince-nez,' (see later in this volume).

Fig,4. 'A Study in Scarlet,' the first Holmes story, in which the detective, solves the murder with methods which bewilder the astonished Scotland Yarders, yet which by today's standards of forensic investigation, would seem to be 'elementary.' Author's copy of unusual copy of STUD, c. 1950.

According to the Metropolitan Act of 1839, county police forces could hire official police detectives from other areas In order to deal with private purposes. And so, Inspector Lestrade is asked by the friends of Mr James McCarthy, to investigate his murder. And it seems likely that Sherlock Holmes was also employed by the Devonshire police in a private capacity for his work on the death of Sir Charles Baskerville, in 'The Hound of the Baskervilles'.

In 1968, the Met police moved into their present modern building at 10 The Broadway, London SW, what was known by them before, as the 'Black Museum', which Conan Doyle visited several times as a prolific crime writer. The Museum, thus described because of the often grim, bloody and dark nature of many of its artefacts, to this day stil houses a unique collection of documents, photographs, and exhibits.

These cover a wide range of subjects, including housebreaking tools which once belonged to Charlie Peace, items relating to some of the notorious Victorian railway murders, and the great London train robbery. There are sections dealing with abortions, Burke and Hare, whose grim story we now know from his letters, once fired the vivid imagination of young Doyle when his uncle took him also to Madame Tussauds, and there are also sections on offensive weapons, espionage, and forgeries. In particular, there's a section which deals with district displays concerning particular crimes. There are things like a loving cup, made from a human skull, and the death masks of famous criminals.

Several of the skulls that belonged to persons executed, are even now on display. Their history was written about by several 19th Century criminologists like 5y3 prolific friend of Doyle, Major Arthur Griffiths who described the lives and bizarre careers of some of these outlandish individuals, especially the 'celebrity' poisoners mentioned elsewhere in volume one of this edition. There are some highly grotesque artefacts for those who feel, in Shakespeare's words, they have not yet 'supped too full of horrors,' including a murderer's severed arms, kept in a tank of formaldehyde, a skeleton and a pickled brain, plus a number of instruments of death and torture.

The Black Museum contains well over a hundred exhibits relating to over 150 years of police history. And many of the artefacts' extensive collections relating to several of the murders and murderers already described in these pages is now on open access to members of the public, although some of it is restricted to that of previous inquirers only, since, as one would anticipate, the nature of the material is somewhat disturbing; as for example, in the exhibits relating to some of the Victorian Ripper crimes.

There is, in addition to this, a mass of other material, comprising police reports, fake documentary and official reports regarding cases of espionage, most of which is kept in climate controlled cupboards, under lock and key, partly because space is limited, but also again, because of the gruesome manner of the items, e.g., police photographs of mutilated murder victims too disturbing to be shown to persons of a sensitive disposition.

Shortly before departing for the Brixton Road, Holmes remarks to Watson that 'Gregson is the smartest of the Scotland Yarders... he and Lestrade are the pick of a bad lot.' STUD.

Holmes' remarks are telling. The police had never been popular with the general public and were frequently satirised in the pages of Punch. Only four years before when Holmes investigated the Brixton Road murder, London had been shocked by the trial of a team of Scotland Yard detectives.

The Yard's first commissioner, Sir Edmund Henderson, had been allowed to increase the Detective Department of the Metropolitan Police to 207.

180 of these men - and some of the detectives chosen to form this elite company were also of European extraction, and of wide and varied background and experience - were to be plain clothes policemen and the other 27 were to work from headquarters.

Gregson and Lestrade, who often collaborated with Sherlock Holmes, came from that small elite whose record of honesty and experience had been sullied by this scandal. The expose came after the trials at the Old Bailey of a gang of swindlers. Harry Benson and Frederick Kurt. These senior detectives, both men of mature years and experience, had been charged with falsely conspiring to obtain an enormous sum of £10,000 from a wealthy French woman, Madame de Goncourt. The trick was to obtain bets from France by posing as an English gentleman who had inside knowledge on the favourites in certain races.

Fig. 5 (above): This remarkable drawing from Arthur Griffiths' 'Mysteries of Police and Crime.' shows police in 1836, trying to quell a political riot in 1836. By the time Holmes began active service in the 1880's, such scenes of disorder were still frequent, but not before on this scale.

When the cheques arrived, they were quickly cashed and the customers of 'Mr. Montgomery', the English gentleman, heard no more. Through the efforts of Inspector Williamson, Benson and Kurt were arrested. The scandal erupted when other members of the gang began to make statements about leading Scotland Yard detectives who were working as accomplices in the operation. Four of these men, Chief Inspectors Druscovitch (a Pole), Palmer, Clarke and Meiklejohn were arrested and charged. Only Clarke was found not guilty at the conclusion of the three weeks' trial. The others were sentenced to two year's hard labour. A report of the Home Office Committee suggested an overhaul of the Detective Department and under Howard Vincent, an enterprising barrister, sweeping reforms were commenced along the lines of the French Surete. The Department was centralised along with its records and thereafter was known as the CID (Criminal Investigation Department). It is not difficult, therefore, to see why Holmes had such little time for the 'Scotland Yarders,' as he called them. Nevertheless, later in his career, his attitude softened towards them. In 3GAB, for example, he remarks that they 'lead the world for thoroughness and method.' At the time of STUD, the official police force had made a few advances and had acknowledged some of the techniques offered by the forensic scientist. However, the bulk of the work pursued by the CID was based heavily on a body of informers who provided inside information on the movements of the underworld.

Fig. 6. The trial of the Scotland Yard detectives. Gregson and Lestrade were most certainly among the 'newer breed' of Scotland Yard detectives

This had existed long before the formation of Peel's New Police. The Bow Street Runners, for instance, had a considerable liaison network with their 'squealers' and one of Peel's reasons for reforming the system was their excessive reliance on this system and the acceptance of bribes. The Met. Police, conservative in their approach, and subject to a rigid hierarchy, were reluctant to adopt new methods unless they had been rigorously proven. Indeed, their inability to solve the Ripper murder has often been put down to this fact. (All but one of the Ripper's victims was removed from the scene of the crime, the bodies washed, and vital clues thus destroyed.) The field was therefore left wide open. But the consulting detective was indeed a rarity. There were of course agencies like the one in Wych Street (now the Aldwych), but their function was limited to matters of civil or domestic dispute. Most private investigators did not have the range or variety of work encountered by Holmes and many of them were employed on what could be politely termed the 'legal borderlands.'

Although Holmes was not always so trusting when he encountered members of the CID, nevertheless, he worked with them in the following stories:

'The Blue Carbuncle', 'The Illustrious Client', 'The Resident Patient'. Then there was also his involvement with detectives in 'The Three Garridebs,' 'The Beryl Coronet,' 'The Bruce - Partington Plans,' 'The Mazarin Stone,' and 'The Naval Treaty.' He is also described as liaising with them in the following stories; 'The Red Headed League', 'The Engineer's Thumb', 'The Empty House', 'The Man with the Twisted Lip', 'The Six Napoleons,' and 'The Noble Bachelor'.

Finally, we have the great detective working with the members of the CID in: 'Lady Frances Carfax', 'The Greek Interpreter', 'The Final Problem', 'The Cardboard Box,' 'Charles Augustus Milverton,' (though strictly speaking, it might be accurately claimed, that in this case, they were, legally speaking, in contempt of the law, since both withheld from police vital eye witness evidence pertaining to a murder); 'The Dying Detective', The Norwood Builder,' 'The Retired Colourman', 'The Second Stain,' 'Shoscombe Old Place,' 'The Sign of Four,' and, lastly, 'A Study in Scarlet'.

Fig.7.. The 'Case of the Yard Detectives on Trial'. A celebrity trial case which brought about necessary reform. From Arthur Griffiths' 'Mysteries of Police and Crime', Vol. 1.

Fig.8. 'At Her Majesty's Pleasure.' The two detectives did hard labour for two years each for their cri: left, Insp. Meiklejohn, and right, Chief Inspector Druskovitch, both senior detectives who worked at Scotland Yard.

Fig. 9. 'New' Scotland Yard, as it appeared in the 1880's to Sherlock Holmes, and where he would have met the likes of Athelney Jones and the redoubtable Lestrade. There were to be subsequent 'new' Scotland Yards, but this surely was the finest of them, architecturally speaking. From Griffiths' 'Mysteries of Police and Crime'.

SHERLOCK HOLMES, CESARE LOMBROSO AND THE BIZARRE THEORY OF ATAVISM

Some Sherlockians still sometimes challenge me and ask me: 'How on earth can you sit and read such twaddle as is contained in Conan Doyle's largely forgotten spiritualist writings like his 'Thew New Revelation' and 'The Case For Spirit Photography,' or even more fanciful book, 'The Coming of The Fairies'? Conan Doyle wrote about spooks he'd thought to have seen; and then claimed all that rubbish about his wife getting in touch with dead folk they'd known a long way back through seances. So where are they now, these relatives, and if there is an afterlife, why doesn't Conan Doyle come back from the otherworld to tell us about it? How could the man who created such a rational genius as Sherlock Holmes ever have convinced himself of all that tosh? It's a complete mystery to me. Well, what's your opinion?'

That led me to thinking about the criminologist, Cesare Lombroso. He, like Conan Doyle, took an interest not only in real life crime but also, like Doyle, showed a deep and abiding interest in Spiritualism.

What exactly was it about this world of ectoplasm, table lifting and table rapping that seemed to attract so many eminent scientists like Oliver Lodge, the renowned physicist, along with Geley, the French scientist rationalist, Richet, and Conan Doyle himself, to their midst and who, just like Conan Doyle, spent many hours and days investigating phenomena, produced by famous mediums, many of whom, like the Italian Eusapia Palladino, were accused, time and again, of downright deception and cheating? Doyle, like these other men, always claimed to be sceptical when it came to 'phenomena,' but was that really the case?

CESARE LOMBROSO AND THE AFTER LIFE

Recently, whilst I was drifting through the labyrinth of the criminology collection of the free library of the website, *www.internet-archive.com*, I came across a biography of the nowadays often derided, Italian criminologist, Cesare Lombroso.

Written in 1911 and originally published in a German edition, this book impressed me by the simplicity of its style and the fairness of its treatment of the great, but some modern criminologists regard as misguided, Italian criminologist.

In fact Lombroso was no less given to generalisations regarding the psychological mind - state and motives for crime, than his now more widely regarded American equivalent, Havelock Ellis, and was certainly the more controversial as a writer. But it was not what the biographer, Hans Kurella, said about Lombroso in his book 'Cesare Lombroso, A Modern Man of Science,' that struck me as important, about his approach to what he described as 'positivist criminology' that amazed me.

Lombroso wrote this:

'To the true criminal, the pangs of conscience are entirely unknown, and a brutish indifference to death is a most frequent manifestation. This is shown very clearly in the turns of phrase met with in the jargon of criminals in relation to the punishment of execution. One of the most sensational trials in recent days — the trial of Heinze and of the prostitute with whom he lived — served to acquaint the general public with the phrase "cut the cabbage" for decapitation. The expression "to sneeze in the sack" corresponds to this (the guillotined head, when severed by the filing knife, is received in a sack); and there are others.'

Fig.10. (above). Cesare Lombroso. Lombroso was a famous Italian criminologist phrenologist, physician, spiritualist, and his theory of 'atavism' was favoured by Sherlock Holmes.. (From www.wikki.domain).

Lombroso gives numerous examples of a perfect equanimity persisting in murderers up to the very moment of death.

One of his reports (*Archivio di psichiatria*, 1891, Section 4) tells us of a murderer who, whilst awaiting his execution, drew caricatures of the spectators. Allied to this indifference, appears to be the puzzling impulse of professional murderers before the commission of a crime, to speak openly of their plans, and even to describe the actual details of the proposed murder. He provides another example:

'Troppmann, although he lied in court during the trial, while confined in his cell, made drawings of the way in which he had committed the murder, as merely negative qualities — due to deficiency in the development of sensibility. Among positive qualities, a characteristic one is the fatuous vanity of many habitual criminals. It is a phenomenon of world- wide familiarity that that which in the life of a human being was at first a means merely, ultimately becomes an independent end — indeed, the sole aim.

'This, (Lombroso goes on to say) 'we find also in the career of the criminal, to whom crime becomes a field for vain display. The art of pocket-picking, of housebreaking, of poisoning, ultimately becomes one pursued for its own sake. 'Some have thought this almost demoniacal; but there is nothing very singular in the practice of an acquired facility from the pure pleasure of its clever performance — art for art's sake. Moreover, we see the same thing also in criminals who secretly destroy property or secretly commit arson. Here the art of remaining undiscovered is cultivated for its own sake.'

Like much of his important work, the finest of all being (surely Holmes would have agreed), his magnum opus and great gift to the criminology of the 19th century, 'L'Uomo Delinquente', Lombroso often contributed many original insights.

When looking at the statistics regarding crime in his own native Italy and indeed, those of many other countries he found certain patterns of behaviour. The modern, often 'safe' view, about this prolific author and his atavism theory is that it was nothing other than one man's theorising and a theory plainly racist in an age of imperialism and most condescending towards members of the non-Aryan, or white Anglo Saxon races.

This is reflected in a recent 'History Extra' internet blog, where the author (admittedly) quotes from an unnamed source: (This is taken from an article written for the 'BBC History Extra' programme in 2019, by Becky Little.)

Fig. 11. A portrait of a typical Italian criminal, according to Cesare Lombroso, from his magnum opus on crime and its causes, the controversial, *L'Uomo Delinquente*.

"Thus were explained anatomically the enormous jaws, high cheek bones, prominent superciliary arches, solitary lines in the palms, extreme size of the orbits, handle shaped or sessile ears found in criminals, savages and apes, insensibility to pain, extremely acute sight; tattooing, excessive idleness, love of orgies and the irresistible craving for evil for its own sake, the desire not only to extinguish life in the victim, but to mutilate the corpse, tear its flesh, and drink its blood."

However, this rather dismissive view of Lombroso's central claim seems to me something of generalisation and an interpretation based not on facts but rather, interpretation.

Lombroso was culpable of making generalisations without always backing statements with evidence. Nevertheless, his reputation for assuming the truth of atavism to be undeniable and thus never showing that he might have modified his theory or look at other possible explanations for the similarities in skeletal structures between criminals, was only properly questioned after Lombroso's death.

To be completely fair about Lombroso, it must be admitted that the black and white stereotypes of the colonial, middle class racist is not altogether true, in empirical terms.

Yet it *is* true that his conclusions often appeared to be based on evidence that was selective. It is also significant that, over the years that followed his initial discovery about the link between skull deformation and certain classes of criminals, he began to admit that other factors could also lead to the creation of the criminal mind and behaviour. As his daughter observed in her popular reissue of the most famous of her father's works in 1911,

'Subsequent research on the part of my father and his disciples showed that other factors besides atavism come into play in determining the criminal type. These are: disease and environment. Later on, the study of innumerable offenders led them to the conclusion that all law-breakers cannot be classed in a single species, for their ranks include very diversified types, who differ not only in their bent towards a particular form of crime, but also in the degree of tenacity and intensity displayed by them in their perverse propensities, so that, in reality, they form a graduated scale leading from the born criminal to the normal individual.'

Indeed, I have a strong suspicion that his rather rapid slide down from one who, in Holmes' era, was regarded as an undeniable authority in the world of Victorian criminology, may have had something to do with his later fascination with, and attempts to prove, the veracity of, an Italian medium, Eusapia Palladino (with whom, among members of the Society For Psychical Research, he also sat, observing and notated the psycho-kinetic behaviour of this extraordinary woman).

He even wrote a popular book on the truth, or otherwise, of mediums, and Spiritualism in general.

It comes as no surprise, therefore, that Conan Doyle had much time for the man, and equally, that his name would be explicitly referenced in the Holmes stories.

Lombroso believed in categorising. He truly believed that from the shape of a person's skull one could determine, without question, if a person might exhibit criminal tendencies.

In his introduction to the edition of the criminologist's famous but highly controversial work 'The Female Offender,.' Douglas Morrison, who was then the governor of Wandsworth prison, wrote this:

'The criminal population exhibits a considerable percentage of anomalies connected with the limbs such as excessive development of the legs; we have also sexual peculiarities such as feminism in men and masculism in women, and infantilism in both.

'Where a considerable number of deep-seated physical anomalies are found in combination in the same individual, we usually see they are accompanied by nervous and mental anomalies of a morbid character. These mental anomalies are visible among the criminal population in an absence of moral sensibility in excessive irritability, and a love of revenge; and a descent to customs and pleasures akin in their nature, to the orgies of uncivilised tribes'.

Morrison, a fervent promoter of Lombroso's theories about criminals, then goes on to comment:

'The criminal population is composed of many types... of casual offenders... juvenile offenders... of insane, weak-minded and epileptic offenders... of habitual drunkards, beggars, and finally, there is a distinct class consisting of habitual offenders against property...'

Lombroso was fascinated by this Italian medium, Eusapia Palladino, an Italian peasant woman, who the Society of Psychical Research, often very objective in its treatment of mediums, regarded with suspicion and who Conan Doyle admitted in a letter to his scientist friend, Oliver Lodge, quite often cheated. However, what I intriguing is that Lombroso claimed that this fiery and irascible medium conformed to the type of female criminal who was often the subject of his investigations of female offenders.

She was scarcely literate, having come from an impoverished peasant background. She was also possibly epileptic, often fiery; and she frequently exhibited fraudulent behaviour to the men of science who sat with her.

One commentator said she was capricious and choleric; at one moment she would be on her knees crying, then would fly at her adversaries and beat them. In the next moment she would be laughing or behaving violently to those who sat with her in many of her seances.

Rather like Sherlock Holmes, the rationalist Cesare Lombroso found he was intrigued by her outbursts of swearing and sometimes lewd and irregular behaviour in front of her all male observers and was highly aware of her blatant sexuality. But also, rather like Sherlock Holmes, when it came to the subject of women, he clearly could not comprehend them, regarding them as

17

an entirely different species. And thus, it comes as no surprise to find that his book about female criminals, entitled 'The Female Offender,' which he regarded highly, because of its reliance on a multitude of statistical evidence collected and analysed by himself and colleagues, was in reality a failed attempt to elucidate female behaviour and often was based on nothing more than a series of assumptions and his own misogynistic prejudice.

LOMBROSO'S FASCINATION WITH THE HUMAN EAR.

Lombroso, like so many Victorians, was completely fascinated by the human ear and had made a rigorous study of the subject; therefore it needn't surprise us in the last when we discover that he ranked the ability of the interpretation and examination of a criminal's ears as of the most useful practices which police might find invaluable.

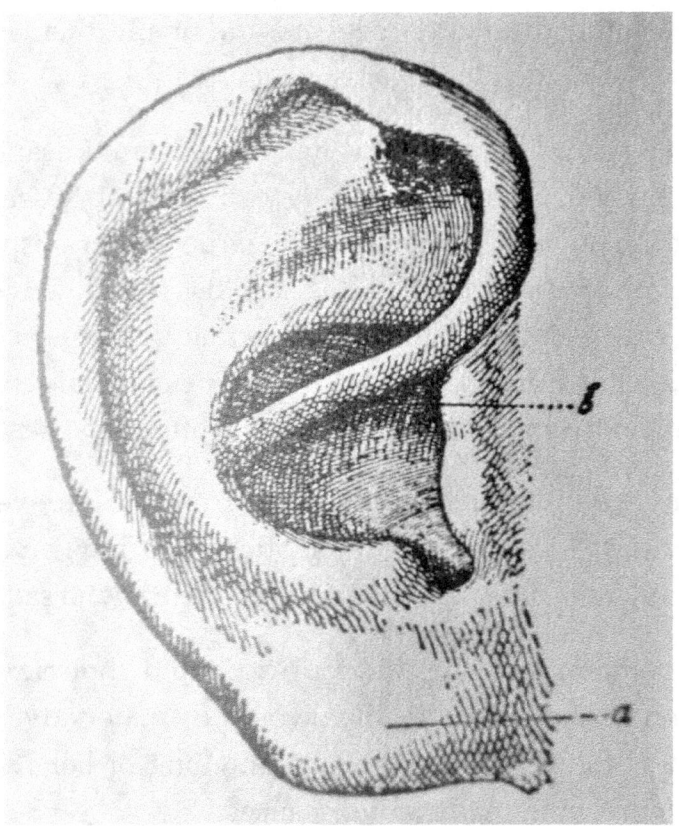

Fig. 12. Lombroso was fascinated by the human ear.

According to Lombroso, 'The external ear is often of large size; occasionally also it is smaller than the ears of normal individuals. Twenty-eight per cent. of criminals have handle-shaped ears standing out from the face as in the chimpanzee: in other cases they are placed at different levels. Frequently too, we find misshapen, flattened ears, devoid of helix, tragus, and anti-tragus, and with a protuberance on the upper part of the posterior margin (Darwin's tubercle), a relic of the pointed ear characteristic of apes. Anomalies are also found in the lobe, which in some cases adheres too closely to the face, or is of huge size as in the ancient Egyptians; in other cases, the lobe is entirely absent, or is atrophied till the ear assumes a form like that common to apes'.

Lombroso's theory that proposed that criminals could not only be recognised, meaured and tested for physiological aspects which would lead to criminal behaviour, was couched in the most extraordinarily abusive and sometimes, racist terminology and observation. Here, for example, is what he had to say about the physiognomy of criminals.:

"In general thieves are notable for their expressive faces and manual dexterity, small wandering eyes, that are often oblique in form, thick and close eyebrows, distorted or squashed noses, thin beards and hair, and sloping foreheads.' he wrote in Criminal Man. 'Like rapists, they often have jug ears, but rapists, however,' he goes on, 'nearly always have sparkling eyes, delicate features, and swollen lips, and indeed most of them are frail, and some hunchbacks.'

Lombroso was highly regarded in his time and often gave advice in criminal cases to Magistrates. In a case where a man sexually assaulted and infected a young girl with syphilis he said that he could single out the unknown perpetrator by simply looking at their appearance in the identification line. He says, 'I picked out immediately one of them who had obscene tattoos on his arm, physiognomy and irregularities and traces of a recent attack of sickness. This is from his book 'Crime it's Causes and Remedies.' Interestingly, however, an entirely different criminal confessed to this crime.

Although Lombroso was greatly influential among intellectuals of his day where his theories were seen as a form of social Darwinism and a development of Darwin's theory of evolution, not all writers and thinkers were happy with his approach. Tolstoy did not believe he was right about criminal types. But his theories were highly popular in the public consciousness. For example, the movie maker Fritz Lang made a film entitled 'M.' about a child sex abuser, who is seen roaming the streets of Berlin. 'My idea was to create the classic description of a Murderer who has big shoulders,' he explained. The resultant portayal of the central character is an individual who is a cruel caricature of the Lombroso criminal type: fleshy, twisted, beetle-browed, dark-jowled, even, it may be said, pig-like. And the idea of the criminal type, it has to be admitted, I also believe, may have even encouraged the Nazi ideology of discrimination among types of people and races later in the 20th Century.

In many ways more empirically conservative in his approach to the examination and collation of evidence was Lombroso's French equivalent, Alphonse Bertillon , who was singled out for praise by Dr Mortimer in 'The Hound of the Baskervilles,' and who enjoyed for many years the respect he rightly deserved by his own and other countries' police investigation teams.

Bertillon's unique method, included creating more than 5 million files and 80000 photographs. The it must have se emed to him an interminable task. He frequently suffer from swollen joints. But when completed, he truly believed that it was more or less impossible for any two people to share exactly the same proportions when it came to the business of creating and then matching body measurements. Using a tape measure, you collected the data you needed from prisoners; and, in his estimation, if 11 unique measurements were recorded for each person, the chances were that people sharing the same measurements would be more than 4 million to one. However, history has proved that he was wrong. The only truly reliable method of unique identification depended on fingerprinting, and only in the mid 20th century was this then superseded by the forensic DNA tests, backed up by the additional resource of fingerprints.

Despite his system coming under attack, what is unique about this French criminologist Bertillon, is that he almost single handed pioneered the investigation and recording of scenes of crimes during an early period, when, by comparison, British police authorities who examined scenes of crime for example in the Ripper case, photographic experts took photographs as evidence of those scenes which some while later was actually destroyed. British detectives had not even considered the usefulness of this method of collation and cross referencing which was perfected by this French investigator. He also developed the mugshot format which is still used today throughout Europe and America.

In the archives of the Paris Prefecture, which is the equivalent of Scotland Yard, scenes of crime photographs were assembled, probably by a private investigator who worked there. In 1903, the private investigators, who put together this remarkable archive of often gruesome and disturbing images, provide us with a very unsettling aspect of violent crime which even then had a profound impact on French Society. (The collection they assembled is available online for those wishing to examine it but cannot be downloaded for copyright reasons.).

EXTRACT FROM 'CRIMINAL MAN,' By Cesare Lombroso's daughter.

('THE DISCOVERY' OF LOMBROSO'S THEORY OF ATAVISM.)

'If we examine a number of criminals, we shall find that they exhibit numerous anomalies in the face, skeleton, and various psychic and sensitive functions, so that they strongly resemble primitive races. It was these anomalies that first drew my father's attention to the close relationship between the criminal and the savage and made him suspect that criminal tendencies are of atavistic origin.

'When a young doctor at the Asylum in Pavia, was requested to make a post-mortem examination on a criminal named Vilella, an Italian Jack the Ripper, who by atrocious crimes had spread terror in the Province of Lombardy, scarcely had he laid open the skull, when he perceived at the base, on the spot where the internal occipital crest or ridge is found in normal individuals, a small hollow, which he called median occipital fossa.

'This abnormal character was correlated to a still greater anomaly in the cerebellum, the hypertrophy of the *vermis*, i.e., the spinal cord which separates the cerebellar lobes lying underneath the cerebral hemispheres. This *vermis* was so enlarged in the case of Vilella, that it almost formed a small, intermediate cerebellum like that found in the lower types of apes, rodents, and birds. This anomaly is very rare among inferior races, with the exception of the South American Indian tribe of the Aymaras of Bolivia and Peru, in whom it is not infrequently found (40%). It is seldom met with in the insane or other degenerates, but later investigations have shown it to be prevalent in criminals.

'This discovery was like a flash of light. "At the sight of that skull," says my father, "I seemed to see all at once, standing out clearly illumined as in a vast plain under a flaming sky, the problem of the nature of the criminal, who reproduces in civilised times characteristics, not only of primitive savages, but of still lower types as far back as the carnivora."'

Readers of the Holmes saga, and especially those fans of 'The Hound of the Baskervilles,' will I'm sure recall the fascination expressed by Dr Mortimer as he quite clearly covets Sherlock Holmes' skull, noting that he had not "expected so dolichocephalic a skull or such well-marked supra-orbital development. Would you have any objection to my running my finger along your parietal fissure? A cast of your skull, sir, until the original is available, would be an ornament to any anthropological museum".

This apparently casual remark by Mortimer, but more importantly, Holmes' reply of endorsement to him, surely marks yet another fascinating link between the detective and the Italian criminologist.

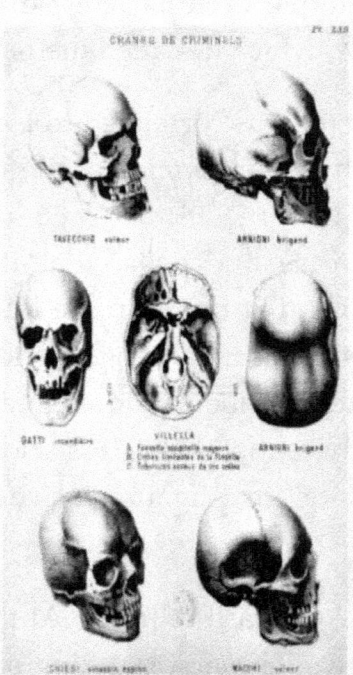

"The Skulls of Malefactors"
by Doctor Léon Ardouin

ANTHROPOLOGY SOCIETY OF PARIS
Meetings of April 17, 1879 and July 17, 1879 respectively

Robert K. Stevenson – Translator and Editor

The skulls of criminals frequently display pathological lesions, a weakly-developed frontal region, and other anomalies, all of which leads one to conclude that a criminal is *born*, not made.

Fig. 12. Lombroso and Dr Mortimer were not alone in believing that skulls of a criminal could be identified from their fissures and nodes. In 1879 two criminologists, Doctor Arthur Bordier and Doctor Léon Ardouin, provided fellow members of the Anthropological Society of Paris with lectures based on their publication, 'The Skulls of Malefactors.'

This might suggest that Holmes is here referring to his study of criminology, which is precisely my point. What he is referring to is Lombroso's adoption of the quasi - science of phrenology, otherwise known in lay terms. as the study of bumps and shapes of the human skull.

SHERLOCK HOLMES AND CRIMINAL TYPES IN CRIME FICTION

As one commentator on Gothic fiction has remarked (and the Holmes stories most certainly exhibit strong features of the Gothic, as it also did the tales of the inimitable Poe, who invented the crime story and also the firt convincing psychopath tale in his 'The Tell-tale Heart'), there is a great connection between the writing of Bram Stoker and Conan Doyle, who, unsurprisingly, both knew each other very well and found common ground in their work in theatre.. But interestingly - and this is rarely pointed out by many commentators, so also did Oscar Wilde, who shared with Conan Doyle in his novel 'The Portrait of Dorian Grey', written at the same time as 'The Sign of Four', the identical notion explored by Stevenson in 'Dr Jekyll and Mr Hyde' to shocking effect, similar in its Lomrosian theory about the nature of evil, though based on a different principle; namely it was this. A man's face might be marked with the signs of immorality or wrongdoing, which he then bears for life, rather like the stigmata of a curse.

In Wilde's 'The Picture of Dorian Grey,' the leading character, a dissolute corrupter of men and women, finds a picture of himself which had been painted years ago and left in an attic. It is then that he rediscovers the entire corrupted trajectory of his life which appears in the face which he sees before him. In Bridget MarshalL's study of the Gothic, and in her comparison of Stoker and Conan Doyle, she sees the twin obsessions of Doyle and Lombroso, as is evident also in the dialogue piece quoted above in HOUN, between Holmes and Mortimer. Here, then, is the link between phrenology and physiognomy which so often is played out in the various description of villains in the Holmes tales. Marshall points out that:

'In the works of the novel, particularly in the Gothic novel, villains are clearly marked. The idea that evil can be seen in the face is important to the characters in the (mainstream 19th Century) novel, as well as readers of the Gothic novel. Certainly other forms of fiction used characters' physical appearance as indicators of their known character, but not to such a degree as in the Gothic novel.' [1]

She concludes that the study and belief of evil, as not only a tangible and real force could be seen in the behaviour of criminals, but also that this Lombrosean theory or notion was reflected in their body shapes and the features of their skulls; and that this view of a kind of physiological corruption based on their behaviour was frequent in the literature of the late 19th Century.

It would certainly help us to understand the widespread belied held by many Victorians, including physicians and moral commentators from both the church and moral commentators, that the prevalence of syphilis among the lower working classes represented a kind of phyisical and deforming curse among those who consorted with known prostitutes; a belief that, as we now know, was based on nothing more than an assumption.

Franz Joseph Gall (1758-1828), the inventor of the theory of phrenology, believed the brain was divided into specific areas, and that each area was responsible for a human characteristic such as pride or wit. The size of each area was linked to the "power of manifestation" of that trait. Gall believed those people with larger "pride areas" of the brain, for example, were more proud.

Gall also explained that it was possible to judge the size of an area, and hence to make judgements about a person's character, by examining the surface of the skull above that area. Promoted via the literary and philosophical societies of middle-class Britain, phrenology boomed between 1820 and 1830. For the new middle classes, phrenology symbolised the progressive nature of science. Phrenological journals, modelled on established scientific journals, were published, and a selection of skulls, models, and charts which accompanied the lectures, helped maintain its reputation of objectivity and rationality.

---

[1] ('The Face of Evil: Phrenology, Physiognomy, and The Gothic Villain,' IOW Studies, online PDF extract).

In spite of his many detractors, Gall was an important figure in the history of neurology. Previously, the mind had been seen as part of the soul and, therefore, as created by God, but people were now beginning to view the mind as a physical aspect of the brain, thus reinforcing the Darwinian view of the evolution of Mankind.

When Lombroso rediscovered Gall's work, and then perceived it in his own attempt to rationalise the behaviour of criminals, he subsequently linked this to his and others' preconceptions, regarding the marked and obvious differences between the physiognomy of the human races.[2]

Lombroso also regarded certain specific human ritual activities as things which brought a perverse satisfaction to the criminal ego. One that he particularly singled out for adverse comment was the art of tattooing, which had become very popular and no doubt spread through the widespread voyages undertaken by members of the Royal and merchant navies of this and other countries. The concept of body art Lombroso found to be just another extension of criminal perversity.

As we know, Holmes himself was much preoccupied with the observation of tattoos, and made frequent comments about them which were far more objective tha Lombroso's. Here is Lombroso's reckoning of the Oceanic art of tattooing.

LOMBROSO AND TATTOOING.

'Among primitive peoples, who live in a more or less nude condition, tattooing takes the place of decorations or ornamental garments, and serves as a mark of distinction or rank. When an Eskimo slays an enemy, he adorns his upperlip with a couple of blue stripes, and the warriors of Sumatra add a special sign to their decorations for every foe they kill. In Wuhaiva, ladies of noble birth are more extensively tattooed than women of humbler rank. Among the Maouris, tattooing is a species of armorial bearings indicative of noble birth.

---

[2] See: Gall, Franz Josef (1835). "On the Functions of the Brain and of Each of Its parts: With Observations on the Possibility of Determining the Instincts, Propensities, and Talents, Or the Moral and Intellectual Dispositions of Men and Animals, by the Configuration of the Brain and Head, Volume 1.'

'According to ancient writers, tattooing was practised by Thracians, Picts, and Celts. Roman soldiers also tattooed their arms with the names of their generals, and artisans in the Middle Ages were marked with the insignia of their crafts. In modern times this custom has fallen into disuse among the higher classes and only exists among sailors, soldiers, peasants, and workmen.

'Although not exclusively confined to criminals, tattooing is practised by them to a far larger extent than by normal persons: 9% of adult criminals and 40% of minors are tattooed; whereas, in normal persons the proportion is only 0.1%. Recidivists and born criminals, whether thieves or murderers, show the highest percentage of tattooing. Forgers and swindlers are rarely tattooed.

'Sometimes tattooing consists of a motto symbolical of the career of the criminal it adorns. Tardieu found on the arm of a sailor who had served various terms of imprisonment, the words, "*Pas de chance.*" The notorious criminal Malassen was tattooed on the chest with the drawing of a guillotine, under which was written the following prophecy: "*J'ai mal commencé, je finirai mal. C'est la fin qui m'attend.*"

'Tattooing frequently bears witness to indecency. Of 142 criminals examined by me, the tattooing on five showed obscenity of design and position and furnished also a remarkable proof of the insensibility to pain characteristic of criminals, the parts tattooed being the most sensitive of the whole body, and therefore left untouched even by savages.

'Another fact worthy of mention is the extent to which criminals are tattooed. Thirty-five out of 378 criminals examined by Lacassagne were decorated literally from head to foot.

'In a great many cases, the designs reveal violence of character and a desire for revenge. A Piedmontese sailor, who had perpetrated fraud and murder from motives of revenge, bore on his breast between two daggers, the words: "I swear to revenge myself." Another had written on his forehead, "Death to the middle classes," with the drawing of a dagger underneath. A young Ligurian, the leader of a mutiny in an Italian Reformatory, was tattooed with designs representing all the most important episodes of his life, and the idea of revenge was paramount. On his right forearm figured two crossed swords, underneath them the initials M. N. (of an intimate friend), and on the inner side, traced longitudinally, the motto: "Death to cowards. Long live our alliance."

'Tattooing, as practised by criminals, is a perfect substitute for writing with symbols and hieroglyphics, and they take a keen pleasure in this mode of adorning their skins.'

To conclude this brief analysis of Lombroso's impact on Conan Doyle's view of criminology, I would suggest that Holmes himself, especially in HOUN, shows a marked tendency in what he believes to be its use to the criminal investigator. As I pointed out in my critical commentary of that work:(*The Annotated Hound of the Baskervilles*),

'Although they make brief and undemanding appearances in the novel, they (i.e. the minor characters' pet obsessions) are still an integral part of it (the plot and its dramatis personae).

'Mortimer's obsession with the apocryphal study of other men's skulls; Frankland's unhealthy fixation over the legal niceties of trespass and Stapleton's quest for rare moths and butterflies (how apt that he should seek to ensnare and then chloroform his small victims!), all reinforce that brooding central image of the great Grimpen Mire. Each man shares an entropic picture of life by which he is also trapped.'

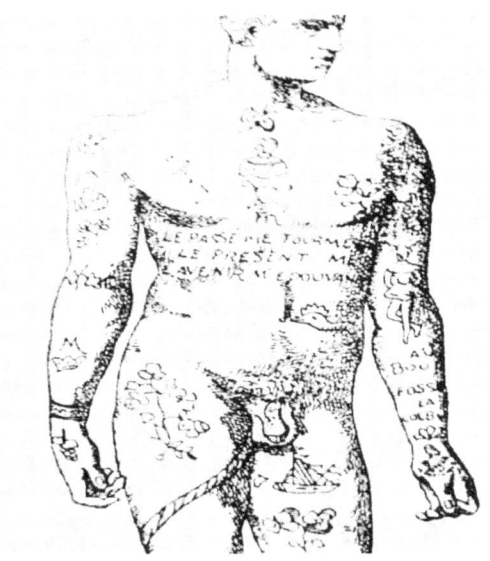

Fig.13. Lombroso, the Italian criminologist, argued that there was a definite link between tattoos and criminals. Illustration from Lombrodo's 'L'Uomo Delinquente.'

ORIGINS OF THE HOUND

POEM: THE CROMER HOUND

By Kelvin I. Jones

Once, whilst walking here

On Cromer's shore,

Battling in the teeth of a grim,

Equinoctial gale,

I thought I heard him

In the storm's din,

Borne on the biting wind,

That black hell hound's

Supernatural wail.

Oft then, when dreaming,

I would hear his bone chilling,

Deadly, death rattle,

Dragging to their doom

Those who dwelt in towers

Of Gothic gloom,

And died beneath his curse

Like cattle.

Years later,

When living here

Beneath those beetling cliffs,

Wet from a winter's squall,

We took the path

That wound through mist,

Until at last,

Chafed by the an east wind's freezing blast,

We came to Cromer Hall.

Instantly I saw this hallowed place,

This arc of dark, crenellated towers;

Glimpsed through undergrowth and ancient trees,

I saw those ruffians, garbed in wig and lace,

And the cursed Hugo,

Praying, on his knees,

That he might not die at the appointed hour.

Bone chilled, we returned home

To glass of port and roaring fire,

Whilst I, like one possessed,

Leafed through crisp pages

Of my Doyleian best,

Drinking in the Gothic gloom

Of a tale seeped in sin, lust

And the curse of ages.

I knew then he had trodden here,

Holmes and his loyal amanuensis,

Heard, like me, the chilling growl;

Watched as it burst through the wicket gate,

Dragging men down beneath the coal - black earth,

There to await their allotted fate.

Here, beneath the towers of Cromer Hall,

Where winds still rage like demons

On this eastern shore,

Where lifeboats launch in the wrack and spume,

So they, who otherwise

Might perish in the sea's spitting wind

And gathering gloom,

May live once more;

There, rising to meet me,

#Stands Baskerville Hall,

And by it stands the Death - Hound's face,

Curtained by a deathly pall;

Black Shuck,

The harbinger of death

And ill luck.

I smell, then, its rank, malodorous breath.

I freeze, stock still with fright,

Seeing its vicious jaws,

Clamped tight,

Burning bright,

Phosphorescent green and blue;

Its eyes like blazing coals,

Red from the hexed stain of centuries.

That hellish hound,

Felled by he of the six- shot Webley,

The swordstick and the cloth cap;

That grim stalker of the dark,

Its voice a weird, unearthly sound,

Its great bulk half veiled by moonlight,

Soaked through with blood and gore.

THE HOUND AND THE BLACK DOG.

'A hound it was, an enormous coal-black hound, but not such a hound as mortal eyes have ever seen.'

-The Hound of the Baskervilles.

The Hound of the Baskervilles has certain features which immediately identify it with the archetypes of Celtic and Old English folklore. Its size and blackness, its blazing eyes and "dripping jaws" link it with its neighbours, as far afield as East Anglia, Yorkshire, Lancashire, Wales and the Channel Islands.

In the Middle Ages the black dog was associated with witchcraft. As the "Black Man" often crops up in witch trials of the period as an alias of the Devil, so the black hound is cited as one of his servants, or alternatively, one of the transformations available to a witch.

An account from Hereford describes how a phantom dog haunted the spot where a witch was murdered by a chimney-sweeper. 'He was as big as a Newfoundland, but very gaunt, shaggy, with long ears and tail, eyes like balls of fire and large, long teeth.'

The luminosity of the hound's eyes is a feature common to all these sightings. The Boggart of Lancashire, a harbinger of death, had 'large, luminous, malevolent eyes.' On occasions, the reports describe the hunter himself as having saucer eyes along with the more instantly recognizable horns and tails.

HOUNDS ON DARTMOOR

The memory of the Wild Hunt features wide and large on Dartmoor and its environs. In addition to the famous "Hound Tor', "Great Hound Tor" and "Hel Tor", places which owe their names to the legend of the Hunt, legends of black and sometimes white hounds abound in the area.

Okehampton Castle is haunted by a black hound. Just north of Throwleigh Village, a sound of phantom ponies is often heard with an accompanying rush of the wind. On Merripit Hill, a local legend tells of a phantom sow and her litter who spend their nights pursuing a dead horse at Cator, only to find nothing but skin and bones on their arrival. At Wallaford, on the Abbot's Way, Squire Cabell's great tomb, which lies outside the church in a porch, is so placed as to keep its evil inhabitant securely entombed. He and his black hounds have an evil reputation there.

Ruth E. St. Leger-Gordon (The Witchcraft and Folklore of Dartmoor) believes that Doyle's hound is based on a satanic version known vaguely as "the Black Dog of Dartmoor" which once used to "scare belated travellers who would then whip up their horses to escape him".

THE HOUND AS CURSE

The theme of Hugo and his descendants, who carry with them the curse of his original sin, has many parallels in the folklore of the West Country. Tetcott in North Devon is haunted by the last of the Arscotts, a huntsman of eccentric ways who "when the full moon is shining as clear as days.... hunteth the country from Pencarrow to Dazzard".

At Braunton Barrows, the ghost of William de Tracey is forced to twist ropes out of sand. As he succeeds in completing this onerous task, a Black Dog appears and burns through the strands with his fiery breath.

In South Devon, on the banks of the Tamar, a pack of hounds escorts its master, a renegade priest. At Dean Combe, at the Pool of the Black Hound, the soul of a weaver, called Knowles, was changed into a Black Dog and is condemned to spend eternity here.

In Cornwall, the ghost of John Tregagle of Trevorder appears at the site of Dozmary Pool. Here, the Devil appeared as a hunter with "two doggies fierce and felte", and struck a bargain with Tregagle. Each day Tregagle did evil in exchange for his soul. Eventually he was struck dead by lightning:

"Then from the blacke corpse, a pale spectre appear'd,
And hied him away through the night
When quickly the yelpes of the hell-houndes are heard,
And to the pursuite bye the bugle are cheer'd,
Whyle behynde thunderes after the spryte.

And stylle, as the trav'ller pursues his lone waye
In horrours, at nyghte o'er the waste.
He hears Syr Tregeagle with shrieks rushe awaye,
He hears the Blacke Hunter pursuing his preye,

And shrynkes at his bugle's dreade blaste.

Ever since, John Tregagle has spent his time spinning a rope of sand or dipping out the pool with a limpet shell and at times being hunted by the Devil and his hounds, at which times he is heard to roar and howl in a most dreadful manner. (Notice the similarity with the story of William de Tracey)

RIVAL CLAIMS

The inspiration of the Baskerville legend has been discussed many times and is possible that his friend, Flecher Robinson may have mentioned the legend to Doyle and that the conversation then turned to the "West Country legend".

But which legend was it?

One theory which is still particularly popular in Norfolk is that Cromer Hall was the inspiration for Baskerville Hall. Cromer Hall is a country house, located a mile south of Cromer, on Hall Road. The present house was built in 1829 by the architect William Donithorne and is a grade two listed building. Built in the Gothic revival style and described as Tudor Gothic by the architectural historian Nikolaus Pevsner, it is constructed in flint with stone dressings and a slate roof.

'The north gabled wing,' (Pevsner comments), 'has a bell tower over the roof with battlements and a short spire. The building has many tall octagonal stone chimneys, some single and some in groups. Adjoining the main house to the north east there are a range of buildings which include stables and a domestic wing. This section is built behind a flint screen wall with three and four centred headed doorways and two stone mullion and transom windows. The entire outside walls are of flint construction, but inside the walls facing the courtyard are of brick construction with low-pitched, hipped, slated roofs. The wing also has octagonal chimneys. The rooms have with glazing bars and there are large four- centred, arch-headed doors'.

Cromer Hall also has a strong possibility as the inspiration for Baskerville Manr thanks to a possible visit to the house by Conan Doyle in 1901. According to local belief, during his visit to Cromer, Conan Doyle and Bertram Fletcher Robinson had dinner with Mrs Benjamin Bond Cabbell at Cromer Hall.

During dinner, Mrs Cabbell told them about her husband's ancestor, Richard Cabell who was Lord of Brook manor at Buckfastleigh and had been killed by a devilish dog. The description of Baskerville Hall in Doyle's novel could equally apply to Cromer Hall:

'The avenue opened into a broad expanse of turf, and the house lay before us. In the fading light I could see that the centre was a heavy block of building from which a porch projected. The whole front was draped in ivy, with a patch clipped bare here and there where a window or a coat-of-arms broke through the dark veil. From this central block rose the twin towers, ancient, crenellated, and pierced with many loopholes. To right and left of the turrets were more modern wings of black granite. A dull light shone through heavy mullioned windows, and from the high chimneys which rose from the steep, high-angled roof there sprang a single black column of smoke.'

Sadly, however, the idea locally that Sir Arthur gained his information from the lips of local philanthropist Benjamin Bond Cabbell himself is almost certainly inaccurate, since Lord Cabell was already dead by the time of Doyle's possible visit, although his widow, Lady Cabbell, had survived her husband, as local records clearly demonstrate. Local legend here tells of how one of Cabbell's ancestors killed his wife and as a consequence was cursed, like his descendants, by a black hound from Hell.

However, it is entirely possible that Doyle visited Cromer Hall, as described in my reconstruction of events, even though there is no direct evidence for it. The Cabbells were well loved in Cromer, especially since Benjamin auctioned off large areas of his estate to encourage local building. (The reader may have noted the variant spelling of the name Cabell.)

There are, of course, a number of Baskervilles. D.A. Redmond, ('A Study in Sources') mentions a Major C.H.L. Baskerville of Croydon, Major H.W.M. Baskerville of the Norfolk Regiment (significant?) and there was a Baskerville Hall in Birmingham. Roger Robinson has even unearthed a Baskerville family at Shiplake in Oxfordshire; and the home at Crowsley Park has a yew alley and a wolf's head crest. Another branch of the family lived at Eardisley Castle, between Hereford and Kington (one of their number, John, was responsible for the famous type- face).

The credit for this next discovery goes to Dr Maurice Campbell who, in addition, unearthed the Black Hound of Hergest, a phantom hound which appeared to members of the Vaughan family, who lived only a mile away from Kington.

According to Dr Campbell, Doyle stayed near Kington when writing The Hound, *although I have not been able to independently verify this.*

Another claim, by J.L. McCowen (Letter to 'The Baker Street Journal', March 977, p48) for the "original Radnorshire Baskervilles" whose home was at Clyro, near Hay-on- Wye, mentions that "Doyle used to visit the Baskervilles at Caemawr". He goes on to say:

'There are two local legends of the death of a poor country girl at the hands of Hugo Baskerville's pack of hounds, and the subsequent deaths in the family. One relates to "The Moor" (the earlier Baskerville home a few miles away) and includes reports of sightings and the baying of a ghost hound.'

Perhaps the most popular of the Baskerville Hall claims was made by James Bliss Austin in 1964. This concerns the legend of Sir Richard Cabell, Lord of the Manor of Brook, who died in 1677.

According to J.L. Vivians, in 'Visitations of Devon', the Cabells of Brooke originated from Richard Cabell of Fromeselwood. Sir Richard was one of the third generation of the Cabells, but the family died out with his own subsequent death in 1677. According to 'Devon Notes and Queries.' (Vol. 7, p. 234), Richard married one Elizabeth Fowell at Ugborough on the 7th January, 1654 (or 1665), and had but one daughter. She in turn carried the estate to the family of Fownes.

Mr J.R. Elliott, the area librarian of Devon County Library, informs me in a letter that 'there is some doubt as to the validity of Richard having the title 'Sir'. ' Several searches made have failed to confirm his knighthood and it seems likely that this was an honorary title, by virtue of his position as 'Lord of the Manor of Brooke.'

Little is known of the historical Cabell. In 'The Reports of the Devonshire Association' for 884 (p94), mention is made of Sir Richard as a "persecutor of the Nonconformists", although in 672 one Richard Bickle took out a licence to preach at the house of Samuel Cabell of Buckfastleigh. Samuel Cabell appears to have been the uncle of (Sir) Richard, and he clearly favoured the Puritans.

J.R.W. Coxhead, in his fascinating study, 'The Devil in Devon', provides the link between the Yeth (Heath) Hounds and the sinister Sir Richard, and it is in this study that the connection with Doyle's legend is assumed. According to Coxhead, "One wild night in the year 677, Cabell died, and throughout the hours of darkness, the jet-black hounds of the Demon

36

Hunt from Dartmoor 'raged and howled around the manor-house. Many superstitious folk..., were convinced that the hell-hounds had been sent to convey the spirit of the wicked landowner to purgatory".

Sir Richard's body lies beneath a pagoda- like building outside the south porch of Buckfastleigh Church. The legend has it that this measure was taken to protect the townspeople of Buckfastleigh from his evil spirit. It is also said that if the visitor pokes his finger through the keyhole of the locked door of the pagoda, he will have it gnawed off.

The body of Sir Richard is weighted down by a second large slab to ensure that he will not walk again.

Charles Merriman (Sherlock Holmes Journal,, vol.9, no 2) notes that Brooke Manor, the Cabell house at Cross Furzes, "has a driveway..., of about three- quarters of a mile in length through a tunnel of trees. to the left of the 4Hall front are some yew trees." The manor is just the type of place that might have appealed to Doyle as the original of 'Baskerville Hall'.

However, when all the evidence is weighed regarding the location is assembled, there is no doubt that, visually, at the very least, Cromer Hall fits the bill with its supreme, and uncannily accurate Gothic style, along with the brooding façade and internal architecture. The large stained glass windows of the interior, with their exquisite cut glass, the vaulting and the wonderful flying buttresses, the magnificent stone structures which reinforced the building; are all perfectly depicted in the Conan Doyle literary version of Baskerville Hall. Clearly evident also are the colonnades and statues; and especially the historical figure of the knight, just outside the main entrance. The spires and the pointed arches all reinforce Conan Doyle's profoundly Gothic vision.

'In the fading light I could see that the centre was a heavy block of building from which a porch projected. The whole of the front was draped in ivy with a patch clipped here and there, where a window or a coat of arms broke through the dark veil. From this central block rose the twin towers, ancient and crenellated and pierced with many loopholes. To right and centre turrets were more modern wings of black granite. A dull light shone through heavy mullioned windows, and from the high chimneys which rose from the steep, high angled roof, there sprung a single black column of smoke.'

If the reader cares to examine the late 19th century photographs of Cromer Hall, he will immediately recognise the similarity regarding the ivy;

the mullioned windows which appear to peer out from the surrounding ivy and the high steeped roof of this dark and very gloomy Gothic building, as it then was before it was cleaned in the 20th century. The origins of Sir Richard's evil reputation are veiled in obscurity. Folk legends frequently arise from popular hatred of figures renowned for their religious intolerance, and there are many parallels of this. Whatever his evil actions were, the legend of Richard Cabell seems certain to have provided part of the idea for Doyle's own story of "the phantom-hound" and the family to which it attached itself.

Fig 15. The front entrance here of Cromer Hall, a photograph taken in 1890, showing the uncanny resemblance to Baskerville Hall. The photograph appears here by courtesy of the present day Cabell family who themselves completely support the local opinion. That Conan Doyle not only. visited the premises when he was staying in Cromer but that he chose this Gothic. Mansion as the original model for his Baskerville Hall.

PARKER: 'A GARROTTER BY TRADE'

When Sherlock Holmes is in Baker Street once more, recovering from his three long Wanderjahre and with his companion and chronicler Dr Watson, who now has recovered from his fainting fit, induced by seeing his long missing friend; the detective explains to him that the man below who stands all day on the pavement opposite 221B, keeping watch on them, was once a garrotter 'by trade.'

Fig. 16. The ferocity of the garrotters' attack knew no limits.

THURS 12 SEPT 1895. DUNDEE COURIER

'Female Garrotters Heavily Punished. Four female garrotters, each under 18 years of age, were sentenced to ten months' hard labour, the Old

Bailey, London, yesterdav, for robbing another woman with violence in Spitalfields.'

Often, the person who was the victim was moved into a state of some confusion, or lack of concentration by a young and attractive woman, who would distract him momentarily, before her two accomplices struck, then rob him of all his precious goods, often comprising a watch, a gold chain perhaps, and other items of expense. These robberies took place in broad daylight, often on the streets of London.

And the man who stands keeping watch on Baker Street during the time Mr. Sherlock Holmes was resident, was an employee of the gang of friends is, we learn, still an employee and works for the professor, under the control of Colonel Sebastian Moran, Moriarty's sharp shooter, himself a leading light of what remains of the gang, most of them now having been arrested.

Parker was, we would well imagine, no different to many other of the typical gang members of the garrotters, a man, perhaps, who turned to crime because of a brutalised background, or who saw the chance to profit from those who had wealth and position in society.

Consider this letter written to a London newspaper:

The account appeared in the 'Cork Examiner' on Friday 13th December 1867.

COMMENCEMENT OF THE GARROTTING SEASON

"The garrotting season seems to have set in severely south of the Thames. A correspondent of The Star writes:-

"On Friday night last, between five and six o'clock, in Crescent-lane, leading from Clapham Common to Clapham Park, my brother was garrotted by two ruffians, who robbed him of jewellery, money and everything in his possession. He is a tall and powerful young man, perfectly able, with a fair chance, to defend himself, but was attacked suddenly from behind (a thick sword-stick knocked from his hand), and immediately rendered powerless, being bonnetted, thrown on his back, and sat upon by a big man, who grasped his throat, stuffing a handkerchief into his mouth, "to keep the chicken from squalling," as it was elegantly expressed, and otherwise brutally ill-treated. Thanks to speedy remedies applied, he is now recovering, but is much shaken, and his throat and features remain swollen and sore…"

In the last five decades of the 19th century, it seemed to many people that the garrotting gangs had become so much a part of daily life, that even the local magistrate did not take the crime very seriously:

SAT 6TH SEPT 1862.

LONDON EVENING STANDARD.

THE GARROTTER ALARM.

TO THE EDITOR.

Sir, — In your report this day of the proceedings at the Marylebone Police-court, I perceive, in the case of two men being charged with an attempt to rob a gentleman in Albany Street about one in the morning, that the magistrate, addressing the prosecutor, remarked, "I suppose you are like everybody else, you have got your head full of garrotte robberies."

Surely, this sneering remark of the magistrate was totally uncalled for, whether, as referring to this particular case, or as applied to the public generally. There is no doubt that the present prevalence of garrotte robberies entails some additional trouble upon police magistrates, and that their patience may be sometimes sorely tried in listening to the details of suppositious attempts at garrotting; but surely when a person has narrowly escaped a premeditated attack from garrotters, and in furtherance of the ends of public justice attends at the police-court to give his evidence, he ought not to expect to be snubbed from the bench; and taunted with timidity.

The worthy magistrate should consider, that if "everybody's heads are full of garrotte robberies," it is really very excusable under the circumstances, although he himself may regard all such absurd fancies as the result of weak imaginations. A remark of this nature, uttered in a jeering tone from the bench of a police court may be of a far more mischievous tendency than the utterer might anticipate. The police, who, of course take their initiative from their superiors, are already too apt to disregard complaints received from unofficial sources, and to treat the public generally as troublesome and absurdly apprehensive. It is needless to point out how this feeling on the part of the police would be strengthened by such a remark as that expressed by the Marylebone magistrate.

I am, Sir,

Yours obediently,

ONE WHO BELIEVES IN GARROTTERS. Dec. 4. 1862.

Besides this description, we have one from another paper of the period, a second account. of how vicious these attacks were. Indeed, in some cases, they led to murder charges being placed before the individual members of the gangs.

One wonders what sort of a man Parker was? We do know from Holmes' brief description and account of him, of his ability to play the Jew's harp. Was he perhaps, Jewish himself? Did he come from Whitechapel, for example?

There was a large Jewish community who lived in Whitechapel. And when in 1904, Conan Doyle visited Whitechapel as a member of The Crime Club to examine the places in Whitechapel, where the targets of the Ripper's fury had been found, he was struck, as were his companions, by the number of Jewish people that were plying their trades there.

Parker and his fellow garrotters had a particular system which they employed and which in fact, had, gone on in parts of London like Whitechapel for many years before Holmes' reference to it. It reached its ascendancy during the mid 19th century so by Holmes' period, it was by no means an innovation.

The name given to the garrotter was, termed, rather affectionately, 'Chokey Bill,' a rampsman who carried with him a bag with which he would have hit his victims, (resembling an eel skin).

It was the gang leader (presumably Parker) who grabbed his prey by the neck. And thus immobilising him or her, he would then assist another gang member to put a scarf or rope around the victim's neck.

During the summer months, when it was considerably warmer, the brutality of these attacks caused great concern, especially during the period just prior to Holmes' arrival in London. They caused so much alarm that calls to concerted public action in newspapers, like the one above, were very popular.

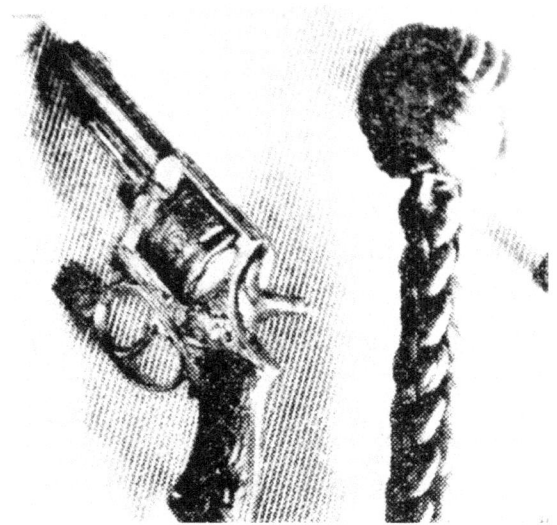

Fig. 17. Weapons used by the garrotters: the revolver and the cosh. The Webley, left, is much like Dr Watson's gun.

One example of their vicious treatment of their victims will suffice. A gentleman; who was an MP, was walking one night in the summer, from parliament to his club in Palmetto, rather as Holmes' older brother Mycroft would often do, as he made his way to the Diogenes Club.

It was in the middle of July that Mr. Pilkington was attacked so savagely and, as it was said, 'in open sight of everyone else'. He was quickly beaten to the ground, trampled on and then left, bleeding. That same night, another man also fell foul of the garrotters. A man called Edward Hawkins was similarly assaulted between St. James and Bond Street. These attacks became more and more frequent as the summer nights held on, and as it grew warmer. A person who was a gunsmith had his hand so badly beaten and twisted, that it had to be amputated, but the victim later died.

Why was garrotting so popular? From the middle to the late 19th century the papers reported it often in urban areas. And it was usually done by gangs of men who carried out these attacks. Many of them, at least from their accounts given by them, in court, claimed to have been displaced persons, having arrived from another part of Britain and having no work. But no one has yet explained exactly *why* it also became popular eventually, even in rural areas. Cases were reported as far away from London as Lancashire, and occurred also in Yorkshire and Nottingham, and Exeter. It became almost a fashionable way of earning money illicitly in Victorian London among groups of certain working class men.. There were even Garrotters' societies, which had been started up. In December 1862, a newspaper called the 'Weekly Despatch' reported:

'The manner in which garrotters, armed to the mouth and teeth,then proceed along the streets at night, clinking their sword canes and short sticks, and ready to draw at a moment's notice their weapons, are thus calculated to strike terror into the breasts of others, as well as those of the Great Enemy'.

In 1863, more people were hanged than in any other year, because of something then known of, and popularly described by the Press, as 'the Bloody Code', a weekly event in Liverpool to dissuade people from violent crime. In July that year, a law was passed, which became known as the 'Garrotters' Act'.

The law provided for a special sentence for the flogging of offenders. In Lancashire, where the cutting of cotton supplies for the American Civil War brought about a great deal of suffering, and therefore, mass unemployment, a huge number of violent robberies of this sort took place. However, the Act of Parliament of 1863 did not stop the corruption and this specific crime remained constant. No one died of a garrotting after that. That was perhaps more chance than anything, but the police by then became stronger in their strategies, and were seen talking, and often in twos, on street corners. as was the case in Whitechapel, for example.

Thus, by these methods, the incidents of garrotting started slowly to diminish. Certainly the public reaction to this crime was regarded as much more serious than any of the other types of armed robbery.

In the summer of 1862, the outbreaks of garrotting seemed to be growing at a tremendous rate. There was no apparent reason for this. In July that year, an MP had been walking home from parliament to his club in Pall Mall. He was very badly beaten and left for dead.

The same thing happened to a distinguished 80 year old, who was assaulted between St James's Street and Bond Street, as he was approaching some temporary boarding houses. Rather often, as was the case with the murders of prostitutes in the east of London, such attackers were very rarely seen.

The public outcry at the crime of garrotting was now immense. There was also in existence, a growing number of people in the middle classes, who were conscious of the way in which it affected their businesses in the retail trade.

For example, a contemporary commission which was formed in 1839, offered the opinion that pickpockets were thriving because people thought that they were safe under the eyes of the 'new' (Peel's, that is) police force, which had recently been brought in. Garrotting may have seemed a safe crime by some persons in authority but many of the attacks were most brutal and had lasting effects on the victims.

The reputation of the pickpockets and muggers was not helped in any way by the somewhat gentle treatment of these criminals in the pages of Charles Dickens' novel 'Oliver Twist,

'Here the organiser of the child picpockets, Fagin, is in fact not depicted as a violent criminal leader, unlike his associate in crime, Bill Sykes, who is to me, the archetypal garrotter..

Fagin was what was known in the underworld as a kitzman, a manager of child thieves. Its original Hebrew meaning, rather ironically, was 'a priest of righteousness').

GROSS ABOUT SHERLOCK: TWO OF A KIND?

In 1891, Hans Gross published his now classic volume about criminology, 'Criminal Investigation'. It was a memorable year both from the point of view of Dr. Watson and that of his friend, Sherlock Holmes. the criminal investigator.

It was the year that witnessed the last of the Ripper murders (Coles, 13 February, 1891) and also, for Holmes, 'the matter of supreme importance' regarding the continued exile of French princes from their country.

In June 1891 Dr. Watson sold his Paddington practice and repossessed his former practice in Kensington and in the following month the first of the short stories, 'A Scandal in Bohemia', appeared in 'The Strand Magazine'.

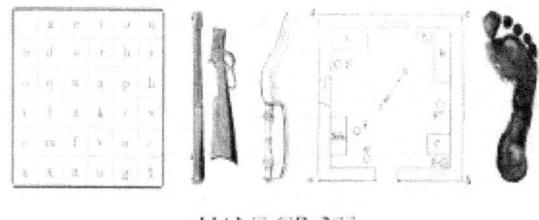

CRIMINAL
INVESTIGATION

A PRACTICAL HANDBOOK
FOR MAGISTRATES, POLICE OFFICERS,
AND LAWYERS

VOLUME 2

HANS GROSS

Fig. 18. This book, by Austrian jurist and criminologist, is of great importance regarding the methods of Sherlock Holmes.

'Criminal Investigation' was a remarkably thorough and painstaking survey of the whole field of detection and its comprehensive range gained immediate respect amongst theoreticians and practical exponents in the field.

The language and approach of Gross's work bears an uncanny resemblance to those early effusions of Sherlock Holmes. As a practical investigator, Holmes had acquired an incredible stock of detailed information to launch on the unsuspecting public. He was fortunate to be alive at a time when publishing had reached its Parnassus.

Any number of monographs, novelettes and beautifully embossed volumes of minor poetry poured from the presses. The availability of cheap wood pulp had revolutionised the publishing world.

Holmes, swept up in the wave of authorship, had produced some authoritative works, among them 'Upon Tattoo Marks' (1878), 'Upon The Tracing of Footsteps,' (1878), 'Upon The Distinction Between the Ashes of the Various Tobaccos,' (1879), 'A Study of the Influence of a Trade upon the Form of the Hand,' (1886), 'On The Variability 0f Human Ears,' (1888), 'The Typewriter and its Relation to Crime,' (1890) and the curious article which had appeared in The 'Fortnightly Magazine' (1881/2) (dismissed by Watson as "ineffable twaddle"), entitled 'The Book of Life.'

The effect which these small, but significant publications had on the minds of other leading criminologists in the field was clearly considerable.

It was slowly being realised that with the advances being made in the experimental sciences, it was no longer satisfactory to call in an expert and rely on his testimony alone. It was the criminologist himself who needed to break new ground.

If we can rely on Watson's tabulation of his friend's 'limits' it would appear that even as early as 1881 Holmes had made considerable inroads into criminology, physiology experimental chemistry and other areas of knowledge.

Like his contemporary to whom he makes an indirect reference, Alphonse Bertillon, the great French criminologist, Holmes recommended that the most practical thing a detective could do was to "shut yourself up for three months and read twelve hours a day at the annals of crime," and pointed out that "It's all been done before, and will be again."

For that reason, Holmes spent much of his professional career absorbing and becoming expert upon a wide range of specialised knowledge, including tobacco ashes, cryptography, newspaper types, perfumes, toxicology, the dating of documents, the typewriter and its relation to crime, bicycle tyres, tattoos, footsteps, the influence of the trade on the form of the hand, and the names and trademarks of the world's major gunmaking firms.

He also showed considerable interest in anatomy, an interest which Watson described as "accurate but unsystematic," and twice applied this knowledge in the form of practical experiments.

Although he claimed to have investigated over five hundred cases in the course of his career, a surprisingly small number (38%) dealt with murder. Fourteen of these 23 resulted in the murderers being arrested or killed, three involved non-human agents, and in all fourteen Holmes made a successful analysis. In five other cases,

Holmes succeeded in identifying the criminal but the murderers escaped the reach of the law, and in four other cases Holmes gave the murderers their liberty, because there were extenuating circumstances involved. Today's forensic scientist would have found the range of murder cases fascinating.

Among the causes of death were gassing, poisoning, asphyxiation, and death from head injuries, comprising a variety of blunt instruments and guns. In the vast majority of these cases, a quick eye for detail at the scene of the crime led Holmes to the murderer with remarkable rapidity.

According to Gross, the investigator had to be prepared to solve 'problems relating to every conceivable branch of human knowledge.

A detective ought to be acquainted with languages He should know what the medical man can tell him and what he should ask the medical man; as well as possessing robust health and extensive acquaintance with all branches of the law'.

In 'Sherlock Holmes - his limits,' Holmes, according to Watson, 'had a good practical knowledge of the British law`, was exceptionally athletic, was 'well up in belladonna, opium and poisons generally', had a 'practical but limited' knowledge of geology and a 'profound' understanding of chemistry. His grasp of anatomy was 'accurate but unsystematic'.

Watson was puzzled by the apparent randomness of his companion's approach but if he had taken the trouble to work it out he would have realised that this was just the sort of practical knowledge a criminal investigator was required to acquire.

Not only did Gross regard the science of chemistry as 'unique in its wide range and its many points of contact with other sciences', he further went on to argue that the biologist, a key connection in the forensic process, and 'primarily concerned with the identification of materials derived from plant and animal sources', would frequently be called on to 'identify seeds, fragments of plant and animal tissue such as splinters of wood and sawdust, hairs and fibres,' and be 'competent to identify blood stains'.

Fig. 19 Like his creator, Conan Doyle, and, like the criminologist Hans Gross, Sherlock Holmes had acquired many forensic skills.

Holmes was well aware of these demands. In 'The Lion's Mane', for instance, we find him resorting to an enlarged photograph in order to identify the type of wounds inflicted on McPherson's back, whilst 'Shoscombe Old Place' opens with Holmes bending over a low-power microscope. "Those hairs are threads from a tweed coat," he observes. "The irregular grey masses are dust. There are epithelial scales on the left, Those brown blobs in the centre are undoubtedly glue."

Clearly, Holmes was obviously well up in this particular branch of investigation, so much so, we find that he has spared time to advise Scotland Yard about the potential uses of the microscope ("Since I ran down that coiner by the zinc and copper filings in the seam of his cuff they have begun to realise the importance of the microscope,").

Much earlier in his career, he had made much of his powers of observation by a description of the unfortunate Henry Baker's billycock, much to the amazement of his Baker Street 'biographer'.

"The lens discloses a large number of hair ends, clean cut by the scissors of the barber," Holmes observes. "They all appear to be adhesive, and there is a distinct odour of lime cream,

'This dust…is not the gritty, grey dust of the street, but the fluffy brown dust of the house, showing that it has been hung up indoors most of the time."

Gross devoted a large section of his vast study to graphology, about which he held a number of reservations:

'If data in greater number were collected, if more cautious and more accurate experiments were made,' he pointed out, 'then it would be possible to individualise, generalise and establish rules thus leading to the increase of knowledge'.

He held the opinion that, because of the complexity and variety of human nature, the student of handwriting needed to serve a long study

. 'Observation and personal study, followed with zeal and regularity, will convince investigators that examination of handwriting has nowadays become a science.'

Gross's style is ponderous, often rather pompous. Was this due to a clumsy translation from the original German or was it just the character of the man himself?)

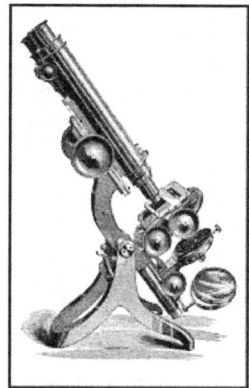

Fig. 20 A late Victorian microscope of the type and design which Holmes and his Austrian counterpart, Hans Gross, would certainly have used.

Holmes' own abilities in the field were undoubtedly exceptional. Not for nothing was he the author of a work on 'Ancient English Charters' (a work that earned him international renown).

From the outset of his career he made it clear to his companion that, like Gross's model investigator, he was perfectly able to 'extract from a writing the character of an individual'. In 'The Sign of Four' he gives Watson a typically arrogant, off-the-cuff demonstration of his powers.

HOLMES: What do you make of this fellow's scribble?

WATSON: It is legible and regular...a man of business habits and some force of character.

(Holmes shakes his head.)

HOLMES: Look at his long letters. They hardly rise above the common herd. That d might be an l, and that l an e. Men of character always differentiate their long letters, however illegibly they may write. There is vacillation in his k's and self-esteem in his capitals'.

It is reasonably clear from the above that Holmes had adopted some such system of classification suggested by Gross, whereby the investigator takes an example of handwriting from a number of people who are known to him and then draws conclusions from them.

'The same procedure will be followed in making lists from every imaginable point of view of age, sex, size, nationality, position, profession, and occupation,' Gross observes.

To Holmes, the classifier of the agony columns and the compiler of the anomalous scrapbooks, this would have presented no problem.

As with graphology, cryptology, or the study of secret messages, was awarded serious consideration in Gross's work.

His examination of the different forms of cryptograms was, like the rest of his work, well researched.

He first of all distinguishes between the two main classes of cypher: substitution cypher, in which the letters of the original text are represented by other letters or symbols, and transposition cyphers, where merely the letters of the original message are switched round.

Gross gives as an example of the simplest substitution cypher the following, where each letter of the message is replaced by the letter which occurs immediately after it in the alphabet, e.g.:

SHADES OF THE PRISON HOUSE

TIBEFT PG UIF QSJTPO IPVTF

The more advanced form of this, known as Playfair, is also described, where a key square, formed from a prearranged keyword, is created.

The keyword is written down in a five letter line, avoiding repetition of letters in that word, then followed by the remainder of the alphabet.

(WORD: ARBITRARY)

A R B 1 T
Y C D E F
G H K L M
N o P Q s
U v w x Y

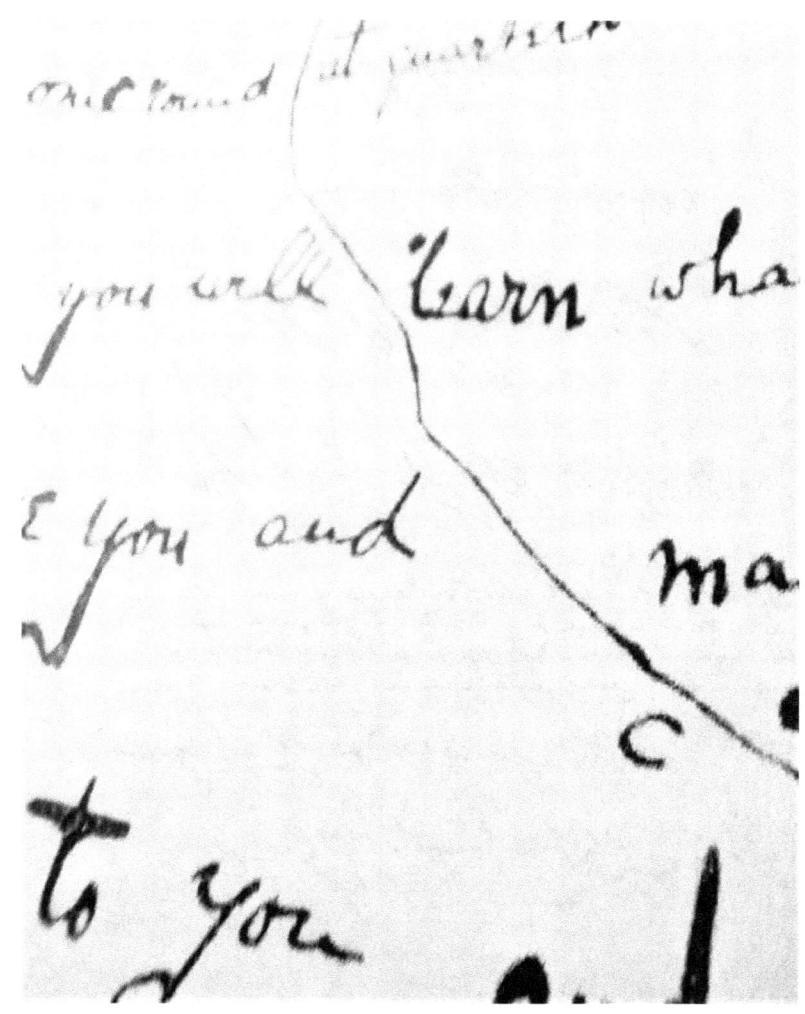

Fig, 21, Handwriting specimen from REIG which helped Holmes solve the case.

There are countless variations of this principle but it is not a type with which Holmes appeared to have been confronted during his career'

.

The type of cypher key used by Porlock in 'The Valley of Fear' is mentioned, however, under Gross's classification as 'Books used for key purposes such as novels, Bibles, etc. The cypher was as follows:

534 C213 127 36 31 417 214|

DOUGLAS 109 293 5 37 BIRLSTONE

26 BIRLSTONE 9 127 171

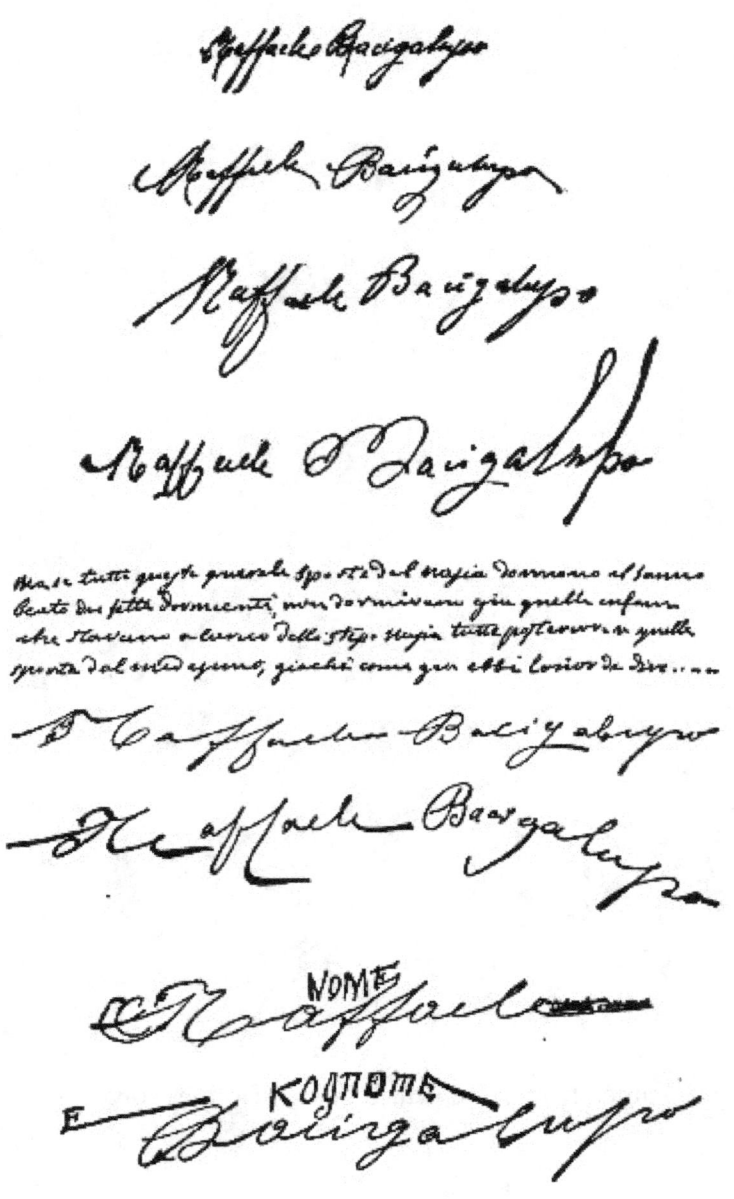

Fig.22. These signatures of criminals, taken from Lombroso's
Classic work on criminology, would have been of great interest
to both Gross and Sherlock Holmes.

Holmes remarks blandly to Watson that "there are many cyphers which
I would read as easily as I do the apocrypha of the agony column... But this is
different. It is clearly a reference to the words in a page of some book."
'Clearly' because Holmes knew this did not fit into the familiar transposition
or substitution category. Holmes' subsequent tracking down of the particular
volume (Whitaker's Almanac) owed much to his familiarity with the type
faces of reference works (a skill which was to prove considerable use to him
in 'The Hound of The Baskervilles'). "The cypher message begins with a large

534..." (hence the volume is a large one)…the next sign is CZ" (indicating a second column) all of which indicates that it is a "large book, printed in double columns and in common use".

"The Bible!" cries Watson. An intelligent guess, but Watson has forgotten that there are innumerable versions of the Bible. Bradshaw is eliminated from the list because its vocabulary is 'terse and limited'. So too is the dictionary.

What's left? An almanac.

As usual, Holmes scores within minutes. In practice it was probably a much more roundabout affair but then Watson had a particular flair for romanticising his companion's abilities. Even so, we may assume that Holmes, by this stage in his career, had acquired considerable expertise in the cracking of cryptograms.

Fig.23. Hans Gross, an unflattering picture of the great Austrian criminologist.
His methods were, like those of Sherlock Holmes, a mixture of cryptography
and graphology.

The keyword is written down in a five letter line, avoiding repetition of letters in that word, then followed by the remainder of the alphabet.

(WORD: ARBITRARY)

```
A R B 1 T
Y C D E F
G H K L M
N o P Q s
U v w x Y
```

There are countless variations of this principle but it is not a type with which Holmes appeared to have been confronted during his career.

The type of cypher key used by Porlock in 'The Valley of Fear' is mentioned, however, under Gross's classification as 'Books used for key purposes such as novels, Bibles, etc. The cypher was as follows:

534 C213 127 36 31 417 214 l
DOUGLAS 109 293 5 37 BIRLSTONE
26 BIRLSTONE 9 127 171

Holmes remarks blandly to Watson that "there are many cyphers which I would read as easily as I do the apocrypha of the agony column... But this is different. It is clearly a reference to the words in a page of some book." 'Clearly' because Holmes knew this did not fit into the familiar transposition or substitution category. Holmes' tracking down of the particular volume (Whitaker's Almanac) owed much to his familiarity with the type faces of reference works (a skill which was to prove considerable use to him in 'The Hound of The Baskervilles').

"The cypher message begins with a large 534, . ." (hence the volume is a large one)...the next sign is CZ" (indicating a second column) all of which indicates that it is a "large book, printed in double columns and in commonuse".

As usual, Holmes scores within minutes. In practice it was probably a much more roundabout affair but then Watson had a particular flair for romanticising his companion's abilities.

Even so, we may assume that Holmes, by this stage in his career, had acquired considerable expertise in the cracking of cryptograms.

In his classic work, 'Criminal Investigation,' Gross warns the reader that the relative letter frequency of the twenty-six letters of English is only a rough estimate and cannot be relied upon where the text is lengthy.

Holmes, in his explanation to the doctor and Inspector Martin, is more explicit.

He notes that "the order of the English letters after E is by no means well marked, and any preponderance which may be shown in an average of a printed sheet may be reversed in a single short sentence. Speaking roughly, T, A, O, l, N, S, H, R, D and L are the numerical order in which letters occur."

Now this is either a remarkable coincidence or proof positive that Gross' work had a place on the bookshelf of 221B, for this order of letters conforms exactly with Gross's own tabulation.

Fig. 24. (above). Sherlock Holmes examines the curious stick-like figures in the cryptographic message left for its recipient in 'The Adventure of the Dancing Men'. Illustration by Sidney Paget, taken from 'The Strand Magazine.

Even more curious is the section of Gross's work entitled 'Footprints'. He goes into the subject at great length and a large portion of the chapter is devoted to the preservation of prints. 'The best material is plaster of paris," he comments. 'To secure best results it is essential to use the best materials and dental plaster is an excellent medium.'

Methods of mixing and applying are discussed as well as ways of speeding the drying process. Could Gross have used Holmes's own 'Art of Tracing Footsteps, with some remarks upon the uses of plaster of Paris.' one is led to wonder? Since the work appeared in 1878, well before Gross's 'Criminal Investigation' made its appearance, the question is well worth considering.

Tracks and Tricks

Perhaps the most famous case in which Holmes used his ability to read footsteps and tracks was 'The Priory School'. This adventure presents the reader with a most interesting example of investigatory field work. Gross deals with animal and vehicle track marks briefly but it appears that Holmes, true to form, had made it his business to acquaint himself with the different forms of bicycle tread, then in current production, in addition to the iron shoes and horse shoes available in different parts of the country. "This, as you perceive, is a Dunlop, with a patch upon the outer cover. Heidegger's tyres were Palmers, leaving longitudinal stripes."

The ingenious trick of attaching cow shoes to a horse's feet and Holmes' equally ingenious and brilliant deduction, based on the irregularities of the prints, are examples of the best type of detective work, and Gross, the great empirical criminologist, would have found much to admire in Watson's account of his friend's skill and insight into the examination of trace evidence.

That Gross' work so impressed the justices, and his fellow colleagues in the police forces of Germany and Austria, owes much to his wide and often very detailed knowledge of the scientific and pseudo - scientific sciences, such as that of psychological motivation. which came under the professor's examination.

Fig. 25.. This German psychiatrist, Krafft-Ebing, first made detailed dnotes on his patients about what were then regarded as 'sexual perversions.' Making a study of violent sexual attacks on victims by those likeJack the Ripper, he attempted to produce a profile of the murderer in his definitive work, 'Psychopathia Sexualis.'

When, later on in his career Gross came to publish his remarkable studies regarding the body language used by criminals and the way this hidden but shared language might be then examined by trained officers of the law and scientific investigators, it soon became apparent in police circles throughout Europe, but especially in Germany, Austria, and France,.

Detectives then realised that a good understanding of the 'criminal mind,' would prove vital in proving solutions in terms of patterns of conduct and most especially signs of ritual murder that might have been, but very usually did not, occur in examples of murder or sadistic attacks of a sexual nature associated, for example, with sexual and obsessive ritual.

Knowledge of this type and a statistical understanding of its meaning by late Victorian investigators might have made a good deal of difference in the Ripper investigation and its disappointing outcome. Gross' work is absorbing reading, not merely because of its comprehensive range in the field of criminology, (it is still used or quoted from as a reference work, even today, and has been continually revised since its first appearance) but also because it reveals to us a contemporary of Holmes, working within roughly similar parameters and with the same apparent zeal, to employ a strictly scientific approach and diversity of interests to the subject matter of crime.

To those students of the man whose cry was so often "Give me data!" it is well worth recommending to those many admirers of the Sherlock Holmes stories and those of us who admire his talented creator and solver of real-life crime, Conan Doyle.

Fig.26. Hans Gross, in later years, whose forensic methods revolutionised what is now usually termed 'criminalistics'.

Fig. 27. High precision lenses like this magnifying lens from 1888, were thought essential to a crime investigation. Photo, c. of D.J. Jones.

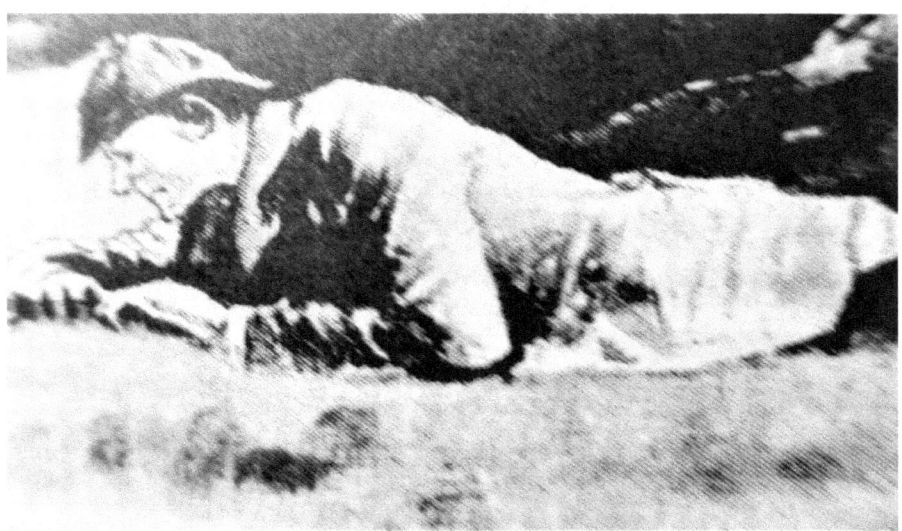

Fig. 28. Hans Gross, like his British colleague, Sherlock Holmes, stressed the importance of footprints and their preservation. A scene here from 'The Boscombe Valley Mystery,' where the explanation of the mystery depends almost entirely upon trace evidence.

Fig. 29. A transvestite Victorian prostitute, posing in a burlesque -
type costume. Such cross dressing photos were popular in the 1880s among some men..

The women of the Sherlock Holmes saga are not infrequently described
to the reader in piteous and oppressed terms. They range from Beryl Stapleton,
who is corrupted and enters a conspiracy with her husband to kill Charles
Baskerville, to Violet Smith. who is forced against her will into an illegal
marriage; ('The Solitary Cyclist'); a woman framed for murder by her
employer's wife, ('Thor Bridge'), a wife whose lover has no option but to beat
her husband to death rather than to witness her being savagely beaten by him,
('The Abbey Grange'); to a daughter locked permanently in a room rather than
submit to her odious father's marital designs upon her, ('The Copper

Beeches'), and finally, to a woman who is drowned with her lover and has one of her ears cut off ('The Cardboard Box').

As William Booth wrote in his polemical essay, which attempted to wag the finger at politicians and the failures of social reform in Britain in the late Victorian age, ('In Darkest England, And the Way Out,' published in 1890, a year bang in the middle of the Holmesian era.):

'We talk about the brutalities of the dark ages, and we profess to shudder as we read in books of the shameful exaction of the rights of a feudal superior. And yet here, beneath our very eyes, in our theatres, in our restaurants, and in many other places, unspeakable though it be but to name it, the same hideous abuse flourishes, unchecked. A young penniless girl, if she be pretty, is often hunted from pillar to post by her employers, confronted always by the alternative, Starve or Sin. And, when once the poor girl has consented to buy the right to earn her living by the sacrifice of her virtue, then she is treated as a slave and an outcast by the very men who have ruined her. Her word becomes unbelievable, her life an ignominy, and she is swept downward, ever downward, into the bottomless perdition of prostitution'.

The story of Miss Kitty Winter, and her vengeful vitriol - throwing attack, aimed at the prosperous businessman and Austrian voyeur, is all the more poignant, perhaps when you consider the period in which this story was being created. For though it was published in March 1923, the story is actually set earlier, in the September of 1902. ('The Illustrious Client.')

London, particularly sections of it, like the Ratcliffe Highway in the East End, and also Shadwell, Spitafields, and Whitechapel - all of these were greatly affected by the trade of prostitution, and I have no doubt that Kitty Winter, in desperation, and plagued by poverty, following the erosion of herself confidence, found herself in need of such a solution.

There were different types of prostitutes. And judging by the drawing which accompanies the 'Strand Magazine story of 'The Illustrious Client,' poor Kitty was not one of the more wealthy whores.

Prostitution in London, particularly in those areas we commented on in the chapters in this series dealing with Jack the Ripper, was literally sectioned up into types of prostitutes. There were, in fact, very few districts of London that didn't boast one variety or another of these women. They counted among their customers, the commercial traveller, who'd come to town on business, (highly likely, in the case of Jack the Ripper), These would have included the commercial traveller; the middle class gentleman and the tradesmen, plus the herds of artisans and manual and factory workers who had come to London for a spending spree, or for a change of scenery.

In the Sherlock Holmes saga, of course, a high class prostitute or 'courtesan,' like Irene Adler, who themselves preferred to be referred to in 'polite society,' were legion. Indeed, many years ago, the esteemed British Sherlockian and social historian, Michael Harrison even wrote a book on the subject, [3] noting therein, that Edward V11th had a whole retinue of distinguished 'courtesans' who, each Christmas, were allowed their own royal carriage in which to travel with him, to Queen Victoria's home in Sandringham, Norfolk, where they disembarked at a small platform, conveniently placed in the woods to avoid them from the public's scrutiny.

This affirmed what I had been informed of by my wife and her sister, who were the grandchildren of Mr Billing, blacksmith from the adjoining village,of Flitcham, who frequently worked on carriages for the Royal Estate, and he most clearly attested his memory of those occasions.

Although 'Bertie's' amorous pursuits may shock us today, he had many male admirers who acted in the same way and did not consider their erotic amusements as a question of morality.

The visitor to London in the 1880s was offered a wide variety of choice when it came to prostitutes.

He would find most certainly what he sought for in the Haymarket or Windmill Street, and the surrounding areas.

The choice of prostitute was extremely varied, according to the needs of the punter, and child prostitution was rampant as Oscar Wilde discovered, initially to his pleasure.

In fact, ironically, the chances of a man being mugged in that area were at their very lowest, compared to areas such as the West End which catered for the more high class 'lady of the night,' as they were then often described.

[3] Michael Harrison, 'Fanfare of Strumpets,' published by W. H. Allen, 1971.

Fig.30. London of the 1880s and 1890s offered a wide variety of prostitutes. This was Mabel Gray, a high class whore who once worked as a shop girl in fashionable Regent Street..

Fig.31. The Canterbury Hall, pictured here in the 1850s, not long after it was erected.

And, because a more well - off person would present a possible means of employment for a whole night, in the 1880s, a number of the popular night houses and casinos in areas such as Cremorne gardens, and the Argyle Rooms, to name but a few, were devoted to drink and dance, activities, which inevitably attracted the work of the prostitutes. And naturally, because the women were obliged to ply their trade, they went to the music halls.in pursuit of the more regular and re wealthy client.

The biggest of these establishments lay in area of Leicester Square where once stood the Empire Theatre of Varieties.

Every night when there was a band playing music, the prostitutes could be seen sitting in parks or in boxes at the theatres or concerts, and there were of course, those of the more richly adorned sort.

Those who, perhaps like Irene Adler, may have accompanied men in the famous Rotten Row, where the horse breakers, as they were described , bore that name as a euphemism for prostitutes.

The whole city of London, we've already mentioned, was infested with ;nests of brothels', according to the newspapers at the time.

As I have also indicated, one of the most notorious areas of all was the Ratcliffe Highway in London in the East End.

At the time when Sherlock Holmes began his career in Baker Street, this street ran parallel with the river Thames from Whitechapel to Stepney.

Thus it was very well placed to serve the huge collection of docks on either side of the Pool of London, where ships anchored prior to delivering their goods to the wharf side.

In every street, in every public house, and often in every lodging house here, were a huge number of brothels, which used to be populated with sailors of all nations. And they were all looking for their appetites to be sated. Where there was a demand for a particular perversity, it very soon was fulfilled by the brothel keepers, as the epic account of one man' sexual odyssey among the fleshpot of late Victorian England, the =anonymously named 'Walter' of the erotic masterpiece, 'My Secret Life', was soon to discover, fulfilled his sexual desires and at one stage, even threatened to bankrupt him. Walter's clientele, he soon discovered, were often women whose work had ceased for various reasons, leaving them with a collection of young mouths to feed. Sometimes they had had criminal convictions such as larceny, or even attacks on rival prostitutes, as in that era a prostitute usually commandeered what was called a 'patch,' or 'pad';meaning that this was regarded as her own, unassailable area which nobody could be allowed to claim was hers.

Fig. 32 (below). The 'Illustrated Police News', showing details of the fifth victim of Jack the Ripper and the crime scene in Berner Street.

Such areas of the Capital were also swarming with a great number of impoverished beggars. At the time when Holmes' resourceful underworld agents roamed these mean streets, in search perhaps of people who had suffered at the hands of predatory men like the odious Gruner, they would soon be seen pleading for pennies in the same breath as they confided obscenities, in the hope of perhaps enlisting a potential client for buggery or oral sex acts in the narrow, ill - lit back streets..

For in the slum areas of all large towns in Britain at that time, there were simply hundreds of displaced young, truant children who had to live by their wits, and had to do so consequently, by begging, stealing or prostituting themselves.

In this context, therefore, we can understand, perhaps even sympathise, with the predicament of Kitty. The attitude of people like the social reformer, William Acton, and to some extent, Henry Mayhew, who remained critical of the Kitty Winters of London, was much influenced by the concept of 'the weakness of women. Of course, they blamed a prostitute and her plight on the shoulders of men. But each then explained it by referring, like the prosperous social reformer, William Acton, to the principle of supply and demand.

When William Acton wrote about the prostitutes of London, he visited the capital in the 1880s and went to a prostitutes' lodging house which had eight rooms. Each of these rooms had been set at two shillings a night. And the landlady informed him that they were each hired more than twice for sexual congress, in the course of just an evening. He then went to a dance room, attached to a pub, where there was often a German band playing. All these sorts of pubs had possees of prostitutes who went there regularly to meet men.

The anonymously, lust - inspired Walter, who we have learned about earlier in this 'Criminal World' series, visited these places often when he frequently made expeditions to slum areas, in order to find cheaper prostitutes that he could afford, since he had then fallen on hard times, at the mid span of his life. And so he had resorted to wearing his oldest clothes, amd masking his face with the peak of a large cap, so he would not be recognised by those who might have seen him elsewhere.

IF he had not done so, he would have been an obvious target, being a man with money in his pocket, and a gold watch on his chain, which would have been quite visible to footpads. Some of the prostitutes of that area who either patrolled the streets, often by now in pairs, following the audacious Ripper crimes, or who attended the many music halls, would encourage more wealthy gentlemen to visit them. Here, once the customer was inside the lodging house, a male companion would then appear; he would be quizzed by the sex worker's pimp and she would then have to yield to his sadistic ompulsions.

Acton, when reviewing the evidence, like many respectable, middle class men of his era would say, that prostitution was fuelled by a number of factors, and perhaps the most important of these was what he termed as 'natural sinfulness'.

The preference to be idle, rather than to work hard to obtain a living, William Acton claimed, did not entirely derive from a state of extreme poverty. He believed that the desire to be a prostitute might be influenced even by genetic factors, thus agreeing with the theories of the misogynist Lombroso who believed that criminals, especially females were born to ctime.

In fact, Acton was not entirely wrong in some of his conclusions. A letter written to 'The Times' newspaper in 1858 by a prostitute, for example, claimed that the thousands of women who were compelled to take to prostitution were poor women, were doomed to toiling on starvation wages, and, if they were simply to allow misery and famine clutch them, they would have to 'render up your body or die'.

In the period when Holmes and Watson witnessed the vitriolic burning of Adelbert Gruner's face, there were literally hundreds of women who had swelled the ranks of prostitutes; women who ranked among their number former dressmakers or hat makers, shoe binders and shop workers.

All these people had suffered as a result of the economic deprivation of the period. And, of all the commentators, perhaps it is Henry Mayhew who provides the most harrowing scenes in the interviews that were conducted by himself and others.

Once thrown upon the rubbish heap of society, these women would have had no hope, other than to ply their trade as a 'drab'. And so did poor Kitty.

We can therefore perhaps better understand the fury of the women who would no doubt have approved of her throwing acid, to wipe the self satisfied smile off the face of that comfortable, well - off Austrian businessman; he who had ruined the lives of so many other women; and who had arranged for a bunch of thugs to attack the French agent, Le Brun with sticks, and as a result, crippled the man for life.

The very visible phenomenon of so many women like the unfortunate Kitty, seen everywhere in London, but also in other British towns, patrolling the streets,and this came to the notice of the 'Pall Mall Gazette' in the July of 1885, when a series of articles commenced, entitled 'The Maiden Tribute of Modern Babylon'.

This series created great alarm. It was regarded as a sensation, an *exposee* which not only had an effect on English Society, but which sent messages throughout Europe France and Belgium, regarding the extreme infestation of prostitution in English society, but especially in London, where such women were seen as 'a disgrace' by a newspaper which was taken seriously by the literate classes, and of course, which is also mentioned by Sherlock Holmes himself.

The public outcry that followed this series was so effective, that it led to a discussion in Parliament where, among MPs, two unrelated things were talked about, but often regarded as synonymous: prostitution and slavery.

Prostitution was regarded by many members of Parliament as a form of slavery, known as 'white slavery', whereby women were seen as victims, unable to control their fate; and a comparison was offered with those people in Greek mythology who every year, were compelled to sacrifice their virginal daughters to the Monster at the Cretan Labyrinth.

In the 'Pall Mall Gazette' article, it was suggested that the women were innocents, sacrificed to the sexual tastes of those men who would then subject them to sadomasochistic acts by wealthy English gentleman, referred to often by French journalists as *'le vice anglais,'* and so 'served as a perversion which became 'the essence of their delight.'

One of the arguments for reform was that the average age of women being in this way abused, was reported by journalists as far below the age of what is now termed in law as 'the age of consent'.

Earlier, in 1880, when Sherlock Holmes was at the commencement of his career. two investigators, Butler and Dyer, published an account of their research into the 'white slave trade ,'and then petitioned Parliament to take action. Butler described 'children, English girls of from 10 to 14 years of age, who have been stolen or kidnapped and carried off from English country villages , and then held captive in Belgium in Brussels, where the presence of 'these children is unknown to the ordinary visitors', and that this human trafficking was 'secretly known only to the wealthy man, who is then able to pay large sums of money for the sacrifice of these innocents'.

Despite the obvious rhetoric of these two commentators, it is a fact that the British Home Office, at that time when Holmes was operating in the capital, was monitoring small groups of English girls who were bound for foreign brothels, especially in Paris. This traffic in under age women in the Sherlock Holmes period was not new, nor was it unusual.

In the summer of 1877, the Belgian consul, Lumley, suggested to Earl Derby, that the average number of young English girls rescued from houses of ill fame in Brussels 'during the last seven years had been 'seven per month.'

Despite this assertion, police inspector David Morgan stated in a report to Parliament that in his division, there could be no white slavery because the 'neighbourhood was too poor.' However, a barrister, Thomas Snagge, who documented the trade in English girls to Belgium, dismissed the evidence because, he declared, 'generally these girls (from Europe) understand the business perfectly well and come over here to be professional prostitutes,' but he then also added that English girls 'were debauched abroad,' and that the women 'were in homes where they were kept as prisoners'. When studying these accounts of the women who were provided in English and continental brothels, and the *modus operandi* which they offered to clients, it became increasingly likely to me that the woman, Beryl Stapleton who posed as Jack Stapleton's sister but was, in reality the wife of Stapleton in the 'Hound of the Baskervilles', was quite likely to have been herself a prostitute. Stapleton may have employed her in his nefarious plans to murder Charles Baskerville and his successor, Henry Baskerville, since she had already assumed a completely fictional identity, calling herself Mrs Vandeleur. when he'd obtained a post at a boys' boarding school.

This fact is supported by evidence in the story of the sadomasochistic treatment by her husband, and persuades me that Beryl Stapleton was one of Stapleton's former clients whom she may have met when plying her trade. most probably in a London brothel.

Fig. 33. (above): Mrs Ronder, wearing a veil to cover her disfigurement in a scene from 'The Veiled Lodger'. She,. like Kitty, was among a number of female victims of male corruption in the Holmes stories.

THE DUDLEY VITRIOL THROWING CASE

Fig. 34. The appalling Dudley vitriol throwing case, sensationally reconstructed here by an unacknowledged artist in 'Police News', June 1885, a case which Holmes would certainly have known of, if we believe Watson's comment regarding his companion's 'knowledge of sensational crime.' The perpetrator was motivated, (as in the case reported in France, and which follows), by jealousy and a desire for revenge. Ellen Bevan had three previous convictions when she was sent to prison in the summer of 1885, but she was subsequently released on licence from the Fulham Refuge on 20 May 1890. She then remained in the south of England, but was again brought before the courts in October 1895, when she was sentenced to 18 months in Wormwood Scrubs for the crime of larceny at St Albans. Newspaper image © The British Library Board.

Express and Echo - Wednesday 23 March 1910
HER REVENGE: Woman Throws Vitriol Over Her Rival IN ALGERIAN THEATRE.

Telegrams from Algiers describe a terrible scene which occurred in the course of a performance at the Nouveau Theatre last night when a woman attacked with vitriol and a razor another woman, whom she accused of enticing away her husband. Her victim was injured in a ghastly way and was crushed among the audience.

Mme. Apasqumo, and the object of her fury, Marie, who has three children, stated she had been deserted by her husband some time ago in favour of the other woman, and had been lying in wait for an opportunity to take her revenge, which occurred last night, when, in the theatre, she found her husband and Marie sitting together. Stealing up behind the unsuspecting pair, without giving anybody a cause to divine her purpose, she suddenly poured the contents of a phial of vitriol over her rival's head, and then, throwing herself upon her, endeavoured to cut her throat with a razor. The agonised shrieks of her victim spread terror throughout the auditorium and, in a moment, there was a rush for the doors, some catastrophe being feared, but those who were sitting in the immediate vicinity, and had witnessed the affair, recovered their presence of mind in time to prevent the completion of the crime. After a struggle, the two women were separated, and Apasqumo was overpowered and arrested. It was then seen that the woman Marie was in a serious condition. She had been horribly disfigured, and was bleeding from several cuts about the neck. A young woman sitting close by had also been burned by splashes of vitriol. After she had been medically examined, it was stated that the throat wounds were not of a dangerous character, but that the result of the vitriol attack would mean she would probably lose her sight completely. Mme. Apasqumo was removed to the police depot, but out of pity for her children, who would otherwise have been left uncared for, was released on bail.

AN ILLUSTRATED GUIDE TO CRIMES AND CRIMINALS
From 'The Strand Magazine', July- December 1897, Vol. 14.

Of all the more hazardous, though thoroughly romantic professions, none is more interesting than that of burgling. The art of burgling and housebreaking has positively developed into a fine art, and although we do not admire the members of the craft, yet every individual representative of it is undeniably interesting. There is something irresistibly tantalizing, yet at the same time fascinating, about your average burglar.

Those of a nervous temperament may look under their beds for a whole twelve month from the 1st of January to the 31st of December. But he is never there. He is a playful fellow - merry man; he likes his joke, for on the very night you forget to peep under the couch where Morpheus receives you for 21 few hours, he is bound to be there, and the next morning you find all your drawers ransacked.

At first you put it down to the dog, but when disappeared, you come to the conclusion that no representative of the canine world who ever barked or picked an honest bone, could. (*In Holmes' time and also for the author of this piece, it certainly was 'new.' It is no longer so, but in my view, as an ex - Londoner, a grand building, nevertheless.]possibly help himself so freely and with so liberal a hand. - KJ*)

The New Scotland Yard Museum will provide much practical information on the ways and means which our friend the enemy utilizes for the purpose of thus annoying you.

Your enterprising burglar shall have what he thoroughly deserves: a complete chapter to himself, and illustrated with his own weapons of warfare into the bargain. Not that we expect that he will be much gratified at the publicity here given to his methods - a publicity which is, all to the [4] advantage of his enemy, the householder, for whom to be forewarned is to be forearmed.

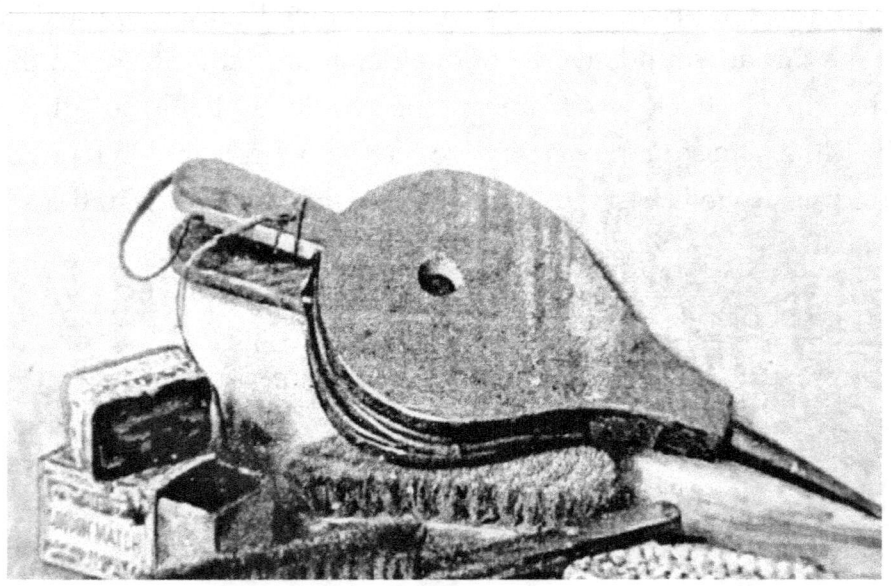

Fig. 35. Type of equipment used by Charlie Peace for smelting down gold and silver plate from his countless burglaries.

---

[4] The elegant lines and exquisite 'Art Deco' feel of this grand old building stand oddly and defiantly in contrast to some of the contemporary architectural monstrosities which desecrate the skyline of my former home city.

Our burglar friends may find a grain of comfort in this fact - that we frankly acknowledge that it is impossible for us to give them as much space in these pages as their unquestionable genius deserves. They are really too inventive, too enterprising. Still, the exhibits in the museum will be of considerable help.

Fig. 36. The Life and Times of Charlie Peace, who did more than any criminal to popularise the 'art of burgling.' A contemporary pamphlet, concerning his escapades.

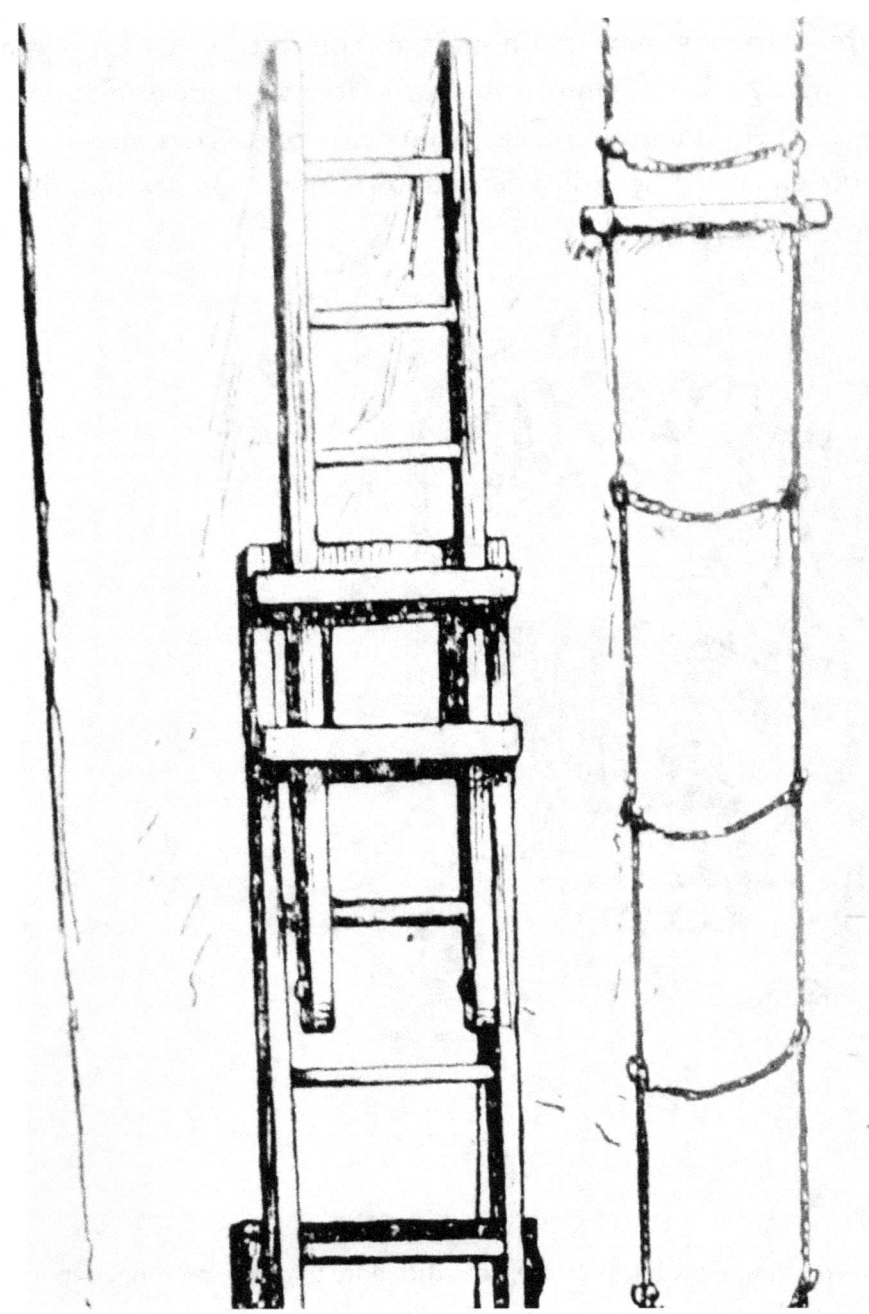

Fig 37. The two types of ladder used by Peace, given to
The Black Museum, shortly after his trial and execution for murder.

Again, a burglar, who was the terror of Birmingham for many years, and who had done fourteen years' penal servitude for burglary and attempted murder, was of the decided opinion that more tools were manufactured in Birmingham than in any town in the country, while the greatest "authority" on burglars' tools in general, and "jemmies" in particular, was the famous American bank burglar, Adams, whose instruments were treasured and preserved at the New York police headquarters. It is probable, however, that most instruments are home-made, or manufactured by an honest - in a strictly burglarian sense - blacksmith.

The first object of housebreaking curiosity you meet with at the New Scotland Yard Black Museum is a complete safe-breaker's outfit, collected at different times by Superintendent Shore, and artistically set out on a board covered with red baize. The dark lantern is at the centre.

Fig. 38. Selection of late Victorian dark lanterns, probably once belonging to Peace. Black Museum.

The steel jemmy surmounts the whole, running in a symmetrically decorative line along the top, and amongst the various items one notices the prising instrument, steel wedges, wood used for obtaining leverage delicately constructed saws, files, and a box of graduated Schultz powder, the latter explosive being used for blowing in a lock when the place where the safe is situated is left totally unattended, and there is no fear of the explosion acting as an alarum.

Burglars' lanterns vary in size - they are known as "darkeys" in the profession, the better class of lantern now in use being of the police pattern; a trifle bulky, perhaps, but nevertheless being very reliable, seeing that they are similar to those of Government make. The group of lanterns at the museum may have cost anything between fourpence and a shilling each, certainly no more. Their owners invariably carry them away, unless disturbed, when they are left behind, as a legacy. The police seldom attach any importance to the finding of a lantern. Yet one or two of them are ingeniously made. There is one made out of a Bryant and May's matchbox. A handle has been put on to the box proper and a space made for the light to come through, so as to he easily covered with the thumb. Such a lantern as this would be used when using a small jemmy. Its companions have a light-hole even smaller still. They are ordinary lanterns with the glass taken out, a piece of tin inserted, and a hole made. Perhaps, however, the most ingenious of them all is a small bottle containing a tiny piece of phosphorus.

Our friend - once the owner of this highly interesting relic - merely had to "shake the bottle," when, lo and behold!…Then a great light shineth!'

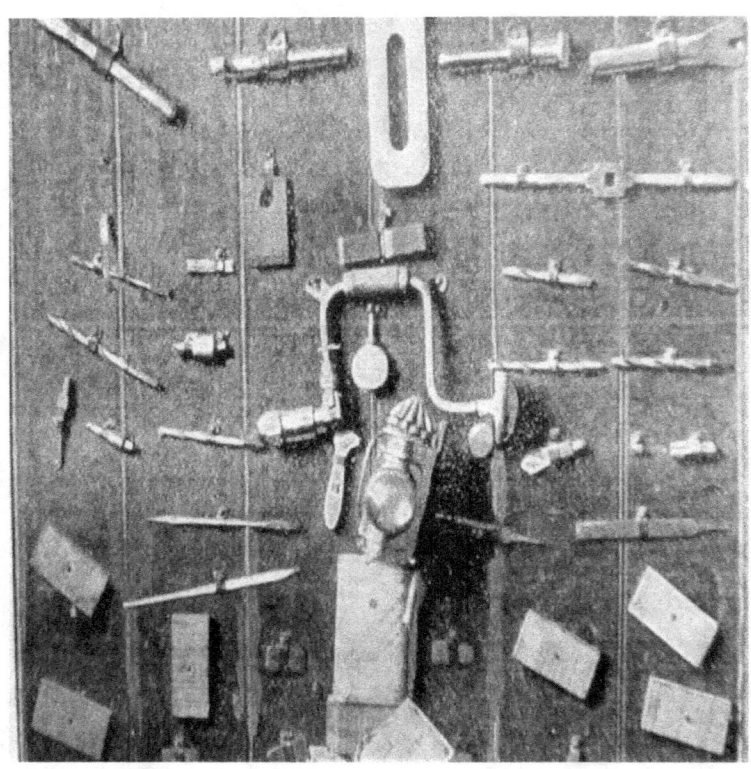

Fig.39 .The famous set of burglary tools, seen here in 'The old Black Museum' at 'NEW Scotland Yard,' which is now, somewhat confusingly, for those who are visitors to the city. 'Old' Scotland Yard.'

(This superb example of Victorian architecture still stands by The River Thames, itself surely a pilgrimage site for serious followers of the adventures of, and the Victorian criminal world of Sherlock Holmes, that place where Holmes would have collaborated with 'the official' police, occasionally providing support for their 'deficiences.' – kj).

The exhibits here comprise samples of probably every tool used in the pursuit of this profession. It has always been an open question as to where burglars and house - breakers obtain their tools. Some three or four years ago it was stated at the Dalston Police Court that one man makes all the burglars' 'jemmies ' in London, and further, that the police knew the man well, were on familiar terms with his own particular trade, but there was positively no law by which he could be arrested or stopped.

(The dark lanterns, pictured in this article, were part of the 'Yard's collection of burglars' essential tool kits. The Holmes stories feature them six times, in SPEC, REDH, SIGN, BRUC, CHAS, and SIXN.)

Fig. 40. There is one other method of gaining light. This is by means of a wax candle stuck in a bit of wax'. However, in this remedy for darkness A need for brightess was created using a piece of phosphorous and a jar.

Perhaps the jemmy was the most popular burglar's tool with which the public would have been on disagreeably familiar terms. They can supply you with any size at New Scotland Yard. Here you have a pretty little thing which is used for safe-breaking purposes. They are all made of the best steel.

This extra long one-it measures 3ft. - is called "The Lord Mayor," whilst its two next sized ones are dubbed "To the Alderman" and "Common Councilman."

It is a significant fact, which has never been satisfactorily explained, that the members of the fraternity of which we are now treating go to the City for names for their jemmies.

Possibly some of them may have comfortable recollections of the Mansion House, and thus take revenge on the Lord Mayor and his colleagues by using them, in the shape of jemmies - for burglarious purposes!

The smaller jemmies are robed in a cloth case; another unscrews in the centre, so as to be more readily carried.

Another is a packing-case opener, such as is used in Covent Garden every day for prising open boxes of fruit. Many are the ways adopted for carrying these.

It is generally believed by the authorities that in the conveying of burglars' tools, cabmen are often in league with the offending parties. A cabman going through the streets at night can jog along unnoticed, especially if a lady and gentleman in evening dress are inside.

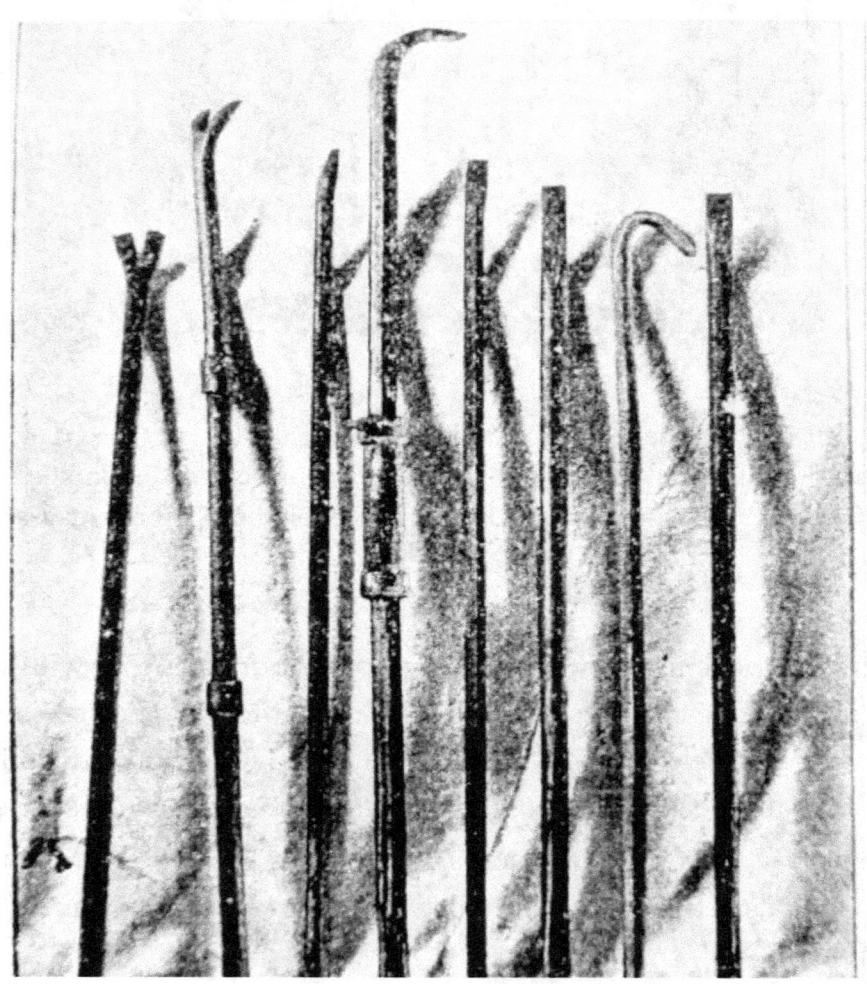

Fig. 41. (Above). A fine set of burglars' jemmies, once part of The Scotland Yard 'Black Museum collection.

The general rule is to carry jemmies down the leg of the trousers or up the sleeve whilst other tools are smuggled into long pockets of the "rabbit " pattern, such as used by the old-time poachers. Perhaps the most remarkable place in which a burglar carried his tools was a euphonium. However, he succeeded in passing through the City as a "wait," and made a fairly good profit out of the night's proceedings. It is not on record whether the constable on point wished him a merry Christmas, or not.

We are inclined to tell a story which we have every reason to believe to be perfectly true. It was told to the writer by a burglar. The burglar stated that in country 'affairs' it is always deemed wise to hide the tools to be used somewhere near to the spot to be operated upon, and not to carry them about the person. He had hidden his tools in a hedge in the morning. When he arrived in the afternoon to the previous. to setting out for the scene of the burglar, he found them gone. Whilst hunting around, he noticed some children romping about in an adjoining field. One little bright-eyed lassie saw him, and leaving her companions, ran up to him and said, in childlike way: "Please, sir, I've found this." "This" was the burglar's tools tied up in a piece of black cloth. The little girl was rewarded with sixpence.

Of skeleton keys there is a very admirable selection at New Scotland Yard. They are made both of iron and steel, mostly of scrap iron, as it is tougher and has no grain in it. Burglars and housebreakers usually make their own skeleton kcys, some of which are very rough. The key is bought in the block, and the wards are cut out as needed. Those shown are of two kinds. The bunch consists of " pick~locks," which are made of stout wire. A housebreaker has to be caught with as many as thirty of these picklocks in his possession. For larger locks, the keys are much stronger. The pretty, little, cloth case was found on a gentleman. These would be used for opening heavy doors.

Of those shown it will be noticed that all save two are made with the wards to both ends. There can be no doubt as to the efficiency of skeleton keys, and lever locks are strongly recommended to the wise, as it would be impossible to open one with a "skeleton."

We now come to the wedges-apparently very small, but incalculably important items in the particular branch of art with which we are now dealing. Wedges may be either of wood or steel, and are used for driving under doors whilst working in a room. They are usually held tight to the door by a gimlet, so that if the housebreakers were disturbed and an attempt was made to open the door, the more the opposing party waned to push outside, the tighter the door would become.

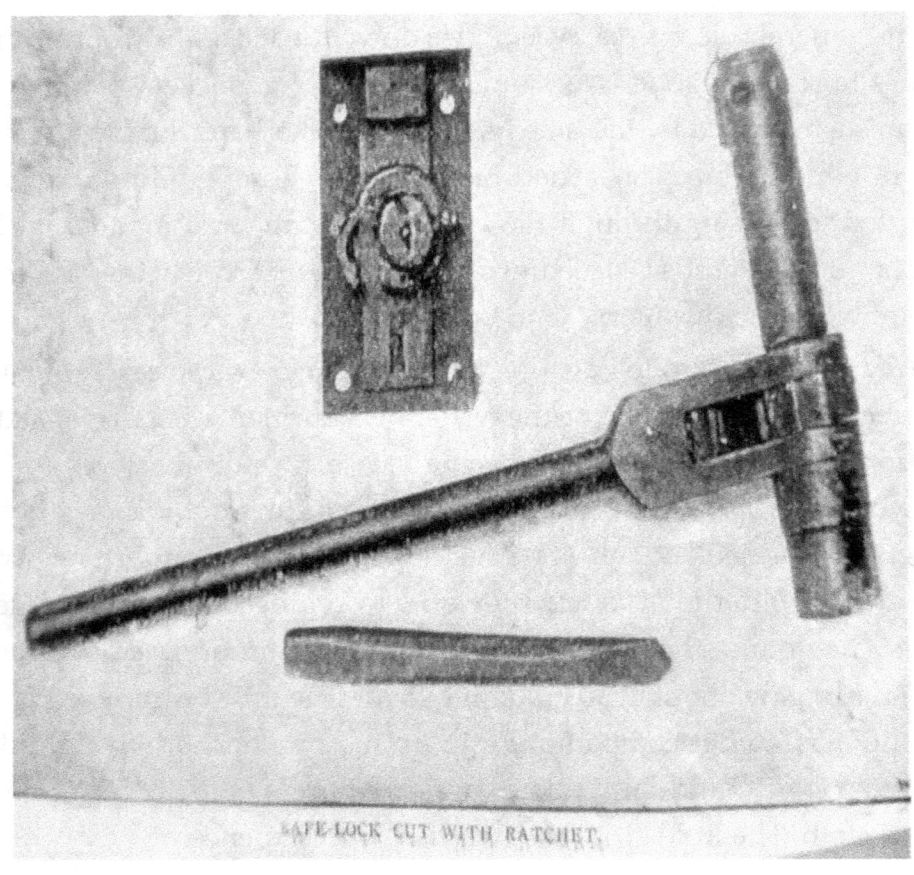

Fig 42. . A ratchet and wedge, used together, were an efficient way of gaining access to a property fast. From The Black Museum collection.

Fig.43. Some of the London cab men were believed to be in cahoots
with members of the burgling community but nothing was proven.

The only hope would be to force the doors and, the thieves in nine cases
out of ten would have ample opportunity to get away.

You may find at Scotland Yard the mahogany leg of a parlour chair, with
a number of wedges by its side, which tells a story of ingenuity as clever as
anything of its kind ever conceived by any novelist. More than that, it reflects
the greatest credit upon the skill our detectives and police officials. These
simple harmless - looking little wedges were quite sufficient to get the criminal
three by twenty years' penal servitude for burglary.

It was 1875. A number of burglaries were being committed in a certain
district of London. Almost invariably the perpetrators were foolish on these
particular occasions, for they left their wedges behind them. These were,
however, treasured by the police. When the men were eventually arrested, it

was found that a chair at their lodgings was minus a leg, and when the wedges were pieced together, and -hey, presto! here was the mahogany leg!

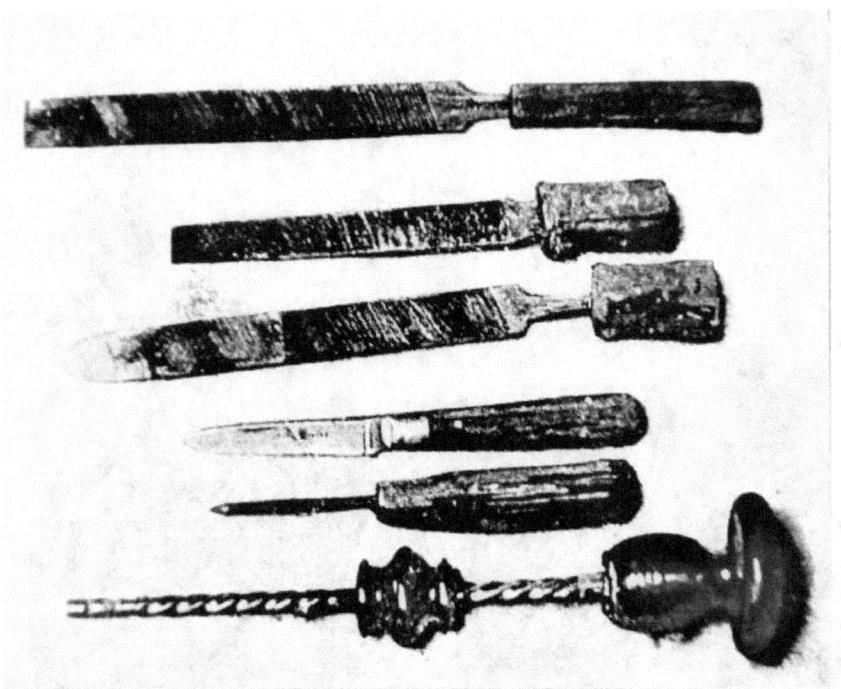

Fig. 46. A set of burglar's picklock tools. Black Museum, Scotland Yard.

Equally interesting and simple little items which tell a big story and carry with them heavy punishments. In this case it is a group of articles comprising a number of bullets, a wooden wedge, a truncheon case showing bullet marks a soft black felt hat, and two chisels.

Above the case is an enlarged photo of some weapons. They are relics of the murder of Police Constable Cole, on December 8th, 1882, by Thomas Henry Orrocks. Orrocks left his lodgings, in a turning out of Dalston Lane, where the affray took place, the old hat, the wooden wedge, and the two chisels being used. He was suspected of the crime.

The discovery was made that he had been practising with a revolver at Tottenham Marshes, and a bullet found in a tree there was identical with those found in the constable's truncheon case. But the most convincing evidence was the fact that when the chisels were photographed, the word "Rock" was found scratched near the handle.

It is a fact, not generally known, that photography can render visible what the eye is quite unable to discern. It was sufficient to trap Thomas Henry Orrocks. Perhaps, however, the button incident is the prettiest example of all.

What a warning to burglars! The relics consist of an old black overcoat with a bone button piece, broken off in a carefully preserved small wooden box.

In January, 1874, a burglary was committed ln the vicinity of Westminster. A little piece of freshly broken - off bone button was foolishly left on the window-sill. This the police kindly and considerately took charge of. A man was suspected, but there was no evidence against him to justify an arrest. But an enterprising police officer clung to that bit of button, and one night, he chanced to come across a gentleman with a button that had a piece missing. "Halloa," he exclaimed, "button broken, eh ?"

"Yes," replied the proprietor of the old black overcoat. " I've lost it. I don't know where it is."

"I know," said the calculating detective. "Here it is! Why, bless me, it just fits, my friend!"

Some of the stolen property was found in his pockets. The cap meant the button fitted. He received a sentence of three years.

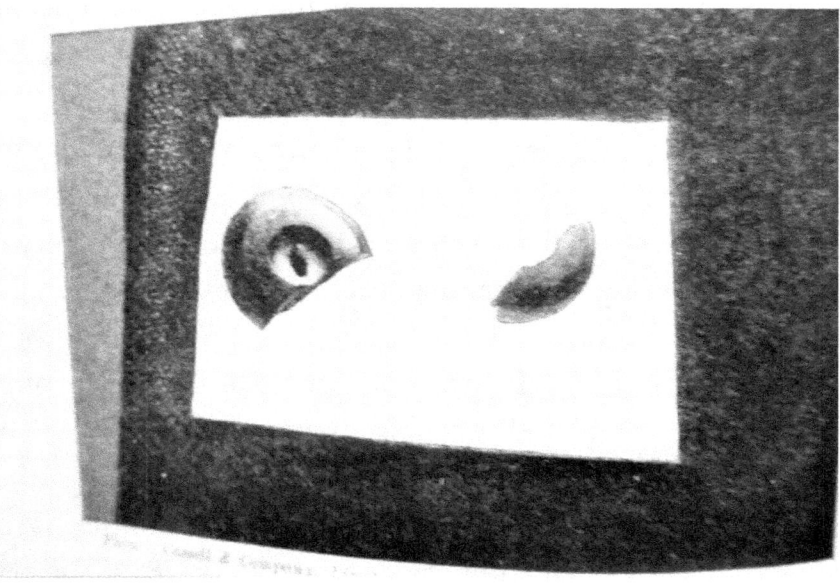

Fig. 47. The small piece of button, discovered at the scene of a famous Victorian murder, and kept in the Black Museum. concerning a vicious burglar who was convicted on the basis of a small piece of broken button - thus being among the first of convictions based upon scene of crime material, and linking the murderer to his victim.

Among the miscellaneous exhibits at the New Yard is a piece of wood cut out of a stable door at Kensington. It is thick and bulky; would take ten minutes or a quarter of an hour to cut; and is a good example of the work done with the ordinary stock and centre bit. It is of sufficient size to allow the hand and arm to go through comfortably, so that the bolt of the door may be drawn back. An artist's palette knife is by its side, which is used for opening window sashes. If your housebreaker found that he had to deal with a patent lock, he would cut the windowpane, by placing brown paper over the glass and working over that, so that no noise is made. But it may bc mentioned that this is rarely done.

An illustration is given of a lock of a safe cut away by a ratchet. It is an ordinary ratchet about 2ft. long. It is in reality a common workman's tool, and is used every day on palings in the streets. Such an article as this is bought in any ironmonger's shop. But who would ever think of using such a tool as this? The instrument for cutting through shutters is rather more ingenious.

This is evidently a home-made tool. It is a steel-cutter and can be made any size by moving the centre-bit. A knife is at each end, being kept in position by a long screw. A hole is made in the shutter first, the graduated screw is inserted, and, as this is driven in, so the knives cut their way. It is surmised that this shutten cutter was not found to answer the purpose for which it was intended, as it is the only one ever found by the police. The other specimen is for wooden shutters - the tridents being so made that whilst one cuts, the other scoops out.

The collection of revolvers is unique and it is hung on the walls of the museum with a decided eye to effect. They comprise weapons of every type and pattern. The two specially selected, which appear above a very formidable dagger, evidently of Eastern manufacture, have their own peculiar history. The small one is the centre of attraction amongst a strange group of relics, consisting of a pair of links, the clasp of a purse, a little piece of steel which fitted inside a bracelet, and even a piece of a heel-tip. The heel-tip corresponded with the footprints of a suspected man, and, together with the remains of the trinkets, helped to bring a verdict of "Guilty." All these are associated with the Muswell Hill burglary of January, 1889. The revolver was used by one of three men who were all subsequently sentenced to penal servitude for life for shooting at Mr. Atkin.

Fig.48. Below.A large presentation case, containing a collection of weapons unique in the annals of British 19th C. cime. Several of the items shown here are believed to have originated at the Yard's Black Museum, following the arrest of Charl Peace but some are from the Muswell Hill and Hoxton burglaries.. Note the popularity of the Webleys, and the often quoted, lead - tipped cosh or 'Neddy,' so enamoured by garrotters like Parker. Photo source: Griffiths, Vol. 2 (q,v.)

The larger revolver, which has an exceptionally heavy central fire, belonged to a top-hat shooter. On July 18th, 1884, a burglary was attempted at Hoxton. The police chased burglars over the roofs of the houses, and a worthy named Wright, who had attempted to make himself look highly respectable in a silk hat, amused himself by clinging to a chimney- pot with one arm, and using the other to practise shooting with, the targets being the constables. Mr. Wright is not likely to play at this very risky pastime again. He is Her Majesty's guest for life in a palatial residence, specially constructed for dispensing hospitality to such gentlemen.

The life preservers are interesting. They hang in a delicious group, just by the window. They are of all sorts and sizes. One swings on a piece of thick cord heavily loaded; another is made of rhinoceros hide. A pretty little invention in these specialities doubles up and fits the waistcoat pocket, the more popular example being made out of a piece of cord, twisted round a short cane with a lead shot at both ends.

The life preservers have a curious companion, a pair of coverings, very rudely made out of coarse linen for the feet, which the burglar puts over his boots out of thoughtful consideration for the slumbers of his victims.

The disguises used and treasured at New Scotland Yard chiefly consist of false whiskers and beards. They are all made of dark crepe hair and fastened to wires, which fit over the ear and keep them in position. The most original idea for concealing the face, however, is given a prominent place. Its wearer was a most unfortunate individual, and there is every reason to believe that he has the warm sympathy of all his brother professionals. He was "specially engaged" on a public house in the New North Road after closing time. He was found under the bed, and hurried to get away, being most determinedly chased by the energetic landlord. The owner of the black billycock, fancying he saw a means of escape, made for a window. But his patent hat and face protector served him a shabby trick. The man only saw a window and not the iron bars between a couple of which his head lodged in, as though specially designed for the purpose. The landlord - who was fortunately blessed with a delightfully humorous disposition, - prodded the "bar" lodger with a sword-stick. The poor man, being then prodded upon, assisted his captor by yelling for the police himself! Result, 5 years.

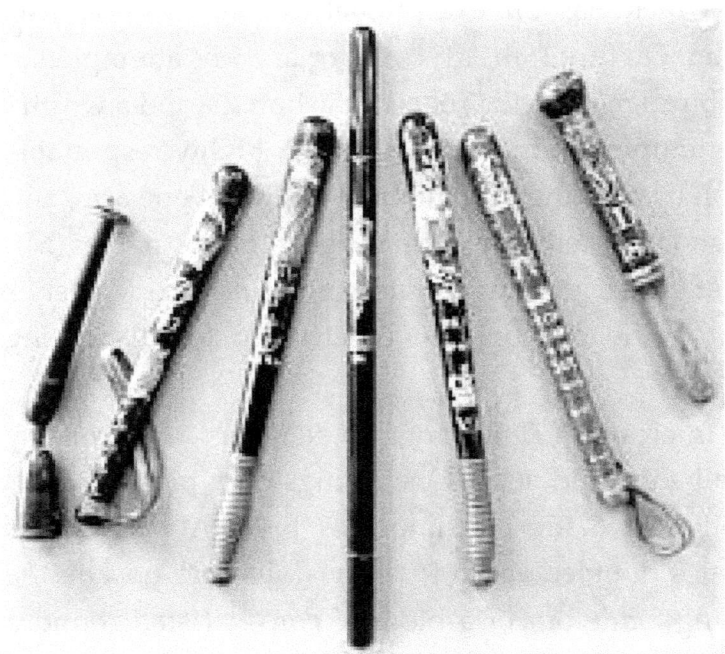

Fig 49, Victorian 'life preservers, often carried ornate designs. C. The London Museum.

Fig.48 . The billycock hat, the type of hat which undoubtedly featured as the more battered equivalent in 'The Blue Carbuncle,' shown here and used in a bungled burglary in London's New North Road.

There are many exhibits at the museum used in this special branch of burglary - rope ladders, treadles, strings, coils of copper wire, gimlets, wedges, woollen stockings to go over boots, etc. The rope ladders, known as 'slings,' are often 5ft. and 3ft. long, and are made with rope treads just sufficient to put the foot in. A hook is at the end, which is lodged on some convenient support strong enough to hold the weight of the man ascending, They are generally carried by winding them about the body.

The wire, string, wedges, socks, etc., in the illustration were found at Ealing when the men escaped. They had 'wired' the house and grounds all over. This is done in order that, if they are chased, the wires, which are placed at ankle height, trip the pursuer up, the thieves themselves knowing of their whereabouts, by putting a piece of white paper in their immediate vicinity.

These are the simple appliances of your truly artistic burglar-the man who has been laying his plans for months, the individual who will pay a hundred visits to the house before he brings about his grand 'coz', who will know the value of every piece of jewellery the ladies are wearing at the dinner-table, and be fully aware of the exact place, where to lay his wily fingers on them in the dressing-room. This is the class of men who are the greatest trouble to the police - these are the best customers of the receivers.

Frequently a man is employed to do all the planning and mapping out for the party who will do the actual job. For this he is paid a certain price - or perhaps a commission on the results of the robbery. This person will draw up a plan of the house as true- though perhaps not quite as artistic as any architect. But he gives the thief the very information he needs, and puts on the map of the house and grounds the exact position where the operator must "beware of the dog."

A man named Connor is credited at New Scotland Yard with being one of the finest adepts at this particular work, of all which have come under their notice. He used to lecture on this peculiar art to young thieves, and whilst in prison, wrote a work giving them practical advice on the subject. The prison officials allowed him to finish his literary effort, and when his time expired, coolly appropriated the same.

No article dealing even in a small way with "Burglars and Burgling" would be complete without some reference to "The King," and the relics of this talented individual are of a highly interesting character.

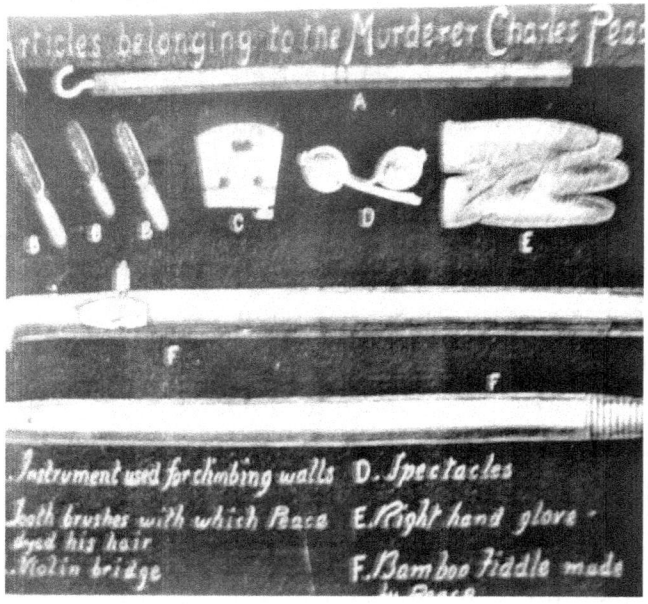

In the image, handwritten labels read:

Articles belonging to the Murderer Charles Peace

. Instrument used for climbing walls   D. Spectacles

. Tooth brushes with which Peace dyed his hair   E. Right hand glove

. Violin bridge   F. Bamboo fiddle made

Fig.50. The smelting pot which was used by Holmes' 'good friend,' Charlie, in which Peace would melt down his gold and silver ornaments, after yet another of his successful burglaries.

THE LEGEND OF CHARLIE PEACE

Charles Peace thoroughly deserved to be crowned the king of all burglars, housebreakers, and scoundrels in general. Peace always worked single-handed. He had no "receiver," and melted down all his own stuff and sold it as a matter of business.

All his stock-in-trade is to be found at the museum. His tools are only ten in number, and comprise a skeleton key, two pick-locks, a centre-bit, a large gimlet, a gouge, a chisel, a small vice (for turning keys on the outside of doors-used when people leave the key in the lock), a jemmy (about 5ft. long), and a knife. With these Peace consistently worked and achieved a success rate which earned him a legendary reputation.

Neither are his blue spectacles and case missing. These he used for purposes of disguise, though when arrested at Blackheath, his face was stained with walnut-juice, in the hopes of passing off as a Mulatto. His ladder was quite a unique arrangement. When doubled up it is to all outward appearances simply a bundle of blocks of wood such as any carpenter might carry home for firewood. But it opens out to a length of some 13ft., working on a bolt, with a hole at one end to hook on a nail in the wall, and so complete facilities were afforded for climbing to window or veranda. In addition to his tools he called into requisition a pony and trap at night. He practically killed the pony with hard work.

The crucible in which he did his melting down is of clay and was found at Peckham. Its interior is much scorched. It is about 6in. deep inside, and the diameter of the orifice is 4in.

Peace was truly magnificent in all he undertook in his own peculiar profession; he positively arose to greatness. In the midst of his burglaries he kept up a fine house at Peckham, with two house-keepers and a servant. His drawing-room suite was worth sixty guineas, a Turkey carpet was laid on the floor, gilded mirrors decorated the walls; and on the grand piano was a beautifully inlaid Spanish guitar worth some thirty guineas.

He lived the life of an independent gentleman. He was passionately fond of music, and on the night of the attempted robbery at Blackheath, he had an at-home concert, and whilst one housekeeper played the piano and another sang, Charles joined in with the violin.

His audacity was such that at the time his name was on everybody's lips, and Scotland Yard was full of him. He visited the Yard disguised as a clergyman and asked a number of questions about himself!

His false arm was a unique idea. He was minus the forefinger of the left hand, and after he left Sheffield on 29th November, 1876, his description was posted at every police-station in the country.

So he made himself this arm which he placed in his sleeve, hanging his violin on the hook when engaged in walking about and taking stock of "crackable" residences; and screwing in a fork in the place of the hook for use at meals.

So, for something like two years the irrepressible Peace walked this earth short of a hand, whilst the police were looking for a man short of a finger!

SUPPLEMENT: PEACE: VICTORIAN FOLK HERO, BUT NOT A MAN OF PEACE.

Arthur Griffiths, the prolific but reliable chronicler of late Victorian crime, (*Mysteries of Police and Crime*) records that, in 1876, Peace was busy organizing several burglaries in the East Riding of Yorkshire.

It is conceivable that the 22-year-old Holmes may well have met this man when he was visiting his parents in the East Riding. (How else would he have known Peace was a violin virtuoso?) Peace, according to Griffiths, who knew him personally, was a very direct man of a practical turn of mind, and it is difficult to see how Holmes' adjective of "complex" could really apply. He was arrested in dramatic circumstances at a house in Blackheath when Holmes was at the height of his career (1878).

By then he was a wanted man, having murdered his neighbour, Mr. Dyson, two years previously. Peace had amorous designs on Dyson's Sheffield wife and had been warned off by Dyson. Undaunted, Peace began to harass Dyson and eventually shot him dead in his own back garden. He later shot a policeman in Manchester, a crime for which another suspect, William Habron, was wrongly convicted. Peace had the cheek to attend Habron's trial in disguise!

After Sheffield, Peace moved to a house in the East Riding, and then to Nottingham, where he carried out a series of warehouse robberies. When things got too hot for him, he moved to Lambeth, London. Then he moved with his lover to Greenwich and thence to Peckham, to a bigger house, furnished principally with the proceeds of his countless break-ins.

The contents of his drawingroom comprised a walnut suite (50 guineas – a fortune in those days), ornate mirrors, Turkish carpets, a bijou piano, a Spanish guitar, and several fine Cremona fiddles, the latter of which would have amused the inhabitants of Baker Street. (Did Holmes obtain his Stradivarius via Peace?)

Peace was greatly and very skilfully accomplished. Maintaining a respectable veneer, he employed several matrons at various rented addresses to guard his "valuables." One aspect of his character would have earned the detective's admiration, for he was a master of disguises, appearing for example in Peckham, as a one-armed man with a hook, and in Greenwich as a kindly churchwarden.

On November 17, 1878, Constables Robinson and Girling were on watch outside No. 2, St. John's Park, Blackheath (the original house still stands). The night was very dark so that, when Robinson saw a candlelight flickering in the kitchen, he knew his chance had come to earn himself some promotion. Peace put up a good fight. After firing five shots, he tried to stab Robinson with a sheath - knife but he desisted once the "bracelets" were clapped round his wrists. His face was stained with walnut-juice, he then claiming to be an American half caste. After a fortnight this alias yielded to another. This time he was Johnson, a labouring type who lived in Peckham. No doubt this facility with disguises would also have amused Sherlock Holmes.

A search of his clothing yielded several pawn tickets which indicated the proceeds of his recent burglaries.

When he was subsequently removed from Pentonville prison to the Leeds Assizes, Peace attempted a daring escape from a railway carriage but succeeded merely in fracturing one of his legs.

He was a true professional, as his collection of picks and skeleton keys in the Black Museum testifies to his skills. Nor was he without a sharp sense of humour. Griffiths recorded this story when he visited him in prison, shortly before his execution:

"What is the good of telling the truth? No one believes you when you do. ... When I was Mr. Johnson of Peckham, I went into the chemist's one morning, smoking an excellent cigar. The chemist said: 'That's a fine cigar." Some weeks afterwards I came across a fine lot of Havanas in a house I visited late at night, and I secured them. The chemist got a box of them. "'There, Mr. So-and-So,' I said, 'I have stolen you these. I hope you'll like them.' He laughed loudly, and no more believed me than before."

When he was arrested at Blackheath he is alleged to have said: "Wot! Only two on yer? I thought the whole bloomin' Force was after me!"

Until the Blackheath capture, Peace remained elusive and an embarrassment to the Yard. Did Holmes contrive his capture?

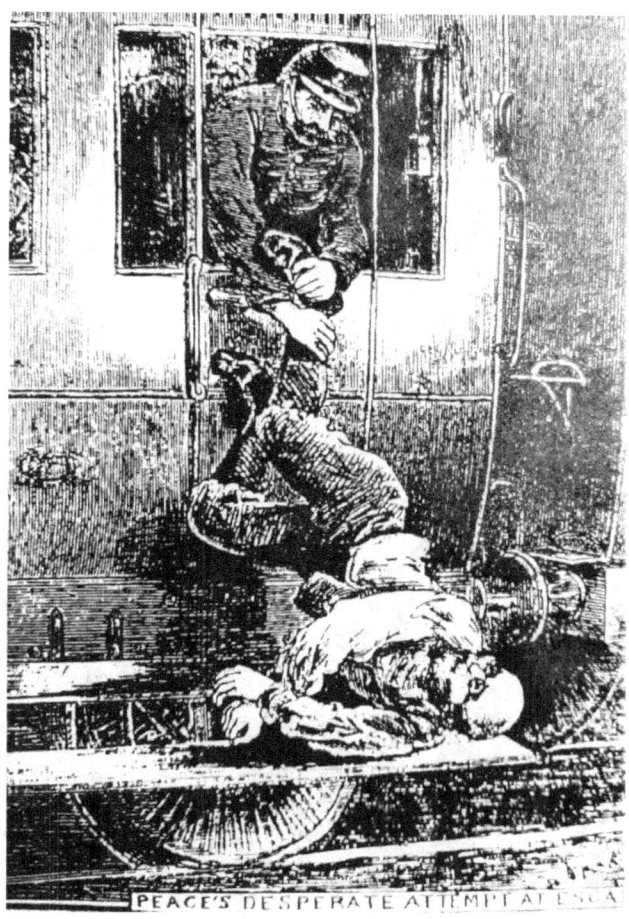

Fig. 51. Peace escaped his captors after a loo request was granted.
He then squeezed his body through a carriage window.

Fig 52. The hanging of Charlie Peace. From a popular chapbook,
published in the year he died, 1879. Author's collection.

HOLMES AND THE ANARCHISTS: A STUDY OF THE YOXLEY OLD PLACE AFFAIR.

Fig. 53. The murder of General Trepoff.

Perhaps it is hardly surprising that those enigmatic revolutionaries, the nihilists, anarchists and socialists occasionally gain a mention in the Sherlock Holmes Saga. However, Conan Doyle was not alone among his contemporaries in providing these intrepid emigrés with a little passing publicity. Joseph Conrad's darkly prophetic 'The Secret Agent' devoted an entire novel to the activities of the Anarchists (it is a meticulously researched piece of fiction). Robert Louis Stevenson, whom Doyle greatly admired, used the Nihilists' bomb - throwings as the subplot of his 'The Dynamiters' (1884); whilst G, K. Chesterton exploited the theme in his story, 'The Man who was Thursday'.

The years 1880-1900 witnessed a phase of intense upheaval in European political ideology and it was from this period that the revolutionaries gained both their birth and subsequent notoriety, both of which are reflected in the fiction of the period.

Of all the European nations, only England resisted this turmoil unscathed. Perhaps the tradition of extreme conservatism that had dogged English politics since the time of Cromwell, acted as a restraint on the British people, or perhaps the iron grip of the Victorian class system provided the ultimate form of resistance to the new '-isms.'

The English, always a pragmatic people, were deeply suspicious of new ideas, even from France. The subsequent fate of Oscar Wilde and his doctrine of art for arts sake is a prime example, where the 'Bohemian' was considered an enemy of society and a figure of decadence who represented a threat to the moral order.

Nevertheless, in late Victorian England, a continual battle was fought between the political fugitives from Russia, Italy and France who settled in London, and the newly established *agentes provocateur* of the Special Branch.

Throughout this period the sensational press continued to publicise the wilder exploits of these ideologically inspired revolutionaries. The press, like the great British reading public, understood little of their beliefs or opinions and was far more interested in their so-called criminal activities.

This state of ignorance is well illustrated in '*The Six Napoleons*,' when the shopkeeper, Morse Hudson, observes:

'Disgraceful sir! A Nihilist plot, that's what l make it. No one but an Anarchist would go about breaking statues. Red republicans, that's what I call 'em. '

Hudson is obviously very confused since he speaks as if he believes these three distinct terms are one.

In fact, nothing could be further from the truth.

In the newspapers of the late '80's and '90's, however, the terms 'nihilism' and 'anarchism' were bandied about in just such a manner, even by the heavyweights of Fleet Street.

Since that time there has been little to alter these misconceptions. Even today, in England, in the mass media, the word 'anarchist' invariably summons up a picture of a destructive hoodlum to the average man or woman, whilst the term 'nihilist' usually creates nothing but confusion.

Nihilism has, like anarchism, a specific meaning. It was first applied in the 1860's to a Russian revolutionary philosophy which advocated the destruction of all types of government, institutions, traditions and class distinctions. There was nothing new in this idea. It had its roots partly in the French Revolution and was clearly defined by (among others) the French philosopher Rousseau. However, the term was first used in Turgenev's novel 'Fathers and Son,' then coming into prominence.

He is described as one 'who does not bow down before any authority, who does not take any principle on faith, whatever reverence that principle may be enshrined in', one who refuses 'to talk nonsense about art, parliamentarianism, trial by jury... while all the time, it is a question of getting bread to eat,' and one who is persuaded that there is no 'single institution' in our present mode of life, in family or in social life, which does not call for complete and unqualified destruction.'

Turgenev's portrayal of the Nihilist philosophy concentrated on one specific and overriding feature: its contempt for sentimentality and tradition. In this respect Nihilism represented a total antithesis to the English way of life, as exemplified in Edmund Burke's philosophical writings. The past had to be done away with, the only truth was that of scientific and material evidence. It is small wonder that England hated the Nihilists.

Stepniak ('Underground Russia', Eng. trans, 1883, Ch,4, p.8.), the author himself a Nihilist, described the development of this new ideology as 'a struggle for the emancipation of intelligence from every kind of dependence.'

The fundamental principle of Nihilism, properly so called, was a belief in absolute individualism. It was the negation, in the name of individual liberty, of all the obligations imposed upon the individual by society, by family life and by religion. a reaction against the moral despotism that weighs upon the private and inner life of the individual.

The Nihilists' sole god was, according to Stepniak, that of pure reason, and Art was irrelevant since it was not explicable in rational terms. The Nihilists' future world was, he believed, a scientific utopia.

In the period 1860-70, Nihilism progressed from being a philosophical and literary movement to that of a practical and militant organisation.

In 1866, the attempted assassination of Emperor Alexander produced an outburst of hysteria and Nihilism's political force was strengthened by the Paris Commune which endeavoured to bring together the various and disparate elements of social democracy.

The next phase in the development of Nihilism was inextricably bound up with the rise of two other important movements: Anarchism and Socialism.

Anarchism shared with Nihilism the two principles of individual freedom and a rejection of government as a repressive and immoral force.

However, where it differed was in its suggestion of a reorganised society, based upon the principle of collectivism.

The principles of Anarchism were announced to the world during the congresses of *The First International* (1864) and later at the Jurassian Federation. However, the first international body of anarchists was founded by Michael Bakunin and Elisee Reclus in 1865. It was anti-statist, atheist and committed to the use of force. Later it was replaced by a secret international Alliance of Social Democracy, founded by Bakunin, at the end of 1868. The aim of the Alliance was to destroy the basis of existing society, and to replace it by a series of federations of self - serving political units.

The offices of the Federation were situated in Geneva, and it was not long before linked branches appeared in France, Spain, Switzerland and Italy. It had been Bakunin's aim for the Federation to join Karl Marx's Alliance but he was refused permission to do this because of certain profound ideological differences.

The clash between the Socialists and Anarchists amounted to this; both believed in the revolt of the working classes. However. Marx maintained that the assumption of political power by the proletariat should be achieved by electoral means, whereas the Anarchists were convinced this should be achieved by force. (Following the massacre of thousands of communards, Marx later changed his views.) But there were other divisive issues.

Bakunin wanted the abolition of the state and the destruction of the very principle of authority.

The principles of Anarchism were announced to the world during the attempt on the life of Count Von und zu Grafenstein; and finally in *'The Adventure of the Golden Pince-nez'*, where the principal characters are Russian Nihilist emigres.

THE BOULEVARD ASSASSIN

By the time he came to write 'The Golden Pince-nez', Conan Doyle had clearly become quite fascinated by the activities of these political revolutionaries.

The story opens with Watson referring to Holmes' 'tracking and arrest of Huret, the Boulevard assassin - an exploit which won for (him) an autographed letter of thanks from the French President and the Order of the Legion of Honour. *'The Golden Pince-Nez'* took place in 1894 and perhaps the most remarkable assassination attempt of that year was that of the French President, Marie Francois Sadi Carnot.

On June of that year, while driving to the Exposition Coloniale, in Lyons, he was stabbed by Cesare Giovanni Santo, an Italian Anarchist. On June 26, 'The Times' had reported that Santo was a 'Nihilist'.

Even such an august newspaper as this suffered from semantic confusion, it seems. Although Santo claimed he had no accomplices, the French authorities, seeking vengeance, arrested some 200 known Anarchists but later released them without charge. Santo was brought to trial on August 3rd but still refused to name his fellow anarchists. The following day he was sentenced to death.

The French police continued to persecute the Anarchists. On the 7th of August, 25 of them were again brought to trial but one week later 22 were acquitted, again through lack of positive evidence.

The extreme mishandling of the Santo affair would obviously have attracted the attention of Doyle who, as we know, had links with the Sureté and it seems obvious that thc opening of *The Golden Pince-Nez* is a distinct reference to the French Anarchists.

'IT WAS SHE.'

The Nihilist identities of both Professor Coram and Anna form the background to this unusual story, and it is clear from reading the story that Doyle had the Petrograd purges in mind:

'We were reformers (Anna tells Holmes), - revolutionists-Nihilists, you understand. He and I and many more. Then there came a time of trouble, a police officer was killed, many were arrested, evidence was wanted, and in order to save his own life and to earn a great reward, my husband (Sergius) betrayed his own wife and his companions. Yes; we were all arrested upon his confession. Some of us found our way to the gallows and some to Siberia. . .'

In my study of the geography relating to this strange but very convincing tale of love, passion and revolution, in the Kent village I revealed to be the place where lay the true location of Yoxley Old Place.

Coram's residence was then known as Rede House, and it was situated near Strood, Kent (not far from Chatham and Rochester). Until its demolition in the 1930's it had formed a magnificent local landmark. And it had connections with a bunch of reformers who fascinated Conan Doyle. The central character's full name in this Russian revolutionary's drama was one Sergei Slepniak-Krauchinsky. A leading figure in the Nihilist movement, he was also acquainted with Bakunin and Kropotkin. (The link between Doyle and Wilde is more fully explored in my 'Sherlock Holmes And The South Eastern,' pp. 19-20)

Fig 54. Conrad's novel, 'The Secret Agent,' helped spread public fear of Russian revolutionaries.

Fig 55. This drawing, illustrating a story by
Eugene Moret in the 'Strand,' shows the widespread fear
  of the political movements in Europe which were later
  defined as 'Anarchism' and 'Nihilism.'

The reader will recall that, following Holmes' return to Baker Street in 1894, it was one Oscar Meunier who created the wax effigy that foiled Colonel Sebastian Moran.

The name Oscar Meunier is an interesting (if unconscious) compound of two revolutionaries: Oscar Wilde, with whom Doyle was personally acquainted, and for whom he had the greatest respect until the author's fall from grace: and Theodule Meunier, a French anarchist.

On 15 March 1892 a bomb, planted by Meunier, was found on a window of the Lobau barracks.

Meunier escaped, wasn't prosecuted and eventually made his way to London where he remained until 1894.

Throughout the spring of 1894 a series of bomb outrages continued to wreak havoc in Paris. On 4 April a bomb thrown into the bohemian Foyot Restaurant blinded the French writer Laurent Tailhade.

The French police were thus gratefully relieved when Theodule Meunier was arrested on the very same day as he was attempting to board a train at

Victoria Railway Station, bound for the Isle of Sheppey. He was later extradited and sentenced to perpetual labour in Cayenne.

On three subsequent occasions Doyle used the term 'Nihilism' in passing, in the Holmes saga (he, like many of his contemporaries, used it as a synonym of Anarchism); once in 'Wisteria Lodge,' where the murders of Don Murillo and his secretary were ascribed to Nihilism; once in *His Last 'Bow*,' where Klopman was described as being the Nihilist who made an attempt on the life of Count Von und zu Grafenstein; and finally in *The Golden Pince - Nez*', where the principal characters are Russian Nihilist emigres.

The Holmes story, therefore, remains an intriguing blend of historical fact and political fiction. And if there was one thing Conan Doyle grasped well with his, as the author put it - 'cerebral tentacle'- it was history.

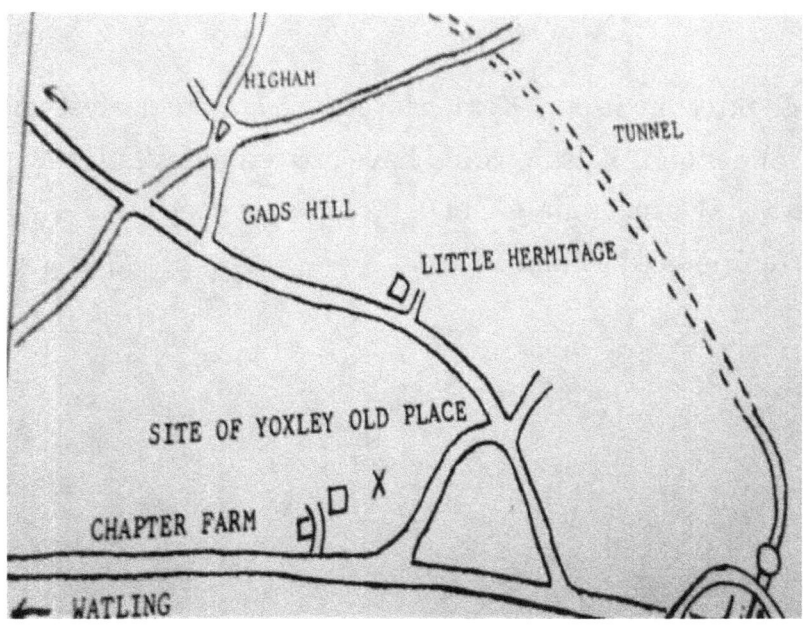

Fig. 56 A diagram showing the whereabouts of 'Yoxley Old Place, near Strood, in Kent.

Fig, 57. High Street in Strood, Kent, near Rochester, the nearest town
to which Holmes and Watson would have arrived to investigate
the 'Yoxley Old Place' affair (GOLD). From a rare postcard
from 1886 (author's collection).

DYNAMITE AND DYNAMITERS

(Written anonymously, in 'The Strand Magazine' of Jan - July, 1894). This fascinating article about Scotland Yard and their ongoing struggles with the terrorist bomb outrages of the 1880s illustrates just how difficult it was to keep control of public fear and anxiety over the issue. 'Dynamite and Dynamiters,' is taken from the Strand Magazine of 1894. January to July, by an unknown writer, and was profusely illustrated. In an earlier edition of the same year, '

The Strand' published an equally interesting tale of terrorism about a French anarchist by the French writer Eugene Moret, entitled 'An Anarchist,' and it describes in vivid detail 'a terrible panic and fright,' depicting the inhabitants of a small town, fleeing in the wake of an explosion. The article begins thus and has something of Holmes' particular style about it):

It is not intended that this series of articles we propose publishing here should in any way give rise to alarm or be an incentive or disturbing thoughts. On the other hand, a better knowledge of how crimes are committed and ultimately carried into effect may provide a course of much needed lessons, usually omitted in one's earlier education.

At New Scotland Yard, a large apartment is devoted to the exhibit of 10,001 records of crime in the shape of actual weapons associated with particularly notorious and sometimes instances of the most historic deeds. A visit to this place is the finest and most complete nerve tester in the world.

The new authorities at New Scotland Yard have kindly placed this room, and its contents, at our disposal. And each of the separate cases, which will contain exhibits of some distinctive branch of offences, requires a chapter, by itself.

The most recently arrived exhibit is one which now possesses a peculiar interest. In the centre of the room is a glass case, which provides an interesting place for mementos of the most important and significant outrages and serious cases of discoveries of explosives, which have called for the attention of the inspectors of explosives, over the last 15 years.

One man, Chief Inspector Colonel Majendie, who trained in India has been associated with this gentleman, as a chemical expert, an explosives expert. There is no better known than this man, a man in the prime of life, of great energy and immense disposition, who may be singled out as engaged in the two extremes of business and pleasure. His business is dynamite.

Fig 58. (Above) the Scotland Yard detective, who took on the quest to investigate the Fenian bomb outrages during the late 1880s was no doubt familiar with Holmes.

The gunpowder and all the associated blasting operatives make him a special person His room at the Home Office, contains slabs of American dynamite, infernal machines and detonators are also present. His rooms at home are covered with portraits of these tuneful youngsters, the bombs. Many of them are in the whitest of white surpluses. While the drawers of his desk are brimming with youthful letters from the past and present choristers of the great St Paul's Cathedral, who he helped to avoid an incident.

He never destroys a dynamite file or relic, or even a chance letter; such is his reputation as the sworn enemy of dynamite. And it was in company with him, that I visited New Scotland Yard and examined, one by one, the contents of the case already referred to, and associated then with the various incidents in which they were designed to play, and in some cases, succeeded in playing so prominent a part. It may be said that the more serious attempts to devote dynamite to the purpose for which it was intended commenced in 1881, when on the 14th of January of that year, an attempt was made to blow up the barracks at Salford, in the Midlands. Very little damage was done to the barracks, but a boy was killed and another one was injured, sadly, in the attempts to destroy life and property.

Only one other death has so far occurred on Christmas Eve of 1892, when a terrible Infernal Machine exploded outside the detective office in the exchange court of Dublin Castle, which was the headquarters of the police. A detective officer was killed instantly. Without including minor or explosions, the numbers of important dynamite efforts from the 1881 to the year 1892 are as follows:

In 1881, nine attempts, in 1882, five attempts, in 1883, ten, in 1884, twelve, in 1885, eight; in 1886, four, in 1887; five attempts; in 1888, but only two in 1889 and 3 attempts in 1890, so now down to 5.

It is not necessary to say that the initial explosion of sulphur in 1881 greatly alarmed the public. Anything found suspicious was at once associated with dynamite. And the earliest relic treasured at New Scotland Yard is a strange looking object, which was found in a tramcar, but owing to the excited state of mind of the British public at that time it was immediately put down as another bomb attack.

Fig. 59. The Salisbury 'Infernal Machine.'

There is, though, some reason to believe that it was nothing more than a model for a new idea in babies' feeding bottles. The inventor never put in a claim for it, but it still remains at the Yard for anybody who can justify his claim to the possession.

By its side is an imitation piece of coal, a deadly weapon if it were used for it is intended to be filled with explosive material, and then thrown in the stoke hole of a vessel in the hope that the stoker may then shovel it into the fire, with some other fuel. Another relic of the same year, 1881, is one of four machines found on the 2nd of July ship at Liverpool in the Bavaria. Six other machines of that type were found in the ship called the Malta, and two days before, similar items were discovered in barrels of cement. They contained lignite dynamite, which is a very cheap clock arrangement for firing dynamite. These machines, in leaden boxes, were about nine inches long by four inches square. A second machine of the 1881 period is made of a clockwork pattern. And this is controlled by a small knife, which falls at the second time, cutting a string, releasing a spring, which falls on a percussion cap. And so it brings about a loud explosion.

An 1882 relic is an interesting one, and its surrounding companions are very curious. Here, in the museum, is the revolver in the picture shown with which O'Donnell, the terrorist, shot Carey, It is of an American pattern and marked 147A in the catalogue, a most ingenious contrivance. Also, in this part of the catalogue in the collection is a tin can, made into two compartments. It was used for conveying gunpowder to Egypt, which is so made that when it is probed by the customs officials to see what it contains, the probe used comes out, and you are then covered with oil. A few samples of a not particularly choice brand of cigars is also shown. A gentleman who has no great love for you, and who fully appreciates the weakness of human nature, seldom refusing a cigar, offers you one out of his case. 'Something very choice, I assure you,' he says. He is a perfect stranger to you but, well, a cigar is a cigar, you accept the offer of benevolent proprietor, who sees you light up, and you puff away, and suddenly when he's called away, the cigar explodes. It contains an explosive wrapped up in a piece of blue paper, and is placed about halfway down the cigar.

But the most interesting relic of 1882 is a little cannister much resembling a diminutive milk can, which is supposed to contain dynamite, and it has never been opened since its receipt at the House of Commons in that year; it is addressed to Mr Forster, who was then the chief secretary for Ireland.

It was not, however, until 1883 that the authorities were fully aroused. The Explosives Act of 1875 had controlled all substances of this kind, but it was not designed to control the criminal use of explosives, although it is true that certain core clauses were found available to this extent, but the Act of 1883

Fig, 60. Clockwork mechanism used by British anarchists, 1880-1890.

was passed by the Commons in a single sitting, and a far - reaching act it was, dealing with every possible phase of the question of explosives.

No wonder this Act was passed! Before the New Year of 1883 many days passed, during which acts of terrorism had been gradually increasing with the threat of the Fenians, of course, and those persons who we regard as either Nihilists, or as Anarchists.

They had been busy in our own kingdom for a number of years since Colonel Majende had first been appointed and they afforded more anxiety and trouble to Colonel Majende and his colleagues than any trio of years since these more serious efforts had been made. Glasgow was the scene of the operations, and on the night of the 20th and morning of the 21st of January, three explosions occurred, in all of which lignite dynamite had been used.

Fig.62. A rare photo, showing the huge devastation of what was once police headquarters at old Scotland Yard during the Fenian and anarchist bombings of 1880s. Amazingly, though, on this occasion, no one was actually killed by this huge explosion.

The first was that at the Cradeston gas works on the south side of the city on the 20th and the remainder at at Fossil Bridge, and at at Buchanan Street, Station, which is a police station. On the 21st. no lives were lost, but considerable damage was done.

Photographs are of the greatest possible use to the expert when engaged in making these experiments, in order to find out the cause of the explosion. A picture at the Glasgow gasworks was taken in the interior of a holder, and shows the perforations of the plates by debris on the side of the hole, opposite to the main opening. These are of course very alarming, but without the fortitude and the best work of explosives teams, we will be in a much less safe condition than we are. However, the most serious case that the Colonel has had to deal with was the discovery at Birmingham on the fifth of April 1883, of a factory of nitroglycerin, and of a large amount of the same substance brought to London.

It is due to Birmingham police who kept their heads, magnificently, because they laid their traps with skill, and communicated with the authorities at the home office, at the right moment. Some of the nitro-glycerine found its way to London. The Birmingham police travelled up to London itself with a man whose luggage consisted of a pair of fishing stockings, containing some 70 pounds of this awful explosive agent. He was duly arrested, and the explosive was lodged at a magazine, near One Edge, and subsequently made into dynamite, and then destroyed.

The October of 1883 brought about two explosions, both on the Metropolitan Railway. The first event occurred between Charing Cross and Westminster, fortunately resulting in no personal or serious structural injury. That however, was not the case on the same night at Praed street, when an explosion resulted in three carriages being practically smashed, while 62 people were injured by the broken glass and the debris.

An important discovery was made on the 16th of January when, in 1884, some slabs of a powder of American lignite were found in Primrose Hill tunnel and it is surmised that these were thrown away by a conspirator as being of no use for the moment, seeing that it was probable that everything was cut and dried for.

In the following month, a quartet of attempted outrages at four London stations took place, one of which was tolerably successful.

On the 26th of January and then in February 1884, there was an explosion in the cloakroom of the Brighton and South Coast railway at Victoria Station, and also subsequently, on the 27th of February and the 28th, while on the 1st of March, discoveries were also made of bags containing Atlas powder with clockwork, that had been destined for Charing Cross, Ludgate Hill and Paddington Station, respectively.

In all these cases the clock device was used and was identical with the one found at Paddington Station, left in a cloakroom in a portmanteau. The authorities were for the moment at a loss to discover how the explosion occurred until the police communicated the fact that a portmanteau had been listed at Charing Cross Station. An extract of some interest from the official report will be recorded here.

'REPORT ON THE PADDINGTON BOMB'

When the clock was found it was taken away. The dynamite had not exploded, owing to the fact that the winder had caught against a little knob which failed to release itself, and when detective Ford expressed a desire to take the clock home with him to show it to his wife, the jolting of the cab was sufficient to partially release the winder and the pistol descended during the night. Of course, the cartridge and dynamite had previously been removed by the inspectors of police!'

We now come to the most deadly of all the weapons used by the dynamiter. This is the bomb that explodes instantly on falling. These enormous bombs, as in the case of the shrapnel shell used by the Artillery, can only be designed for one purpose of human life; and they are essentially man - killing machines.

On April the 11th, 1884, three metal bombs containing dynamite were found in the possession of one Daley at Birkenhead, who subsequently was sentenced to penal servitude for life. It should be stated here that Daley at his trial suggested these bombs might be used for killing fish. 'Yes,' said Col. Majendie, pointing to those found on Daley, 'but nobody would care to fish with those.'

From the same year, 1884 , no fewer than three Explosions occurred on the night of 30th of May, and on the same night a bag was found in Trafalgar Square containing Atlas powder , where 14 people were injured by the explosion, which occurred about 15 seconds later. Also another one at the Junior Carlton Club, a short distance from the residence of William Wynn in St. James's Square, which the raiders evidently mistook for parts of the Intelligence Office and the Home Security office.

It is probable that this was used also at Southover. Possibly, a bag was lobbed over the area railing but accidentally lodged in a window recess of the morning room, where the most serious effects of the explosion were felt. The windows of the house were much shattered by the third explosion of this night, which took place at 9:20 p.m., at old Scotland Yard, the former residence of the detective police force, outside a room used by some of the detective staff. The explosion brought down a portion of the building, doing considerable damage to some carriages standing there at the time, in proximity to the buildings, and actually injuring several people there.

An explosion also occurred in 1884 on December 13th, and it took the form of a considerable charge of dynamite or other nitro compounds under

London Bridge, where little damage was done. But there is no doubt that the perpetrators of the deed were themselves killed, since Colonel Majendie found what he thought to be the remains of a person who was blown up in a boat used in the transaction, though very little damage was done, fortunately, and enough just to believe that some of the bridges that span the river Thames might need special protection.

The last of the three bad years was 1885, when a brass tube or fuse for filling and firing nitro-glycerine compound was set off on a Sunday in Liverpool. It was an ingenious bomb in which sulfuric acid was used. Finally, there was a trio of bombing events: on 3rd of January 1885, the 24th of January 1885, at the Tower of London, scattering The Stand of Arms and implements of War, but the most effective of these was in the old banqueting hall.

They think that a man carrying in his pockets explosives did this.

There are more instances, but looking at them all, it is remarkable to imagine not only the bravery of the police but also of the courage and commitment of the officers on the ground; but also how thankful they are to the cooperation of the public for alerting them to these terrible infernal machines.

CRIME, GENDER & CORRUPTION: THE TREATMENT OF WOMEN IN THE SHERLOCK HOLMES STORIES

Conan Doye's Gothic masterpiece, '*The Hound of the Baskervilles*' contains one of the most explicit references to flagellation throughout the whole Sherlock Holmes story cycle. The abuse and exploitation of women is, of course, a dominant theme in Conan Doyle's work and his work on the reform of the Divorce Laws is well known. [5] However, in no other story is the incidence of sexually motivated violence more clearly illustrated than in 'The Hound'.

In the tale, Beryl Stapleton is found in their Dartmoor cottage by Holmes and Watson,, tied to a timber in the centre of the bedroom.

This is no sudden outburst, but a deliberate, definite act of premeditated and sustained sexual sadism.

In his perceptive article: 'Upon the Victorian Reticence of John H. Watson M.D,' Dean Dickensheet suggests that the truth about Beryl's treatment may have been far worse than Watson leads us to suspect ('Baker Street Miscellanea', Summer 1980, pp 6- 9 & p. 38):

"Stapleton, having bound his recalcitrant wife to the beam, stripped her to the waist (at least) and savagely beat her upon the back and (probably) breasts, exhibiting the diablerie of a man attempting to disfigure those desirable charms which he believes he has lost to another."

Following this inhuman act, Stapleton then trusses his victim like a mummy, no doubt sating his perverse lust for "bondage."

Doyle did not have to include this episode in his narrative. The fact that he allowed it to remain says something for his artistic integrity. (The reader may recall how he refused to allow '*The Cardboard Box*' to be reprinted in '*The Memoirs*' because of its sex and violence). What is he doing is to enlist the reader's sympathy for the plight of this abused woman, thus making more credible her renunciation of Stapleton, but also highlighting the plight of many women in late Victorian England who suffered the indignities of an abusive relationship.

---

[5] Conan Doyle was one of the most vociferous and active members of the Divorce Law Reform movement, often writing to the newspapers about the topic.

The discovery of the tortured and defiled Beryl Stapleton has been described by Doyle's biographer, Owen Dudley Edwards, as 'the novel's true heart of darkness' and he has cited this as the reason why the novel has no happy ending. ('*The Quest for Sherlock Holmes*', Mainstream Publishing, 1983). Stapleton's manipulation of others, combined with his own inability to master his sexual desires, creates the fatal flaw in his personality and remains utterly, and disturbingly, convincing.

In many ways 'The Hound' is a triumphant piece of writing, despite its occasional unevenness and sometimes heavy - handed approach. It is truly a very dark novel, about disturbing and hidden matters, about the primeval in all of us; and it deals honestly, and in greater detail than many of the short stories, with themes such as avarice, lust, perversity, corruption, cruelty and fear. The supernatural element is exploited by Doyle to considerable effect, for it reinforces the tragic reality of the work's dramatis personae. Far from being mere caricatures, as John Fowles once suggested, Doyle's puppets dangle and dance in a most convincing way. Human nature here, in this Gothic novel, is dwarfed by the unreasoning primal forces which have given birth to the hound and its legend.

And it is also a thoroughly atheistic and cynical work. There is no reconciliation at the conclusion of this tangled skein of events, and no easy solution. Illusion and superstition are as much in evidence by the end of the novel as at the beginning. It is with some disbelief, therefore, that we read of the hound, being purchased from a London dealer called Ross and Mangles. Stapleton, the villain of the piece, is no melodramatic monster, but precisely the kind of cold and inexplicable psychopath who we read about in today's newspapers.

'*The Hound of The Baskervilles*' is a mature novel, occurring at a crucial time in the author's career. It should not surprise us, therefore, to find that its central themes of both guilt and retribution should predominate. In this tragic novel, the anti-romantic depiction of human relationships convinces us by its consistent realism.

The drama of this "dream-work" is worked out at a number of levels, but it is at the symbolic and numinous level that Doyle achieves most success. The all-engulfing metaphor of The Mire and the dynamic and destructive hound, tower over human aspirations, and threatesn to obliterate them altogether.

'The Hound' marks a turning point in the Holmes cycle, for it is from here onwards that Holmes begins to assume a more detached (and often cynical) role. The later stories often deal with the problems of violence and abuse in human relationships (e.g.'The Veiled Lodger,' 'The Illustrious Client,' 'Lady

Frances Fairfax'), particularly between the sexes, and one can trace this theme back to 'The Hound' and its literary and biographical genesis.

Conan Doyle's 'Hound of the Baskervilles' was written at the turn of the century, and thus shares with other significant popular novels of that period the Gothic overlay, which works like Bram Stoker's 'Dracula' and Robert Louis Stevenson's 'Dr Jekyll and Mr Hyde' enjoy.

There is the ever - present threat in the novel of moral and psychical disintegration and regression – indeed, regression, in terms of atavism, enters at two points in the narrative: when Dr Mortimer discusses the Hottentots with Sir Charles and also when, having examined the portrait of Hugo Baskerville, Holmes discovers a striking likeness between Stapleton and the evil ancestor. In Stapleton, we see the sins of the past worked out in the transgressions of the butterfly - collecting psychopath.

In the early to mid-Victorian period, authors such as Charles Dickens borrowed typically Gothic motifs – the innocent abandoned in a threatening environment for example, or the mysterious stranger with secrets to hide – and adapted them to contemporary Britain to highlight modern concerns. Stories such as 'Oliver Twist' *(1838) and* 'Bleak House' (1853) used Gothic imagery as a means of drawing attention to the social illness afflicting the poor in London. The urban slums, with their dark streets and seedy areas of vice and squalor are parallels to the ivy-clad castles and catacombs as the main settings for Gothic terror.

Later still in the Victorian fin de siècle, the scene changes again: it is no longer the physical landscape that provides the location for Gothic tales but rather, more disturbingly, the human body itself. Works such as Stevenson's 'Strange Case of Dr Jekyll and Mr Hyde' (1886); Oscar Wilde's 'The Picture of Dorian Gray' *(1891);* and Arthur Machen's 'The Great God Pan' (1894) all follow this parallel path.

H G. Wells' 'The Time Machine' (1895) and Bram Stoker's 'Dracula' (1897), both explore the theme of the human mind and body changing and developing; mutating, corrupting and decaying.

In Stapleton's case we are dealing with a corruption of the mind, as also occurs in 'The Picture of Dorian Gray', where the painting found in the attic symbolises the gradual moral decay of its subject, as Dorian descends further and further into moral dissolution. In 'Dracula,' moral decay and physical dissolution occur among the populace, as the Count's quest for a mass vampiric attack on the city begins to have an effect.

This descent into madness and distorted fantasy is reflected in the character of the madman, Renfield, who is psychically linked to the Count and becomes his unwilling agent. This idea of psychical control, which leads to moral contagion is also reflected in Conan Doyle's lesser known short novel, 'The Parasite.' In Doyle's relatively unsuccessful but unjustifiably overlooked narrative, the principle of moral and psychical contagion is convincingly described. The mesmerist who the central character deals with, is, moreover, a woman of foreign extraction and this is a theme Conan Doyle refers to in several other of his novels and short stories.

In the short story entitled 'The Case of Lady Sannox,' for example, the central female character, the toast of London society, is carrying on a flagrantly open sexual affair with Douglas Stone, an arrogant, young surgeon. Lord Sannox is thought by Stone to be a clueless old fool, unaware of the liaison. After discussing with the Lady his plan to murder her wealthy husband, so that they can then marry, Stone is hired by a heavily disguised Turkish man to perform a questionable operation on his wife whose lip, ostensibly, has been poisoned.

Dr. Stone has to operate on the woman without seeing the whole face, since, as we know, Muslims don't tolerate strangers seeing a wife''s face. Dr. Stone accepts, and surgically removes the upper lip from the woman. But just after the mutilation, Stone then realises that he has unwittingly disfigured his mistress. The incognito Turkish man is then revealed as Lord Sannox, who has planned hideous vengeance upon his wife and her lover. Lady Sannox meets her lover when she is treading the boards and thus carries with her, as defined at the time by her occupation, the hint of loose morals. Her lover is straight out of Wilde's 'Picture of Dorian Gray' – a man of perverse sexual interests whom Doyle expertly and subtly describes as follows:

'Douglas Stone had finished his dinner, and sat by his fire in the study, a glass of rich port upon the malachite table at his elbow. As he raised it to his lips, he held it up against the lamplight, and watched with the eye of a connoisseur the tiny scales of beeswing which floated in its rich ruby depths. The fire, as it spurted up, threw fitful lights upon his bold, clear-cut face, with its widely-opened grey eyes, its thick and yet firm lips, and the deep, square jaw, which had something Roman in its strength and its animalism.'

This story, like 'The Hound,' features a female character who is by nature, both adulterous and sexually passionate. Beryl Stapleton, who hails from Costa Rica, is certainly not a Muslim, but she is clearly very voluptuous, and the admiring Dr Watson who has had an 'experience of women encompassing three continents,' gives her the full treatment with his overtly purple prose:

117

'I could not doubt that this was the Miss Stapleton of whom I had been told, since ladies of any sort must be few upon the moor, and I remembered that I had heard someone describe her as being a beauty. The woman who approached me was certainly that, and of a most uncommon type. There could not have been a greater contrast between brother and sister, for Stapleton was neutral tinted, with light hair and grey eyes, while she was darker than any brunette whom I have seen in England - slim, elegant, and tall. She had a proud, finely cut face, so regular that it might have seemed impassive were it not for the sensitive mouth and the beautiful dark, eager eyes. With her perfect figure and elegant dress, she was, indeed, a strange apparition upon a lonely moorland path.'

There are most clear indications that Conan Doyle was himself attracted to women who bore a physical similarity to Beryl Stapleton and Lady Sannox – dark, sultry and passionate. An early photograph of his second wife and reputedly platonic lover, Dr Doyle – though we only have Conan Doyle's word for this[6] – shows a highly attractive young woman with dark hair who can certainly be accurately described as 'sultry' and sexually desirable.

An almost identical female character type is also evident in the female protagonist of *'The Problem of Thor Bridge,'* where The 'Gold King,' an enterprising and exploitative capitalist, meets a sultry South American woman, one Maria Pinto, then, some years later, loses interest in his wife and craves the love of and sexual fulfilment with, an attractive young governess:

'I met my wife when I was gold-hunting in Brazil,' the 'Gold King,' *(J. Neil Gibson, tells Holmes.)* 'Maria Pinto was the daughter of a Government official at Manaos, and she was very beautiful. I was young and ardent in those days, but even now, as I look back with colder blood and a more critical eye, I can see that she was rare and wonderful in her beauty. *It was a deep rich nature, too, passionate, wholehearted, tropical, ill-balanced, very different from the American women whom I had known.* (My italics – KJ). Well, to make a long story short, I loved her, and I married her. It was only when the romance had passed — and it lingered for years — that I realized that we had nothing — absolutely nothing — in common. My love faded.'

As with the unforgettably attractive Beryl Stapleton, when Dr Watson finally gets the chance to meet the accused governess, Miss Grace Dubar, in her prison cell, he almost swoons with admiration at her full bloodied charms:

'I can never forget the effect which Miss Dunbar produced upon me. It was no wonder that even the masterful millionaire had found in her something more powerful

---

[6] See my detailed and revealing investigation of the Doyle menage in 'The Curious Case of The Dog In The Night-Time, Cunning Crime Books, 2021.

than himself - something which could control and guide him. One felt, too, as one looked at that strong, clear-cut and yet sensitive face, that even should she be capable of some impetuous deed, nonetheless there was an innate nobility of character which would make her influence always for the good. *She was a brunette, tall, with a noble figure and commanding presence, but her dark eyes had in them this appealing, helpless expression of the hunted creature who feels the nets around it, but can see no way out from the toils* (my italics – KJ).

Like Beryl Stapleton, and also, like Jean Leckie, these are women of great physical charms, all of them tall, highly intelligent, very passionate and often swarthy skinned. They are far and away more interesting to the reader and, of course dear impressionable Dr Watson than someone like the scheming, cerebral and manipulative Irene Adler, of 'dubious fame.' Each of them is trapped by the machinations and manipulations of men. Each of them is locked in a desperate three - way relationship (Beryl – Sir Henry Baskerville – Jack Stapleton), from which there is no obvious escape. Each, in the imagination of the author, represents illicit sexuality, intelligence and virtuousness and voluptuousness which is desirable but unobtainable – an exact parallel to Conan Doyle's real - life amorous dilemma.

The Holmes tales are peppered with mysterious women with tragic pasts. As W.W. Robson observes in his introduction to the Oxford edition of 'The Hound':

'They are in different ways victims of masculine oppression: for all the social conservatism of the Holmes stories, they carry within their identity a latent old-fashioned feminism. Beryl Stapleton and Laura Lyons are the chief examples of exploited women in 'The Hound,' whose social protest turns on the varieties of that exploitation both as objects and as agents. To the we might add, in a minor way, Mrs Barrymore, the victim, not of her husband but of her brother, and of the culture which questioned her right to have human feelings at all.'

The role and function of abused females is nowhere more at large than in another Gothic novel of this period, 'Dracula,' published in 1897 more than three years before 'The Hound.' The fates of both Mina Murray, Jonathan Harker's fiancée and her friend Lucy Westenra, as they succumb to the Count's sinister persistent predation, forms the very heart of this Gothic novel. As Robert Humphrey points out in his insightful essay, *'Ideals of the Victorian Woman as Depicted in 'Dracula''* (Online essay in 'The Artifice', 2014):

'If Mina is on one end of the spectrum, then the three daughters of Dracula are on the complete opposite end of the spectrum. These three women are a representation of the Victorian belief toward women of impurity (i.e., a vastly negative, immoral, sinful idea toward women of this nature).

Stoker is linking hyper-sexual females with vampires/vampirism, and vampires/vampirism is linked to evil. If A=B and B=C, then A=C. So, through association, Stoker is linking hyper-sexual females with evil. This is likely how Stoker, and many other Victorians, viewed the sexualized and unchaste women in society in Victorian England.'

Fig.. 63. Jean Leckie presented to Doyle his ideal of desirable womanhood: passion, intelligence, vivaciousness, a brooding manner and a simmering sexuality.

All this points to an unresolved oedipal conflict on behalf of the author - a conflict which continued to dog him even in his later years and which may well have contributed to his quest for the "proof" of the world of spirits. In a sense, Conan Doyle's dream world, so graphically conveyed in 'The Hound,' was found to be ultimately unsatisfactory to its author.

It is curious that 'The Hound's appeal lies far more in its appeal to the supernatural than to any display of the scientific method of its central character, Holmes. Indeed, Holmes is quite significantly marginalised in-the novel and exhibits little of his usual ingenuity and vision. The novel's power comes from its mythic foundation and its ability to portray the destructive and repressed side of human nature.

The way in which Conan Doyle weaves this dark side of our natures with the features of the Dartmoor landscape provides the ultimate strength of the writing. In fact, nowhere else in the Holmes saga, does he achieve this degree of power or intensity. The rational explanation of the legend and the curse seems strangely at odds, therefore, with this exploration of the mythic throughout the novel. Perhaps, by the time that Conan Doyle penned his late masterpiece, he was already slipping into that world of the unseen, that hidden world of spirits which provided the focus for the remainder of his public career and private life.

In an illuminating article in the volume 'Violets and Vitriol', by Diana Barsham, the author [7] describes Conan Doyle's dichotomy regarding his fictional creation. Sherlock Holmes she reveals, as we all had suspected, is someone who has a problem with women and is clear evidence of the author's own apparent confusion. She also notes that whilst in the earlier stories Sherlock Holmes appears to be asexual and a cynic as regards women, in general his behaviour towards individual women is beyond reproach, if somewhat paternalistic. The article entitled *The secret marriage of Sherlock Holmes and other eccentrics readings,* by Michael Atkinson, suggests that women are often portrayed in the Sherlock Holmes stories, as they often are in much crime fiction that followed that of Doyle. The narrative construction is often designed to reveal the truth and the truth is actually revealed through a woman. However, much like a a woman, e.g., Irene Adler, truth often averts her face from him. Atkinson explains that the repressed level of truth is female in nature in detective stories and resists the intellectual constructs which are imposed on it; plus, the truth is very often female in nature; and that this explains Doyle's own ambivalence towards the Sherlock Holmes stories. [8]

Sherlock Holmes will, on the one hand, often decry or seem to criticise the actions of women; while on the other hand, often defend and be remarkably protective of women, as in his clients, e.g. in *The Copper Beeches* and of course the classic story of the predatory men in *The Solitary Cyclist,* where his female client, Violet Hunter, is forced into an illegal marriage ceremony.

---

[7] 'Violets and Vitriol', ed. S. E. Dahlinger, Calabash Press, 2004.

[8] 'The Secret Marriage of Sherlock Holmes', Michael Atkinson, Univ. Of Michigan Press, 1998.

Even though he is seen often to protect women,, Holmes remains very cool and distant, as he appears to us, in the *Sign of Four*, when he first meets Watson's betrothed, Mary Morstan, Even as late as the story of 'The Lion's Mans, when Holmes is living alone in Sussex, he takes a long time to determine the importance of the relevance of the *femme fatale*, Maud Bellamy, thus showing in the story a lack of understanding and empathy with women. One of his most frequently quoted comments about women crystallises this ambivalent attitude:

'The Motives of women are so inscrutable. Do you remember the woman at Margate whom I suspected for the same reason. No powder on her nose - that proved to be the correct solution. How can you build on such a quicksand?'

To Holmes, women are unpredictable and subject to flights of fancy or irrational behaviour. In many of the later stories, women, in particular, hold the key to the solution of the crime, but especially so in 'The Golden Pince-Nez' which as we have seen, is about a Russian lady who reclaims her past by concealing herself from a sinister cigarette - smoking scholar.

I have always believed this character in 'The Golden Pince Nez' to be a representation of the theosophist, Madame Blavatsky, about whom Conan Doyle was quite preoccupied and obsessed. I believe he saw her actually as a personification of womankind and he also saw her as a personification of the occult Teachings of Eastern religion, particularly that of Buddhism which he makes several references to in the Holmes stories.

In his youth, Doylee was obsessed with the concepts of karma and reincarnation, although these did not feature in his later spiritual inspiration. Madame Blavatsky herself, who was a disciple of a Brotherhood whose members had the ability to summon up apparitions and make astral journeys was unmasked when her letters were was finally revealed as a hoax. Doyle was deeply disappointed and regretted that she had taken to this course of deception. As he says in his memoirs of her: 'The woman undoubtedly had real psychic powers, whatever their source'.

We see, therefore, that the character of Holmes himself is a projection of Conan Doyle's subconscious and his obvious confusion about women to a very great degree. Like his creation, the seemingly asexual and quite possibly latently homosexual Sherlock Holmes, Doyle appeared often to toy with the principles of esoteric religions and beliefs but is never quite able to commit himself about their efficacy; or to make a final judgement as to their acceptability.

As Diana Barsham perceptively reveals in her essay (sic.) Holmes' continued and frequent encounters with women in the later stories, written in the period of Doyle's career when he had met and subsequently married his own *'femme fatale,'* Jean Leckie, often do contain images of the abuse or exploitation, and even the disfigurement of women, so vividly delineated when describing the beaten and much ravaged Beryl Stapleton of 'The Hound'.

In the long story, 'Wisteria Lodge,' the central character, Miss Burnett, is humiliated, drugged with opium , then pushed into a railway carriage; in 'The Disappearance of Lady Frances Carfax', a lonely, wealthy and naive widow, is buried alive by a scheming fraudster, the Reverend Holy Peters; in 'The Devil's Foot,' the victim, Brenda Tregennis, becomes a motive for murder, while in 'The Veiled Lodger', and also in 'The Illustrious Client', Conan Doyle seems haunted by the connection made in his later Holmes stories by the theme of hideous disfigurement, a theme which had preoccupied him so much in the earlier non - Holmes story of 'The Case of Lady Sannox.'

Even more disturbing, in my opinion, is the role of victim as the subject of predatory male lust, which is the cenral plot of perhaps the last recorded case of Sherlock Holmes, entitled 'The Creeping Man'. In this bizarre tale, the ageing and clearly almost impotent Professor Presbury, so desires a renewal of his youth and full sexual vigour, that he embarks on injecting himself with a serum taken from the gonads of rhesus monkeys. On the eve of his marriage, he attempts to satiate his overwhelming lust, by trying to break into his daughter's bedroom in order to enjoy incestuous sex. The sense of loathing and terror experienced by this young woman at seeing the half wolf, half satyr figure at her bedroom window, speaks volumes, regarding Conan Doyle's depiction of the 'man beomes beast' nightmare that so frequently assailed his complex imagination:

'My room is on the second floor. It happened that the blind was up in my window, and there was the bright moonlight outside. As I lay with my eyes fixed upon the square of light, listening to the frenzed barkings of the dog, I was amazed to see my father's face looking in at me…If that window had opened, I think I should have gone mad…'

A SELECT BIBLIOGRAPHY ON CONAN DOYLE, WOMEN AND SEXUALITY IN THE SHERLOCK HOLMES STORIES

Doyle, Georgina. **Out of the shadows**: the untold story of Arthur Conan Doyle's first family; Georgina Doyle. Ashcroft: Calabash Press, 2004. An account of Doyle's marriage to Louise Hawkins, Jean Leckie and his relationship with his children Mary and Kingsley. The book reveals much about the impact of Jean Leckie on the author.

Duncan, Alistair - **An entirely New Country** – ebook, 2019. A detailed record of Doyle's residence at Windlesham, Sussex during the period of his second marriage.

Edwards, Owen Dudley. **The Quest for Sherlock Holmes:** a biographical study of Arthur Conan Doyle; Edinburgh: Mainstream Publishing, 1983. A discussion of how Doyle's boyhood experiences shaped his literary attitudes and writing.

Green, Richard Lancelyn. **A Bibliography of Conan Doyle;** by the late Richard Lancelyn Green and John Michael Gibson; with a foreword by Graham Greene. New revised and expanded edition with addenda and corrigenda. Boston: Hudson House, 2000. A scholarly and indispensable descriptive bibliography of Doyle's output.

Jones, Kelvin I. **Conan Doyle And the Spirits: the spiritualist career of Arthur Conan Doyle.** Thorsons Books, 1989. Useful insights into the sources of Doyle's supernatural and gothic tales and especially the effect of his personal relationships on his creative output.

Lycett, Andrew. Conan Doyle: **The Man Who Invented Sherlock Holmes**. Weidenfeld and Nicolson, 2007. A far ranging and lucid account of Doyle's life and especially his relationship with Jean Leckie and Louise Hawkins.

ON SEXUALITY AND GOTHIC REPRESSION IN 19TH CENTURY LIERATURE

Anne Williams – **'The Horror, The Horror**: Recent Studies in Gothic Fiction.' MFS Modern Fiction Studies - Johns Hopkins University Press Volume 46, Number 3, Fall 2000.'

Jones, Kelvin I. – **'The Annotated Hound of the Baskervilles,'** which contains several seminal essays on the literary genesis of 'The Hound.'

Jones, Kelvin I. – **The Carfax Syndrome:** Vampirism and Sexuality in the Sherlock Holmes stories, Sir Hugo Publications, 1989.

Jones, Kelvin I – **Sherlock And Porlock** – Literary Influences in the Sherlock Holmes stories. Cunning Crime Books, 2019 (revised edition).

Howard, Jacqueline & "Robert Mighall: **'A Geography of Victorian Gothic Fiction: Mapping History's Nightmares,'** in **'Romanticism'** ('On the Net 20')

Valdine Clemens. **'The Return of the Repressed: Gothic** Horror from The Castle of Otranto to Alien.' Albany: SUNY P, 1999.

Bigelow, S Tupper. **The Singular Case of Fletcher Robinson.** Baker Street Gasogene,1, no 4, April 1962. De Waal, 2469.

Rosenberg, Samuel – **'Naked Is the Best Disguise'** – A Freudian interpretation of several of the Holmes stories. Penguin Books, 1974.

Freud, Sigmund – **'The Interpretation of Dreams' and 'Totem and Taboo'.** The Complete Works of Sigmund Freud. Pergamon E-book edition, 2019.

Redmond, Christopher - **'In Bed with Sherlock Holmes':** **Sexual Elements in Arthur Conan Doyle's Stories of the Great Detective.** Simon & Pierre, Toronto, 1984.

A STUDY OF A SCARLET STUDY: The origins of Doyle's detective mysteries.

The appearance of 'A Study in Scarlet,' in 1887, marked the literary genesis of Sherlock Holmes. To Sherlockians the world over, this was indeed cause for rejoicing, but what of the rest of the reading world? The truth is no one took a great deal of notice of his first foray into the minds of the Victorian reading pubic in December 1887.

In January 2021, The Sherlock Holmes Society of London was a very pensionable 70 years old. Did anyone else, apart from Sherlockians, take notice of Conan Doyle's gift to the development of the crime story genre? I, for one, believe that they did so.

What of the occasional taster of the detective story, or the eclectic reader, who sometimes allows himself the indulgence of a good murder mystery? And what of that legion of writers who preceded and succeeded Sir Arthur Conan Doyle?

To whom is owed the debt of originality?

To put it another way, is Sherlock Holmes a mere isolated phenomenon (as many Sherlockians would sometimes have us believe), a jewel in the crown of late-Victorian literature, or is he a culmination, a landmark, an extraordinary synthesis of ideas that would propel crime fiction into the now most popular and perhaps enviable of all literary genres in the 21st Century?

The publishing history of that first slim volume, demurely entitled 'Beeton's Christmas Annual,' need not be retold here. At first, it attracted little attention from the reading public, and very scant notice from the critics. Significantly, however, the illustrated weekly, 'Graphic,' wrote of it at the time, giving it a passing, if brief, but nevertheless encouraging mention.

A year later, 'A Study in Scarlet' appeared under its own title, carrying in a rather clumsily bound volume, six dreary little sketches by Doyle's doomed, epileptic and often drunken father. The critic for 'The Graphic' this time wrote: 'Nobody who cares for detective stories should pass over 'A Study in Scarlet'. The author has equalled the best of his predecessors …He has actually succeeded in inventing a brand - new detective… The plot is… daringly constructed… There is no trace of vulgarity or slovenliness, too often characteristic of detective stories… Besides being exceptionally ingenious, it may be read with pleasure by all those (who) do not care for such things in a general sense.'

It is, one has to admit, a rather limp review, carrying with it the inference that the 'new detective story' was somehow, no doubt because murder seemed to persons of sensibility, a rather sordid and distasteful new genre, most distasteful. Was the writer of this review correct in saying that the work would "never have been written" but for Doyle's illustrious predecessors?

And was he at all accurate in his assertion that here was a "brand new detective," and here was a "daringly constructed plot"?

Perhaps the most significant influence on Doyle's conception of the detective was that doomed, but gifted alcoholic genius, Edgar Allan Poe, who, in three short tales of detection, created the psychological formula that has survived a century and more, of variation and elaboration at the hands of lesser writers. Disregarding 'The Gold Bug' for a moment (a story of mystery and analysis, but hardly a detective story in the strict sense), these stories comprise The Murders in the Rue Morgue, The Mystery of Marie Roget, and The Purloined Letter. Their structure has been loosely described by Howard Haycraft, in his classic 'Murder for Pleasure,' as the physical, the mental, and the "balanced" type, respectively.

It is, however, the very first of these tales which exhibits the features adopted by Conan Doyle, viz. that the more outré the features of the case, the more simple is its explanation, and that when all impossible solutions have been discarded, the residual solution shall be the only acceptable one. Apart from the basic structure of the mystery and its solution, Doyle incorporated much more of Poe into his own conception than perhaps has been admitted by previous critics of his works, but whose legacy and influence Doyle was only too ready to admit when he later embarked on a literary tour of America.

The opening chapters of 'A Study in Scarlet' fascinate the reader with their vivid delineation of a Bohemian and vain amateur investigator, dedicated to the doctrine of 'deductive.'

The word 'deductive' and its abstract noun, deduction. are both misleading, for what Holmes applied himself to, with such consummate ease, was induction, as was so ably demonstrated by the late Italian crime writer and semeotics scholar, Umberto Eco's analysis. Doyle's flesh-and-blood psychological realism of the work, in STUD however, is both an interpretation, yet an improvement, on Poe's preface to' The Murders in the Rue Morgue'.

Doyle's mentor Poe, writes: 'As the strong man exults in his physical ability... so glories the analyst in that moral activity which disentangles .... He is fond of enigmas, of conundrums, of hieroglyphics; exhibiting in his solutions of each a degree of acumen which appears to the ordinary apprehension preternatural. His results brought about by the very soul and essence of method, have, in truth, the whole air of intuition... *The analytical power should not be confounded with simple ingenuity; for while the analyst is necessarily ingenious, the ingenious man is often remarkably incapable of analysis* ...It will be found, in fact, that the ingenious are always fanciful, and the truly imaginative never otherwise than analytic.' (*My italics- kj*).

Poe's portrayal of Dupin as analyst, and man of science, solving crime for reasons purely of intellectual pleasure, is a clear prediction of Holmes. But there is much more both to Dupin and Holmes than a basic ratiocination.

These literary figures are essentially projections of their authors' egos, heroes whose skill and imaginative powers exist to create a dramatic conflict in the narrative that must be resolved. Champions of mind over matter, expert reasoners, men of vast and often obscure knowledge, they are both to some extent superhuman figures set against the forces of darkness.

Many followers of the chronicles of Sherlock Holmes believe that Edgar Allan Poe was not only the originator of the fantasy and supernatural horror story - a fact acknowledged by the 'King of Horror,' Steven King - but that he also created and defined the modern crime story. Define? Maybe, but not 'invent'.

Although Edgar Allan Poe is credited as the creator of the detective story and the character type known as the amateur sleuth, C. Auguste Dupin and his ratiocinative ability, these were clearly influenced by several other French sources. These prototypes were regarded as *'romans policier'* – accounts of the detective's pursuance of crime, not puzzles or 'mysteries.'

Two likely sources are Voltaire's *Zadig: Ou, La Destinée, Histoire orientale* (1748; Zadig: Or, The Book of Fate, 1749) and François-Eugène Vidocq's *Mémoires de Vidocq*, chef de la police de Sûreté jusqu'en 1827 (1828-1829; Memoirs of Vidocq, Principal Agent of the French Police Until 1827, 1828-1829). Poe mentions Zadig in 'Hop Frog' and thus most likely knew the story of Zadig's ability to work out the description of the king's horse and the queen's dog by examining tracks on the ground and hair traces found on nearby bushes. Poe also makes a reference to Vidocq, the first real-life detective (in 'The Murders of the Rue Morgue' as a "good guesser," but one who could not see clearly because he held the object of investigation too close. In the tales of Vidocq there is very little in the way of rational or inferential deduction which we find later in Dupin and Holmes.

Poe's creation of the ratiocinative story also derives from broader and more basic interests and sources. To begin with, there was his interest in the aesthetic theory of Samuel Taylor Coleridge, who himself identified greatly with the woe of Goethe and other nineteenth century German Romantic writers like Schiller. In many of Poe's most well - known critical essays, for instance, in his 1842 review of Nathaniel Hawthorne's 'Twice-Told Tales' (1837) and particularly his theoretical articles,'Philosophy of Composition' in 1846 and "The Poetic Principle" in 1848, Poe, ever the original thinker, developed his version of the theory of the artwork as a form in which every single detail helps to create the overall effect - a distinctly Holmesian approach. This organic aesthetic theory influenced Poe's creation of the detective genre, in which every detail, even the most minor, may be a clue to the solution of the story's mystery.

The development of the mystery and detective genre also reflected itself in the influence of the Gothic novel and, throughout the evolution of the detective story, this element persisted. A typical early example is Wilkie Collins' 'The Moonstone' and it is no coincidence that in Doyle's first attempt at a crime story, 'The Mystery of Cloomber,' the Gothic element is exceedingly strong, as it continues to dominate in 'The Sign of Four' the second Holmes novel and, of course, the overtly and creepily Gothic 'The Hound of the Baskervilles 'which Doyle referred to as 'a real creeper' in a letter to his mother. The Gothic house as a scene of crime is clearly embedded in Conan Doyle's tortured and frequently guilt - ridden consciousness, even in his now forgotten first foray into that rank, gloomy, and often incestuous quagmire of the late Victorian genre that still today continues to haunt modern writers like Susan Hill in her 'Woman In Black,' which is profoundly Doylean:

'Once out of sight of Branksome and there was no sign of the works of man save only where the high, white tower of Cloomber Hall shot up, like a headstone of some giant grave, from amid the firs and larches which girt it round. This great house, a mile or more from our dwelling, had been built by a wealthy Glasgow merchant of strange tastes and lonely habits, but at the time of our arrival it had been untenanted for many years, and stood with weather-blotched walls and vacant, staring windows looking blankly out over the hill side. Empty and mildewed, it served only as a landmark to the fishermen, for they had found by experience that by keeping the laird's chimney and the white tower of Cloomber in a line so they could steer their way through the ugly reef which raises its jagged back, like that of some sleeping monster, above the troubled waters of the wind-swept bay.'

The traditional English Gothic novel, based on the idea of concealed sin, or in some extreme cases, graphically described scenes of rape and incest (as in Matthew Lewis' 'The Monk,'), filled with mysterious and apparently inexplicable happenings, like the detective puzzle, moves inexorably toward a conclusion that will explain everything that is, on the surface, inexplicable to the reader. The first gothic novel, Horace Walpole's 'The Castle of Otranto" (1765), and Mary Radcliffe's subsequent 'Mysteries of Udolpho', (1794) with their cryptic clues, were, in effect, both very early sources of the detective story but with supernatural and Gothic components.

A third source of the newly invented detective mystery lay in Poe's utter fascination with codes, cryptograms and puzzles. In an article in a magazine in 1839, he offered to solve all cryptograms submitted and in a follow-up article in 1841, said that he had indeed solved most of them.

In 1841, Poe published several articles on cryptography, under the title 'A Few Words on Secret Writing'. Poe's favourite system of cryptography was the use of a 'key-phrase'. This is a sentence of 26 letters, which match the letters of the normal alphabet. Poe's articles were about cryptography in its most recognizable form, namely an incomprehensible string of letters or symbols that is clearly a cipher. But there is a more advanced form of cryptography, in which the secret message is hidden inside an apparently meaningful 'cover' text.

Although Poe demonstrated his skill as a solver of puzzles in many magazine articles, the most impressive fictional depiction of his talents as a cryptographer occurs is his story 'The Gold Bug.'

William Legrand, the central character in "The Gold Bug', shares some characteristics with Poe's famous detective, Dupin. Legrand is from an illustrious family, but because of financial problems, has been reduced to near poverty. Although he is of French ancestry from New Orleans, he lives alone on an island in South Carolina. Like Dupin, he alternates between melancholia and enthusiasm, (q.v. Holmes) which leads the narrator (also like the narrator in the Dupin stories) to suspect that he is the victim of a type of madness – a form of monomania.

Legrand discovers a piece of parchment on which he finds a cryptogram with directions to the buried treasure of the pirate Captain Kidd.

As with the Dupin stories, 'The Gold Bug' focuses less on action than on the explanation of the steps toward the unveiling of the mystery. To solve the puzzle of the cryptogram, Legrand shows the basic Holmesian qualities of the amateur detective's close attention to detail, information about language and mathematics, considerable knowledge about his opponent, Captain Kidd, and, most significantly, a perceptive intuition and a sharp reasoning ability. These are significant in our understanding of Poe's legacy to Conan Doyle, as, indeed is the fascination with cryptograms, which appear not only in 'The Adventure of the Dancing Men' but also, very significantly in 'The Valley of Fear,' when Holmes receives a coded message from his agent, Porlock.

Poe's famous Gothic stories of psychological obsession, appear, on first reading, quite different from his ratiocinative stories of detection. In fact, they have a very similar structure. Both types of story depend on a guilty secret that has to be exposed; in both types of narrative, the central character is an eccentric; and both types of story are, in fact, elaborate puzzles filled with clues that must be pieced together before the solution is finally revealed to the reader.

It is in the Auguste Dupin stories, however, that Poe develops most of the conventions of the detective story. The first of these three stories, 'The Murders in the Rue Morgue,' is the most popular because it combines inexplicable events with impressive feats of deductive reasoning. The narrator, the forerunner of Dr. Watson, meets Dupin in this story and very early recognizes that he has a double personality, for he is both highly imaginative and yet coldly analytical. The reader's first encounter with Dupin's deductive ability takes place even before the murders occur.

Dupin explains his method of 'mind reading.' by which he followed the narrator's thought processes by noticing small details and associating them. This method is, as we discover with Holmes, by no means original to the Conan Doyle method, and is demonstrated in the very first version of 'The Cardboard Box.'

Dupin's knowledge of the murder of a mother and daughter in the Parisian Rue Morgue is gained by the same means that any ordinary citizen might learn of a murder—the sensational French newspapers.

As with Sherlock Holmes and many of his subsequent rivals, Dupin scorns the methods of the professional investigators as being insufficient. He argues that the police find the mystery insoluble for the reason it should be easy to solve, that is, its bizarre nature. Therefore, the ease with which Dupin solves the case, is in contrast to its insolubility by the police, who, as in the Holmes saga, are frequently denigrated.

The heart of the story focuses on Dupin's explanation of how he solved the crime rather than on the action of the crime. The points about the murder that puzzle the police—the contradiction of several neighbours who describe hearing a voice in several foreign languages, the fact that there seems to be no perceivable means of entering or exiting the murder room; these factors assist Dupin to solve the mystery. He accounts for the foreign-sounding voice by deducing that the criminal must have been an animal; he explains the second point by following a mode of reasoning based on a process of elimination, to determine that apparent impossibilities are in fact possible. When Dupin shows that an escaped orang-utang committed the murder, the prefect of police complains that Dupin should mind his own business. Dupin is not impressed by this reaction.

'The Mystery of Marie Rogêt,' although based on Dupin's solving of a crime primarily from newspaper reports, is in reality based on the murder of a girl, Mary Cecilia Rogers, near New York City. Because the crime had not been solved when Poe wrote the story, he made use of the facts of the case to tell a story of the murder of a Parisian girl, Marie Rogêt.

The story ostensibly begins two years after the events of 'The Murders in the Rue Morgue,' when the prefecture of police, having failed to solve the Marie Rogêt case himself, worries about his reputation and asks Dupin for help. Dupin's method is that of the armchair detective and is more like that of a case which might have been solved by Sherlock Holmes' reputedly 'smarter' brother, Mycroft. He examines copies of the newspapers that carry descriptions of the crime and then methodically examines each one.

In 'real' life, it was Poe's knowledge of the conventions of the novel that enabled him to deduce the correct conclusion of Charles Dickens's novel 'Barnaby Rudge: A Tale of the Riots' of '80, (1841) , the previous year, when he had read only one or two of the first episodes. By this means, Dupin eliminates the various hypotheses for the crime proposed by the newspapers, and then proposes his own hypothesis, which is confirmed by the confession of the murderer.

Dorothy L. Sayers has lauded 'The Mystery of Marie Rogêt,' as a story 'for connoisseurs', and 'a serious intellectual exercise rather than a sensational thriller, like "The Murders in the Rue Morgue." However, the most complex of the Dupin stories must surely be 'The Purloined Letter' where the solution is based to a great extent on political intrigue. As with the other Dupin stories, the basic premise of the missing letter tale can be found in Doyle' much later 'Second Stain' Holmes story.

Poe was certainly highly inventive and set the benchmark high for future writers of the crime genre, but none of his successors have quite achieved the apparent fluidity of style that Conan Doyle mastered in those 56 short stories and four novels of his; nor does Poe possess Conan Doyle's facility with dialogue. Doyle is a master of the form of the detective story. His characters are entirely credible; his stories are nearly all highly convincing, and they often carry within them the disturbing darkness and characters of the Gothic genre. The darkness of each crime solved is dispelled by the ratiocination of Holmes, who is a less imposing and far less loquacious form of Dupin, but a detective who frequently shares his *fin de siecle* despair' regarding the world of crime and criminals.

Fig. 64. This nightmarish illustration of the Rue Morgue
tale is by the artist Aubrey Beardsley and appeared in an edition
of the Poe book printed in 1894.

SHERLOCK HOLMES: THAT 'TRIFLING MONOGRAPH' ON HANDWRITING

By Sherlock Holmes

The ideas I set before you that I formerly espoused in 'The Book of Life' have not changed fundamentally over twenty years as a private consulting detective and I still adhere to them. The identical principles set forth there may also be applied to the study of handwriting.

Regarding the appreciation of manuscripts, the most divergent opinions exist. Some people have made a science of it and yet, do not know how to sufficiently appreciate the results of their examination, while others consider the knowledge so many persons pretend to possess, as the mere product of their imagination.

No detective is obliged to form a decision on one side or the other, but he must take up a position on the subject and form an opinion upon it, whether he believes in the study of graphology or not. Before the detective decides this, we would advise him to give the matter careful consideration, for no sooner do we in a matter of human knowledge, establish a certainty about it, no matter how wide the limits may be, we then find that knowledge cannot be limited. In other words, all knowledge is capable of development, but how far, we do not know.

No one will deny that it is worthwhile for educated persons to form an opinion about graphology. At least everyone will agree that the writing of an uneducated labourer looks very different to the writing of an educated lady, and that the child does not write like the old man, and that the writing of a farm labourer will not be mistaken for that of a learned man. However, as soon as you have gone so far, you must confess that there is such a thing as graphology, because you have acknowledged that the principles of it have to be correct.

One can go further and talk about pedantic, interesting, nervous, fickle, energetic handwriting and moreover, recognise the writing of an aristocratic lady or the soldier, or the merchant, or the scholar. By this means one has already gone a long way to demonstrate the rudiments of graphology and admitted that the things established by an examination of handwriting are capable of a wider and more scientific development.

If data in greater numbers were collected, and if more cautious accurate experiments were made, then it was surely be possible to individualise and generalise and thus, establish rules, leading to our increase of knowledge.

There is a line in some subjects beyond which we cannot go and this is easy to see. Would anyone, for example, maintain that, the study of the connection between the lines of the hand and the fate of the criminal should be advanced to a science? Perhaps not, but as regards pure graphology, there are acknowledged facts and it is therefore permissible to think that it is capable of development.

As early as the 17th century, work on the subject appeared, namely the 'Ideographia Prosperi Aldorissi', by Camillo Boldo.[9] At the beginning of the 18th century an anonymous book was published in Paris entitled 'The Art of Judging the Character of Men By Their Handwriting.' Goethe and Lavater were interested in the subject and Henza, who for a considerable time published appreciations of manuscripts in the 'Leipzig Illustrated Journal' also wrote a volume entitled *''Die Chiro-Grammatomantie.'* Other well-known experts have also written on the subject as, for example, Zim-mali, Meiidius, Machmer and many others have also written treatises from which the detective can learn many things to help him in his profession.

We may say at once that there are few people so well fitted to be handwriting experts as the trained detective. The latest and perhaps the best work on the subject is Ames 'On Forgery, Its Detection and Illustration,'

We must now proceed to briefly consider the aims of study and experience calculated to confer higher-order skill handwriting expert. Here are the citeria:

1st. The process of understanding handwriting should be seen as a continuum.

2nd. The detective should familiarise himself with the publications devoted to writing and phases of penmanship, involving careful preparation models for an engraver and the critical scrutiny of plate reproductions.

3rd. The preparation of critical, technical, literary and scientific instructions for the student of penmanship should be observed.

---

[9] Camillo Baldus or otherwise often spelt as Camillo Baldo, was one if the very first Western intellectuals to try and define personality and character interpretation from specimens of handwriting. printed and manuscript works covering a wide range of subjects. He wrote a number of books but perhaps the best known of these is his essay on graphology, 'Trattato Come Da Una Lettera Missiva Si Conoscano La Natura E Qualità Dello Scrittore', the first detailed investigation of the subject, published in 1622 when Baldi was over 70.

4th. The accumulated experience arising from previous examinations of disputed writing and the verdicts of juries in cases on which the expert has been previously employed, should be considered.

5th. The occupation of an engraver or lithographer should be considered when the frequent reproduction of handwriting and especially autographs, is involved.

6th. The professional observation of handwriting in any line of financial commercial business tends to confer skill. It will be worth saying that an investigating detective of experience and intelligence must at least have followed the fourth line of preparation laid down by Ames. Although a study of books like those mentioned above will be of great service, more important still are observation, followed by analysis and deduction. Thus, the process of examining handwriting may become a science.

The examination of manuscripts is of value to the detective in two ways: it enables him to know his man and next, renders it possible for him to solve the preliminary question, namely, "are the presumptions sufficient to assume the two writings are identical and to warrant the employment of an expert on the subject?"

A detective is in a better position than anyone else to obtain the knowledge necessary for this, for not only has he to examine many writings, but he nearly always comes to know the author of them. He can therefore verify the conclusions he has arrived at when examining writing, by personal dealings with the writer. Every criminal record offers, from this point of view, ample material; in the notes and signatures of the investigating detectives colleagues and clerks, and the signatures and writings of witnesses and accused persons, and especially in letters and other documents which form part of the papers in a case, sufficient material is thus to be found. All that is necessary is for the detective to take a close interest in the subject.

The writing specimen provided must be studied and the results obtained from the examination should be compared with the information obtainable from other sources as regards the individual in question. Finally, one must try to find out when things are not clear, and where a possible mistake in judgement has been formed - all this is easy to say, but the work itself requires much time and trouble.

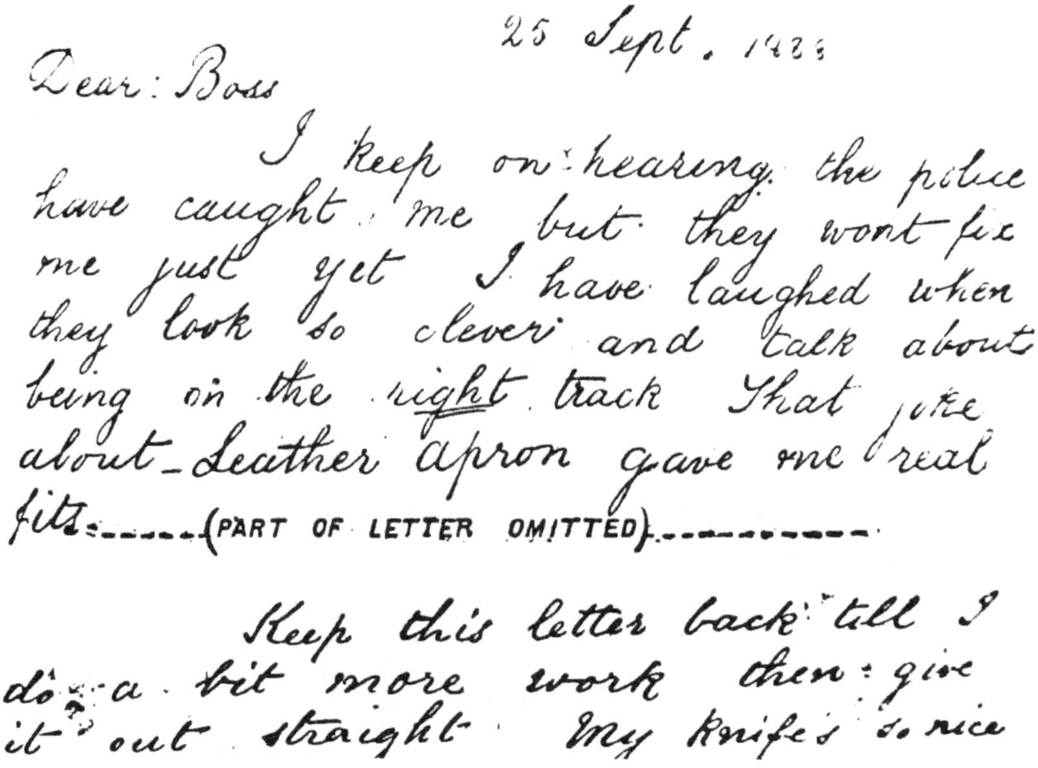

25 Sept. 1888

Dear: Boss

*I keep on hearing the police have caught me but they wont fix me just yet I have laughed when they look so clever and talk about being on the right track That joke about Leather apron gave me real fits*____(PART OF LETTER OMITTED)_____

Keep this letter back till I do a bit more work then: give it out straight My knife's so nice

Fig.65. If investigators of crimes were better acquainted with the mehods by which we can interpret character and personality, like this letter, which was supposed to have been written by Jack The Ripper, our apprehension of murderers of this nature might well improve.

As regards the first part of the work, it is necessary to proceed in the most methodical way. In the first place, it is required to become familiar with all forms of letters, generally used by old people, who have learned handwriting many years before: but in doing so, it must not be forgotten that the employment of such forms is no absolute proof that the writer is an old person. Certain people have had an old writing master and his character is not very independent often employing for a long time afterwards, the lessons they have first learned.

There are also people have taken to the habit of using antiquated letters out of sympathy for the archaic 'bore' or old person. There are also old people who have preserved their youthful character and like to do everything as young people would do: they follow the fashion or the form of letters as they would an old-fashioned garment and sometimes will adopt new forms of letters. But this is exceptional, and as a general rule, people do not change the writing to which they have become accustomed – especially when well advanced in life.

Ames, in his classic study, cites two cases of character reading from handwriting which show what store he lays by the fashion in writing.

Not long since, the writer was present with a party of ladies and gentlemen, where the reading of character from handwriting was the subject being discussed. One of the ladies took from her pocket two letters and, handing them to him, asked an expression of his opinion respecting the authors.

Inspecting one of them, he said: "the writer was upwards of 60 years of age, a methodical, careful, experienced businessman and probably the head of a corporation." Inspecting the writing of the other letter, he then commented, "The writer of this letter is between 30 and 40, a keen, active man of affairs, probably the secretary of the corporation or a large business."

The lady who had sought out this opinion at once clapped her hands, saying that nothing could be more truthful, adding that one was the president of the savings company and the other was secretary of a corporation. She said, "I would just like to have you explain to me how you could tell that." The reply was, taking the first one: "Here is a strong, clear, legible, practised hand, methodical, without change, or erasure, from beginning to end, and it is written in a round shaped hand, which must have been learned more than 45 years ago, as this school of writing has not been taught in this country since that period. This, together with a dignified and deliberate appearance of the writing, fixes his age at over 60 years, while the practised style of the letter indicates a large experience in the business world. The good judgement and accuracy manifested in the writing shows corresponding traits in business affairs."

As to the other letter, he said: "This is an elegant, Spenserian hand, which must have been learned at a much more recent date, and hence by a younger man. It is written with great facility, indicating young and well - trained muscles and the composition and subject matter is such as to indicate one trained and familiar with the business world. Here, therefore, is a man not above middle life and possessed of the requisite qualifications for the active duties of secretary or chief clerk of the large business enterprise."

Having determined this question of age, the next thing to be done is to see whether the writing examined is by one who writes little or very much. This presents no difficulty in that may not be easy to express in words what is meant by a 'running' hand. Everyone knows how to distinguish an awkward and heavy or embarrassed script, from a free, practised and flowing style.

This is exceptionally easy. A more difficult question is to discover the gender of the writer; yet, even when one is not accustomed to examining writing, one may make the distinction without mistake. A little experience and practice soon make it almost impossible to commit an error.

The next problem concerns the exterior form of the writing and consists of classifying the writing of men according to their professions. Thus, it is easy to recognise the rapid and legible writing of learned men and which may sometimes present a peculiarity where the characters bear a certain resemblance to print. The writing of soldiers is more like that of trades people, but it is clearer and more energetic – more sure of itself. The writing of civil servants and other officials can be as a rule only described as untidy. The schoolmaster, who finds himself obliged to set beautiful copies before his scholars, is incapable of committing himself often to the luxury of writing of his own choosing, and in everyday life he still writes copies.

When carrying out the study of manuscripts, a document, like a deposition, should never be handled without an attempt to gain profit by that study. First look at the signature and read all that you can read from it. Then, relying on the facts set out, the accuracy of the opinion formed from that may be verified. For example: "Artisan, 40 or 50 years old, open hearted, trustworthy, honest small in stature, careless." Then the description, profession, and so on, is looked at and the opinion is found to be accurate.

Another mechanical method of seizing upon peculiarities in writing may be mentioned. All that is necessary to be done is to go over the writing simply with the eyes, following the outlines of the characters. But this must be done quickly as if you were writing yourself.

It is important to re-examine a piece of writing for the purposes of verification, when one has subsequently become better informed about a certain individual. For example, the writing of an accused may have been examined and an opinion formed about him, but the whole work should be done over and over, and the two results re-examined when, subsequently, his guilt or innocence has been definitely established.

The only correct method is to study and examine the characteristics of each piece of writing apart and then to compare the results obtained, but not the writings themselves. Only after having carefully done this, can the two documents be compared together for resemblances and differences.

It is useful, whenever writing is to be examined critically, to draw certain lines which enable characteristic peculiarities to be discovered. These lines are horizontal or demarcating lines: four of them should be drawn, such as may be seen in the writing books of children, but instead of being straight, these lines will be broken, joining the upper and lower extremities of all the letters. The straightest line will be that joining the lower edge of the letters without loops or tails. Taken together, the four lines will then represent characteristic peculiarities important for comparison.

But if the writing has been forged, the line will therefore be interrupted, though the characteristic distances between the lines may not be lost. If the case is an important one, the documents should be photographed.

The photographs may then be handled at will and many things often discovered in them which may be missed when examining the original document itself. Interruptions in words taken singly are important. As a rule, words are written without stopping and in one continuous flow, but there are several exceptions:

1.When the word is so long that one is obliged to move the forearm which rests on the table, then the palm will also be moved.

2. When also, in long words, near the commencement of the word, an I has to be dotted, or a t stroked. When these signs come at the end of the word, as a rule, one writes the word before placing the sign, but in other cases the word is usually interrupted in the middle, the sign being placed, and the word continued.

An example would be the word 'misunderstanding.' Most writers would stop after the third S and dot the I, then go on to the end of the word before dotting the eye in ING and finally stroking the t.

3. When certain letters do not join easily with others; example, S, or after certain capital letters B, Z, D, etc; sometimes also after certain small letters, for example g, d, or 1: and finally, one sometimes breaks off in the middle of the letter itself, for example, p d, k.

4. When the person writing has got into a habit of breaking off frequently without any particular reason.

In every case such interruptions should be characteristic of all pieces of writing, and must be studied minutely. In the case of disputed documents, it will be noticed that the interruptions are few and cannot be therefore explained by the above stated reasons.

As to spelling, this proves absolutely nothing. The forger might know how to spell and yet intentionally introduce mistakes in his writing. also make many mistakes in his ordinary writing, while in the forged document he may have looked up some of the words in a dictionary and thus corrected them.

The graphologist, Ames, gives some interesting information regarding tracing. There are, he says, two general methods of perpetrating a forgery. One is by tracing and the other is by free handwriting. Tracing can only be employed when a signature or writing is present in the exact form of the desired reproduction. It can be done by placing the writing to be forged on a transparency over a strong light, then superimposing the paper on which the forgery is to be made. The outline of the writing underneath will appear plain enough to trace it with a pencil. This tracing is then blackened on the obverse side. However, a forgery done by means of tracing can have certain limitations. Instead of the mind being occupied by the usual function of supplying the matter to be recorded, it devotes its attentions otherwise. Thus, the hand no longer glides naturally over the paper, but moves slowly with a halting and vacillating motion, as the eye passes to and from the copy to the original, moving under the specific control of the will. Evidence of such a forgery is manifested in formal, broken, nervous lines, the uneven flow of the ink and the often retouched lines and shades.

These proofs are unmistakable when studied with the aid of a microscope. Also, the evidence is often provided by a careful comparison of the disputed writing, noting the pen pressure or absence of any of the delicate and unconscious forms and shades characteristic of the standard writing. Again, the forger rarely possesses the requisite skill to exactly reproduce the features of the original by the tracing. Many of the minutiae of the original writing, are more or less microscopic, and for that reason they pass unobserved by the forger. Outlines of writing to be forged are sometimes simply drawn with a pencil and then worked up in ink. Such outlines will not usually provide so good an imitation as to form, since they depend on the imitative skill of the forger.

In concluding these trifling observations on handwriting, the author must add that there are distinguished experts now in handwriting, who often proceed in conformity with very scientific principles. To these we may confidently approve of their competence, but we must not also neglect to make our own observations in order to compare them with those of the expert, in the interests of the enquiry.

WHEN CONAN DOYLE MET JACK THE RIPPER

INTRODUCTION

According to the 'Encyclopaedia Brittanica,'

'In the late 19th century, French psychologist Pierre Janet appropriated the label 'idée fixe' for use in a clinical context. He applied the term to any inflexible and often irrational belief, such as a phobia, typically linked to a traumatic memory, that slips from conscious control (becomes 'dissociated') and subsequently dominates a person's mental activity'.

For example, the eating disorder anorexia nervosa, characterized by self-starvation, would be the outward expression of such an *idée fixe*. To treat the illness, Janet submitted, psychologists must address not only the patient's aversion to eating but also the *idée fixe* and the related traumatic experience that lie at the root of the condition.

According to Dr. Watson, in his account of the story of the 'Adventure of the Six Napoleons', 'There are no limits to the possibilities of mono mania. There is the condition which the modern French psychologists have called the '*idee fixe*', which may be trifling in character and accompanied by complete sanity in every other way.

A man who has read deeply about Napoleon or who had possibly received some hereditary family injury through the Great War might conceivably form such an *idee fixe* and under the influence be capable 'of any fan tastic outrage'. It might be said that Sir Charles Baskerville's obsession with the legend of 'The Hound.' resulted in an *idee fixe*, which consequently led indirectly to the termination of his life.

This notion was a popular one with Conan Doyle and can be seen at work in other non-Holmes stories; for example, in his horror story, 'The Brown Hand,' and most of all in his often ignored novella, 'The Parasite.'

Interestingly, for fans of the Holmes stories, it has often been noted that obsession formed also an immense subject for the originator of the entire crime genre, Edgar Allan Poe.. The most original example of this, surely must be 'The Tell - Tale Heart,' in which Poe vividly conveys the emotional state of intensity of his central character, a deranged psychopath, through the use of a monologue. This form of short story has since become a favourite type of narrative to portray criminals suffering from what psychiatrists would define as 'a disassociated state of mind.'

The card index filing system used by detectives at the Yard at the time of the Ripper murders which might therefore have led them to their man, The Ripper, was very primitive, to say the least, and did not have the flexibility, or investigative connections, that the modern day detective affords.

From our reading of the Sherlock Holmes stories, we know that Sherlock Holmes was an expert on handwriting analysis. Cyphers, footprints and distinctive marks on paper, plus the effects of a particular livelihood on the hand of a person who pursued his or her occupation; all these and others were part of his expertise. In fact, his knowledge was as wide as was that of his maker, Conan Doyle, and it was extremely precise.

It comes as no surprise therefore, to imagine that Conan Doyle would have solved the Ripper enigma. He was most concerned, as he said in the interview in the magazine Titbits, in 1894,. that the police had simply not asked handwriting experts to look at the handwriting examples and see if they matched any of the letters that their relatives had produced.

In fact, it does not seem that the police actually compared newspaper reports at all. Yet, Conan Doyle, living as he was during that period of these murders in the area of Portsmouth in Southsea, would have been able to take advantage of 'The Portsmouth Evening News'. This newspaper published very graphic accounts of the murders. Therefore, Conan Doyle was in receipt of all of the forensic evidence he needed regarding the identity of The Ripper.

LETTERS FROM THE CRIME CLUB

If we're looking at providing a solution regarding handwriting we must admit such analysis is vitally important. We know that Doyle would have analysed the message in the letter that was seen by him at the Black Museum. And we also know that he assumed that the murderer was of foreign extraction, or had lived abroad, possibly for a long time. He also was of the opinion, although this must remain purely a conjecture, that the man who committed the crimes may have been of American origin. (This was the 'dear boss' letter which was sent to the Criminal Agency in September of 1888.)

There was a also a theory at one time which was popular with the ex - commissioner of Police, Robert Anderson, that the Ripper could have been a person of Jewish extraction. When the information by Anderson was finally leaked to the press, this caused a great deal of hostility among the largely dominant East End Jewish community. Anderson, the person responsible for making this view, published an article in Blackwoods Magazine in March 1910, Part Six , where he writes as follows;

'One did not need to be a Sherlock Holmes to discover that the criminal was a sexual maniac of a virulent type, that he was living in the immediate vicinity of the scenes of the murders. And he was not living absolutely alone. His people knew of his guilt and they refused to give him up to justice.

'During my absence abroad, the police had made a house to house search for him. Murders are rare in London and the Jack the Ripper crimes are not within that category. And if the police investigating the case of every man in the district would know the circumstances were such, that he could go and come and get rid of his blood stains in secret. And the conclusion we came to was that he and his people were low class Jews. For it is a fact that people of that class in the East End will not give up one of their number to Gentile justice, and the results proved that our diagnosis was right on every point. For I may say at once that if Scotland Yard had powers such as the French police possess, the murder would have been brought to justice.

'Scotland Yard can boast that not even the subordinate officers of the department will tell tales out of school. And it would ill become me to violate the unwritten rule of the service. The subject will come up again. And I will only add here that the Secord Ripper letter, which is preserved in the police Museum at New Scotland Yard, is the creation of an enterprising London journalist. I will only add that the second individual whom we suspected was caged in an asylum. The only person who had ever had a good view of the murderer at once identified him. But when he learned that the suspect was a fellow Jew, he declined to swear to him'.

There was an immediate reaction to Anderson's claims in this interview in the Jewish Chronicle of the 4th of March 1910, when a journalist attacked Anderson for his overt racist views. The journalist observed that this theory was nonsensical and that it condemned a whole neighbourhood of immigrants by tarring them with the same brush.

What proof did Robert Anderson have to support this view, the journalist asked. In fact, the only very detailed description of what the killer may have looked like comes from an eyewitness statement made shortly after the last of the five so -called classic murders, ending with the murder of Jane Kelly in the September of 1888.

In the statements made to the police the eyewitness has this description of the Ripper and it comes from a document from a Metropolitan Police address, in Commercial Street, dated the 12th of November 1888;

'The description of the witness who saw the victim, a 'gentleman' describes him in vivid and clear detail, The report states:.

'Age about 34, height about 5ft 6ins.,complexion pale, dark eyes and eyelashes. Slight moustache cut off at each end and hair dark. Very surly looking, dressed in a long, dark coat, collar and cuffs trimmed and trim. The dark jacket under a light waistcoat, dark trousers, dark felt hat turned down in the middle. Button boots, decorated with white buttons; he wore a very thick gold chain, a white linen colour, a black tie with horseshoe pin and of respectable appearance.'

That is a report given by George Hutchinson, who was one of the detectives who gained access to that witness statement.

And now we look at further significant evidence, The suggestion that the Ripper was of foreign extraction has been favoured by many people. And this is supported by some of the phraseology used in the letters that the Ripper ostensibly sent, either to the Central Press Agency or to the police directly.

The first offender profile was in fact assembled by detectives of the Metropolitan Police about the personality of Jack the Ripper. Police surgeon Dr.Thomas Bond was asked to give his opinion on the extent of the murderer's surgical skill and knowledge.

Bond's assessment was based on his own examination of the most extensively mutilated victim and the post mortem notes from the four previous canonical murders, in his report to the police.

Following his detailed analysis of the body, or what might better describe as the remains of the killer's last victim Mary Kelly, dated November 10, 1888, he mentions the sexual nature of the murders. He deduced,that these feelings were coupled with elements of misogyny and rage. Dr. Bond also attempted to reconstruct the murder and interpret the behaviour pattern of the offender, and soon thereafter, he came up with a profile or signature of the personality traits of the offender to assist the police. The profile explained that five murders of seven in the area at the time the report was written had been committed by one person alone who was both very physically strong, composed, and daring.

This unknown offender would be quiet and harmless in his outward appearance, and that he was probably middle-aged, and neatly dressed'; also that the attacker most probably, wore a long cloak to hide the bloody effects of his attacks out in the open. He would be a loner, without a solid occupation, eccentric, and very mentally unstable. He might possibly suffer from a condition called Satyriasis, a sexual deviancy that is today referred to as hypersexuality or promiscuity. Bond also mentioned that he believed the offender had no specific anatomical knowledge and that he would not be able to confirm the oft- stated view that he might have been. a surgeon or a butcher. Bond's summary profile further explains:

'The murderer must have been a man of physical strength and great coolness and daring... subject to periodic attacks of homicidal and erotic mania. The characters of the mutilations indicate that the man may be in a condition sexually, that may be called Satyriasis.'

As a doctor in general medical practice, both in Birmingham and Southsea, it is entirely likely that Conan Doyle would have previously come across this condition, known in Victorian times as Satyriasis. It is also very possible that he may have acquired a copy of the most famous autobiographical account of this condition, written by the enigmatic and anonymous 'Walter.' In that century, 'satyriasis' was a condition most commonly applicable to men and for which there was apparently no obvious cure, apart from frequent doses of bromide, or when this did not work, through barbaric practices such as penile cauterisation.

Conan Doyle himself had also written a detailed study of the symptoms of tabes dorsalis, a discreet account of the disease of syphilis and he had even written a short story about it. This may be of some significance and may provide The Ripper with an additional motive for the attacks.

Doyle also used the subject of syphilis as the theme for 'The Third Generation.' In this rarely read tale, later reproduced in Doyle's 'Round The Red Lamp,' a young aristocrat visits his GP with a skin condition diagnosed as a *'strumous diathesis'* – otherwise known as scrofulathen. The name given to the condition by Doyle is a euphemism for syphilis.

The young man is told by his doctor that he must not even consider going through with his marriage, and that he has been cursed by an hereditary illness. References are made to his ancestor's 'hereditary blight.' The afflicted visitor then makes this impassioned plea:

'"But where is the justice of it, doctor?" cried the young man, springing from his chair and pacing up and down the consulting-room. "If I were heir to my grandfather's sins as well as to their results, I could understand it, but I am of my father's type. I love all that is gentle and beautiful— music and poetry and art. The coarse and animal is abhorrent to me. Ask any of my friends and they would tell you that. And now that this vile, loathsome thing—ach, I am polluted to the marrow, soaked in abomination! And why? Haven't I a right to ask why? Did I do it? Was it my fault? Could I help being born? And look at me now, blighted and blasted, just as life was at its sweetest. Talk about the sins of the father — how about the sins of the

Creator?" He shook his two clinched hands in the air — the poor impotent man with his pin-point of brain caught in the whirl of the infinite.'

During the period when Doyle was practising as a doctor, the 1880s, there was a relatively new view of human sexuality gaining ascendance. Several 'authorities' on the subject regarded male sexuality as a biological imperative, which added fuel to many writings on the male gender; but these assertions in turn were countered often by those who argued that 'civilisation' enabled humans to transcend animal instincts.

This view acquired a public voice through the 'Social Purity Campaign' against the sexual 'double standard', and for the need for male as well as female continence outside marriage. Though the female Purity campaigners were sometimes mocked as 'puritans' who had failed to attract a spouse, the movement succeeded in raising public concern over brothels which, especially in the East End of London, had reached a record high at the time when the Ripper struck; and there was a theory that Jack the Ripper may have contracted syphilis from a prostitute, and that this in turn, might have been precisely why he took his own form of barbaric vengeance on the unfortunate sex workers. His decision to remove the uterus of one victim has been interpreted as a direct attack on the "essence of being a woman" – and experts believe he removed it, in order to mark his hatred of womankind.

I believe it is entirely convincing that Doyle shared this view of the Ripper's profile.

One other thing about the killing spree, which has attracted previously only scant notice, has been the possible use of the River Thames as a useful getaway route. In that period, the Thames was where people often got their drinking water from. However, it also acted as an important water-highway through the city.

In the novel by Charles Dickens 'Our Mutual Friend,' Jesse "Gaffer" Hexam – a waterman, is the father of Lizzie and Charley, who makes a living by robbing corpses found in the river Thames. His former partner, Rogue Riderhood, turns him in for the murder of John Harmon after Harmon's body is supposedly dragged from the river. A search is mounted to find and arrest Gaffer, but he is discovered dead in his boat.

In this Dickens novel the great river and conduit is described in eloquent detail, lying in the midst of that vast overflow of London, where it is seen, not only as a huge and tainted sewer, but also as a place of secrets and concealment. The two characters depicted, earn a strictly and unpredictable illegal living by fishing dead bodies out of the murky waters. Hexam and the daughter Lizzie , make a meagre and perilous living by robbing corpses found in the Thames. His former partner, Rogue Riderhood, turns Hexam in for the murder of John Harmon after Harmon's body is supposedly dragged from the river. A search is mounted to find and arrest Gaffer, but he is discovered dead in his boat. Hexam has been thus retrieving corpses and taking the cash from their pockets, before handing them over to the authorities. Papers in the pockets of the drowned man identify him as Harmon.

In the novel, Dickens uses many images that relate to water.

Phrases such as the "depths and shallows of Podsnappery," and the "time had come for flushing and flourishing this man down for good", are examples of such imagery. Some critics see this visual imagery as excessive, thus creating a feeling of caricature, but in the case of these descriptions of the great river, this only serves to intensify the connection between the reader's fear of criminality and the sense of the river as a living but malign being in which terrible secrets may soon be revealed.. Thus, Dickens' account of the River Thames carries within it the dark and disturbing Gothic horror of Poe which so frequently imbues the work of Conan Doyle; and both writers have a great knack in their description of the uncanny, This extract from Dickens makes the comparison

'Allied to the bottom of the river rather than the surface, by reason of the slime and ooze with which it was covered, and its sodden state, this boat and the two figures in it obviously were doing something that they often did and were seeking what they often sought. Half savage as the man showed, with no covering on his matted head, with his brown arms bare to between the elbow and the shoulder, with the loose knot of a looser kerchief lying low on his bare breast in a wilderness of beard and whisker, with such dress as he wore seeming to be made out of the mud that begrimed his boat, still there was a business-like usage in his steady gaze. So, with every lithe action of the girl, with every turn of her wrist, perhaps most of all with her look of dread or horror; they were things of usage.'

In the 1880s the River Thames would have been shrouded in virtual blackness at night, and anyone who either worked on the river or might have given a large tip to a lighterman, would have escaped arrest or even challenge by the Thames River Police. The River Police, who operated with both the Met. Police but also the City Police Force, had far fewer numbers. They had at their disposal several small, low bottom boats and three steam launches. Doyle favoured the idea of The Ripper using The Thames as a dark tunnel where the he could be entirely undetected and invisible from the riverbank, and this image is beautifully delineated in 'The Sign of Four,' where in the penultimate chapter of this Holmes story, one of the murderers, Jonathan Small, is chased by a steam launch down to Gravesend where Small attempts an escape by launching himself from the boat straight into a bank of mud.

In my trilogy of books, 'The Criminal World of Sherlock Holmes,' I have conjectured that it is certain that Jack the Ripper used the river, following his dastardly butcheries in Whitechapel. This is a highly likely scenario. After dusk, an impenetrable gloom fell on its dark waters, thus enabling many criminals to escape without even a trace into the various parts of the city.

In the middle of the 19th century, Henry Mayhew and other social commentators were able to comment on the great number of robberies committed on the River Thames. These declarations differed in value, for example, from 'The little ragged child stealing a piece of rope or a few handfuls of coal from a barge,' to 'the lighterman carrying odd bails of silk, worth several 100 pounds. Looking to the long lines of shipping along each side of the river, these river criminals relied on the vessels that daily ploughed their way along its route. They were able to slip aboard the dense shipping in the docks and then emerge, laden with untold wealth. And thus we should not be surprised at the level of almost unseen crime which flourished along the river's course.

The river had its own populace, some of whom belonged to, or depended on the criminal classes. The 'mudlarks,' so called, consisted of boys and girls who varied in age from eight to fourteen. These were, in their appearance, much like the Baker Street Irregulars. Many of them were described in Sherlock Holmes' time as 'coal light workers,' groups of mainly Irish youths, employed by older men, who were made to get coal from the ships illegally, which often their mothers would then take in the street and exchange for food. The children would get between the barges, lift up one end of the canvas and knock the pieces of coal into their mouths, which they would then pick up afterwards at the dock side. They frequently sold these coals in and among the lower classes of people for a few half pence each. When arrested by the Thames River Police, some of the Mudlarks obtained short term spells of imprisonment from three weeks to a month. But other, more repetitive offenders, were sent to Reformatories for two to three years.

Further up on the Thames from where Holmes and Watson entered the police steam launch, could be seen at low tide groups of older women picking up coals in the bed of the river. One particular woman, described as 'a robust creature dressed in an old cotton gown with a straw bonnet tied round with a handkerchief, who wanders about in the waters of the river, without shoes and stockings', was often seen in the neighbourhood of Blackfriars Bridge, where also could be seen small groups of ragged dressed females 'from 10 to 50 years;. Some of them, the account goes on to describe, started their career with stealing rope or coal from barges, then proceeded to take the more valuable copper from vessels, and afterwards went down in the cabins and stole other goods.

There was even a class of boys who sailed the river in very ancient boats, and often got on board into craft under the pretext of sweeping. They would leave the barges laden with coffee, sugar or rice, stealing anything that they could get their hands on. They were again described as 'ragged and wretched in appearance'. When pursued by the Thames River Police, they would take to the water like rats, splashing through the mud.

These youths were expert swimmers, and ranged from 12 to 16, attired, or rather, dis-attired in a similar way to the other ragged boys in the metropolis, and in appearance, much like the Irregulars. Some of them were healthy, some slept in barges and others inhabited some of the local lodging houses. In the summertime, they would sleep in the open barges, and often, in the winter, cover themselves with old hessian sacks to keep warm.

It is quite conceivable that some of the Baker Street Irregulars may have drawn their number from these gangs of children, often termed 'river rats.'

The level of unseen crime on the banks of and in the waters of the River Thames was notable, all of which gives, in my opinion, credence and support to the idea that the Ripper may also have had links to some of the criminal fraternity, who may have may supported him either invisibly or unknowingly. There was a great degree of smuggling of contraband goods on the river by foreign seamen, upon their arrival from foreign ports, in the shape of tobacco, coal, handkerchiefs and jewellery.

Mayhew reports how, one morning, while running by the Tower of London, a policeman once spotted a group of chimney sweeps who had stolen merchandise from a boat and were leaving in a steam vessel, carrying with them some large bags. On searching the bags, he found several packages of manufactured tobacco. The chimney sweeps were arrested, and discovered to have in their possession £100 each. They were sentenced to six months each in prison, and having refused to pay their fines, were then imprisoned for an additional spell.

I had for long entertained the notion that the lightermen, who plied their craft and helped to convey people up and down the River Thames may have had what was tantamount to a season ticket with Jack the Ripper, and if Conan Doyle's convincing theory that the perpetrator of these crimes may have been an American, it would have been only too easy for a lighterman to convey him down river to Gravesend from where boats headed across the Atlantic and beyond, even to the shores of the USA.

The reputation of the lightermen who plied their trade in these river taxies during that period was not above reproach. Mayhew, for example, quotes an account of two men who, in April 1858, were charged with robbery from barges at Wapping. They received quantities of dye, wire, and other commodities near the London Docks. They then loaded the stuff into an empty barge alongside two barges, then took a chest of dye from one of them and a case of wire card from the other, to the value of £25. Then they took the barge with the stolen property on board to Rotherhithe, landing at the Elephant Stairs, where they were taken away in a cart.

The property was never recovered. But the two men were sentenced to 18 months at the Criminal Central Court. Mayhew comments that many of the lightermen were often 'dissipated in their habits, and then resorted to thieving when they lacked money.' And that they spent time dancing, in the concert rooms on the notorious Ratcliffe Highway, a place also mentioned by Holmes. They generally were known to cohabit with prostitutes and they were 'an entirely different class of men.' He compares them to the River pirates, who also lived with prostitutes, but who were generally smarter and better dressed.

In case anyone thinks that Mayhew's descriptions are exaggerated, my own family history has a light to shed upon the matter of the reputation of the lightermen. When, at the end of the 19th century, my great uncle was found dead, his stiffening body stretched out on top of steps leading down into the river, in the region of Greenwich, it was discovered that he had been robbed of his takings as a newsagent. And because there were no witnesses to the crime, the perpetrator of this vicious murder was never discovered. Hence, the reputation that the River Thames had as a cloak of invisibility, under which crimes often could be committed, was a view which was shared by many Londoners of that time, including my grandfather Frederick Morrison.

According to Adrian Conan Doyle, the author's son, in a letter sent to Tom Cullen, a researcher, Adrian had this to say about his father's views regarding Jack The Ripper:

'I do remember that he considered it likely that the man (the Ripper) had a rough knowledge of surgery and probably clothed himself as a woman to approach his victims without arousing suspicion on their part.'

As was proved several times in the George Edalji case, Doyle understood much about psychological profiling and how it worked; unlike some members of the metropolitan police, it must be admitted. He would therefore have both read and thoroughly comprehended what Hans Gross, the famous contemporary of Conan Doyle and his detective, had to say about this method of investigation, which, as we know, began with the first ever criminal profile, that of the Ripper himself.

In Gross's classic work about the motives of murderers, 'Psychological Crime Investigation', the Austrian ex-magistrate wrote this:

'If we stop with the phenomena of daily life and keep in mind the ever-cited fact that everybody recognizes at a glance the old hunter, the retired officer, the actor, the aristocratic lady, etc., we may go still further: the more trained observers can recognize the merchant, the official, the butcher, the shoe-maker, the real tramp, the Greek, the sexual pervert, etc.

'Hence follows an important law -- that if a fact is once recognized correctly in its coarser form, then the possibility must be granted that it is correct in its subtler manifestations.'

A most Holmesian statement which might have had the sage of Bake Street himself nodding in agreement. Gross then goes on to explain:

'The boundary between what is coarse and what is not, may not be drawn at any particular point. It varies with the skill of the observer, with the character of the material before him, and with the excellence of his instruments, so that nobody can say where the possibility of progress in the matter ceases.

'When he speaks of stupid and intelligent faces, he is a physiognomist; he sees that there are intellectual foreheads and microcephalic ones, and is thus a craniologist; he observes the expression of fear and of joy, and so observes the principles of imitation; he contemplates a fine and elegant hand in contrast with a fat and mean hand, and therefore assents to the effectiveness of chirognomy; he finds one hand-writing scholarly and fluid, another heavy, ornate and unpleasant; so he is dealing with the first principles of graphology;--all these observations and inferences are nowhere denied, and nobody can say where their attainable boundaries lie.'

So did Doyle know the name of the Ripper? I think he did but he was not going to disclose it. We can be certain that, among the papers and books sold which formed that great collection of criminological works owned by Doyle but auctioned after the writer's death in 1930, there might have been some clue into the final revelation of the man the world subsequently knew as 'Jack The Ripper'.

Is it at then at all possible, to demonstrate that Conan Doyle had quietly and discreetly worked out the identity of this enigmatic killer?

The period of murders under consideration extends initially from August 31st to November the ninth, 1888. During that time, five prostitutes were murdered in the East End of London.

In my opinion, there was an additional murder which was the murder in Castle Alley near a railway arch. This murder is perhaps worth considering as worthy of inclusion, and also since, from the extensive reports in Doyle's copy of The Portsmouth Evening News, we might then deduce, by inference, that Doyle would have gathered much of his data during this period. We might, like him, assume that the attacker wore female attire, and, as some of the detectives under the instructions of Commissioner Macnaghten speculated, bore the signs of an interrupted attack by a man disguised as a woman.

Prior to the 'railway arch murder, however, the so-called 'canonical' Whitechapel murder victims were as follows:

Mary Ann Nichols, who was killed at Buck's Row in Whitechapel. on August the 31st. Then, Annie Chapman, also a person earning money from immoral earnings, who was killed in Hanbury Street, on September the eighth in that same year.

Next was a woman called Elizabeth Stride, who died on September the 30th at Berners St., Catherine Eddowes, who died at Mitre Square.

Lastly, on September 30 of the same year, Mary Jane Kelly, who was gruesomely slaughtered at a place called Miller's Court on November the ninth, 1888.

A look at the murders prior to the railway arch murder reveals that each of the victims had their heads almost completely severed and also this kind of detail was reported in the newspaper which Doyle would certainly have read when he was a GP in Southsea.

In addition to these details, in five of these cases, the woman's abdomens were gouged, or opened. The very last murder was reported in an unusually graphic depth and detail in the Portsmouth Evening News. And it was this bizarre nature and gruesome detail, which got into the newspapers of the period. No one seems to have taken much consideration of the thoroughness of information in the news reports. However, this totality of factual detail provides a very detailed and an obvious series of links, which we can then comprehend and trace in a forensic chain.

Conan Doyle visited Scotland Yard's Black Museum, on December the second, 1892, four years after the Whitechapel Ripper murders. He would already have scrutinised the reports given by the attending surgeons who investigated the state of the bodies and also given talks to the Crime Club mmbers.

153

And here now is something which, up to this moment, has never been considered in any depth.

Conan Doyle would be interested in the perversity of the crimes, especially in connection with the knowledge that he had acquired from his reading of the forensic analysis of psychotic behaviour, which he would have read about, not only in Krafft Ebing's classic study 'Psychopathia Sexualis' , but also in the work of the Austrian judge, and renowned Austrian criminologist, Hans Gross.

I believe that Conan Doyle then used his literary skills and his formidable imagination to come to a well- informed view of the possible identity of the Ripper.

Conan Doyle, who himself, led something of a double life, enjoying the affections of Miss Jean Leckie. was no prude when it came to writing about women. He was, of course, a contemporary of Edward the 7th, whose reputation regarding high class whores was legendary, And his Christmas visits to the royal household at Sandringham, when he could be seen accompanied by a virtual tribe of whores was widely known. The libidinous aspect of his life as successor to the throne has been well documented in. many different media. But perhaps the best study of the huge tribe of women who profited from their association with this profligate. man in upper class English society has best been described in Michael Harrison's epic book, 'A Fanfare of Strumpets, (W.H. Allen, 1971), In which he describes not only Edward's compulsive addiction to harlotry, but in addition, the strong grip which this sort of sexual addiction had on a large number of upper class royal hanger - on. Small wonder is it therefore that the career of his own son, the Duke of Clarence, as a flagrant homosexual and as a possible contender for the role of the Ripper has been the subject of yet another royal biography by Mr Harrison. [10] Yet, regarding Bertie's son the, circumstantial evidence seems unconvincing, since at the time of most of the Whitechapel murders, the Prince was at Sandringham.

Several of the Ripper theorists have shown interest in the theory that the mass murderer of the 1880s was inspired to commit the murders of prostitutes because he had contracted some form of venereal disease. Among upper class

---

[10] Clarence: The Life of H.R.H. the Duke of Clarence and Avondale (1864-1892). Prince Albert Victor, Duke of Clarence and Avondale (Albert Victor Christian Edward; 8 January 1864 – 14 January 1892), was the eldest child of the Prince and Princess of Wales (later King Edward VII and Queen Alexandra). From the time of his birth, he was second in the line of succession to the British throne, but did not become king or Prince of Wales because he died before both his grandmother Queen Victoria and his father.

men, like those who were considered 'favourites' of the phallically prolific, and gambler extraordinaire, Bertie, much care had to be taken to avoid contamination. In fact, the plague and almost phobic fear of venereal disease. is a theme often re-visited in the autobiography of the man known as 'Walter' in his 'My Secret Life,' where fear of contracting one of these numerous diseases reaches morbid proportions in the later accounts of his experiences with prostitutes. And rather as it appears in many of his letters to polce, the Ripper uses the same type of language when describing his experiences among the poorer prostitutes, using word like 'whore.' 'drab,' and 'doxy.'

Just three years before the Ripper murders, Conan Doyle published an interesting document as part of his submission for a higher medical decree. Its title was:. 'An Essay Upon the Vasomotor Changes in Tabes Dorsalis' (Doctoral thesis). University of Edinburgh. hdl:1842/418.

when it came to the reinvention of the ideas he purloined from his predecessor, the American literary genius, Edgar Allan Poe. He had studied both the previous forms of the genre and - this was perhaps the most significant fact of all - he had accumulated a vast library of works relating to crime and criminology. Conan Doyle had learned much about the psychology and modus operandi of the dark world of 19th century crime.

When it came to writing convincing crime fiction, this author soon discovered that, with apparent ease, he could not only shock, but also intrigue readers.

But Conan Doyle had some distinct advantages over other writers. He had a degree in medicine, and he knew a great deal about the structure and the effects of many lethal poisons. This new writer also knew what a profile of a killer would be like; he had studied the methods of master poisoners like Palmer and Pritchard; and the burgling antics of the master thief, Charlie Peace; and in these stories, he employed this data and his formidable skill as a creator of realistic dialogue and convincing plots, to good use. He was about to conquer the world with his fictional forensically self-trained detective in the formative year for Conan Doyle of 1888.

MURDER AND BLOODY MAYHEM

Conan Doyle's bloody revenge tale, 'A Study in Scarlet', would be the first of many of these tales, bringing fame and prosperity to its young and ambitious writer, featuring a central protagonist, a detective with the unlikely name of Sherlock Holmes

As the years followed, these tales would eventually establish 'Sherlock Holmes' as a household word.

Now, over 150 years after his first appearance between the pages of the modestly produced 'Mrs. Beeton's Christmas Annual,' Holmes has been allowed into that rare Parnassus of public domain characters, like Count Dracula and, perhaps, more pertinently, Dr. Jekyll; and not least, of course.the elusive and enigmatic master of disguise, the man or woman the world still can never forget, that Scarlet Pimpernel, not of crime fiction, but of real-life Victorian crime, Jack the Ripper,

The appearance of Doyle's master sleuth coincided with the very firscriminal profile and also Richard Krafft Ebing's book, Pyschopathia Sexualis. This book is perhaps one of the most neglected of all 19th Century works on human sexuality and what was then regarded as the subject of sexual 'deviance'. It was controversial because of the liberal attitude to sexual behaviour which it proposed, and also of the information it provided– much of it described by Krafft Ebing's patients in considerable and very frank detail. So explicit and uncensored was the material that Krafft Ebing - rightly so in the period when he was writing - reproduced some of these passages in Latin.

Considering sexuality to be the "the most important factor in social existence," Richard von Krafft-Ebing soon gained a reputation as one of the most well-known early sexologists, especially considering the influence he had on not only the field of sexology, but also of psychology in general.

I first encountered this writer when I was conducting research into late 19th Century criminology, in preparation for an edition of the ten monographs on criminology 'reputedly' written by Sherlock Holmes. Any student of these remarkable and innovative Holmes stories by Doyle will know how authentic is the scientific methodology espoused by Doyle's fictional creation. As a doctor of medicine the author had a scientific training, which is why the Holmes stories are so utterly convincing - far more so, in my opinion, than those by the original pioneer of crime fiction, Edgar Allan Poe, to whom Doyle acknowledged his debt.

Doyle was writing his stories in the 1880s and 1890s for a largely female, middle - class audience, which is why the subject of 'deviant' sexuality is only ever briefly hinted at in the tales.

The one story which comes very close to an explanation and exploration of a crime motivated by sexual jealousy and savage violence is 'The Adventure of the Cardboard Box'. The content of the story was considered by Doyle himself to be so controversial that, when it came to transferring it to the edition of collected tales, known as 'The Memoirs of Sherlock Holmes,' he simply left it out for fear of affecting younger, more sensitive minds.

Yet, another of his tales, 'The Case of Lady Sannox' – not a Holmes tale – concerns the husband of a Moslem woman who, as a cruel punishment for committing adultery forces her to endure facial disfigurement. It is certain to me, reading the story, that Doyle was as interested in the origins of perverse sexuality as many other writers of the period but was forced to sublimate these themes for the benefit of his predominantly female reading audience.

I had not encountered Krafft – Ebing's work until I viewed the television 90s drama entitled 'The Curious Case of the Silk Stocking,' in which Watson's new bride – an American - is seen recommending 'Psychopathia Sexualis' to Holmes.

It is certain to my mind that Holmes, whose knowledge of criminology and criminal cases was described by his chronicler, Dr Watson, as 'profound', would have encountered this work, much as Doyle certainly did.

We also know that Doyle had read the work of the criminologist and Austrian judge, Hans Gross, a fact which was confirmed for me by a conversation I had with Sherlockian friend and Doylean book collector, the late Richard Lancelyn Green in 1987. Richard explained that he had purchased in an auction a copy of Gross's best seller.' Criminal Investigations, a Practical Textbook,' although his copy of the book, signed by Gross and dedicated to 'my dear friend, Dr. Conan Doyle,' was in the original German, as 'Handbuch für Untersuchungsrichter als System der Kriminalistik and was a first edition having been published in 1893. The purpose of the book was to make up for a deficiency in criminalistics. Gross wrote it as an instruction guide for police investigators and magistrates. Indeed, as I then pointed out to Richard, neither the book nor its dedication were surprising to me sinee by 1893, the Holmes stories had become highly popular in many countries and that Doyle could speak and write fluent German, having completed his school career under the Jesuits, when he was sent to Feldkirk in Germany. Indeed, Doyle's admiration for Gross is indicated by the fact that he based the plot of the late Holmes story, 'The Problem of Thor Bridge,' on a real life case which Doylelifted from Gross's 'Criminal Investigation.' Here, a jealous wife commits suicide but stages it to look like murder by standing on a bridge, attaching a revolver to a piece of thick string, at the end of which a large stone has been attached, and which, when fired, ricochets the revolver into the lake beneath her., thus incriminating her husband's much younger lover.

There is no doubt at all to my mind that Doyle would also have obtained a copy of Gross's other pioneering work of criminology, 'Criminal

Psychology,' the first English edition of which was not published until the turn of the century. By contrast, however, Krafft Ebing's monumental book was available in translation long before that and it is my strongly held conviction that Conan Doyl.e would certainly have owned his own copy of this pioneering work; and I am equally convinced that the police surgeon who created the world's first Scotland Yard profile , Dr Bond, had also read it.

PROFILE OF THE RIPPER

Modern works on what is now politely termed as 'sexology' scarcely mention the name of Krafft - Ebing. This is curious and, in some ways inexplicable, since it was he who first defined such terms as 'sadist' and 'masochist,' and was able to illustrate by examples what these terms meant.

As we now know, the sadistic nature of the crimes committed against his exclusively female victims, place the Ripper squarely in the frame as a sexual psychopath.

Richard Krafft-Ebing was born in Mannheim, Baden, Germany, on August 14, 1840. He received his education in Prague and studied medicine at the University of Heidelberg.

First published in 1866, Psychopathia Sexualis ("Psychopathology of Sex") went through a dozen editions and many translations. The book was developed as a forensic reference for doctors and judges, in high academic tone. In the introduction to the book, it was noted that the author had "deliberately chosen a scientific term for the name of the book to discourage lay readers." He also wrote sections of the book in Latin for the same purpose. Despite all these efforts to 'scholasticise' the more intimate observations in the work, it very soon became highly popular with lay readers: it reached twelve editions in his lifetime and was translated into many languages.

Psychopathia Sexualis was one of the first books about sexual practices that studied homosexuality and bisexuality. It proposed consideration of the mental state of sex criminals in legal judgements of their crimes, and during its time, it became the leading medico–legal textual authority on sexual pathology.

Krafft Ebing was as influential in his day as people like Sigmund Freud, and it must be said that his conclusions were drawn from a much wider database than the conclusions arrived at by Freud. Published originally in 1886, Krafft Ebing's work documents a number of clinical case studies of his own patients, and is known for being one of the first works to study female sexual pleasure and homosexuality along with topics such as necrophilia, incest, and paedophilia.

Born into an aristocratic family in Mannheim, Germany, Krafft-Ebing was the oldest of four siblings. His mother was the daughter of a well-known lawyer, whom Krafft-Ebing lived with while studying at the University of Heidelberg. It was there that he, along with his grandfather, developed an interest in the deviant sexual behavior of criminals and mental patients.

Because of this interest, he decided to become a psychiatrist and though he taught as a professor of psychiatry at several different universities; he also worked in private psychiatric asylums, and was an advocate for the reform of the treatment and diagnosing of the mentally ill.

So what, you may ask, has all this do with Jack the Ripper? My answer is: a great deal.

Believing sexuality and "sexual feelings" to influence all social aspects of life, particularly the formation of religions, Krafft-Ebing begins Psychopathia Sexualis with a brief history of sex, which is notable for its inclusion of other cultures and religions than his own, though he believes them inferior to Western, Christian societies.

Women, he writes, were once merely the "chattel" of men, but through the course of human history have, thanks in part to Christianity, become individual beings, with rights and freedoms of their own. For the 1880s, this represented a highly enlightened view.

The twelfth and final edition of Psychopathia Sexualis presented four categories of what Krafft-Ebing called "cerebral neuroses": paradoxia, sexual excitement' occurring independently of the period of the physiological processes in the generative organs; anaesthesia; absence of sexual instinct#; and, most important of all when we are when considering sexual motivation of the Riper crimes, hyperaesthesia, increased desire, and, most importantly for Ripperologists and Conan Doyle, satyriasis .

Krafft-Ebing proposed a theory of homosexuality as biologically anomalous, and originating in the embryonic and foetal stages of gestation, which evolved into a "sexual inversion" of the brain. In 1901, in an article in the Jahrbuch für sexuelle Zwischenstufen (Yearbook for Intermediate Sexual Types), he changed the biological term from anomaly to differentiation. His primary focus is on sexual behaviour in men, there are sections on Sadism in Woman, Masochism in Woman, and Lesbian Love. Several of the cases of sexual activity with children he deals with were committed by women.

Krafft-Ebing's conclusions about homosexuality are now largely forgotten, partly because Sigmund Freud's theories were more interesting to physicians (who considered homosexuality to be a psychological problem), but principally, because he incurred the enmity of the Austrian Catholic Church when he psychologically associated martyrdom (a desire for sanctity) with hysteria, and masochism.

In a footnote added to the 1915 edition of Three Essays on the Theory of Sexuality (1905), Freud urged that homosexuals should not be segregated from mainstream society. As readers of Krafft Ebing will observe, late on in his career, and in the later editions of the book, a more tolerant attitude to 'deviant' sexual behaviour is espoused under the headings of; paraesthesia, perversion of the sexual instinct, i.e., excitability of the sexual functions to inadequate stimulus.

In his book, Krafft Ebing uses and refers to various forms of the condition that most police surgeons presumed the Ripper would have experienced when he attacked his victims. Here is one example of a patient who was referred to:

'Case 13. For three years the generally respected farmer D., married, aged 35, has manifested states of sexual excitement, with increasing frequency and severity, which, during the past year, have become true paroxysms of satyriasis. It was impossible to discover hereditary or other organic cause. D. was compelled, at times when his sexual excitement was excessive, to perform the sexual act from ten to fifteen times in twenty-four hours, without deriving any feeling of satisfaction.

'Gradually he developed a condition of general nervous hyper-irritability (erethisme general) with increased emotional irritability to the extent of pathological outbreaks of anger, and impulse to over-indulgence in alcohol, which induced symptoms of alcoholism. His attacks of satyriasis became so violent that consciousness was interfered with, and the patient raged about in blind impulse to then commit sexual acts. He demanded that his wife give herself to other men or to animals in his presence; that she allow copulation with him, presentibus jiliabus, because this would afford him greater enjoyment. Memory for the events at the height of these attacks, in which the extreme irritability even led to outbreaks of maniacal rage, was entirely wanting. D. himself thought that he must have had moments in which he no longer had control of his senses, and without satisfaction from his wife, would have been compelled to seize the next best female. After an attack of violent emotion, these attacks of sexual excitement suddenly disappeared entirely.'

When one examines in detail (and there is a lot of detail in the Scotland Yard reports kept by the police surgeons of the time, each man being eminent, like meticulous Dr Bond, in his field of forensic expertise). The obsession with acts of mutilation, deliberate and calculated acts of sexual sadism and humiliation is everywhere evident in the Whitechapel murders and, moreover, to a degree that is almost sickening and overpowering. The shocked demeanour of the police on entering the claustrophobic confines of the room in Miller's Court and being the first to witness there that awful scene of the dissected body, gives us the immediate impression that the Ripper was unique in the nature of the crimes achieved. However, this is not so.

There were several similar cases which occurred in both Europe and America, and it comes as no surprise to us, when on viewing the body of the murder victim in the empty house in Brixton, in the Holmes tale of 'A Study in Scarlet' Holmes then remarks on a similar case 'occurring in Utrecht last year.' This no coincidence, for, in rural France, in 1891, Joseph Vacher, a serial murderer, known as 'the killer of little shepherds,' attacked and sadistically murdered at least eleven male adolescent farm workers in a case which was highly publicised.

The investigation was led by one of France's leading criminologists, Alexandre Lacassagne, who in later years would certainly have been known by Conan Doyle. The French equivalent, however, was in most respects, unlike his English counterpart; the latter murderer being regarded as a professional middle class individual. In Vacher, however, the Frenchman is described as a drifting, rootless vagrant, driven by blood lust and the urge to kill and rape his victims.

According to Krafft- Ebing's theory, these acts of blood lust were like those experienced by the Ripper:

'Sadistic acts vary in monstrousness with variation in the power of the perverse instinct over the individual afflicted, and with variation in the strength of opposing ideas are weakened by original ethical defect, hereditary degeneracy, or moral insanity,' wrote Krafft – Ebing. 'Thus, there arises a long series of forms which begins with capital crime and ends with silly acts which afford the perverse desires of the sadistic individual merely symbolic satisfaction. Sadistic acts may be further differentiated with reference to their nature : either as they are indulged in after consummated coitus, by which the *libido nimia* remains unsatisfied; or, with diminished virility, as they are used to stimulate the diminished power; or, finally, where virility is absolutely wanting, as they become an equivalent for the impossible coitus, for the induction of ejaculation.In the last two cases, notwithstanding the impotence, there is still intense libido; or there was, at least, intense libido in the individual at the time when the sadistic acts became habitual. Sexual hyperesthesia is always to be regarded as the basis of sadistic inclinations.

'The impotence which occurs so frequently in the psychopathic and neuropathic individuals here considered, as a result of excesses indulged in from early youth, is usually dependent upon spinal weakness. Often, too, there is a kind of psychical impotence, induced by concentration of thought on the perverse act with simultaneous fading of the idea of normal satisfaction. No matter what the external form of the act may be, the mentally perverse predisposition and instinct of the individual are essential to an understanding of it'.

THE REAL JACK THE RIPPER

By now I was beginning to see a definitive profile of Jack the Ripper. And the picture I was getting certainly supported most of Conan Doyle's suspicions, as confirmed in that interview with readers of 'Tit-Bits' magazine he provided in 1894.

But why, I asked myself, did Doyle say nothing more and when, many years later, he provided a series of real-life famous crime articles for the Strand Magazine, did he not include his previously stated theories about the mystery of The Ripper?

WHY DID DOYLE NOT SHARE MORE OF HIS OBSERVATIONS REGARDING THE RIPPER MURDERS?

In the next part of this examination I will list the reasons for the crime writer's reluctance to provide the proof of this man's identity, a proof that I am certain, he shared and was privy to by Sir Janes Macnaghten, the Commissioner for the Met. Police, who took on his role at Scotland Yard, shortly after the last of the 'canonical' Ripper cases was investigated in 1888. This commissioner was not only in possession of prime facie evidence about his chief subject but, like Conan Doyle, Doyle's friend in The Crime Club, the writer and ex-military man, Major Arthur Griffiths, he was a leading light inthe British Freemasons, as was Conan Doyle.

Perhaps more significantly, if the knowledge he possessed about the Ripper's identity were leaked, there would have followed severe repercussions among many senior politicians of the time, including the monarch himself, Edward the Seventh. And further, that when Conan Doyle learned the truth about the man that he had known well and often played against, in Surrey, where the Ripper lived and whose cricket club and town he frequently visited in Kingsley, Surrey, Conan Doyle took the decision to resign his membership as a freemason as a precautionary measure.

But it was not only the subject's residence in Surrey which troubled Conan Doyle. He was also troubled by the fact that he had played cricket against this man's cricket team for Surrey in at least three matches in the summer seasons prior to the subject's mysterious and inexplicable death in the Christmas of 1888, the year of the last and most savage of the East End slaughter of unfortunate prostitutes, Mary Kelley, in Mitre Court.

Conan Doyle had been a keen cricketer all his life, (and continued to play until 1912ever since he had been taught by the Jesuits at Stonyhurst College (1873-1875) to play the game, and later in his literary career, he was privileged to bowl out the famous living legend of late Victorian cricket, W. G. Grace. Doyle was possessed of a strong right arm and he was taller than the average cricketer, being over six feet.

Doyle continued to play until 1912. He played in 440 matches, and for more than 50 different teams. The main teams were: Portsmouth (49 matches between 1884-1890), Hampshire Rovers (26 matches between 1890-1907), Norwood (71 matches between 1891-1894) and Marylebone Cricket Club aka M.C.C. (96 matches between 1899-1912). He played 10 first-class matches between 1900 and 1907.

He also played with his friend and secretary Alfred H. Wood, with his brother-in-law and writer Ernest W. Hornung and with other writers like J. M. Barrie or P. G. Wodehouse (in Authors and Allahakbarries teams).

To Doyle, the game of cricket was a sacred cow. It affirmed both its players as downright moral and trustworthy citizens of the 'great Empire; but also was a reminder of the players; loyalty to that wider community.

His love of the game was s profound and he believed it to be character building among the late Victorian adherents who played it. And not least among that tribe were many of the writers of the period. In an article he published in the Flintshire Observer 1899, he explained (2 November 1899, p. 6)

"… it was only in times of national excitement, such as we were now experiencing, that we found the true value of the love for games which ran in our veins. We were the one free country of Europe, and it was our duty to keep ourselves fit, as we were compelled to do so. "Talk about calling out the reserves," he continued, "why, they had only commenced to call them out; the real reserves were the lovers of sport, the yachtsman, the rider to hounds, the cricketer, the football player — in a word, you all." If England were in a hole we should have to trust to our sporting men to pull her out. The State had thought it right, to attend to the mind of the child, and they had only got to extend the principle by looking after the physical welfare of the country it they wished to keep the nation at the head."

The theory here espoused by the now celebrity author and soon to be knighted Dr Doyle, would not have been so widely supported had the public come to know in the newspapers that The Ripper was an accomplished cricketer like himself and that he too had learned the game at public school. Therefore, when he did find out the truth about this man, Doyle, understandably, kept the solution a secret.

THE CHIEF SUSPECT: THE FACTS

(For the information that follows, I am indebted to the author, Christopher J. Morley, and his E-book, 'Jack the Ripper: A Suspect Guide' (2005

Bearing in mind Sherlock Holmes' warning that 'there is nothing more deceptive than an obvious fact about the man who might fit the frame for The Ripper.

Montague James Druitt was born at Westfield, Wimborne, Dorset, on 15 August 1857, the second son of seven children, to William and Ann Druitt. His father William was a doctor, as was his brother Robert and his nephew Lionel. Montague was educated at Winchester, and at New College, Oxford where he graduated in 1880 with a third-class honours degree in the classics. While at Winchester he became heavily involved in the debating society, choosing political topics for his speeches.

That same year he took up a teaching post at a boys boarding school at 9 Eliot Place, Blackheath, run by Mr George Valentine.

In 1882 he started a second career in law and was admitted to the Inner Temple on 17 May. On 29 April 1885 he was called to the bar, and rented chambers at 9 King's Bench Walk. The law list records him as a special pleader for the Western Circuit and Hampshire, Portsmouth and Southampton Assizes.

Druitt is often described as a failed barrister; if this claim were true he would have been asked to vacate his chambers. He was successful until 1885 when things started to go wrong in his life. First his father died, at the age of 65, from a heart attack.. Then his mother began to show signs of mental instability and became suicidal and delusional; she would later attempt to take her own life with an overdose of Laudanum. She was admitted to the Brook asylum in Clapton, London, where she remained until 31 May 1890, when she was sent to the Manor House asylum, Chiswick; she died there from a heart attack on 15 December 1890.

Suicidal urges appeared to be a trait in Ann Druitt's family, her sister had also spent some time in an asylum after attempting suicide, and their mother committed suicide while insane.

On, or about, the 30 November 1888, Montague John Druitt was dismissed from his teaching job at the school, for what the press described as, 'serious trouble'. What exactly this serious trouble was, is unknown, but has led to speculation that it was due to a homosexual act with one of the pupils.

While there is no evidence to support this, it does remain a possibility. Druitt was considered a successful handsome man, yet there is no record of any female companions during his life.

Druitt was last seen alive on 3 December 1888. When his eldest brother William, learned that Montague had not been seen for over a week and had been dismissed from his teaching job, he went to investigate, and found a suicide note amongst his brother's possessions which read, 'Since Friday I felt I was going to be like mother, and the best thing for me was to die'.

Montague John Druitt's body was fished out of the Thames, around 1:00pm, on Monday 31 December 1888, by Henry Winslade, a waterman. The corpse was believed to have been in the water for about one month. The body, which was fully dressed and bore no injuries, was brought ashore and searched by P.C. George Moulson, who found four large stones in the pocket of his overcoat, £2 and 17 shillings two pence in coinage, two cheques, one for £50, and one for £16, and a first class season rail ticket from Blackheath to London, also a second half return Hammersmith to Charing Cross, dated 1 December, a pair of kid gloves, a white handkerchief and a silver watch with a gold chain.

The inquest was held at the Lamp Tap, Chiswick, before Dr Thomas Diplock. It was concluded that Druitt had committed suicide whilst of unsound mind. He was subsequently buried in Wimborne Cemetery on 3 January 1889.

Of course, none of the above cumulative evidence necessarily proves that Druitt was The Ripper.

However, as we shall soon see, when circumstantial evidence can be observed as a wide series of correlations, we are then left to the conclusion that:

'When you have eliminated the impossible, whatever remains, however improbable, must be the truth.'

That is another of the sayings of Conan Doyle's immortal creation, Sherlock Holmes.

FURTHER FACTS REGARDING DRUITT AND BLACKHEATH

If Druitt was The Ripper, then he most probably drank in The Princess of Wales, the pub right next to the Blackheath railway station (he was in the hockey team that was based there), and he would have walked up and down the hill to catch trains from Blackheath station to Charing Cross. From here he could also connect swiftly and easily with Whitechapel by rail, or quite inconspicuously, by hansom cab.

At Blackheath he would have been spoiled for choice regarding which train to catch to Charing Cross, for trains arrived at 16 and 18 minute intervals because the station at Blackheath had the luxury of serving passenger trains supplied by the London, Brighton and South Coast Line and trains of the South Eastern Line.

Whitechapel station itself was originally opened in 1876 when the East London Railway (ELR, now the East London Line) was extended north from Wapping to Liverpool Street station. The ELR owned the tracks and stations but did not operate trains. From the beginning, various railway companies provided services through Whitechapel including the London, Brighton and South Coast Railway (LB&SCR), the London, Chatham and Dover Railway (LC&DR), Great Eastern Railway (GER) and the South Eastern Railway (SER).

The boys' prep school where in 1880, Druitt taught in Blackheath, 9 Eliot Place and where he decided to embark upon a teaching career, is now residential, but then was home to several schools. Montague John Druitt Druitt's father died of a heart attack in 1885, and three years later his mother committed suicide. He was dismissed from the school for some "serious trouble", but it exactly what remains a mystery. His body was found floating in the Thames on December 31st 1888.

THE CRICKET LINK

Druitt was nominated for membership of the Morden Cricket Club in 1883, and elected on May 26 of the next year. His subscriptions (which were unenviable) were nevertheless paid in full at the time of his death. Druitt was later appointed treasurer and honorary secretary of the Blackheath Cricket, Gottball and Lawn Tennis Company in 1885. His address was then given as 9 Eliot Place, Blackheath.

Where exactly were this man's 'digs'? Of this we cannot be entirely certain, but it is certain that from the rail station they would have been in easy striding reach of the station or he could have taken one of Mr Tilling's speedy cabs from the nearby cab rank which was adjacent both to the station and the pub.

One of the police reports implied that there was additional evidence against him that could not be brought to light, and that he was "sexually insane," which was a Victorian euphemism for homosexuality.

There is a far better account of the whole story which I shall quote at length from here, provided on the Ripper website, www.casebook.org., by Peter Birchwood, including a very detailed analysis of the evidence regarding Druitt and for which I am mot grateful. Here is, for the reader's benefit again, a list of items discovered with Druitt's body when it was discovered by th waterman at Chiswick:

Four large stones in each pocket

£2.17s.2d cash

A cheque for £50 and another for £16

Silver watch on a gold chain with a spade

guinea as a seal

Pair of kid gloves

White handkerchief

First-class half-season rail ticket from

Blackheath to London

Second-half return ticket from Hammersmith

to Charing Cross dated December 1, 1888.

THE DRUITT FAMILY

Druitt was the second son of a medical practitioner, William Druitt, born August 15, 1857 in Wimborne, Dorset. Researcher Peter Birchwood allows us a glimpse into Druitt's family from his researches into the 1881 census:

Dwelling: Westfield House

Census Place: Wimborne Minster, Dorset, England

Source: FHL Film 1341505 PRO Ref RG11

Piece 2093 Folio 13, Page 19

William DRUITT M 60 M Wimborne,

Dorset, England

Rel: Head

Occ: F.R.C.S. Not Practising

Anne DRUITT M 51 F Shapwick, Dorset, England

Rel: Wife

Georgiana E. DRUITT U 25 F Wimborne,

Dorset, England

Rel: Daughter

Edith DRUITT 13 F Wimborne, Dorset, England

Rel: Daughter

Occ: Scholar

Ethel M. DRUITT 10 F Wimborne, Dorset, England

Rel: Daughter

Occ: Scholar

Ann FLIPP U 35 F Spetisbury, Dorset, England

Rel: Servt

Occ: Cook

Edith DENNETT U 25 F Wimborne, Dorset, England

Rel: Servt

Occ: Parlour Maid

Sophia E. RIDOUT U 23 F Gosport,

Hampshire, England

Rel: Servt

Occ: House Maid

Educated at Winchester and New College, Oxford, Druitt was later to graduate with a third-class honours degree in the classics in 1880 (Sugden).

While at Winchester, however, Druitt was heavily involved in the debating society, choosing mostly political topics for his speeches. He was known to denounce the Liberal Party as well as Bismark's influence as "morally and socially a curse to the world." His last speech contended that while previous generations believed 'man is made for States, it is a 'vast improvement that States should be made for man, as they are now.'

As much a sportsman as a speaker, Druitt was granted a spot in the Winchester First Eleven (cricket) in 1876 and was a member of the Kingston Park and Dorset Country Cricket Club. He was noted to have had formidable strength in his arms and wrists, despite his gaunt appearance in surviving photographs. Druitt also became quite talented at Fives, winning the Double and Single Fives titles at Winchester and Oxford. On March 9, 1875, he placed third in a cricket ball throwing event at Winchester, with a toss of over ninety-two yards.

Immediately after graduation, Druitt began teaching at the boarding school in Blackheath. In 1881 Druitt was introduced into the local membership of the Blackheath Hockey Club and later began to play for the Morden Cricket Club of Blackheath.

The next year, in 1882, Druitt again decided to focus on a law career, and was admitted into the Inner Temple on May 17. On April 29, 1885, he was called to the bar. The Law List of 1886 places him in the Western Circuit and the Winchester Sessions. The next year he is recorded as a special pleader for the Western Circuit and Hampshire, Portsmouth and Southampton Assizes (Sugden).

In 1885 his father passed away as a result of a heart attack, leaving a total of £16,579 inheritance, but leaving Montague and his two older brothers a slim cut. Tragedy struck again in July of 1888, when his mother Ann (née Harvey) succumbed to mental illness and was confined in Brook Asylum in Clapton. Yet through this tumultuous time it seems as if Druitt had managed his affairs quite admirably.

He was nominated for membership of the Morden Cricket Club in 1883, and elected on May 26 of the next year. His subscriptions (which were unenviable) were nevertheless paid in full at the time of his death. Druitt was later appointed treasurer and honorary secretary of the Blackheath Cricket, Gottball and Lawn Tennis Company in 1885. His address was then given as 9 Eliot Place, Blackheath.

And so it went that Druitt seemed to have been able to cope with the loss of both his parents within the small space of three years. But in late November of 1888, it seems that one final straw had broken the camel's back, as Druitt was found on Monday, December 31, 1888, floating in the Thames.

According to his brother William's testimony (who identified the corpse), Druitt was dismissed from his post at Blackheath School for some unknown reason (some authors have taken to suggesting that Druitt was dismissed for his homosexual tendencies, which caused him to molest his students. This is pure conjecture). The date of his dismissal is ambiguous, as can be seen in the only known report to survive of the inquest testimony, copied in part below from the Acton, Chiswick, and Turnham Green Gazette of January 5, 1889:

"William H. Druitt said he lived at Bournemouth, and that he was a solicitor. The deceased was his brother, who was 31 last birthday. He was a barrister-at-law, and an assistant master in a school at Blackheath. He had stayed with witness at Bournemouth for a night towards the end of October. Witness heard from a friend on the 11th of December that deceased had not been heard of, at his chambers for more than a week. Witness then went to London to make inquiries, and at Blackheath he found that deceased had got into serious trouble at the school, and had been dismissed. That was on the 30th of December. Witness had deceased's things searched where he resided, and found a paper addressed to him (produced). The Coroner read the letter, which was to this effect: - "Since Friday I felt I was going to be like mother, and the best thing for me was to die." Witness, continuing, said deceased had never made any attempt on his life before. His mother became insane in July last. He had no other relative

As Sugden points out, the date given of December 30th is both ambiguous and impossible. The wording alone makes it possible that it was in reference to either William's inquiries or Druitt's dismissal. If it was in reference to the former, it is doubtful that William would wait nineteen days after receiving word that his brother was missing to inquire into his whereabouts at Blackheath School. If it referred to the latter, however, it is impossibly incorrect, as Druitt was discovered the day after the 30th of December, and was estimated to have been in the water for upwards of three weeks or more. Sugden concludes, with reasonable certainty, that December 30th is a misprint for November 30th, a date which makes much more sense.

Assuming it was November 30th on which Druitt's dismissal, occurred, the few facts of the case fall nicely into place, assuming therefore it was his dismissal which finally prompted his suicide. The 30th was a Friday, which hearkens back to his suicide note: 'Since Friday I felt I was going to be like mother, and the best thing for me was to die.' Also, remember that among his possessions were two cheques for £50 and £16, respectively. They may have been settlement cheques of Druitt's salary, written upon his dismissal. Finally, there was also found an unused return ticket from Hammersmith to Charing Cross dated December 1.

Still another question arises: when did Druitt commit suicide? His tombstone places the date at December 4th, most probably by William's testimony that "on the 11th of December [the] deceased had not been heard of at his chambers for more than a week." Yet notice the use of the word 'more' -- this suggests a date before the 4th of December. Sugden places the date as December 1st, the day after his dismissal.

This paints a picture of a successful barrister, suddenly overwrought by his dismissal at his second job in Blackheath. He accepts his two settlement cheques from his former employer and sulks home, thoughts of suicide entering his mind. The next morning he writes his note, walks toward the Thames with four stones in each pocket, perhaps glances at his cheques one last time, and throws himself into the icy water.

,It all seems to make sense.

Everything, except for motive, that is. Druitt was still a successful barrister, and the school position was only a secondary means of earning money. He was rather high and well-known in the social stratus, and could easily have found another job if need be. So why the suicide?

Two prominent possibilities arise -- first, the aforementioned implications of his homosexuality. Still, only conjecture, but perhaps his vice was discovered and he couldn't bear the embarrassment.

More plausible, however, was that Druitt's mind was slowly deteriorating. The death of his father in 1885, and the committal of his mother only six months before his death could very well have played a heavy part in the matter. Furthermore, mental illness seems to have run in the Druitt family. Ann Druitt, his mother, attempted suicide by overdosing on laudanum. Her mother before her had committed suicide, and her sister had tried to kill herself as well. Montague's oldest sister killed herself in old age by jumping from an attic window.

And so it must stand -- suicidal tendencies ran in the Druitt family, and it most probably was an overreaction at his dismissal which prompted him to follow suit. Regardless, the inquest was held Wednesday, January 2, 1889 before Dr. Thomas Diplock at the Lamp Tap, Chiswick. It was concluded that Druitt committed suicide 'whilst of unsound mind.' Unfortunately, the coroner's papers no longer exist.

And so the story of Montague Druitt ends.

But his alleged involvement in the Whitechapel Murders begins.

The description of this suspect differs slightly in Macnaghten's memoranda and Scotland Yards public record files. The former reads:

'Mr. M.J. Druitt a doctor of about 41 years of age & of fairly good family, who disappeared at the time of the Miller's Court murder, and whose body was found floating in the Thames on 31st Dec: i.e. 7 weeks after the said murder. The body was said to have been in the water for a month, or more -- on it was found a season ticket between Blackheath & London. From private information I have little doubt that his own family suspected this man of being the Whitechapel murderer; it was alleged that he was sexually insane.

The Scotland Yard file reads:

'A Mr M. J. Druitt, said to be a doctor & of good family, who disappeared at the time of the Miller's Court murder, & whose body (which was said to have been upwards of a month in the water) was found in the Thames on 31st December - or about 7 weeks after that murder. He was sexually insane and from private information I have little doubt but that his own family believed him to have been the murderer'.

Now empirical vidence which supports Druitt's being the Ripper is all but non-existent. In fact, his only true link can be made in his appearance and his likeness to many witness accounts.

All but one witness gave estimate of age close to Druitt's (31): P.C. Smith (28), Israel Schwartz (30), Joseph Lawende (30), and George Hutchinson (34-35). Elizabeth Long gave an age of forty, but she admitted she did not see the suspect's face.

As for appearance, three major witnesses report the Ripper as having a moustache (which Druitt had), although the colour varies from "dark," to "brown," to "fair." Druitt was also of respectable appearance, always known to have been well-dressed. All witnesses except for Lawende (who said the suspect had the appearance of a sailor) support this possibility: Long described a man of 'shabby genteel,' while Smith and Schwartz both labelled the man as respectable; and Hutchinson went so far as to descibe him as prosperous-looking,' but, 'In terms of build, however, Druitt falls short. Then he goes on to say this:

'He was a slender man, while witnesses described the man as being from medium to heavy build, stout, and broad shouldered. Almost unfailingly, the suspect was labelled consistently as "foreign-looking" and "a Jew."

Other problems arise as well. It is generally accepted that the Ripper was an inhabitant of the East End (Sugden), but Druitt had little or no experience in or around the area of Whitechapel. He was living at 9 Eliot Place, Blackheath during the murders. But could that address have been used as a "base" for the murders?

Sugden cites contemporary train schedules in order to disprove this theory. According to him, there was no all-night train service between London and Blackheath. The last train leaving Blackheath in 1888 left at 12:25 AM and the earliest leaving London for Blackheath was at 5:10 AM. Although for the Nichols (3:40 AM), Chapman (5:30 AM) and Kelly (4:00 AM) murders the Ripper may have been able to jaunt over to the station and take a train back to Blackheath with very little time wasted, waiting for the first train to arrive, this *does not hold* true for Stride (1:00 AM), Eddowes (1:44 AM) or Tabram (2:30 AM).

'If the Ripper had killed them and needed to take a train back to Blackheath, Sugden claims, he would have to remain in the area for "perilous hours" just asking to be detected. Still, he admits, the killer could have remained in a common lodging house for some time, although a respectable man such as Druitt in such a place would seem suspicious.

Tom Cullen, noted Druittist, argues that Druitt's known chambers at 9 King's Bench Walk could have been used, as they are within walking distance of the East End. Yet Sugden again refutes this, citing the Ripper's known movements on the night of the double murder. King's Bench Walk was west of Mitre Square (the site of the second murder), and yet the killer is known to have gone north-east directly after killing Eddowes and dropped her apron in Goulston Street. Would the killer have risked detection by entering the lion's den northward if he had indeed planned to find refuge to the west?'

When Macnaghten says in the memoranda, "from private information I have little doubt but that his own family believed him to have been the murderer," one must look closely at the diction of that statement. Notice how he has little doubt *but not absolute evidence*.

We have no clues as to who the informant was whom Macnaghten refers to, but from the way he words his statement, it would seem as if it would have been a Druitt family member. And yet if one of Druitt's relations had informed Macnaghten that they believed he may have been the Ripper, would Macnaghten not rather have said he had evidence that Druitt's family believed him to be insane?

This leads one to believe that perhaps Macnaghten was basing his claims on hearsay and rumour, rather than actual private information he himself received.

Another statement made by Macnaghten was that the Ripper's brain, "after his awful glut on this occasion (Kelly's murder), gave way altogether and he committed suicide; otherwise, the murders would not have ceased."

And yet there is still, to this day, no evidence which shows that serial killers cannot simply stop killing. According to Sugden, "more recent experience ... seems to demonstrate the contrary."

Furthermore, there are other additional reasons besides suicide, which could have prevented the Ripper from continuing his crimes after Kelly, such as incarceration (in prison or an asylum), emigration, accidental or natural death, or even a bout of sickness. Even more damning is the statement that "despite the dramatic increase of such crimes in recent decades, no major offender is known to have committed suicide. (Sugden)"

What's worse are the many errors in Macnaghten's notes regarding Druitt. He stated that Druitt lived with his family, but records show that he lived alone at 9 Eliot Place. He stated that Druitt had committed suicide around the 10th of November, three weeks before it actually occurred. He stated that Druitt was about 41 at the time of his death, overestimating by ten years. Finally, he mentions Druitt as being a doctor, when he was in fact, a barrister and schoolmaster.

Still, Macnaghten was an intelligent man, and it is doubtful he would have placed such merit in a suspect without due cause. Perhaps more evidence or documents will be found in the future which may shed some light on Macnaghten's motive to point the finger at Druitt.

Regardless, the case for Druitt being the Ripper seemed almost cemented by Daniel Farson in 1959, upon his discovery of a man who claimed to have remembered a pamphlet being distributed in Australia around 1890, entitled "The East End Murderer -- I knew him."

Its author, claimed Mr. A. Knowles (Farson's informant), was Lionel Druitt, Drewett or Drewery. The fact that Lionel Druitt, who was Montague's cousin, had left to live in Australia in 1886 only excited the investigators more, and they left to research the possibility.

The men were horribly disappointed. All they found was a shoddy story of a Mr. W. G. Fell of Dandenong, who claimed to have definite proof of the Ripper's identity, but refused to give it out unless he received a £500 reward. No one by the name of Fell was ever recorded living in Dandenong in 1890.

And so it appears, that the pamphlet memories of Mr. A. Knowles represented just a confusion of facts between Druitt and Deeming. The Melbourne Evening Standard of April 8, 1892 carried the headline; "JACK THE RIPPER: DEEMING AT ALDGATE ON THE NIGHT OF THE

WHITECHAPEL MURDERS." This was denied by Deeming's attorney, who rightly proclaimed that he (Deeming) was serving a sentence in South Africa during the fall of 1888. Nevertheless, it was found that Deeming assumed the name of Druin or Drewen shortly after arriving in Australia in 1891.

Although there is no proof, it is most likely that Knowles' memory confused Deeming's aliases with Druitt's name, and that either the aforementioned headline or a similar one (of which there were many in those days) had prompted belief in a pamphlet.

And so remains the case of Druitt. His acceptance as a Ripper suspect must lie in the belief that Macnaghten had more information than he wanted others to know -- information which he claims he destroyed so as not to cause an uproar.

I will contend that Druitt could have committed the murders in time to return to his cricket games, especially in the cases of Nichols and Chapman. If those two queries can be answered in the positive, then Druitt deserves recognition as a leading Ripper suspect. If not, his inclusion as a suspect must be attributed to the sole opinions of Macnaghten, based on hearsay and memory'.

THE SOLUTION TO THE IDENTITY OF THE RIPPER: HAS IT ALL TO DO WITH CRICKET, OR 'BOYS, PLAY UP, AND PLAY THE GAME!

Consider then, the case for Mr Druitt knowing and being acquainted with Mr Doyle thus far.

1. Both were members of the Blackheath Cricket Club. Blackheath Cricket Club has been part of the sporting fabric of the area, joining forces with Blackheath Rugby Club in 1883 to purchase and develop the Rectory Field as a home ground in Charlton, which frequently was the venue for matches in which Doyle and the captain of the opposing team, Druitt, played against each other. Blackheath Cricket Club hosted 84 first-class Kent County matches between 1887 and 1971.

2. Doyle, a keen rugby player, was also a member of the Blackheath Rugby Club, founded in 1858, which is one of the oldest documented rugby clubs in the world and was located until 2016, at Rectory Field on Charlton Road. The Blackheath club also organised the world's first rugby international (between England and Scotland in Edinburgh on 27 March 1871), and then

175

hosted the first international between England and Wales ten years later – the players meeting and getting changed at the Princess of Wales public house on the Heath.

3. The Morden cricket team, of which Druitt was captain, twice had a match in the gardens of The Cedars, Lee, and on one of these occasions, Conan Doyle would have played against the Morden side.

IN CONCLUSION

To my way of thinking, the case against Druitt is convincing. This man's profile fits that of Jack the Ripper neatly. Druitt had motive and opportunity. He could convey himself from Blackheath quickly to the east end of London. and commit the murders, as Doyle belived, then retreating to his father's chambers and afterwards travelling down the Thames .

Hhere, the river and its riverbanks were almost completely clothed in darkness and often fog. Most likely, as Doyle believed, Dritt would have allayed the suspicions of his victims possibly posing as a woman.

In addition, many of the eyewitness accounts of people who saw a suspect at the time of the murders. correspond well with that of Montague Druitt.

Also, consider this: what we know of the family and of what became of them would suggest a profound psychological disturbance in the character of this man.

Now the fact that Doyle did not give his name when interviewed by the magazine, Titbits in 1894 is. I believe, connected to Conan Doyle's membership of the Freemasonry Society. And it is also a fact that not only Doyle but also Druitt and the commissioner, Macnaghten were also members. Interestingly, Conan Doyle resigned his membership in the very year that followed the death of Montego Druitt, He never once referred to this fact, which was most unlike him.. It was only renewed many years later, after he had been politically active and proved himself worthy as a loyal member of the Empire when he served as a Hospital Doctor in South Africa during The Boer War. After then rejoining, his membership of the Freemasons continued until his death in 1930. I truly believe that not only did Conan Doyle discover the truth about his cricket playing friend but I also believe that he was probably very shocked when he discovered the facts about Druitt's. personality and his hatred of women, particularly prostitutes. When informed by the commission of police. About the facts of Druid's life, of his psychopathic personality and that the man had been a Freemason., Doyle then agreed With the commissioner.to make no public acknowledgement of the man's identity as a killer.

And in order to do the honourable thing - for it must be admitted that he was an honourable man – Conan Doyle resigned his membership of the Secret Society of The Freemasons.

'YOU KNOW THAT PARTICULAR QUARTER'

"You know that particular quarter, the monotonous brick streets, the weary suburban highways. Right in the middle of them, a little island of ancient culture and comfort, lies this old home, surrounded by a high sun-baked wall mottled with lichens and topped with moss, th. sort of wall - "
"Cut out the poetry, Watson," said Holmes severely.

- 'The Retired Colourman.'

There were two separate occasions upon which Mr Sherlock Holmes was brought to Lee. One was in the June of 1889, when he was called upon to investigate the curious affair of the disappearance of Mr Neville St. Clair, and the other occasion concerned the investigation into the disappearance of the wife of Josiah Amberley, a retired "colourman" whose residence was at "The Haven" in Lewisham.

Dr Watson, it will be remembered, was called out one evening by a friend of his wife, whose husband, Isa Whitney, was known to have been in an East End opium den called 'The Bar of Gold'. It was here also that Dr Watson met the disguised Holmes and the meeting led to the opening of the adventure later chronicled as 'The Man With The Twisted Lip'.

Holmes chose the hansom cab for his sojourn into this town of Kent (it is academic perhaps that in the previous year it had been transformed into the administrative county of London). If he had taken the train from Charing Cross, his journey would have been longer and more inconvenient. Lee, Blackheath or Lewisham stations were available to him via the North Kent line. Borne on an extensive viaduct, the traveller passed through the suburbs proper - "squalid alleys and clamorous streets gradually giving place to large market gardens," as the S.E. Railway Guide of the time put it.)

The "seven-mile drive" from Swan Lane to The Cedars would have cost five shillings in Holmes' day and the shortest route covered would be six and a half and not, as Holmes tells us, "seven miles". The journey, during which Holmes tells Watson, "We have touched on three English counties in our short drive, starting in Middlesex, passing over an angle of Surrey and ending in Kent," would start from Upper Thames Street and the "broad balustraded bridge" which they flew over would of course be London Bridge. From London Bridge they would continue down Southwark High Street, turning left along Great

Dover Street, and coming out into the Old Kent Road. They would then carry on into New Cross Road. From here they would turn right just after reaching New Cross Station into Lewisham Way.

The Cedars, Lee, where Conan Doyle may have unwittingly played cricket against Montague Druitt, believed to have been Jack the Ripper, by Melville Macnaghten, the Metropolitan Commissioner for Police. A rare photograph has been discovered from the period when Doyle was courting Jean Leckie and writing 'The Man with the Twisted Lip,' in which this remarkable Victorian villa features as the home of the business man, Neville St. Clair.

Watson tells us. "We had been whirling through the outskirts of the great town until the last straggling houses had been left behind, and we rattled along with a country hedge upon either side of us. Just as he (Holmes) finished, however, we drove through two scattered villages, where lights still glimmered in the windows."

The first of these two "scattered villages" can easily be identified as "Newtown" (no longer marked on modern maps), centred around Lewisham High Road; the cab would then come into the country once more with only a few scattered houses such as Llawrenn Villa and Stone House along the route. Then, after coming out of Loampit Vale, the cab would swing round into Lewisham Road, thus coming into the second village of Lewisham, (now, sadly, largely an urban wilderness.).

The cab here would turn left up Belmont Hill and the cab's destination, 'The Cedars', would be on its left. It is worth noting that The Cedars still stands today, and its outward appearance is still the same as it was in Holmes' day. All that has been altered is the inside of the building. A newspaper report of the 1920s tells us that "Messrs Hodson propose to commence almost immediately the development of 15 acres, forming part of the grounds of The Cedars. The mansion is, we understand, to be converted into flats."

"It is worthy of note that it is proposed to retain the outward appearance of "The Cedars", the only alterations contemplated being to the interior."

Watson describes "The Cedars" as "a large villa which stood within its own grounds." A description of The Cedars as it was in 1888 one year before Holmes' visit, still exists, and we are told that, 'The mansion is scarcely seen until we turn a belt of trees and find it close at hand: and the approach at once reveals the beauties to be seen beyond.

'In the front is a border of the finest collection of rhododendrons, with the clematis Virginian creeper and jasmine overhanging the windows in rustic form; and the venerable cedar of Lebanon, near the conservatory, at the top of the lawn . . .

'Northward we look across the railway towards Blackheath at the head of the dell with the shrubberies at each side of the steep slopes which are dotted with trees; and include a fine plantation of the *pinus Australasia* and *excelea* of the Himalayas.'

That plant and many similar Himalayan species Holmes was no doubt to meet later, if we are to recognise his interest in botany. (Witness his words in "Wisteria Lodge"; "With a spud, a tin box, and an elementary book on botany, there are instructive days to be spent,')

We are told by Holmes that "My room at The Cedars is a double bedded one". We also know that Holmes was "staying there while I conduct the inquiry". It will be remembered too that this was one of the cases that nearly foiled Sherlock Holmes, were it not for an all-night sitting in which he reached his solution "by sitting upon five pillows and consuming an ounce of shag".

The question has often been raised as to how Holmes reached his results, for there is no real explanation given.

Mr Bernard Davies (in the 'Sherlock Holmes JournaJ') points out that part of the explanation may be that Holmes knew St. Clair through his acting days. But admirable as this deduction is, it does not give us the answer to the question as to what gave Holmes the key to the problem. Mr Davies suggests quite correctly that "this was a case… of some chord of memory struck by chance as in "The Lion's Mane." Now we know, and Holmes knew, that the name of the beggar suspected of murdering Neville St. Clair (and who was St. Clair in disguise as it turned out) was called Hugh Boone. This alias has its factual origins and, although Holmes found that "it is always awkward doing business with an alias," the derivation of the name is easily discovered.

A Boone family once lived at Lee in an ancient red brick mansion, surrounded by a moat, in the Old Road, for many years called "Boone Mansion", and which was pulled down in 1824. However, the Boone family left a memorial behind then in the form of some thirty alms houses, built in 1826. These alms houses faced Brandram Road, which leads into Belmont Hill, and which comes out almost opposite "The Cedars". Neville St. Clair would obviously have been aware of their existence as they were only a few hundred yards from The Cedars, and it thus was quite natural that he should gain his alias from this source.

The close proximity of these alms houses leads one to suspect that they also gave Holmes the clue to the true identity of 'Hugh Boone'. If he had seen the name, as is most likely, for he had been staying at "The Cedars", it may have well set off a train of thought in his mind which after the coaxing influence of the shag tobacco and the Eastern divan, produced that rare outburst of self-criticism: "1 think, Watson, that you are now standing in the presence of one of the most absolute fools in Europe, I deserve to be kicked from here to Charing Cross."

The stationary type of begging practised by Neville St. Clair [11] was in fact much rarer than it is now generally supposed. Begging was illegal then, as it is now, and a person who drew a crowd round him in a busy thoroughfare was liable to attract the attention of a constable. The problem of begging in the capital had been partly created by the increased vigilance of the municipal police who drove the vagrants of the countryside into the metropolis. In the "paddingkins" or cheap lodging houses of the great city they could dodge the police much more efficiently and their anonymity served as an added protection. In the case of Hugh Boone, alias Neville St. Clair, he avoided prosecution by pretending "to a small trade in wax vestas." The competition was fierce and often vicious in those days. To succeed at begging you not only had to contend with the police; you also had to hold your pitch against competitors.

The procedure of "standing a pad on a fakement" (this involved carrying a card round your neck detailing your claim to charity, tragic past history, etc.) was at the best risky. The blind beggars (the genuine ones, that is,) were best off. Gonorrhoea, for which there was no cure, and smallpox, rife among the lower classes, claimed many victims and the blind man with his dog became a familiar object of Victorian sentiment. Sham blindness was surprisingly uncommon, mainly because it did not often go undetected for very long. If the police didn't realise it, then your own kind soon would.

Boone faked a limp according to Holmes, but "in other respects he appears to be a powerful and well nurtured man." Perhaps that was just as well, for he would have attracted little sympathy from his begging colleagues. But it was of course his appearance which drew in the money.

The return journey to Bow Street at 4.25 the next morning after Holmes all-night vigil would take approximately the same route as before. However, the cab would turn into the New Kent Road this time, and thence to the Elephant & Castle, turning off onto the London Road. At St. Georges Circus they would then turn into the Waterloo Road and as Watson notes "passing down Waterloo Bridge Road we crossed over the river". Here, however, arises one of those peculiar anomalies of unintended Watsonian misdirection, for we are told that "dashing up Wellington Street (we) wheeled sharply to the right and found

---

[11] Begging was regarded almost as if it were a profession by the late Victorians.

ourselves in Bow Street". Now Wellington Street passes straight into Bow Street itself, the police station being on the right - hand side opposite Covent Garden Opera House. What is unaccountable is that Watson should have thought that they turned right at the end of Wellington Street to arrive at Bow Street. All I can suggest is that the cab turned right into Martlett Court, down by the side of the police station, and that Watson, seeing the name of Wellington Street a few seconds before, assumed that by turning right they were presumably turning into Bow Street.

It was not until many years later that Holmes and Watson once again visited Lee. The Neville St. Clair case took place in 1889 and Watson did not mention the locality again (Except for a fleeting reference of the residence of Mr John Scott Eccles at 'Popham House' Lee,) until he chronicled the affair of 'The Retired Colourman.'. …Both Mr Gavin Brend and Mr W.S. Baring-Gould date this case as 1898. This is deduced from the information Holmes supplies: "Retired in 1896, Watson. Early in 1897 he married a woman twenty years younger than himself . . . And yet within two years he is . . . as broken a creature as crawls beneath the sun."

It is assumed that Amberley was a "broken" man within two years of his retirement, by both commentators. However, it is just as logical to suppose that he degenerated to this state within two years of his marriage. This would fix the date of the case as 1899.

The identity of 'The Haven' is slightly more difficult to trace than that of 'The Cedars' where we now now know that Montague Druitt once played cricket against a team headed by Conan Doyle.

Watson tells us that after leaving Amberley's house, he "had driven to Blackheath Station". Later we are told by Holmes that "it is only a few hundred yards to the station (from Amberley's house)." The station referred to could be Blackheath Station or Blackheath Hill Station, the latter being nearer the centre of Lewisham. One is tempted to pick Blackheath Hill Station at first, but the station mentioned is specifically "Blackheath Station". A further objection to Blackheath Station is that it is in the village of Blackheath itself, and as Lewisham is mentioned as Amberley's residence, the station that Watson would have come from was, one presumes, Lewisham Junction. In fact, though, Blackheath Station is just on the parish boundary line between Blackheath and Lee and by the London Government Act of 1899, Lewisham and Lee were united, forming a metropolitan borough. Thus, Amberley's house could still legitimately be referred to as being in "Lewisham".

By 1889, Lewisham had become a sprawling suburb with a population of 92,000 people. Unlike today, however, it was still largely dominated by the middle classes. Men like Josiah Amberley were typical of the residents of this expanding borough. According to a local travel guide of the 1880s:

'The station itself stands on high ground, "the fields (rising) abruptly above it to the top of the hill, and . . . covered with villa residences and pleasant gardens. There are handsome and convenient district churches", remarks 'The Handbook of Kent '. . . 'The "Grammar School", founded by the Rev Abraham Colfe, 1650 is on Dartmouth Hill, . . . and is in . . . the hands of the Company of Leather-sellers".

It is in the vicinity of the Grammar School that Amberley resided.

Belmont Hill, which was then a narrow and steep country lane (now a busy main road) formerly had only three buildings: The Cedars, The Rectory and St Margaret's Church. At the Blackheath end of this hill, however, originally stood a house called "Belmont" which was built in 1830. This house would only have stood a few hundred yards away up the hill from Blackheath Station, and we can be tolerably certain that this is the site of the house to which Watson gave the obviously disguised name of "The Haven".

The whole of the area north of Blackheath Station comes within the parish of Blackheath, and not Lee, so the general southerly direction to which the house would have lain is also correct. (*"When you have excluded the impossible, whatever remains . . . must be the truth"* - Holmes).

Watson, being a habitual addict of the hansom cab, would have taken one from Blackheath Railway Station. We find in 'Butts Historical Guide to Lewisham, Lee, Blackheath & Eltham', 1878, the following information: "Cab stand - opposite Blackheath Railway Station for four carriages. T. Tilling owner. Stable yard adjoining with 15 other cabs". The close proximity of the cab stand would be yet one more good reason for Watson to go to Blackheath as opposed to Lewisham Station, for he could then indulge in his Victorian habit, while Holmes, whose efficient expediency is notorious, obviously found it an advantage to bundle the "writhing and fighting" Mr Amberley into a waiting cab which would then speedily conduct him to the custody of the police under Mackinnon, no doubt awaiting the arrival of their miserly guest at the station. There is also mentioned in the Guide a "pocket time book . . . published monthly, price one halfpenny". But no doubt Holmes was satisfied with his Bradshaw.

Of even more interest, however, is the list of fare rates. In Holmes' day a twelve - month first-class season ticket fare between London and Lewisham (and Holmes and Watson always travelled first-class) cost twelve pounds, which approximates to something like an eightpenny daily return fare.

The railways were not without their problems in those days. Blackheath [12] like Lewisham, was experiencing an expansion of population during the years of Dr Watson's visit and the pressure on the rail traffic grew in proportion. In 1877, the railway bridge had been widened to accommodate more trains. Lengths of sidings, stables for the railway companies' horses and coal yards for local merchants all helped to expand the area.

By 1883 the Bexleyheath Railway Company was floated to build a line from Crayford to Lee via Bexleyheath, but the South- Eastern Railway pushed them out. The new line was finally built between 1891 and 1895. In 1897 the station was considerably improved. Cast iron canopies were built over the platforms and the platform was widened. In the year following Watson's visit the station experienced a visit from no less an august personage than Queen Victoria.

As for "The Haven", the original building with its "high sun- baked wall" as Watson described it, was demolished in 1907 and as there is an unfortunate lack of detailed description about the house in local contemporary guides and documents, it is indeed a shame that Watson was told to "cut out the poetry" just when his monologue was becoming interesting. However, it is of interest that this stood only about half a mile away from, and stood on the same road as "The Cedars".

To Holmes at least, who knew this area, it probably brought back pleasant memories. Indeed, if he was as well acquainted with the area as evidence suggests, he no doubt knew Blackheath well and may, if we are right in assuming his eternal obsession with guides and directories of all kinds, have even had a copy of 'Bradshaw's Descriptive Railway Handbook of Great Britain and Ireland'. (We know of course that he had the standard Bradshaw). This gives us an interesting picture of Blackheath as Holmes must have seen it.

"(This heath) is now a favourite resort of the inhabitants of London who come in crowds during the holidays and summer season - donkey riding being a favourite amusement. The heath is exceedingly picturesque and commands several very fine views".

It is comforting to remember that since Holmes and Watson's day the heath is one of the very few landmarks that have survived the onslaught of time. But then for the eager pilgrim there is always "The Cedars" to visit, where Jack the Ripper played cricket with Conan Doyle.

---

[12] Even as a youth, Blackheath was much regarded as an affluent area.

DR THORNDYKE AND SHERLOCK HOLMES

In his 1941 essay, "The Art of the Detective Story," R. Austin Freeman describes the beginning of what would become his greatest contribution to mystery and detective literature — the inverted tale:

'Some years ago, I devised, as an experiment, an inverted detective story in two parts. The first part was a minute and detailed description of a crime, setting forth the antecedents, motives, and all attendant circumstances. The reader had seen the crime committed, knew all about the criminal, and was in possession of all the facts. It would have seemed that there was nothing left to tell. But I calculated that the reader would be so occupied with the crime that he would overlook the evidence. And so it turned out. The second part, which described the investigation of the crime, had to most readers the effect of new matter. All the facts were known; but their evidential quality had not been recognized.'

Twenty years after the appearance of Sir Arthur Conan Doyle's immortal detective, Sherlock Holmes, a Gravesend doctor, R. Austin Freeman, published his first detective novel. Entitled 'The Red Thumb Mark,' it posed one of the most successful scientific detectives in English fiction, Dr. John Thorndyke. The story concerns the theft of a parcel of diamonds from the safe of an old man, John Hornby. In the safe is found a small scrap of paper marked with a bloody thumbprint. When suspicion falls on Hornby's nephews, Walter and Reuben, they refuse to be fingerprinted by the police.

Later on, Hornby's wife shows the authorities a "Thumbograph" machine, given to her as a novelty by Walter some time earlier, along with several thumb-prints of her friends and relatives, including one identical to that in the safe. Thorndyke's subsequent involvement in the case and the revelation that the fingerprint has been forged, involving a sophisticated gelatine process, forms part of the scientific interest of this early novel.

Freeman's indebtedness to the already famous sage of Baker Street is apparent from a reading of this now rare classic of detective fiction. The novel opens with a chance meeting between the storyteller, Jervis, and Thorndyke at the upper end of King's Bench Walk. From the very first words uttered by Thorndyke, we are in familiar territory: "My dear Jervis," [Thorndyke] exclaimed, as we clasped hands warmly, "this is a great and delightful surprise. How often have I thought of my old comrade and wondered if I should ever see him again.. ."[13] Like Dr. Watson, it transpires that Jervis is in straitened circumstances, and also, like Dr. Watson, on completing his training as a doctor, finds himself facing a cruelly indifferent world:

"My story is soon told," I answered, somewhat bitterly. "It is not an uncommon one. My funds ran out, as you know, rather unexpectedly. When I had paid my examination and registration fees the coffer was absolutely empty..! have, in fact, been earning a subsistence, sometimes as an assistant, sometimes as a locum tenens. Just now I've got no work to do...."

As with Doyle, the character of Jervis bears a strong resemblance to the impecunious author himself. Freeman lived in the south-east of England for most of his literary career, as did Doyle. Born in Soho, London, in 1862, Freeman attended a number of private schools before taking up the study of medicine. Doyle was impressed by the methods of his Edinburgh mentor, Dr. Joseph Bell. Intriguingly, Freeman also was fascinated by the forensic methods of one of his medical instructors, Dr. Alfred Swayne Taylor, though he did not know him personally. Taylor, who was born at Northfleet, Kent, in 1806, became a student of Guy's Hospital at age 16 and later studied medicine in France and Switzerland. In 1831 he was appointed to the Chair of Medical Jurisprudence, a post he fulfilled at Guys for 46 years. He earned subsequent fame in appearing at the trial of Palmer, the notorious poisoner. [14]

The methods of Dr. Thorndyke show that same zest for logical and inductive synthesis displayed by his illustrious predecessor. He frequently lectures the obedient Jervis but, unlike Holmes, shows considerable patience towards his enthusiastic disciple:

"It is easy to trace a connection when one knows all the facts," he said at length, "but it seems to me that you have the materials from which to form a conjecture.... I think, when you have had more experience, you will find yourself able to work out a problem of this kind. What is required is constructive imagination and a rigorous exactness in reasoning...."

---

[13] The similarity between the financial straits of Jervis and Watson is mot similar.

[14] Mentioned by Holmes in SPEC.

Physically, Thorndyke exhibits that same aquiline profile as Holmes. He has a "quiet strength" and "magnetism." He is "tall" and possesses a "handsome, symmetrical face...Yet, though it was as immobile as a mask of stone, it conveyed an impression of intense attention – almost of watchfulness.. "[15]

Born in July 1870 (which would make him sixteen to eighteen years younger than Holmes, according to your chronological predilection), Thorndyke was educated at the medical school of St. Margaret's Hospital, London, where he later rose to the position of Medical Registrar, Pathologist, Curator of the Museum, and Professor of Medical Jurisprudence. Unlike Holmes and Watson, he and Jervis were fellow students. When Jervis meets up with Thorndyke, his companion tells him: "(I) hung about the chemical and physical laboratories, and in the meanwhile took my B.SC. and M.D."

Here we have a ghost of the young Holmes frequenting the chemical laboratory at St Barts:

The grave of R. Austin Freeman, in Gravesend cemetery, Kent, I discovered whilst school - mastering in the town many decades ago. Now the headstone has been lovingly restored by the fans of his Dr Thorndyke narratives. And I am glad to also mention that the enterprising publishers, MX books, has brought out an entire collection of the Thorndyke stories.

".. when I first took these chambers, I had practically nothing to do. I had invented a new variety of medicolegal practice and had to build it up by slow degrees, and the natural consequence was that, for a long time, it yielded nothing but almost unlimited leisure... "[16]

Here is the mirror of the young Sherlock, filling in his too-abundant leisure time by studying at the British Museum reading room and gaining expertise in the various forensic fields of which he was eventually to become a master. Like Holmes, Thorndyke specializes in acquiring the most abstruse kinds of knowledge about subjects which may have a bearing on his cases. He is an expert on the subject of anatomy. In 'The Red Thumb Mark', for instance, he undertakes a masterly series of deductions and inferences based on the observed figure of an aged stationmaster. The scene is highly reminiscent of the duel between Mycroft and Sherlock in GREE:

---

[15] Cf.

[16] Ch. I.: 'A Study in Scarlet'

"I seem to have noticed that peculiar, splay-footed gait in station-masters, now that you mention it."

"Quite so. The arch of the foot has given way; the planter ligaments have become stretched and the deep calf muscles weakened.... "[17]

Where Freeman differs from Doyle in this respect is in the detail of Thorndyke's analyses; and it is this aspect of the Thorndyke novels which some readers have disliked. In the Holmes saga the expertise of the detective is alluded to rather than elaborated upon, thereby imparting to Holmes a continual mystique. Thorndyke is more pedantic; there is no real mystery about him, and he is always at pains to explain his methods to Jervis in the most minute and sometimes tedious detail.

When Thorndyke is sent a batch of poisoned Trichonopoly cigars (one recalls Holmes's own observations on the subject of Trichonopolies in STUD and SIGN), he again shows a remarkably close connection with his illustrious predecessor by commenting upon the typed message that accompanies the package. Possibly Thorndyke had read Holmes's own monograph, "The Typewriter And Its Relation To Crime":

"What is much more striking is the address on the label. It is typewritten and, as you say, typed very badly. Do you know anything about typewriters?"
"Very little."

"Then you do not recognise the machine? Well, this label was typed with a Blickensderfer – an excellent machine... " [18]

Freeman's own opinions about his creation are intriguing. According to Ellery Queen Magazine he once wrote this:

"[Thorndyke] is an investigator of crime but he is not a detective." Dr. Freeman then went on to explain this distinction in detail, proving that "the technique of Scotland Yard would be neither suitable nor possible to [Thorndyke]. He is a medico-legal expert and his methods are those of medico-legal science." Difficult as it is to disagree with Dr. Freeman on matters

---

17 The Red Thumb Mark', p. 159

18 'Fingerprints: 50 Years of Scientific Crime Detection', Douglas G. Browne & Alan Brock, London, Harrap, 1953, p. 59-61.

pertaining to Medical Jurisprudence, we are certain that we merely voice the sentiments of all critics and readers when we insist that Dr. Thorndyke is not only a detective but one of (to quote E.M. Wrong) "the greatest... now in business."

The distinction is perhaps a fine one, but one that the student of the Holmes saga will surely recognize. Freeman went much further than Doyle in pushing forward the lay-reader into the areas of forensic science: Doyle was content to keep these areas in the background where they acted as a foundation stone, providing credibility for his creation. As Douglas G. Browne and Alan Brock observe:

'.. if Holmes in his heyday is always a little behind the march of progress in this particular field, and Thorndyke usually abreast of it, Austin Freeman's technical interests covered a wider range than Conan Doyle's. Holmes placed little confidence in fingerprinting, either as an aid to detection or as a means of registering convicted criminals. The years during which his famous 'Adventures' and 'Memoirs' appeared include the period that saw the first tentative consideration of the system, its adoption, and its vindication; yet there are only four casual references to fingerprints in the series...'

On the other hand, one should not get the impression that Holmes was, by comparison with Thorndyke, relatively ignorant about forensic matters. As I have demonstrated elsewhere, [19] there are numerous indications as to his expertise and wide reading in the literature of criminology. In NAVA he discusses the Bertillon system of anthropometry, expressing "his enthusiastic admiration of the French savant," while in HOUN he objects most strongly when Dr. Mortimer compares him to his peer.

The personality of Thorndyke shares other similarities with Holmes. According to Robert Anstey, K.C., one of his more objective colleagues, he was an "inscrutable man; silent, self-contained, and even secretive, in spite of his genial exterior."[20] In 'The Red Thumb Mark' the character is a little different: boyish, exuberant and more outward going. Thorndyke's secretiveness, like

---

[19] Queen's Quorum, Gollancz, 1953, p. 56, n.

[20] 'The Cat's Eye', ix.

that of Holmes, is an essential feature of the plots; unlike Holmes, however, he can be far more loquacious when the solution of the mystery needs to be stated.

As Dorothy Sayers has pointed out, Thorndyke goes to great pains to keep Jervis informed: Thorndyke can cheerfully show you all the facts. You will be none the wiser, unless you happen to have an intimate acquaintance with the fauna of local ponds; the effect of belladonna on rabbits; the physical and chemical properties of blood; optics; tropical diseases; metallurgy; hieroglyphics; and a few other trifles.[21]

In his 'Aspects of the Modern Short Story,' Alfred C. Ward has provided an interesting comparison between Doyle and Freeman, which comes down heavily on the side of Dr. Thorndyke. Freeman's story, 'An Anthropologist At Large,' shows off Thornyke's deductive skills when presented with a battered hat. According to Ward the process of deduction is much sounder and more scientifically constructed than that of Holmes in BLUE. Ward concludes:

'The fact is, that Holmes was a poseur first and an amateur detective afterwards. His amazing success is rather a put-up job between him and his creator; and his occasional failures are a confidence trick, to suggest that there is really no deception in his triumphs. Thorn-dyke, on the other hand, is a straightforward scientific investigator, with very little nonsense about him. Perhaps, he is a somewhat too well-oiled piece of mechanism to be a satisfactory fictional character; and he has none of those memorable personal mannerisms which have made Sherlock Holmes more real to the multitude than is the whole police force. Story for the sake of story is more generously given by Conan Doyle than by Austin Freeman...'[22]

Ward's criticisms are worth considering. There is certainly something of the poseur about Holmes, noticeably in the earlier stories (STUD and SIGN). The Holmes of STUD is, if anything, too remote, too self - contained. By the time of 'The Adventures' we see a softening of the profile and a more expansive personality emerging. It is this aspect of Holmes which has alienated a number of readers, yet fascinated devotees. Though Thorndyke may be straightforward, there is certainly nothing straightforward or predictable about Holmes. The frequent introspection, the occasional dramatic outbursts, the flashes of sensitivity and artistry all serve to provide depth and richness of

---

[21] 'Introduction to 'Great Short Stories of Detection, Mystery and Horror', Gollancz, 1928.

[22] 13 'Aspects of The Modern Short Story, A.C. Ward, p. 211-26, Univ. of London,1924

characterisation which we miss in Freeman's work. What is also absent – particularly in the novels – is the variety and eccentricity of character types of which Doyle is clearly a master.

The Holmes stories provide such a broad and vivid canvas of the Victorian social strata that at times they assume an almost photographic clarity. (REDH is perhaps the best example of this). Freeman's stories are much lighter altogether and lack that Dickensian richness which made the Holmes saga so popular. Where Austin Freeman succeeds is in his perfection of the form as pure detection. The psychological realism of the stories is particularly satisfying, especially in the so-called "inverted stories" where the crime is described in minute detail, and we follow the criminal's motivation and actions inch by inch. The research is immaculate and goes far beyond anything that Doyle conceived; and there is a much greater consistency in plot construction. Perhaps the most interesting inference to be drawn from a comparison of Thorndyke and Holmes is this: that whilst Holmes is clearly the father and Thorndyke the son, they inhabit radically differing worlds.

The Thorndyke stories hark back to the turn of the century. There is a definite nostalgia about their settings which it is impossible to ignore. Yet the link between literary precedent and its offspring also conceals an antithesis of aims. The Holmes stories are conceived of as an entertainment. Unwittingly, perhaps, they also strike psychological depths in all of us (consider SPEC, for instance, with its complex incestuous overtones and phallic imagery), which the Thorndyke stories do not).

Dr. Thorndyke is pre-eminent as a scientific investigator; he instructs. And because he is first and foremost an instrument of reason, his demonstrations seem mechanical and somehow too correct. Holmes, on the other hand, occupies that twilight world between science and creativity. In this respect he has much more to do with Poe's Dupin and the Romantic consciousness that produced him, than the cool reasoner of Freeman's superbly reasoned narratives.

SOURCES

Norman Donaldson,' In Search of Dr. Thorndyke', Bowling Green Popular University Press, 1971. R. Austin Freeman, 'The Red Thumb Mark'', Collingwood Bros., 1907, Repr. Remploy, 1979. 'R. Austin Freeman, Dr. Thorndyke: His Famous Cases (As Described By R. Austin Freeman)', Hodder & Stoughton, 1929, Repr. 1965. A.C. Ward, 'Aspects of The Modern Short Story', Univ. of London, 1924.

FOOTNOTE: Austin Freeman and A. Conan Doyle: A Comparative Timeline

1876. Doyle begins his medical studies at the University of Edinburgh. There he meets two men who influence the choice of his future novel heroes: Professor Rutherford and Dr Joseph Bell. The latter, a Professor of Surgery, carried out deductions on his patients and their diseases which gave Doyle the idea of a detective using the same methods.

1887: Freeman first trains as an apothecary, then studies medicine at Middlesex Hospital, qualifying in 1887. In 1887, Doyle also writes his first Sherlock Holmes adventure, A Study in Scarlet. The manuscript is rejected by several publishers before Ward, Lock & Co. buy it for the paltry sum of £25.

1889. During a dinner hosted by J. M. Stoddart, an American agent of the Lippincott's Magazine, Conan Doyle and Oscar Wilde are hired to write two stories. Published in 1890, Wilde writes 'The Picture of Dorian Gray 'and Conan Doyle The Sign of Four,' the second adventure of the detective.

1891 (November), Doyle writes to his mother: "I plan to kill Holmes in the sixth adventure. He prevents me from thinking of better things." His mother starts to find more plots; Holmes gets a reprieve.

1891 Freeman returns to London after suffering from blackwater fever. Unable to find a permanent medical position, he decides to settle in Gravesend and earn money from writing fiction, though continuing to practise medicine.

1892. Doyle and his wife move to Davos, Switzerland, where the air is healthier for his wife suffering from tuberculosis. Not far away are the Reichenbach Falls, a gorgeous, magnificent and terrifying framework for a dramatic end.

1901 – 1902 'The Hound of the Baskervilles', a retrospective tale, appears in The Strand Magazine.

1903 An American publisher convinced Conan Doyle to resurrect the detective, offering him a large sum of money. Then, thirty-three new stories will be published between September 1903 (The Adventure of the Empty House) and March 1927 ('The Adventure of Shoscombe Old Place').

1906 The health of Doyle's wife Louisa worsens. She dies on 4 July 1906. This drama plunges him into a state of depression.

1907: First Thorndyke story, 'The Red Thumb Mark', published by Hodder And Stoughton, 1907. Shortly after, Freeman pioneers the inverted detective story.

1909: 'John Thorndyke's Cases,' first published, Jan. 1, 1909.

1910 Conan Doyle intervenes to restore the truth in the Oscar Slater case, a German Jew accused of murder and sentenced to death. Convinced of the innocence of the man, he seeks to prove it.

1930: Freeman's 'The Mystery of 31 New Inn' written; first published. After many years campaigning and travelling widely as a spiritualist, Conan Doyle dies.

SHERLOCK HOLMES AND THE NORFOLK CONNECTION

Conan Doyle set no less than three of his Sherlock Holmes stories in Norfolk, a county of which he was immensely fond and which he frequently visited during his busy career as a writer and campaigner. Doyle, who once owned a thoroughbred Norfolk racehorse, and visited often one of his in-laws here, had already set one of his earlier Holmes stories, 'The Gloria Scott', on the Norfolk Broads.

Strangely, the inception of his later but perhaps most famous Holmes adventure, 'The Hound of The Baskervilles', began, not in the west, but in the east of England.

In the April of 1901, Conan Doyle, having returned from his adventures in South Africa, decided to go on a golfing holiday in Norfolk. Doyle had been demoralised by his experiences in the Boer War and had contracted enteric fever. He needed to recuperate. What better idea then, than to spend a few days with his old friend and journalist, Bertram Fletcher Robinson, who'd returned from South Africa on the same ship, at the Royal Links Hotel in Cromer, a prestigious place he had already visited set on a cliff top above the town itself in 1897, when he spent a week's vacation here with his wife Louise and son Kingsley.

We are informed by John Dickson Carr (and Adrian Conan Doyle) that Doyle stayed at The Royal Links Hotel in 1901, where he and Robinson hatched the idea of writing 'The Hound of the Baskervilles,' and that the two men did this sometime in March. Richard Lancelyn Green, that eminent scholar, subsequently discovered that Doyle and Robinson actually stayed at the Royal Links Hotel in not March, but late April of that year, as a local newspaper, 'The Cromer And North Walsham Post,' reported. This date was also verified from the accounts notebook of Doyle, in which a sum of £6. 6 shillings for two days' residence, is recorded there.

In fact, Doyle and his first wife Louise went on holiday to Cromer in 1897 and knew the place well, as a letter from September 16th, 1897, demonstrates (p. 390, 'Arthur Conan Doyle: A Life in Letters'.) And as we now know, based on the revelations unearthed by Richard, in the publication, 'Radical Rethinks on Hound and Horse: The Edinburgh Physician, A Lady and Mr Robinson,' a Sherlock Holmes Society publication, September 2002), in the third week of March 1901, Doyle was, in fact, screened off from the outside world, snugly ensconced in Sussex at The Ashdown Forest Hotel, where in fact, he stayed with his lover, Jean Leckie, and his beloved mother, incognito, having booked the hotel without any other guests.

Richard Lancelyn Green found another anomaly: biographers Carr and Doyle wrongly assigned the date of a letter written to Doyle's mother from Dartmoor as April 2nd, 1901. The correct date was actually June 2nd, 1901. We also know that by the end of May 1901, when Doyle made his tour of Dartmoor, at least half of the MS had been written.

This grand hotel is no longer there, having been demolished in the 1940s, following a devastating fire, but in its heyday, it attracted the rich and famous to this luxurious setting.

Today, the setting is equally tranquil, for a dense wood covers most of the hill over which the hotel once enjoyed its stunning outlook and the fields beyond are still a popular walking place for local residents. A contemporary guide describes it in detail:

'The Royal Links Hotel, Cromer, situated on the heathery hills towards Overstrand, is the largest hotel in the district. It stands in its own picturesque grounds of seven acres and contains one hundred and fifty rooms. The grand coffee room, drawing room, billiard room, smoke room, and extensive lounge, all on the ground floor, are fitted with every modern improvement, while a hydraulic lift gives easy access to the floors above. In the grounds of tennis and croquet lawns, bicycle house, stabling for visitors etc. The Royal Links Hotel affords an ideal hostelry for golfers and all lovers of scenery and good air. Adjoining, on the Lighthouse Hills, are the links of the Royal Cromer golf club, which for picturesqueness cannot be surpassed. The course consists of 8 holes. Within 20 minutes of the Broads, private steam launches to up to any number of persons can be ordered at the hotel office.'

Conan Doyle, a keen handicap - challenged golfer, but ace cricketer and all-round sportsman, had been here once before with Fletcher Robinson, enjoying a brief golfing interlude, and this was his second visit with the journalist. The Royal Cromer Golf Club itself still exists.

When Doyle and Robinson arrived at Cromer railway station, in late April, 1901, cold winds beat the high cliffs and the temperatures were lower here than in the south. Robinson, who was a veritable mine of information about legends and folklore, soon began to regale his golfing companion with gothic tales.

In his memoir ('The Chronicles of Addington Peace,' Harper, 1905), he recalled how 'One raw Sunday afternoon when a wind rushed off the North Sea,' the two men sat lounging in the comfort of their private sitting room at the Royal Links.

Robinson began to tell Doyle about the legends of Dartmoor, one of which concerned a spectral hound.

However, there is also a very local connection to the hound legend. Both men would certainly have been aware of the East Anglian Legend of Black Shuck, for this was a tale which had its roots in the very place they were staying. But how did the idea come about?

The seaside town of Cromer, a grand collection of late Victorian and early Edwardian hotels, guest houses and flats, was in its heyday, when Conan Doyle stayed here to begin writing 'The Hound' and was also visited by Oscar Wilde.

There are several theories about this. A local story has it that one of the waiters at the hotel told the two men about Black Shuck, explaining that it was in weather like this that the phantom hound could often be seen patrolling the headland. He went on to explain that his own father had seen the beast running along the beach and became aware of its fierce red eyes. A second story has it that Doyle or Robinson may have picked up a local guidebook, a slim volume entitled 'The Norfolk Coast,' which had been issued by the newspaper, the 'Norfolk News'. In the volume was the following curious entry:

'Old Shuck is the grimmest apparition of the Norfolk coast. He takes the form of a huge black dog with a single flashing eye and a mouth that breathes forth fire, and to encounter him is an omen of dread significance: it means that you will die before the year is out. It is, perhaps, the oldest phantom in England; it has haunted our lonely roads for centuries. Probably it is of Norse origin - the Black Hound of Odin - and came to this coast with the Scandinavian raiders. Its lair is some secret place known only to itself, but some of its favourite haunts are known, and not many years ago there were men and women whom nothing would induce to venture into them after nightfall. When the wind howled around their isolated homes, it was the baying of Old Shuck they heard, and they trembled in their beds.'

There is also a tale told along the coast of a practical joke played upon some fishermen by an auctioneer at Cromer.

'Knowing that the fishermen would be leaving a house about ten o'clock at night - the hour suggests the kind of house - the joker captured a black ram, wreathed round with clanking chain, and kept it concealed behind a bank until the men came along the road. Just as they were passing the hiding place, the ram was pushed down the steep bank right into the midst of them. The result of this dramatic appearance of "Old Shuck" was a most disgraceful flight and no fishing for days!

The third, and most popular version of events describes how Robinson introduced Doyle to the story of Richard Cabell (later to become the demonic Sir Hugo Baskerville). Robinson would have known of the story since he had a home in Newton Abbot, not that far from Dartmoor.

What really transpired between the two men we shall never really know. Some commentators claim that the idea for the murder mystery was originally Robinson's and that Doyle wanted to embark on a collaboration but later changed his mind. There is some circumstantial evidence for this theory. There are (curiously) three versions of the dedication of The Hound. The earliest states:

'This story owes its inception to my friend, Mr Fletcher Robinson, who has helped me both in the general plot and in the local details - ACD.'

However, in his preface to the 'Complete Sherlock Holmes,' Doyle later wrote:

'Then came the Hound of the Baskervilles. It arose from a remark by that fine fellow whose premature death was a loss to the world, Fletcher Robinson, that there was a spectral dog near his home on Dartmoor. That remark was the inception of the book, but I should add that the plot and every word of the actual narrative was my own.'

Which, then, are we to believe, and why the shift in Doyle's explanation? This inconsistency has provided the foundation for a bizarre theory, recently espoused by a writer who claimed that Doyle had poisoned Robinson with laudanum and did away with him. Sadly, however, the author in question overlooks the fact that Robinson died of typhoid. It does seem possible, however, that Doyle may have owed much to Robinson's ghastly tales.

We know, for example, that Robinson later showed Doyle the rocky outcrops of the moorland, the prehistoric dwellings, the gloomy walls of Princeton prison. When Doyle arrived in Cromer he had done with Holmes, having sent him to his watery grave at the bottom of the Reichenbach Falls. Since the tale first appeared in its book edition in 1902, following its serialisation in 'The Strand Magazine' between August 1901 and April 1902, we can assume that he must have had a very quick change of mind about his detective.

Amid rounds of golf and long walks along the coastal path to Sheringham and Mundesley, did Robinson and Doyle merge in their combined imaginations the mysterious landscape of Dartmoor and the phantom hound of Cromer? Certainly, in the West Country Cabell legend there was no hound of hell.

The huge, jet-black creature with flaming eyes bears a great resemblance to Black Shuck. Several authorities describe the creature as being the size of a calf and the very origin of the name means demon, from the Anglo Saxon "Scucca" or "Sceocca".

Some say that to witness the hound portends death within a year. This fits well with the demise of the unfortunate Sir Charles.

Conan Doyle's description of Baskerville Hall bears an uncanny likeness to nearby Cromer Hall and it is my strong belief that Doyle had Cromer Hall in mind when he wrote this, for the correspondence is uncannily similar and contemporary photographs bear out this likeness:

'The avenue opened into a broad expanse of turf, and the house lay before us. In the fading light I could see that the centre was a heavy block of building from which a porch projected. The whole front was draped in ivy, with a patch clipped bare here and there where a window or a coat-of-arms broke through the dark veil. From this central block rose the twin towers, ancient, crenellated, and pierced with many loopholes. To right and left of the turrets were more modern wings of black granite. A dull light shone through heavy mullioned windows, and from the high chimneys which rose from the steep, high-angled roof there sprang a single black column of smoke.'

Significantly, also, until the great storms of 1987, Cromer Hall also had a Yew Alley - which plays such a major part in the book.

When the two men finally departed the Royal Links Hotel, they went their separate ways: Robinson to take up a lucrative position as editor of "Vanity Fair" and Doyle to work at fever pitch on what he described in a letter to his mother as a "real creeper". However, it is curious to reflect that the Dartmoor hound may have had its origins in the legend of the hell hound, Black Shuck.

But then truth is often stranger than fiction.

NOTES

The once grand Royal Links Hotel was consumed by fire in the 1940s. According to one eye – witness, 'I Was There Ron Jackson - a Memory of Cromer'. Internet site:

'In 1949 the Royal Links which had hosted Royals and the glitterati of the day was the first to fall to the contagious bout of fires which mysteriously began to sweep the area. Imagine that wonderful central staircase (with no fire doors of course) what a chimney that must have made. At some time during the night (it's funny how things seem to start at night) with the place unoccupied and no doubt the owners abroad, it went up like a torch. If you walk along the cliff path now, there is absolutely nothing to see of what had been a flagship hotel. The ballroom, which was situated lower down by the Overstrand Road in which they once made an early 'Come Dancing' programme, on which Marie and I actually appeared on screen around 1961, followed its parent's firey fate in 1978. I guess the site was worth more than the building and of course houses have replaced it.'

On Sun Aug 12th 2018, Jamie O. Leeson commented:

The ballroom ('Links Pavillion') became a popular music venue of the 70s, hosting the Who, Thin Lizzy and I believe the sex pistols and countless others! There is a blue plaque on the building that stands in its place that is part of the Cromer country club

THE COUNT AND CARFAX: A VAMPIRIC INVESTIGATION

'And near him is a priest
Still schism – whole:
He loves the censer – reek
And organ roll,
He has leanings to the mystic,
Sacramental, eucharistic.
And dim yearnings altruistic
Thrill his soul.'

-Conan Doyle, 'Through the Magic Door.'

Abraham "Bram" Stoker (November 1847 - 20 April 1912) was an Irish writer very well known for his novel 'Dracula'. He was also a friend of Arthur Conan Doyle. He was at Doyle's second marriage on 18 September 1907. In that same year he conducted and wrote an interview with Conan Doyle: 'Arthur Conan Doyle Tells of His Career and Work, His Sentiments Towards America, and His Approaching Marriage.' (See Appendix).

When Bram Stoker managed The Lyceum Theatre in London, he produced the Conan Doyle play, 'A Story of Waterloo', (based on the Doyle story, 'A Straggler of '15.

Conan Doyle wrote in his autobiography:

'I had written a short story called "A Straggler of '15," which had seemed to me to be a moving picture of an old soldier and his ways. My own eyes were moist as I wrote it and that is the surest way to moisten those of others. I now turned this into a one-act play, and, greatly daring, I sent it to Henry Irving, of whose genius I had been a fervent admirer ever since those Edinburgh days, when I had paid my sixpence for the gallery night after night to see him in "Hamlet" and "The Lyons Mail." To my great delight, I had a pleasing note from Bram Stoker, the great man's secretary, offering me £100 for the copyright.'

Stoker was a Sherlock Holmes fan; he thought he could use the character as a model in a first version of Dracula, as a specialist of psychic research named Singleton, with a policeman named Cotford and a Watson-like history teacher named Max Windshoeffel.

Stoker and Conan Doyle both collaborated with other writers on the serial novel: 'The Fate of Fenella,' in 1892.

. What is The Carfax Syndrome?

*"You spoke of some bones, Mr. Mason. Could you show them before you go?" —
Sherlock Holmes, 'Shoscombe Old Place.'*

"What have we to do with walking corpses who can only be held in their graves by stakes driven through their hearts?" asks Sherlock Holmes of his friend, Watson, in the 'Adventure of the Sussex Vampire'. The question is a challenging one; the answer, I would suggest: "quite a deal more than it would seem." Holmes the rationalist, you will remember, scoffs at the idea that vampires can exist in this curious story about a young woman whose fifteen-year-old stepson attempts to poison her young baby. "This Agency stands flat-footed upon the ground. The world is big enough for us. No ghosts need apply." The supernatural held no place in the affections of Sherlock Holmes the analyst. The pure light of reason was what mattered most to him.

At first glance Holmes' rhetorical question seems reasonable enough. It is only when one comes to examine the details of the 'Sussex Vampire' that a glimmer of doubt arises. A Peruvian lady is suspected of being a vampire when she is caught by her nurse in the act of "leaning over her baby and apparently biting his neck."

Holmes' solution to the problem is provided by his observation of the family spaniel, Carlo, who it appears, has been used as a guinea-pig by Jack, the culprit. The young boy had fired poison darts tipped with curare at the animal. The mother, knowing that the deadly poison had been used on her baby, but wishing to protect the stepson, took the most direct course of action and sucked the poison from the wound in its neck. All well and good, you might say. But what do we know about curare?

1. It is a poison that paralyses the thorax and chest muscles

2. It kills within minutes or has no effect at all. (W.S. Baring-Gould's point).

Surely, therefore, the dog should have died immediately when pierced by the dart? No. It was merely paralysed. Surely then, if the dose wasn't fatal, it would have had "no effect at all." No joy here either. What do we deduce, therefore? That the dog had a back injury anyway' Or that the boy, in a fit of remorse, "sucked some of the poison from the dog's wound?"

Two further points to which I would like to draw your attention. Firstly, Ferguson's description of the nurse's discovery. "As she ran into the room she saw her employer, the lady, leaning over the baby and apparently biting his neck. There was a small wound in the neck, from which a stream of blood had escaped." Now if you sucked poison from a wound, especially that of a baby's, the very last thing you would do would be to bite the skin. Also, "as he saw his wife rise from a kneeling position beside the cot, (he) saw blood upon the child's exposed neck and upon the sheet. With a cry of horror, he turned his wife's face to the light and saw blood all round her lips. It was she — she beyond all question — who had drunk the poor baby's blood. " Note the absolute certainty about her husband's observation. There is no doubt in his mind that his wife is guilty of vampirism. More important, is the sheer amount of blood on the "child's exposed neck and sheet". Now why should there be that amount of blood spilled if the woman had really been sucking poison from a wound? Secondly, there is the condition of the mother to consider. She is kept away from the child in a locked room. But when Watson sees her, she is described in the following way:

'On a bed a woman was lying who was clearly in a high fever. She was only half conscious... seeing a stranger, she appeared to be relieved, and sank back with a sigh upon the pillow.... She lay still while I took her pulse and temperature. Both were high...'

The question here arises: why is the woman in this condition? It cannot be because of the poison, for that would have killed her if she had swallowed it. "Mental and nervous excitement" is the cause, according to Watson. But that does not account for the peculiar languor she exhibits, nor her "half conscious" condition. To anyone sharp enough to spot it, the Peruvian lady is clearly the victim of a vampiric attack. High fever and a semi-cataleptic attack were commonly reported symptoms in nineteenth century Romania. And not just in Romania. In Malay, for instance, where the vampire is known affectionately as the 'Bajang.' Symptoms like these are described as 'convulsions, unconsciousness, or delirium, possibly for some days together or with intervals between attacks.'

These curious aspects of the 'Sussex Vampire' appear even odder when one considers the opening of Watson's narrative. Holmes asks Watson to "Make a long arm and see what V has to say," He was, of course, referring to his commonplace book, his anomalous scrapbook in which details of all his previous cases were kept. Among the many fascinating entries, Holmes reads out the following:

"Good old index. You can't beat it. Listen to this, Watson. Vampirism in Hungary. And again, Vampires in Transylvania."

The question must surely be asked: what on earth is such an entry doing in the index of a rationalist like Holmes, a man who professes that "no ghosts need apply"? Unless of course, like everything in the commonplace book, it is there for a purpose...?

But before I ask the unwilling reader to "switch on to a Grimm's fairy tale" (to use Holmes' phrase) I would draw his attention to a number of Sherlockian syndromes, (Syndrome - "a group of related things, events or actions". The discovery of the syndrome in the Holmes stories was first pointed out by Sanuel Rosenberg in his study, "Naked Is the Best Disguise"), each of which serves as a foundation stone for the hypothesis to follow.

. Tomb Robbing in the Canon

The opening and despoiling of tombs is an activity long associated with the cult of the vampire. In the classic vampire story this is usually done in order to impale the suspected vampire and seal off the resting place. Anthony Masters notes in 'The Natural History of the Vampire,' that 'for hundreds of years tombs were continuously being opened and shut. This natural curiosity about the dead could be likened to the little boy who discovers the corpse of a bird and with full ceremony conducts a funeral service. Once buried, the bird will be dug up time after time, 'to see how it is getting on.'

It is interesting to observe how many night-time vigils there are in the Holmes stories. The list is a long one but, for examples, I would refer you to 'Red-Headed League,' 'The Hound of the Baskervilles,' 'Charles Augustus Milverton.', 'The Man with the Twisted Lip' and 'The Empty House.'

The night-time vigil is the classic prelude to the destruction of the vampire, the difference with Holmes being, that he seeks to apprehend the malefactor, not to destroy him. Holmes and Watson go further than this. However, we find a classic example in 'The Adventure of Shoscombe Old Place,' where they break into Sir Robert Norberton's family crypt, ostensibly to discover whether he has done away with his sister and incarcerated her there. But not content with this, Holmes himself breaks open a coffin.

"He turned and tore open the coffin-lid behind him. In the glare of the lantern I saw a body swathed in a sheet from head to foot, with dreadful, witch-like features, all nose and chin, projecting at one end, the dim, glazed eyes staring from a discoloured and crumbling face."

What is the reason for such drastic action? To prove his point? Hardly necessary, surely, since Sir Robert is only too glad to explain the circumstances of his wife's unfortunate illness and death. I would maintain that there is expressed in the above passage, a certain necrophiliac pleasure, a fascination with the charnel house, which is also conveyed by Watson in an earlier description of the interior of the crypt:

"Striking a match, he illuminated the melancholy place — dismal and evil—smelling, with ancient crumbling walls of rough-hewn stone, and piles of coffins.... Holmes had lit his lantern, which shot a tiny tunnel of vivid yellow light upon the mournful scene."

The other occasion on which Holmes rips open a coffin is in 'The Disappearance of Lady Frances Carfax'. In this case, the act is perfectly justified by the circumstances, since the unfortunate Lady Carfax has been drugged and smuggled out of a house, incarcerated with a workhouse corpse, to her premature burial.

This theme of premature burial was one that haunted the imagination of the eighteenth and nineteenth centuries, much beloved also by Edgar Allan Poe; and it may well have been a contributory factor in the emergence of the vampire myth. There is a further syndromic parallel for the astute Holmesian in the name of Sir Robert's dead sister — Beatrice. Now Beatrice was, of course, and Conan Doyle would certainly have remembered this, the subject of a short story by Edgar Poe (his favourite obsession was that of premature burial), in which the dead woman haunts the storyteller by her vampiric presence. Moreover, the idea of incarcerating one's dead relatives in the family vault finds further echoes in 'The Fall of The House of Usher' and 'The Black Cat'. Conan Doyle's admirers need hardly be reminded of his debt to Poe!

4. Underground Chambers, Old Houses.

In nearly all vampire stories, the house, or castle appears as a microcosm of the tomb itself. It is a crypt in miniature and the terms used to describe it are usually something in the manner of "decaying, crumbling, rambling, dark, labyrinthine," etc. Out of curiosity, I decided to reread these adventures of Holmes in which the action takes place at night. To my amazement I found that, without exception, the descriptive language there reflected the pattern of vampiric locations.

In 'The Adventure of the Engineer's Thumb', for instance, the young man Victor Hatherley is lured to a remote house in the country where he is expected to co-operate on an engineering scheme.

"It was a labyrinth of an old house, with corridors, passages, narrow winding staircases (says Hatherley) and little low doors.... There were no carpets and no signs of furniture above the ground floor while the plaster was peeling off the walls and the damp was breaking through in green unhealthy blotches."

Just like a tomb, in fact, and indeed the house is intended to be one, as Hatherley discovers to his cost.

(It is fascinating to compare Hatherley with Jonathan Harker, the hero of Stoker's Dracula. Like Harker, Hatherley is young, a bachelor, somewhat naïve, and imprisoned by a man of evil intentions in a remote spot. There is even a similarity in the surnames.)

Space prevents me from enumerating all these locations. But there are two more which I think illustrate the point. The first is from 'The Red-Headed League,' when Holmes and Watson descend into the bank vaults with Mr. Merryweather to lie in wait for the villain, John Clay:

'... a massive iron gate... was opened, and led down a flight of winding stone steps... Mr. Merryweather stopped to light a lantern, and then conducted us down a dark, earth-smelling passage, and so, after opening a third door, into a huge vault or cellar, which was piled all round with crates and massive boxes.'

The second of these is the forbidding Baskerville Hall which, as a Gothic location, needs no further comment. But to the reader of 'Dracula,' there is more than just a superficial resemblance to the Transylvanian Castle Bran. Even the countryside possesses echoes of the Hungarian terrain. Watson notes that 'the fertile country' is left behind, that the 'road in front of us grew bleaker and wilder.' Around the Hall are stunted oaks and firs. The sterility of the place is overwhelming. The lodge itself is 'a ruin.., with weather beaten pillars on either side, blotched with lichens ...'

Stoke Moran, scene of the infamous Dr. Grimesby Roylott's dealings, bears a marked similarity to Baskerville Hall. It too was "of a grey lichen-blotched stone, with a high central portion and two curving wings, like the claws of a crab..." a very animate and terrifying description, which is unsurprising, given the incestuous overtones of the tale.

But now I wish to add another element into this 'tangled skein' by the idea of 'old dark houses' in the Sherlockian Canon and, amazed that their number was legion, idly turned the pages of my copy of 'Dracula'. And what should I now discover? That the name of the house near Purfleet to which the Count conveys his harem of vampires from his native land is CARFAX. Purely a coincidence? Well, consider the following points:

Holmes discovers Lady Frances Carfax in a coffin - not the most usual of resting places for a live woman.

Holmes visits Dr. Schlessinger, the villain of the piece, and surveys that coffin in "a great dark house in the centre of Poultney Square."

The Carfax of Bram Stoker's story (the name is a corruption of *Quatre Face*, according to Harker) is "very large...gloomy" and dates back to medieval times. Close by is an old chapel. It is in an isolated position and surrounded by high walls.

In a much later Holmes story, 'The Adventure of Lady Frances Carfax,' Doyle re-enacts the claustrophobic horror of a premature burial as a distinct *homage*, I suspect, to the great crime story progenitor, Poe, when a woman is chloroformed and her body pushed into a coffin along with the corpse of a workhouse inmate.

. The **Physical Resemblances**

Throughout the Holmesian saga, there runs a marked similarity of types of persons who are recognisably villains.

The most outstanding example, I would imagine, is Moriarty himself. Now, in order to state the facts of this particular syndrome, the reader must indulge himself in a few quotations. The first is a description of 'The Napoleon of Crime.'

"He is extremely tall and thin, his forehead domes out in a white curve, and his two eyes are deeply sunken in his head. He is clean-shaven, pale and ascetic-looking ... his face protrudes forward and is forever slowly oscillating...in a curiously reptilian fashion."

The second? — well, guess.

"His face was a strong — a very strong aquiline, with high bridge of the thin nose and peculiarly arched nostrils; with lofty domed forehead and hair growing scantily round the temples, but profusely elsewhere ... the chin was broad and strong, and the cheeks firm but thin. The general effect was one of extraordinary pallor."

207

Now who is this?

"I do not think that I have ever seen so thin a man. His whole face sharpened away into nose and chin, and the skin of his cheeks was drawn quite tense over his outstanding bones. Yet this emaciation seemed to be his natural habit, and due to no disease."

And this?

"A large face, seared with a thousand wrinkles and marked with every evil passion, was turned from one to the other of us, while his deep-set, bile-shot eyes, and his thin fleshless nose gave him... the resemblance to a fierce old bird of prey."

And this?

"A light streamed down the stairs ... and the man who bore it was framed in the Gothic archway. He was a terrible figure, huge in stature and fierce in manner... a strong, heavily moustached face and angry eyes ... glared round him into every recess of the vault."

Or how about:

"His eyes were positively blazing. His face was deathly pale, and the lines of it were hard, like drawn wires."

For the record: the third of these is Colonel Lysander Stark, villain of 'The Engineer's Thumb,' the fourth is Dr. Grimesby Roylott, of 'The Speckled Band' and the fifth Sir Robert Norberton of 'Shoscombe Old Place.' The second and sixth are both descriptions of Count Dracula himself.

You will see now why I found it necessary to quote these at some length. All these Holmesian villains (although Norberton does not strictly qualify) have certain features in common. They are all of them tall, possessed of great strength, pale and ascetic, with deep-set, penetrating eyes. They are also all highly intelligent."They are, indeed, as the reader has by now guessed, prototypes of the Byronic vampire.

. The Face at the Window, in 'The Creeping Man'

The final syndrome (q.v.) is perhaps the most perplexing, because I have not myself yet fully understood its significance. The first point to consider relates to two adventures (both late in the saga), 'The Adventure of the Yellow Face' and 'The Adventure of the Blanched Soldier'. In the first of these, Mrs. Munro, formerly Mrs. Hebron, shuts away her coloured daughter and encourages her to wear a mask because she is too ashamed to tell her second husband the racial identity and truth about her previous partner The second concerns an isolated case of leprosy which afflicts a young man, Godfrey Emsworth. He too is shut away and like the young daughter of Mrs. Munro, the sight of the blanched face frightens an unintended observer.

Both adventures occur in large rambling houses and both possess a hint of the supernatural. But the description of the face in 'The Blanched Soldier' is revealing.

"He was deadly pale — never have I seen a man so white. I reckon ghosts may look like that... There was something shocking about the man, Mr. Holmes. It wasn't merely the ghastly face glimmering as white as cheese in the darkness. It was more subtle than that — something slinking, something furtive, something guilty..."

Here, crystallised, is the classic horror/shock recognition one encounters so frequently in the vampire story. The paleness appals the observer — but more than that. There is something deeply disturbing about the pallor of this man — something which evokes a deep current of guilt. It is the sudden glimpse into a face that reveals man's bestial side — the side that none of us dare admit.

This fear or loathing of transformation or "otherness" is the basis for an entire story (again, one of the late adventures), 'The Adventure of the Creeping Man,' as well, of course, as 'The Yellow Face' where the topics of racial impurity and the albino child are interestingly explored by Conan Doyle.

Why does Professor Presbury's faithful wolfhound, Ray, endeavour to bite him? Simply because he has been taking a serum, derived from anthropoids, monkey testes, to put it plainly, tabooed by the medical profession, but which it was believed, by certain people at the time, including Presbury, conveys remarkable strength and virility on the user. Unfortunately, it also provokes a curious case of atavism in Professor Presbury.

"The passage was dark save that one window half-way along it threw a patch of light. I could see that something was coming along the passage, something dark and crouching".

Howard Elcock's powerful drawing which accompanied the publication of 'The Adventure of The Creeping Man' shows Professor Presbury transformed into a Mr Hyde-type monstrosity.

'Then suddenly he merged into the light and I saw that it was he. He was crawling, Mr. Holmes — crawling! He was not quite on his hands and knees. I should rather say on his hands and feet, with his face sunk between his hands.'

Shock/horror again, but this time it is produced by the sight of a man reverting to his more ancient origins. Jonahan Harker's feelings also "changed to repulsion" and terror when Jonathan sees 'the whole man (i.e. the Count) slowly emerge from the window and begin to crawl down the castle wall, face down, with his cloak spreading about him like great wings'.

Holmes' own comment on this species of behaviour is one that I find puzzling. "The highest type of man may revert to the animal if he leaves the straight road of destiny." Fear of the 'other side' but this time fear that perhaps has been rationalised? suddenly became aware that a face was watching me out of one of the upper windows.'

Compare the observer's following reaction to the 'Yellow Face. "I don't know what there was about that face, Mr. Holmes, but there was something unnatural and inhuman about the face... The colour was what impressed me most... something set and rigid about it, which was shockingly unnatural."

Shock, the sense of something "unnatural," against nature, are here both apparent.

And now for the Grimm's fairy tale. We have seen that throughout the Sherlockian Canon there are a considerable number of parallels with vampiric themes and, in particular, Bram Stoker's classic horror tale, 'Dracula'. What evidence is there to support the theory that Holmes himself may have been involved in the battle against the Hungarian Count who bears such a striking resemblance to Professor James Moriarty?

Bram Stoker's novel was published in 1897. We have Jonathan Harker's word for it that "seven years ago we all went through the flames." That would mean the incidents of the story belong to 1890.

According to the Sherlock Holmes biographer, William Baring-Gould, Holmes disappeared in April 1891, a date with which I concur. In the year 1890 there were only seven reported cases, and only three of these were chronicled by Watson. These were 'Wisteria Lodge' (24-9 March 1890), 'Silver Blaze' (25

September 1890 — 30 September 1890), and 'The Beryl Coronet' (19 December-20 December 1890).

But we know that in late December of that year Holmes paid a 'service to the royal family of Scandinavia,' and was engaged on 'a matter of supreme importance to the French Government.'

On September 18 and 25 three reports were carried by London newspapers, two of them concerning vampiric attacks on young children ("The Escaped Wolf" — 'Pall Mall Gazette,' 'A Hampstead Mystery' and 'The Hampstead Horror' both in 'The Westminster Gazette.") Holmes, we know, bought as many of the London papers as he could lay hands on, and was intimate with their typefaces. What are the chances of his ignoring these reports? Slim in the extreme, I would suggest:

Some while during 1890 and 1891 Watson's second wife, Mary Morstan, died. From what cause? Watson does not say. Nor does he even hint at the fact that she is dead. This has struck several commentators as odd in the extreme.

Holmes had in his commonplace book an entry concerning vampires in Transylvania. Why Transylvania? Vampires exist (if at all) all over Western Europe (and the east).

As we have seen, there is internal evidence to suggest that Holmes (or Watson) was not telling the truth about the Peruvian Lady in 'The Sussex Vampire.' It appears much more likely that she was really a vampire. Did Holmes or Watson not wish to alarm the public's sensibility by telling the truth?

In the light of the above, I would suggest the following:

1. That Holmes knew Stoker well and therefore became involved in the Dracula business. This is not as fanciful as it may appear when one considers that:

a) Holmes was well acquainted with Oscar Wilde, as we have already learned. As we also know, there is a parody of him in 'The Sign of Four,' where he appears as Thaddeus Sholto. Now Wilde also was of course a good friend of Bram Stoker and was enamoured of his wife, Florence, before the two married. (For a full examination of this, see S. Rosenberg's "Naked is the Best Disguise," Ch. 5, where the parallel is shown to be uncontradictable. He was also a frequent visitor to the newly opened Lyceum Theatre, where Stoker was then the manager.)

b) Ten years before the Dracula affair, Holmes had been involved in the Case of Vambery, the Wine Merchant (August 1880-January 1881). I conjecture that this Vambery was none other than a relative of the adventurer and

Hungarian professor, Arminius Vambery, the man who gave Stoker a considerable amount of information regarding the legend of the vampire in Transylvania and who furnished him with evidence relating to the Voivoide Dracula, who was indeed the basis for the Count. Vambery spent many an alcoholic hour in Stoker's Beefsteak Room where, along with other guests, Irving and Stoker indulged themselves at the Lyceum. It is more than probable (although not conclusive) that Vambery provided the foundation for Dr Van Helsing, Stoker's learned Dutch hero.

2. That when the hunt for the vampire turned to Europe, Holmes also went abroad, joining Harker, his wife and their companions and that, en route, he became involved in performing services for the royal family of Scandinavia and the French Government.

3. That Miss Mary Morstan died, not of consumption (S.C. Roberts) nor of heart-trouble (T.S. Blakeney) but as a result of a vampiric attack and that this fact alone spurred Holmes to investigate and cast aside his veil of rationalism. The evidence for this last assertion is scant, I will admit. Yet is it not strange that the Lyceum Theatre should provide the meeting place of Miss Morstan and the agent of Thaddeus Sholto in 'The Sign of Four'? (We know Holmes went to the Lyceum on their Wagner nights, which were at that time extremely popular.)

Even stranger: what of the identity of the coachman who meets the detective and his client but who is never revealed to us? All we do know is that he was "a small, dark, brisk man." Bram Stoker fits that description to a tee.

It is interesting that, on several occasions, Miss Morstan nearly faints, that elsewhere Watson describes her "white arm and hand" and "absorbing melancholy" and, that when speaking of her father, she suddenly cuts short her account and "put(s) her hand to her throat."

'These are deep, dark waters, Watson...'

THE HORRIFIC CONCLUSION

What are we to make of all these constant literary echoes and references between Doyle and Stoker? Firstly, we know that the two men not only collaborated with each other regarding the composition of a novel but that this literary collaboration extended to a theatrical production. Doyle not only attended Stoker's wedding but was in quite regular contact with the author, both on a personal and a business basis. There is also a postcard in existence in which Doyle talks enthusiastically of the copy of 'Dracula' which he has recently finished reading. I reproduce it verbatim here:

'My dear Bram Stoker, I am sure you will not think it an impertinence of me if I write to tell you how very much I have enjoyed reading 'Dracula.' I think it is the very best story of diablerie I have read for many years. It is really wonderful how, with so much exciting interest over so long a book, there is never an anti-climax.' - (Claremont, Eastbourne, August 20th, 1897).

Doyle's familiarity of tone and his praise for the Stoker novel indicates to us how close the two men were – and not just as business and creative partners. It is fascinating to learn that, whilst on a recuperative holiday with his new wife Jean Leckie, Doyle stayed at the Poldhu Hotel on the Lizard in Cornwall, some ten miles or so from Helston, the main town for the Lizard, and where I worked and lived as a secondary school teacher for many years. Whilst researching a slim monograph, concerning the roots of the story, 'The Adventure of The Devil's Foot' – a relatively late Holmes tale, published in 1910 – I discovered through my researches, that Doyle had spent a fortnight at the hotel (now a care home); however, I could not prove it. Then two items later came to light: photographs of Arthur and Jean, taken in March 1907, above Kynance Cove (a Lizard beauty spot) and in the possession of that intrepid and scholarly fellow Holmesian, the sadly departed Richard Lancelyn Green; plus a postcard sent from the hotel to Bram Stoker in March 1907, headed 'The Poldhu Hotel,' which ran thus:

'Dear Stoker,

Am having a rest cure. Only hope yours is doing you as much good as mine...'

Here it was, then, that on this bleak and windswept landscape, eerie even in daylight (I can vouch for it), that Conan Doyle summoned from the depths of his dark Celtic imagination the idea of the 'Satanic' visitation, a vision of an hallucinogenic nightmare, and the themes of death and revenge much explored by his friend, Bram Stoker.

In the summer of that same year he was to write 'The Adventure of The Devils Foot', a tale of – to use his own terminology – 'diablerie.' The story also contains a most moving episode where the friendship of Holmes and Watson is tested to the absolute limits. And with his new love, Jean, his first wife Louise's death from tuberculosis, often mistaken in Romania by peasants as evidence of a vampiric attack, and his old and valued Irish acquaintance, Bram Stoker, the bonds of friendship were very much on his mind.

Doyle's praise from one popular 1890s author to another is proof that 'Dracula' much appealed to the dark and disturbing side of Conan Doyle's psyche. No wonder he found Stoker's novel so appealing. To Doyle, the Count, with his stench of moral and physical corruption, would have been a close equivalent to the late Professor Moriarty, whose tentacles spread into the bowels of the Victorian criminal underworld and the city, with its 'dark, Satanic mills' which dogged the life of the poor.

Like the Count, Moriarty has a heart of ice, a complex mind and an acquisitive nature. The Professor is, as we have seen, the embodiment of Doyle's *id*, whence sprang his intense and vivid creativity.

During his lifetime Doyle presented a persona which was opaque and impenetrable. Through a glass, very darkly, we see his heroes and villains stride the pages of his various novels and short stories, but Doyle, unlike his Irish fellow countryman and contemporary Oscar Wilde, never once allows us into his inner sanctuary. To Wilde it was the life of the artist that overshadowed the work; to Doyle it was the work which overshadowed the life until, eventually, he was summoned into a defence of the world of shadows. Sometimes, he admitted that he was indeed Sherlock Holmes; at other times, he denied it completely, once writing back to a critic: 'Please grasp this with your cerebral tentacle: The doll and his maker are never identical.'

APPENDIX:

From The Daily Chronicle: 14th February 1908: Interview between Bram Stoker and Arthur Conan Doyle.

'My first book! That was written when I was six years of age! But if I am to tell you about myself, I suppose I had better begin at the beginning."

The speaker was lying on a chintz covered sofa in the pretty drawing-room of his house at Hindhead, down in Surrey. The forenoon sun was streaming in through one of the mullioned windows, of which the bars were softened by the delicate fringe of green of the creepers which spread all along them. The whole room was full of soft light, which showed the fine old furniture and the multitude of dainty knick-knacks to perfection. Even the many quaint and pretty pictures seemed to stand out from the walls.

From where I sat the whole of the lovely valley, at the very head of which the house stands, lay before me. Due south it falls away, spreading wider as it goes, till its lines are lost in distance, an endless sea of greenery. Far away there are ranges of hills piling up, one behind the other, in undulations of varying blue. Even the whole sweep of the horizon visible from our altitude is like a wavy sea. Nearer at hand, the wonderful green of the valley is articulated by the minor curves and slopes, the trend of surrounding hills. The mighty carpet of green is of the fresh young bracken, whose shoots seem close and are like little croziers wrought in emerald. Against this the rising pine trees seem like dark masses. Close to us, beyond the vivid patch of tennis lawn, are some masses of colour which are simply gorgeous amid the expanse of green. Great shrubs of yellow bloom, clumps of purple rhododendron, luxuriant alder, with masses of snowy flowers starred in their own peculiar green. An expanse which, whether seen from near or far, in unity or detail, simply ravishes the eye with its myriad beauties.

We had motored up the previous afternoon from Guildford, some twelve miles distant. The last seven miles of the journey up the steep, winding road shows one of the loveliest scenes in England—a scene that brings at every new phase fresh memories of Turner. Indeed, Turner himself loved this piece of the old Portsmouth road. Is not one of the weirdest pictures of the Liber Studiorum, "Gallows Hill," taken from it? But here was the crown of it all—that wide expanse seen beyond this foreground of idyllic beauty.

THE UNDERSHAW HOME AT HINDHEAD, SURREY
by Bram Stoker

Conan Doyle built his home Undershaw in the western angle at the joining of the road from Haslemere with the Portsmouth Road, just below the very top of the hill. It stands on a little platform lying below the road. As north and east of it is a thick grove of trees and shrubs, it is completely sheltered from stranger eyes except from down the valley. It is so sheltered from cold winds that the architect felt justified in having lots of windows, so that the whole place is full of light. Nevertheless, it is cosy and snug to a remarkable degree, and has everywhere that sense of "home" which is so delightful to occupant and stranger alike. Throughout it is full of interesting things got together for their interesting association with the author's life and adventures, for their prettiness, or as curios, or works of art.

'Undershaw,' Arthur Conan Doyle's famous literary home, where he and his wife entertained the rich and famous, enjoying a prosperous lifestyle, owing chiefly to the phenomenal and world – wide success of his Sherlock Holmes stories, an achievement which, he frequently pointed out, never ceased to perplex him..

The owner of this almost fairy pleasure house is a big man, massive and burly, and of great strength. His head and face are broad and strong. His eyes are blue with a peculiar effect in light, for they seem to have two shades of blue in the iris. His voice is strong and resonant—a very masculine voice.

The "interview" which followed was the result of many questions. The subject of it was most kind and amenable, thoroughly understanding everything and willing to enlighten me as I required. But he is not naturally a pushing man or an egotist, and it was necessary to keep him resolutely to the point of his own identity. I say this as his various statements were so lucid and illuminative that I think it better to give them in his own words in the sequence of a direct narrative. After all, there is nothing like a man's *ipsissima verba* to show the reality of the individual through the mistiness of words. I omit questions except where necessary, and only venture to add comment or description where such may add to the reader's enlightenment.

A NOTE TO THE READER by Kelvin I. Jones.

This detailed and revealing interview by Stoker with the creator of the immortal detective, Sherlock Holmes, was first published in America in the 28 July 1907 issue of The World (New York). And then re-published iin the UK under the subsequent title "Sir Arthur Conan Doyle Tells of His Work & Career" in the February 14, 1908 issue of The Daily Chronicle.

'My first book! That was written when I was six years of age! But if I am to tell you about myself, I suppose I had better begin at the beginning."

The speaker was lying on a chintz covered sofa in the pretty drawing-room of his house at Hindhead, down in Surrey. The forenoon sun was streaming in through one of the mullioned windows, of which the bars were softened by the delicate fringe of green of the creepers which spread all along them. The whole room was full of soft light, which showed the fine old furniture and the multitude of dainty knick-knacks to perfection. Even the many quaint and pretty pictures seemed to stand out from the walls.

From where I sat the whole of the lovely valley, at the very head of which the house stands, lay before me. Due south it falls away, spreading wider as it goes, till its lines are lost in distance, an endless sea of greenery. Far away there are ranges of hills piling up, one behind the other, in undulations of varying blue. Even the whole sweep of the horizon visible from our altitude is like a wavy sea. Nearer at hand the wonderful green of the valley is articulated by the minor curves and slopes, the trend of surrounding hills. The mighty carpet of green is of the fresh young bracken, whose shoots seem close and are like little croziers wrought in emerald. Against this the rising pine trees seem like dark masses. Close to us, beyond the vivid patch of tennis lawn, are some masses of color which are simply gorgeous amid the expanse of green. Great shrubs of yellow bloom, clumps of purple rhododendron, luxuriant alder, with masses of snowy flowers starred in their own peculiar green. An expanse which, whether seen from near or far, in unity or detail, simply ravishes the eye with its myriad beauties.

We had motored up the previous afternoon from Guildford, some twelve miles distant. The last seven miles of the journey up the steep, winding road shows one of the loveliest scenes in England—a scene that brings at every new phase fresh memories of Turner. Indeed, Turner himself loved this piece of the old Portsmouth road. Is not one of the weirdest pictures of the Liber Studiorum, "Gallows Hill," taken from it? But here was the crown of it all—that wide expanse seen beyond this foreground of idyllic beauty.

UNDERSHAW HOME AT HINDHEAD.

Conan Doyle built his home Undershaw in the western angle at the joining of the road from Haslemere with the Portsmouth Road , just below the very top of the hill. It stands on a little platform lying below the road. As north and east of it is a thick grove of trees and shrubs, it is completely sheltered from stranger eyes except from down the valley. It is so sheltered from cold winds that the architect felt justified in having lots of windows, so that the whole place is full of light. Nevertheless, it is cozy and snug to a remarkable degree, and has everywhere that sense of "home" which is so delightful to occupant and stranger alike. Throughout it is full of interesting things got together for their interesting association with the author's life and adventures, for their prettiness, or as curios, or works of art.

The owner of this almost fairy pleasure house is a big man, massive and burly, and of great strength. His head and face are broad and strong. His eyes are blue with a peculiar effect in light, for they seem to have two shades of blue in the iris. His voice is strong and resonant—a very masculine voice.

The "interview" which followed was the result of many questions. The subject of it was most kind and amenable, thoroughly understanding everything and willing to enlighten me as I required. But he is not naturally a pushing man or an egotist, and it was necessary to keep him resolutely to the point of his own identity. I say this as his various statements were so lucid and illuminative that I think it better to give them in his own words in the sequence of a direct narrative. After all, there is nothing like a man's ipsissima verba to show the reality of the individual through the mistiness of words. I omit questions except where necessary, and only venture to add comment or description where such may add to the reader's enlightenment.

DOYLE'S IMAGINATIVE FORBEARS.

"My people on the father's side," said the creator of "Sherlock Holmes," "we all artists of a peculiarly imaginative type. My father, Charles Doyle, was in truth a great unrecognised genius. He drifted to Edinburgh from London in his early youth, and so he lost the chance of living before the public eye. His wild and strange fancies alarmed, I think, rather than pleased the stolid Scotchmen of the 50's and 60's. His mind ran on strange moonlight effects, done with extraordinary skill in water colors; dancing witches, drowning seamen, death coaches on lonely moors at night and goblins chasing children across churchyards."

All these pictures were in the room, or in some of those adjacent. With them were a host of others, delicate fancies and weird flights of imagination. There was one tiny picture of a little fairy carrying a branch and leading a beetle by a string, which was daintily sweet.

"I have myself no turn for this form of art at all beyond a very keen color sense which makes a discord of shades perfectly painful to my eye. I suppose, however, that there is a metabolism in these things, and that any sense I have for dramatic effect corresponds, or is an equivalent, in some degree, to the artistic nature of my father, whom, by the way, I in no degree resemble physically. But my real love for letters, my instinct for story-telling, springs, I believe, from my mother, who is on Anglo-Celtic stock, with the glamour and romance of the Celt very strongly marked. Her I do resemble physically, and also in character, so that I take my leanings towards romance rather from her side than my father's. In my early childhood, as far back as I can remember anything at all, the vivid stories which she would tell me stand out so clearly that they obscure the real facts of my life. It is not only that she was—is still—a wonderful story-teller, but she had, I remember, an art of sinking her voice to a horror-stricken whisper when she came to a crisis in her narrative, which makes me goose-fleshy now when I think of it. I am sure, looking back, that it was in attempting to emulate these stories of my childhood that I first began weaving dreams myself.

A SIX-YEAR-OLD AUTHOR.

"When I was six I wrote a book of adventure—doubtless my mother has it still. I illustrated it myself. It must be an absurd production, but still it showed the set of my mind. When I went to school I carried the characteristic with me. There I was in some demand as a story-teller. I could start a hero off from home and carry him through an interminable succession of wayside happenings which would, if necessary, last through the spare hours of a whole term. This faculty remained with me all my school days, and the only scholastic success I can ever remember lay in the direction of English essays and poetry. I was no good at either classics or mathematics; even my English I wrote as pleasure.' not as work.

AT SCHOOL IN GERMANY.

"After leaving Stonyhurst I was sent to a 'finishing' school in Germany, the Tyrol. There again my tendency to letters asserted itself. I started and edited a school magazine. Although the German acquired was indifferent, I think I had great benefit from the small but select English library. Macaulay and Scott, I remember, were my favourite authors. But I was and am still an omnivorous reader, with very catholic sympathies. There is hardly anything which does not interest me. I have sometimes tested myself by going into a large library and noting which of the books I am tempted to take down. I think that if let loose in such a place on a wet day my first choice would be military memoirs; but I am deeply interested also in criminology, in all sides of history, in science—so far as I can follow it—in comparative theology—if it is not ruined by the heavy touch of the writer—in travel—if the author has the skill to keep a glamour over his picture—in any form of fiction. Indeed, it would be difficult to name any form of true literature which does not give me intense pleasure.

STUDYING MEDICINE IN AULD EDINBORO.

"In 1876 I drifted into the study of medicine. The reason largely was that my people lived in Edinburgh"—he pronounces the word in Scotch fashion, "Edinboro"—"and there is a famous medical school there. For four years I went through the curriculum. My people were not at that time wealthy, and it was a struggle to keep me at college. So I compressed my classes into the winter, and devoted each summer to serving as a medical assistant, and so earning a little money to help to pay the fees. I served in this way in Sheffield, in the country districts in Shropshire, and finally in Birmingham —a billet to which I returned three times. The practice lay mostly in the slums of that great city, and I certainly saw a large variety of character and of life, such as I could hardly have known so intimately in any other way.

"The one trouble to me in this arrangement of my life was that I had no means of gratifying the love of athletics which was very strong within me. I used to box a good deal, for that consumed little time; but my cricket and football were neglected. I can say, however, that I have played for my university in both cricket and Rugby football. I had then no time or chance of being a constant player; I feel justified, therefore, in taking it out at the other end. I played a heavy match at football when I was forty-two years of age, and I still, at the age of forty-eight, play cricket twice a week. So I claim now the debts which were not paid me in my youth.

SURGEON TO AN ARCTIC WHALER.

"When I was nearly twenty-one a friend of mine who had been surgeon to a whaler in the Arctic seas told me that he was unable to return that summer, and offered me the billet. I was away for seven months in the Greenland ocean. I came of age in 80 degrees north latitude.

"This was a delightful period of my life. There are eight boats to a whaler, and the eighth, which is kept as a sort of emergency boat, is manned by the so-called 'idlers' of the ship. These consisted, in this case, of myself, the steward, the second engineer and an old seaman. But it happened that, with the exception of the veteran, we were all young and keen; and I think our boat was as good as any."

As he spoke he could not fail to remember the harpoons hanging on the staircase wall. They seemed to account for this enthusiasm. He went on:

" One of the truest compliments I ever had paid me in my life was when the captain offered to make me the harpooner as well as surgeon if I would come for another year. When you think that a whale was then worth some £2,000 and that hit or miss depends on the nerve of the harpooner, I am proud to think that the skipper, old John Grey, should have offered me such a post.

"On returning home from the Arctic I took my degree, having been thrown back one year by the fact of going North. I was twenty-two when I qualified, and, thanks to my numerous assistantships, had a very varied experience behind me.

DOWN THE WEST AFRICAN COAST.

"Almost immediately afterward I was offered the post of surgeon to a steamer going down the west coast of Africa. I was again most fortunate in my captain, and the voyage was a delightful one. We were away four months and the pleasure of my experience was only marred by my getting the rather virulent fever which prevails on that coast. Two of us got it, and the other man died, so that I suppose I may call myself lucky.

"On my return to England I settled in practice, first in Plymouth and then, after a few months, at Southsea, the fashionable suburb of Portsmouth. My adventures in that rather romantic period, and all my mental and spiritual aspirations, are written down in 'The Stark Munro Letters', a book which, with the exception of one chapter, is a very close autobiography.

"In this period my literary tendencies had slowly developed. During the years of my studentship my life was so full of work that, though I read a great deal, I had little time to cultivate writing. After starting in practice, however, I had much—too much—time on my hands; and then I began to write voluminously.

"Most of it was, I think, pretty poor stuff; but it was apprentice work, and I always hoped that with practice I might learn to use my tools.

"FINDING HIMSELF" IN LITERATURE.

"Every writer is imitative at first. I think that is an absolute rule; though sometimes he throws back on some model which is not easily traced. My early work, as I look back on it, was a sort of debased composite photograph in which five or six different styles were contending for the mastery. Stevenson was a strong influence; so was Bret Harte; so was Dickens; so were several others.

"Eventually, however, a man 'finds himself,' or rather perhaps it is that he grows more deft in concealing the influences which blend with one another until they form what means a new and constant style.

"I suppose that during those early years I wrote not less than fifty short stories. The first appeared in 1878 while I was still a student. It was in Chambers's Journal and was called 'The Mystery of the Sassassa Valley'. I had three guineas for it. After receiving that little check I was like a beast that has once tasted blood, for I knew that whatever rebuffs I might receive—and God knows I had plenty—I had once proved I could earn gold, and the spirit was in me to do it again. It was a delightful opportunity for carrying into actuality the dreams of my youth. I had to earn money by some form of work, and that was the sort of work I longed to do.

TEN YEARS OF ANONYMITY

"For ten years I wrote short stories; roughly, from 1877 to 1887. During that time I do not think I ever earned £50 in any year by my pen, though I worked incessantly. Nearly all the magazines published the stories anonymously—a most iniquitous fashion by which all chance of promotion is barred to young writers. The best of these stories have since been published in the volume called The Captain of the Pole Star! Sometimes I saw my stories praised by critics, but the criticism never came to my address. The Cornhill Magazine, Temple Bar and London Society were the chief magazines in which my stories appeared.

"Finally in 1887 I wrote A Study in Scarlet, the first book which introduced Sherlock Holmes. I don't know how I got that name. I was looking the other day at a bit of paper on which I had scribbled 'Sherringford Holmes' and 'Sherrington Hope' and all sorts of other combinations. Finally at the bottom of the paper I had written 'Sherlock Holmes'. 'A Study in Scarlet' appeared in a Christmas number of Beeton's Annual. The book had no particular success at the time, though many people have been good enough to read it since.

"MICAH CLARKE" AND "THE WHITE COMPANY".

"My next book was 'Micah Clarke,' a historical novel. This met with a good reception from the critics and the public; and from that time onward I had no further difficulty in disposing of my manuscripts. When two years later I wrote 'The White Company' I felt that my position was strong enough to enable me to give up practice. I still clung to my profession, for I came to London and started as an oculist. After six months, however, this also seemed unnecessary, and I finally retired. I have not indulged in my profession since, except when I went campaigning."

That he did good service in that noble profession in the South African war is attested not only by his book on the record of the Langman Hospital, but by a noble silver bowl which stands at a corner of his house in Hind-head, on which is inscribed:

"To Arthur Conan Doyle, who at a great crisis—in word and deed— served his country."

When he had come to the part in his history where he had started his bark on the sea of literature, I think he considered that his duty with regard to the interview. In obedience to my request, however, he went on. I wished that the American people might hear some special comment on their own affairs:

DOYLE'S AMERICAN TOUR

"In 1894 I went on a lecturing tour to America. I had no hopes of any success in the matter; my idea was simply to see a country in which I took a deep interest, and to pay my expenses while I was so doing. Major Pond, however, in his enthusiastic way fixed up a considerable programme for me, so that I was forced to do rather more than to pay my expenses and rather less in the way of seeing the country. I was there, all told, between four and five months, and the fact that I was lecturing had the one advantage that it took me into some of the byways and smaller towns that I should not have otherwise visited.

"I came away from America with a deep admiration for both the country and the people; and much touched by all the kindness and even affection which I had encountered. It has left a lasting impression on my mind which the lapse of thirteen years has in no way effaced. I want to go again without having any work to do, and I want to go out West and Southwest. One feels that society with its highly organised life is to some degree the same everywhere throughout the world, but that the real distinctive America is that portion which is still finding itself, as it were, and has not yet set into its final form.

"I read Wells's book on the subject the other day; it seemed to me to be very deep and very suggestive. I should think that Americans need not mind frank criticism from such a man as he, for his own mind is essentially democratic and American.

"But the fact is that these various dangers and drawbacks which one sees— the dangers of the great trusts—the dangers of violent labor unions— the dangers of the multi-millionaire—the dangers of individual character and violence becoming too strong for the organised legal machinery of the community—all these things are probably prominent problems to be solved by the human race, and only showing up in America because things move faster there and are on a large scale. But always behind the turmoil are ranked the millions of steady, solid, law-supporting citizens; and one knows that in the end all will be well.

"As I am speaking of America I remember one incident that comes back vividly to my mind. When I was there a strong wave of anti-British feeling was passing over the country. It was not shown offensively to the stranger within their gates, but one could hardly pick up any sort of newspaper without reading what was painful and usually untrue about one's country. On one occasion at Detroit this feeling showed on the surface. A small supper was given to me by some kind and hospitable friends at a club there. We looked upon the wine when it was red, and at a late stage of the evening, politics having come up, one of the company made a speech in which he made a severe attack upon Great Britain. I asked my friend Robert Barr, who was in the chair, to allow me to answer the attack. This I did, speaking my mind out of the fulness of my heart. I think no one who was present could fail to have been surprised at the way in which after events bore out my remarks. What I said practically was:

"'You Americans have lived, up to now, within a ring fence of your own. Your country has become so vast, and you have so much to do in peopling it and opening it out, that you have never had to think seriously of outside international politics, and you have lived to some extent in a world of prejudice and of dreams. This period is now drawing swiftly to an end. Your country is filling up, and soon you will have surplus energies which will lead you on into world politics and bring you into closer actual relationships with the other powers. Then your friendships and your enmities will be guided, not by prejudice nor by hereditary dislikes, but by actual practical issues. When that days comes—and it is coming soon—you will find that the only people who will understand you—who will see what your aims are and who will heartily sympathise with you in them, are your own people, the men from whom you are sprung. In a great world-crisis you will find that you have no natural friend among the nations save your own kin; and to the last they will always be at your side!'

"Well, within three years came the Spanish war—the suggested European coalition against America—the strong attitude of Great Britain upon the subject. It was as good an illustration as one could desire of the prediction which I had made in my speech.

"We know very well on this side that if the case were reversed and we ourselves had to look for sympathy and understanding, all minor contentions would vanish in an instant and we should find a strong and true friend by our side."

A HAPPY ANNOUNCEMENT

One little personal piece of information was given by Sir Arthur Conan Doyle which may make a fitting conclusion to this interview. It was the news of his approaching marriage. Sir Arthur is engaged to a young lady, Miss Jean Leckie of Crowborough, to whom he is to be married in September. His face lit up as he finished: "I am the most lucky of men. May I be worthy of my good fortune.

THE VICTORIAN DETECTIVE: SHERLOCK HOLMES IN CONTEXT

In its origins, the detective method is closely connected with early Romantic ideas about the nature of the imagination. As we have seen, Edgar Allan Poe set the precedent of the detective as an impure rationalist; and it has frequently been pointed out how the methods of Dupin and his disciple Holmes rely not on deduction, but induction. This is a method which requires the mind to make certain leaps of the imagination.

The classic example of the detective psychology can be witnessed in the famous mind-reading episode, which Conan Doyle took from Poe and adapted in 'The Adventure of the Cardboard Box." Dupin is fascinated by that same element of the irrational and bizarre that characterises the Sherlock Holmes stories. The detective faith is founded on the maxim that "once you have eliminated the impossible, whatever remains, however improbable, must be the truth", and the detective, by temperament, ignores the normal social conventions. Thus the narrator of Poe's story describes his friend's odd conduct in the story of 'The Murders in the Rue Morgue.'

'At the first dawn of the morning we closed all the massive shutters of our old building, lighting a couple of tapers which, strongly perfumed threw out only the ghastliest and feeblest of rays. By the aid of these we then busied our souls in dreams-reading, writing, or conversing, until warned by the clock of the advent of darkness. Then we sallied forth into the streets, arm in arm, continuing the topics of the day, or roaming far and wide until a late hour, seeking amid the wild lights of the city that infinity of mental excitement which quiet observation can afford.'

The whole *fin de siécle* atmosphere has been vividly prefigured by Poe in this passage; and the latent elements of this atmosphere were to flourish magnificently in the euphoric character of Sherlock Holmes. The natural order has been reversed, and the detective is described as one whose interest lies in the perverser fringes of humanity. While inactive, the detective "busies his soul" with the stuff of dreams by means of opium or cocaine (Holmes was an inveterate drug addict). But while active, he assumes a kind of Wanderlust; a restless spirit of social inquiry consumes him. He paces the streets of the city. In such moments he completely identifies with the morality and the angst of his society.

In the later Victorian detective, the man of common sense and practical acuteness, characterised by Wilkie Collins and Dickens, gives way to a much more complex personality. The later detective is a civilized gentleman and a dandy who flirts with *fin de siécle* aestheticism. Whereas Holmes is an eccentric Bohemian who keeps his tobacco in the Persian slipper, Dickens' Sergeant Cuff in Dickens' early novel, 'Bleak House', has no time for fanciful ideas or speculative theories about the fate or nature of Mankind. By contrast with Holmes, he is a down-to-earth pragmatist.

"If we could fly out of that window hand in hand (says Holmes), hover over this great city, gently remove roofs, and peep in at the queer things which are going on, the strange coincidences, the plannings, the cross-purposes, the wonderful chains of events, working through generations, and leading to the most outre results, it would make all fiction with its conventionalities and foreseen conclusions most stale and unprofitable."

The detective story thrived on the sensibility of the age, in order to preserve the values that it believed in. The detective is an instrument of control, armed with the newly- emergent science of the age and with its liberal hopes, and he sits like a moral guardian at the very centre of the Victorian consciousness. Here was a rich character, a persona of his author but with a flexible, autonomous existence that was not entirely dependent on the other more manipulated characters of the narrative. In this way, the detective represented a new challenge to the strict conception of character which had previously dominated the novel. The convention, observed on the whole by writers like Dickens and Thackeray, showed a marked degree of stylisation.

Dickens' novels are especially interesting in the peculiarly unreal and somewhat grotesque nature of their characters. Dressed in a distinctive manner, with a particular eccentricity of speech to offer, a Dickens character approaches the nature of a formula that can be set to work at the author's will.

A convention such as this shows a refusal to deal realistically or at any depth with the inner lives and motivations of human beings. Dickens' world is invariably a world of surfaces and symbols, where characters only act to prove who they are, though I would point out that this is not strictly true of 'Oliver Twist,' where the sharp social observation which begins with the intended corruption of the innocent young Twist by Fagin and Sykes, ends horrifically and viciously with the vicarious and senseless beating to death of Sykes' girlfriend, Nancy. The detective, however, was not responsible for any major changes in the Victorian conventions about plot. If anything, he served to reinforce them.

The plot of a mid-Victorian novel frequently asserts the existence of an unbreakable chain of consequences. Such a convention assures the author and reader that any moral action will be complemented by its just conclusion. Characters who transgress the moral order fall prey to a series of fatalities, as in all truly Gothic novel, and the detective novel, as we see most sharply revealed in the detective fiction of Edgar Allan Poe, is essentially Gothic both in tone and in structure. A mere glance also at Conan Doyle's early, but far less successful offering of his 'Mystery of Cloomber', also illustrates this point. Here, in 'Cloomber,' however, Doyle does not yet have and has not invented his detective, the man of scientific reason and moral order, to show us the moral imperative at work.

The detective works to preserve this moral order. The plot of the detective novel operates in reverse, from the occasion of the crime, and in reading the crime novel, the author is asking us to rationalise the event. In a modern context, the detective may be seen as the *psychoanalytical attempt to reconcile individuals to society.*

The detective succeeds most in his enquiries, when he is able to manipulate the guilty feelings of his subjects. 'The Moonstone' shows this method working to its best effect. The problem of guilt which always surrounds the heart of the mystery, often derives from the idea of the curse, a theme that recurs persistently in the Victorian detective novel. (The most popular example of this is 'The Hound of The Baskervilles'.)

The idea of the curse was, of course, not new to nineteenth century literature. Wordsworth and Coleridge ('The Ancient Mariner,') had both given the subject a Romantic treatment. The Romantic notion is that the curse originates from a sin that is committed against the natural and moral order of the universe. The killing of the albatross in 'The Ancient Mariner' is the most famous example. The curse owes something to the Christian notion of Original Sin. 'The sin of the father will be visited on the children.' and it is believed that the only hope of deliverance lies in a reconciliation with natural forces. The curse theme eventually found its way into the detective fiction of the nineteenth century, where it was dealt with in a more realistic context.

It is clear from an examination of the conventions of the Victorian novel that there was a vast territory of the mind that the major writers of the age felt they were incapable of exploring. These conventions helped to maintain what has been called an 'official consciousness'. Steven Marcus has shown in his now often regarded masterpiece of mid-Victorian attitudes to sexual pleasure and conventional views about the erotic, 'The Other Victorians,' how the massive expansion of pornography during the period arose from these writers' inability to deal with the rapid change of sexual roles that the age was undergoing.

The Victorian consciousness was quite unprepared to discuss those areas of the psyche associated with the irrational and subconscious, except in the examples we have of its Gothic fiction. But in both the underground pornography of the time and in its expanding popular fiction, there was a constant awareness of what the political or moral consciousness often feared to discuss.

As we shall see in the concluding essay of this collection, Robert L. Stevenson described this situation of a split consciousness in 'The Strange Case of Dr. Jekyll and Mr. Hyde.' Dr. Jekyll is (like Dr. Watson) a man of normal and conventional sensibility; respectable, rational and morally sound; prior, that is until the commencement of his chemical and biological experiments. But, as the reader is soon to discover, unable to reconcile private desires with public duty, he witnesses the whole moral order of which he is an important representative, crumble into chaotic confusion.

What is then unleashed is the grotesque immergence of a monster of primitive desire, a creature with a phenomenal capacity for hatred, and who delights in [23] acts of seemingly vicarious and sadistic pleasure. And so the suppressed forces that lay in wait in Dr. Jekyll now roam unleashed and unchecked, in the desperate and morally abandoned Mr. Hyde.

'Dr. Jekyll and Mr. Hyde' and Poe's 'Murders in the Rue Morgue' both deal with a recurrent theme in the detective story- the brutal and seemingly motiveless murder landscape of much of the best of our 20th century crime

---

[23] Lecter is a serial killer who eats his victims. Before his capture, he was a respected forensic psychiatrist; after his incarceration, he is consulted by FBI agents Will Graham and Clarice Starling to help them find other serial killers .Lecter first appeared in a small role as a villain in Harris' 1981 thriller novel 'Red Drago.'

writers, but more markedly in the bleak depictions of modern psychotic villains in, for example, the early crime novels of Ruth Rendell, and the motiveless murder of innocent victims in the hideously convincing Hannibal Lecter series.

The senseless and unmitigated violence of these vicious acts of savage murder is always emphasised, and this is no less apparent at the birth of the crime genre in Poe's 'Murders In The Rue Morgue.' Mr. Hyde also sets about his victim with an 'ape-like fury' while Poe's ape severs a woman's head in a paroxysm of fury, which is never provided with a rational explanation.

The perverse crime frequently introduces animal or barbaric forces as an agency for the crime's accomplishment; and the more perverse the crime, the more bizarre is the agent. The Holmes stories have a list that would fill a grotesque menagerie, ranging from a giant rat to a worm that induces insanity.

'The Speckled Band,' perhaps the classic Holmes story, and considered by Doyle as his favourite of the series, describes the attempt of Dr. Grimesby Roylott, an incestuous and phallic villain in both his behaviour and appearance, to destroy both his step-daughters, through means of a ventilator, that connects his own room with theirs. He is able thus to unleash a swamp adder on them to gain his financial control of their inheritances. The second stepdaughter is spared her gruesome fate as Holmes lies in wait in her room and beats the snake back through the ventilator. The creature subsequently attacks and kills its master. The overtones of this story are fairly explicit; what is very important is the role of the detective as a moral agent and his psychological relationship to the author and his society. The forces being dealt with in stories such as this one are irrational, terrifying and uncontrollable. None of the authors I have discussed feel they can allow these subliminal forces their full reign. The ape must be brought back to captivity, the snake beaten through the ventilator, and the Hyde in Dr. Jekyll extinguished. And the detective provides the expiation of these irrational forces. Thus, the detective can be seen as a mythic figure in the late Victorian mind. While embodying their aspirations, he became in the imaginations of his creators and in the collective subconsciousness of the Victorians, many of which provided for these stories' female readers, a superhuman moral force, working out the conflicting drives of a divided consciousness; and often attempting to reconcile reason with desire. So Holmes still lives on, as a perpetual ideal of moral good, a chivalric knight, vanquishing the dark shadowlands of the Victorian mind.

COINERS AND CRACKSMEN OF THE CANON

It is with little surprise that we discover a large number of burglars and forgers crossing the path of Mr Sherlock Holmes. The age during which he embarked on his illustrious career was confronted by both types of criminal in numbers that it had probably never before witnessed. The forger (or coiner) flourished because of the proliferation of reproduction processes that had burst upon the world of the Victorians from as far back as the 1860s, thus making the duplication of documents all the easier to perform, whilst the wild spread of suburbia north and south of the Thames made the task of the cracksman more challenging than ever before.

Although the investigation of forgery occupies a central place in only one of the sixty adventures recorded by Dr Watson (ENGR) it is clear from inference that Holmes had a number of other dealings with a variety of forgers active during the 80s and 90s. As far back as 1881, Holmes advised Lestrade on the details of one such case, then being handled by the 800-strong C.I.D. The detective branch of the Metropolitan police had been experiencing a rough ride. Three chief inspectors had got into the toils of a gang of betting swindlers, and suffered criminal convictions in 1877; and recently the plain-clothes division had experienced an influx of 'better educated' types, many of them accepted because of their linguistic abilities. This clearly did not extend to the likes of Tobias Gregson for whom the word 'RACHE' meant an abbreviation of Rachel and not the German for 'revenge'. The C.I.D. was then young in years and experience, and therefore Holmes was clearly a useful court of appeal. Lestrade had 'got himself into a fog recently over a forgery case' and Holmes had come to the rescue. Later Holmes was himself to investigate the Conk-Singleton forgery case (SIXN), and the activities of John Clay (REDH),

Archie Stamford (SOLI), Arthur H. Staunton (MISS) and Victor Lynch were all guilty of the crime. Forgery (defined as 'the fraudulent alteration of writing to the prejudice of another man's rights') was common enough among the lesser criminals.

There was a great trade in faked testimonials and the marking of watches and jewellery. But as regards forgery proper, i.e. the manufacturing of phoney cheques, bank notes and coinage, this was carried out by a small band of highly skilled criminals.

It is with little surprise therefore that we discover a large number of burglars and forgers crossing the path of Mr Sherlock Holmes. The age during which he embarked on his illustrious career was confronted by both types of criminal in numbers that it had probably never before witnessed.

Forgery (defined as 'the fraudulent alteration of writing to the prejudice of another man's rights') was common enough among the experts. John Clay and Victor Lynch, who remained quite aloof from the actual distribution of the currency undoubtedly belong to this category.

The coiners who manufactured the 'hard' currency worked hand in glove with the 'smashers' or 'utterers' who up and down the country distributed the false coinage into the general currency. Fairs and country markets were an obvious place to unload large quantities of the stuff. Silver currency was the favourite commodity since it offered its practitioners an easier fake than gold and it was the main product of Dr Becher, the accomplice of Colonel Lysander Stark. Stark's remote house in the Esher countryside with its huge hydraulic press designed to create the amalgam used as a substitute for silver was typical of the coiner's practice. Silver coining wasn't an easy business and usually required a team of skilled workmen to perform it. According to Inspector Bradstreet, the Becher gang 'have been turning out half crowns by the thousand' and were 'coiners on a large scale.'

There were a number of different alternatives available. The traditional system involved making a counterfeit out of a metal plate and then impressing it with a hammer and die. The flats were then treated with nitric acid to produce a silvery surface. Coins could also be struck from pewter. But both these processes took time and were laborious. Silver plated coins made from bronze medallions soon supplanted them. An alloy made from tin, copper and a small amount of antimony was employed; and this was then cast into a plaster of Paris mould. Each mould was made in two halves and these had to fit exactly to make the facsimile coin convincing.

Once the castings had been prepared in this way they were then connected to the negative lead of a battery and immersed in a solution of cyanide, where a piece of silver, connected to the battery's positive lead was also placed. The silver then transferred itself in a thin deposit to the surface of the coins.

From a reading of 'The Engineer's Thumb,' it is apparent that Dr Becher was employing a system somewhat similar to this, although with the added refinement of a hydraulic press. The walls of his house , it will be remembered, were of wood, but the floor consisted of a 'large iron trough'. When Victor Hatherly came to examine it, he discovered 'a crust of metallic deposit all over it'. Probably the coins were placed in the trough, covered in a solution of acid and then subjected to an electrical current when the press made contact.

The forging of paper money earns but scant attention in the Canon, but it is probable that John Clay and Victor Lynch were both involved in the process. The chief place of production for forged bank notes was Birmingham. From there, they were brought in bulk to London, where they were intermittently distributed. The reproduction of a Bank of England note was no real problem. The ink and design could be exactly copied, but the essential problem lay in obtaining the special paper, manufactured by the Bank's own paper mills. At one such establishment (Laverstoke Mill in Hampshire) the security was lax enough to enable a man and wife team, the Burnetts, to filch as much as three hundred sheets. The Burnetts, whose accomplice, (a worker at the mill) was suspected and confessed to his complicity in the crime, were eventually traced to London where they were arrested by the City police.

But it was the forging of cheques that offered the most promising opportunities to the aspiring criminal. Cheque forgery (of which Count Negretto Sylvius was a willing exponent in MAZA) was both simple to arrange and lucrative to carry out once the cheque book itself had been purloined. In the Victorian age cheques were not, as now, individually numbered and hallmarked, so cheque fraud depended on finding a customer of that bank with a big enough bank account. Usually cheque 'sharps', as they were called in the underworld, worked in pairs; the Beddington brothers were typical of this arrangement (STOC).

The most secure method was to employ a third person who, under the impression that he was working for a respectable partnership, carried out the villains' intentions quite unwittingly.An advertisement was placed in a newspaper offering employment to a junior clerk at a high rate of salary. He was then interviewed at a suite of vacant offices, introduced to his prospective employer and sent out with the dud cheque to the bank, where he was asked to cash it. Having done this, he handed the money over to the employer and returned the next day, only to discover that all trace of the business had vanished.

This use of a stooge was the trademark both of John Clay, who used Mr Jabez Wilson as a 'front' to his attempted robbery of the City Suburban Bank (his job was to copy out the A's of the Encyclopaedia Britannica), and the Beddington brothers who employed Hall Pycroft to copy out a Paris trade directory.

The unfortunate Victor Hatherley, thus loses a thumb as the result of becoming an unwitting participant in the coining operation of the psychotic and mysterious Dr Lysander Stark.

Beddington's clever use of Pycroft's handwriting in order to impersonate the young stockbroker's clerk reveals him as an expert in the art of forgery, a gift that enabled him to rob the firm of Mawson and Williams of a hundred thousand pounds-worth of American railway bonds. This was big money and scores high in the annals of forgery. As business expanded and larger amalgams were formed, forgery, embezzlement and fraud became both easier and more popular.

As far back as the 1860s, for instance, Leopold Redpath obtained £150,000 through forgeries on the Great Northern Railways Company and another man, Beaumont Smith, produced £350,000 of fake exchequer bonds. But the risks were grave. In the face of a life sentence or transportation for life it is not surprising that Beddington's brother should attempt to hang himself.

Burglary was an altogether more common crime among the lower criminal classes and proved to be a major headache for the police force of the 1880s and 90s. Charlie Peace, whom Holmes eulogised about (ILLU) and claimed was a great artist, was perhaps outstanding in the field and noted for the daring quality of his crimes. He had in fact been arrested and tried long before Holmes commenced his career and was active mainly in the Blackheath area, after shooting a Blackheath constable and was ultimately executed for a murder in Sheffield some two years previously.

By the time 'A Study In Scarlet' appeared in in 'Beeton's Christmas Annual', so many burglars were armed either with revolvers or clubs, that revolver drill was instigated among the Metropolitan police and all policemen on night duty in the outer area of the city were allowed to carry stout sticks, a situation which led the satirical Mr Punch to comment:

'Now Robert has a pistol,
Just like William Sykes's hobby,
So Bobby is a match for Bill,
And ten to one on Bobby!'

The burglars in the Canon number many. Among the more infamous gangs were the Randalls, a father and two sons team who operated in the vicinity of Lewisham and Sydenham (ABBE), and the Beddington brothers, already mentioned. John Clay was an expert cracksman and the notorious Stapleton was suspected of several break-ins further afield than Devonshire.

The fraternity of the gang was apparently common among cracksmen at this time. According to the historian Chesney 'the most successful cracksmen tended to live in more or less respectable districts and sometimes in a style that the most prosperous pick-pocket could hardly rise to, these masters of the craft kept servants, ate and drank luxuriously, enjoying the 'choicest wines' and adorned their women extravagantly'.

The gang itself was an amalgam of different types and a fairly ad hoc affair, at that. The comfortable, almost middle class = status of the cracksman himself is more than evident in the character of John Clay whose hands are 'white, almost womanly' and who protests on capture, 'I beg that you will not touch me with your filthy hands.' The 'one or two scores' that Holmes intended to settle with Clay no doubt originated from an earlier period, when his methods were no match for the elusive cracksman, whose pattern was to lay low for several weeks after a 'job' and to remain constantly mobile. It was not uncommon for certain august figures in the 'trade' to travel up and down the country as 'guest artists'. All this made the job of the official police force more difficult to perform, but for Holmes, who could adopt a variety of disguises and who had contacts among the criminal fraternity (Shinwell Johnson and Porlock, to name but two) the task was easier.

'Cracking a crib! as it was called (also the name it is affectionately referred to in REDH and REIG), or breaking and entering, involving a skilled and often a complicated procedure. As regards the techniques employed by Mr Clay and his associates, little has changed since those far off days except the substitution of electrical for manual equipment. As Holmes, a first - rate cracksman himself, realised (CHAS), the first essential was to gain inside information into the movements of a house's inhabitants, and ideally to gain a confederate on the inside. Then, it was a much easier job than today, since all the big houses which were worth 'doing' could be relied upon to possess a large staff of domestic servants. The complicity of a servant was easily gained since butlers, footmen and kitchen staff were relatively mobile and forged references easily obtainable.

Besides, these individuals were often paid low wages so that the temptation to open a door or window at a pre-arranged time of the night in exchange for a large sum of money must have seemed extremely attractive.

But even if the servant was not consciously involved in the attempted burglary, much could be gleaned from a garrulous kitchen maid regarding the movements of the premises' owners. The infatuation of Charles Augustus Milverton's maid Agatha, with Holmes, posing as a rising young plumber, Escott by name, is a good example of this particular technique of interrogation:

'I have walked out with her each evening, and I have talked with her. Good heavens, those talks! However, I got all I wanted. I know Milverton's house as I know the palm of my hand.' – Holmes.

One of the functions of the canary (although in this capacity he or she was frequently referred to as the 'crow') was to carry the cracksman's tools to and from the chosen rendezvous. The point about this was that, if caught on his way to or from the crime, charges could not be levied against him.

The carrying of burglary tools about the person at night is as much an offence as the crime of burglary itself, and in view of this, Holmes's own escapade in Hampstead appears decidedly risky. It is in fact one of the many instances where he exposes Watson to unnecessary danger (the drug-taking episode in 'The Devil's Foot' is another). It seems odd that Holmes didn't think to employ the usual method of employing a hansom cab in order to convey him swiftly back to Baker Street, for this was usual amongst cracksmen. The most common approach was to pay a cabbie a large sum for the night's services (and no questions asked), which included the precaution of using false number plates. He would then wait at some distance from the site of the break-in and drive up on a pre-arranged cue. The goods were then carried swiftly inside and conveyed to a 'fence'.In addition to his burglary of the Milverton household, Holmes also broke into the premises of Hugo Oberstein (BRUC), Baron Von Gruner (ILLU), Josiah Amberley (RETI) and Holy Peters (LADY).

It is interesting that Holmes again comments in RETI, 'Burglary has always been an alternative profession, had I cared to adopt it,' and when accused of being 'a common burglar' he replies (to Holy Peters) 'so you might describe me'. Indeed, his lawless attitude of breaking into Peters's premises without even a search warrant has not gone unnoticed by commentators. Are we to assume that Holmes was serious in describing burglary as an 'alternative profession?' Were there links in his past with the fraternity of cracksmen, including Charlie Peace himself, that he did not wish to be revealed?

These are fascinating questions to which there appear to be no immediate answers.

SHERLOCK HOLMES ON HIMSELF, CRIME, CRIMINALS AND THE ART OF DEDUCTION

Fig. 64. "I am a brain, Watson. The rest of me is a mere appendix." This self-defining comment by Sherlock Holmes, about his approach to crime and the methods he proposed, occurs in 'The Mazarin Stone'. A wonderfully evocative illustration by my esteemed friend and great Sherlockian artist, Douglas Walters, which served as the dust jacket of the elegant volume, 'Canadian Holmes: The First 25 Years', published by The Bootmakers of Toronto,

"My name is Sherlock Holmes. It is my business to know what other people do not know."

— The Adventure of the Blue Carbuncle.

"No man burdens his mind with small matters unless he has some very good reason for doing so." – A Study in Scarlet.

"No: I am not tired. I have a curious constitution. I never remember feeling tired by work, though idleness exhausts me completely."
— The Sign of Four.

"I could not rest, Watson, I could not sit quiet in my chair, if I thought that such a man as Professor Moriarty were walking the streets of London unchallenged."
-The Empty House.

"I should be very much obliged if you would slip your revolver into your pocket. An Eley's No. 2 is an excellent argument with gentlemen who can twist steel pokers into knots. That and a tooth-brush are, I think, all that we need."
- The Speckled Band.

"If a gentleman walks into my rooms smelling of iodoform, with a black mark of nitrate of silver upon his right forefinger, and a bulge on the side of his top hat to show where he has secreted his stethoscope, I must be dull indeed if I do not pronounce him to be an active member of the medical profession."
-A Scandal in Bohemia.

"It is a capital mistake to theorize before one has data. Insensibly one begins to twist facts to suit theories, instead of theories to suit facts."

-A Scandal in Bohemia.

"The strangest and most unique things are very often connected not with the larger, but with the smaller crimes, and occasionally, indeed, where there is room for doubt whether any positive crime has been committed." -The Red-headed League.

"Beyond the fact that he has at some time done manual labour, that he takes snuff, that he is a Freemason, that he has been in China, and that he has done a considerable amount of writing lately, I can deduce nothing else."

-The Red-headed League.

"It is usually in unimportant matters that there is a field for observation, and for the quick analysis of cause and effect which gives the charm to an investigation. The larger crimes are apt to be the simpler, for the bigger the crime, the more obvious, as a rule, is its motive."

- A Case of Identity.

"It is my business to know things. Perhaps I have trained myself to see what others overlook."

- A Case of Identity.

"It has long been an axiom of mine that the little things are infinitely the most important."

-A Case of Identity.

"1 can never bring you to realize the importance of sleeves, the suggestiveness of thumb-nails, or the great issues that may hang from a bootlace."

- A Case of Identity.

"Never trust to general impressions, my boy, but concentrate yourself upon details. My first glance is always at a woman's sleeve. In a man it is perhaps better first to take the knee of the trouser."

-A Case of Identity.

"I think of writing another little monograph some of these days on the typewriter and its relation to crime. It is a subject to which l have devoted some little attention."

- A Case of Identity.

"Singularity is almost invariably a clue. The more featureless and commonplace a crime is, the more difficult is it to bring it home."

- The Boscombe Valley Mystery.

"Circumstantial evidence is a very tricky thing. It may seem to point very straight to one thing, but if you shift your own point of view a little, you may find it pointing in an equally uncompromising manner to something entirely different."

-The Boscombe Valley Mystery.

"You know my method. It is founded upon the observance of trifles."

-Th¢ Boscombe Valley Mystery.

"The ideal reasoner would, when he has once been shown a single fact in all its bearings, deduce from it not only all the chain of events which led up to it, but also all the results which would follow from it. As Cuvier could correctly describe a whole animal by the contemplation of a single bone, so the observer who has thoroughly understood one link in a series of incidents, should be able accurately to state all the other ones, both before and after. We have not yet grasped the results which reason alone can attain to."

-The Five Orange Pips.

"What can you gather from this old battered felt?"
"Here is my lens. You know my methods."
"I can see nothing."
"On the contrary, Watson, you can see everything. You fail, however, to reason from what you see. You are too timid in drawing your inferences."

-The Blue Carbuncle.

"It is always awkward doing business with an alias."
  - The Blue Carbuncle.

"... Watson, I am not retained by the police to supply their deficiencies."

-The Blue Carbuncle.

Holmes: "You have come in by train this morning, I see."
Helen Stoner: "You know me, then?"
Holmes: "No, but I observe the second half of a return ticket in the palm of your left glove."

- The Speckled Band.

"When a doctor does go wrong he is the worst of criminals. He has nerve and he has knowledge. Palmer and Pritchard were among the heads of their profession."

243

- The Speckled Band.

"I had come to an entirely erroneous conclusion, which shows, my dear Watson, how dangerous it always is to reason from insufficient data."

-The Speckled Band.

"Circumstantial evidence is occasionally very convincing, as when you find a trout in the milk, to quote Thoreau's example."

-The Noble Bachelor.

"It is an old maxim of mine that when you have excluded the impossible, whatever remains, however improbable, must be the truth."

- The Beryl Coronet.

"You have given prominence not so much to the many *causes célébres* and sensational trials in which I have figured, but rather to those incidents which may have been trivial in themselves, but which have given room for those faculties of deduction and of logical synthesis which I have made my special province."

-The Copper Beeches.

"Crime is common. Logic is rare. Therefore it is upon the logic rather than upon the crime that you should dwell."

-The Copper Beeches.

"The days of the great cases are past. Man, or at least criminal man, has lost all enterprise and originality. As to my own little practice, it seems to be degenerating into an agency for recovering lost lead pencils and giving advice to young ladies from boarding-schools."

-The Copper Beeches.

"My dear Watson, you as a medical man are continually gaining light as to the tendencies of a child by the study of the parents. Don't you see that the converse is equally valid? I have frequently gained my first real insight into the character of parents by studying their children."

-The Copper Beeches

"

Fig. 66. The arrest of the murderer, Wainwright, who murdered his grl friend, then dissected her, sealing her body parts into tubs, which then leaked on the high road. He is pictured here, posing to police as an innocent bystander, indicating the trail of blood, from the cab carrying her body parts. One of several murderers mentioned by Holmes..

"It is my belief, Watson, formed upon my experience, that the lowest and vilest alleys in London do not present a more dreadful record of sin than does the smiling and beautiful countryside… There is no lane so vile that the scream of a tortured child, or the thud of a drunkard's blow, does not beget sympathy and indignation among the neighbours, and then the whole machinery of justice is ever so close that a word of complaint can set it going, and there is but a step between the crime and the dock. But look at these lonely houses, each in its own fields, filled for the most part with poor ignorant folk who know little of the law. Think of the deeds of hellish cruelty, the hidden wickedness which may go on, year in, year out, in such places, and none the wiser."

- The Copper Beeches.

"It has always been my habit to hide none of my methods, either from my friend Watson, or from anyone who might take an intelligent interest in them."

-The Reigate Squires.

"You may not be aware that the deduction of a man's age from his writing is one which has been brought to considerable accuracy by experts."

- The Reigate Squires.

Holmes: "I clambered over the fence into the grounds."
Percy Phelps: "Surely the gate was open?"
Holmes: "Yes, but I have a peculiar taste in these matters."

- The Naval Treaty.

"Elementary. It is one of those instances when the reasoner can produce an effect which seems remarkable to his neighbour, because the latter has missed the one little point which is the basis of the deduction."

-The Crooked Man.

"You come at a crisis, Watson. If this paper remains blue, all is well. If it turns red, it means a man's life."

- The Naval Treaty.

"There is something in common between these hands. They belong to men who are blood relatives. It may be obvious to you in the Greek 'e's, but to me there are many smaller points which indicate the same thing. I have no doubt that a family mannerism can be traced in these two specimens of writing".

- The Reigate Squires.

"There is no one who knows the higher criminal world of London so well as I do. For years past I have continually been conscious of some power behind the malefactor, some deep organizing power which for ever stands in the way of the law, and throws its shield over the wrong-doer."

- The Final Problem.

"Your neighbour is a doctor?" he said, nodding at the brass plate.
"Yes. He bought a practice, as I did."
"An old, established one?"
"Just the same as mine. Both have been, ever since the houses were built."
"Ah, then you got hold of the better of the two."
"I think I did."
"But how do you know?" '
"By the steps, my boy. Yours are worn three inches deeper than his."

-The Stockbroker's Clerk.

"Well, we may save the police some little trouble in that direction," said Holmes, glancing up at the haggard figure huddled up by the window. "Human nature is a strange mixture, Watson. You see that even a villain and a murderer can inspire such affection that his brother turns to suicide when he learns that his neck is forfeited...."

- The Stockbroker's Clerk.

"From the point of view of the criminal expert, London has become a singularly uninteresting city since the death of the. late lamented Professor Moriarty ... the community is certainly the gainer, and no one the loser, save the poor out-of-work specialist, whose occupation has gone. With that man in the field one's morning paper presented infinite possibilities."

- The Norwood Builder.

Fig 67. 'The late, lamented Moriarty,' as Holmes ironically describes his foe, seen here in the steely grip of his nemesis and adversary, as they tussle at the edge of the awesome precipice of The Reichenbach Falls. Drawing by Sidney Paget from 'The Final Problem', which appeated in 'The Strand Magazine.'

"The faculty of deduction is certainly contagious, Watson."

- Thor Bridge.

"I can discover facts, Watson, but I cannot change them."

-Thor Bridge.

"It is not really difficult to construct a series of inferences, each dependent upon its predecessor and each simple itself. If, after doing so, one simply knocks out all the central inferences and presents one's audience with the starting-point and the conclusion, one may produce a startling, though possibly a meretricious, effect."

-The Dancing Men.

"Every problem becomes very childish when once it is explained to you."

-The Dancing Men.

"I am fairly familiar with all forms of secret writings, and am myself the author of a trifling monograph upon the subject, in which I analyse one hundred and sixty separate ciphers; but I confess that this is entirely new to me."

- The Dancing Men.

"A bicycle certainly, but not *the* bicycle. I am familiar with forty-two different impressions left by tyres."

-The Priory School.

"One should always look for a possible alternative and provide against it. It is the first rule of criminal investigation."

-Black Peter.

"l would ask you, how could one compare the ruffian who in hot blood bludgeons his mate, with this man, who methodically and at his leisure tortures the soul and wrings the nerves in order to add to his already swollen money-bags?"

- Charles Augustus Milverton.

"You know, Watson, I don't mind confessing to you that I have always had an idea that I would have made a highly efficient criminal... See here. This is a first-class, up-to-date burgling kit, with nickel-plated jemmy, diamond-tipped glass cutter, adaptable keys, and every modern improvement which the march of civilisation demands."

-Charles Augustus Milverton.

"I think there are certain crimes which the law cannot touch, and which therefore, to some extent, justify private revenge."

-Charles Augustus Milverton.

"l propose to devote my declining years to the composition of a textbook which shall focus the whole art of detection into one volume."

-The Abbey Grange.

"Perhaps when a man has special knowledge and special powers like my own, it rather encourages him to seek a complex explanation when a simpler one is at hand."

-The Abbey Grange.

"You will remember, Watson, how the dreadful business of the Abemetty family was first brought to my notice by the depth which the parsley had sunk into the butter on a hot day."

-The Six Napoleons.

"I choose to be only associated with those crimes which present some difficulty in their solution."

-The Cardboard Box.

"Look out of this window, Watson. See how the figures loom up, are dimly seen, and then blend once more into the cloud-bank. The thief or the murderer could roam London on such a day as the tiger does the jungle, unseen until he pounces, and then evident only to his victim."

- The Bruce-Partington Plans.

"It is fortunate for this community that I am not a criminal ... Suppose that I were Brooks or Woodhouse, or any of the fifty men who have good reason for taking my life, how long could I survive against my oum pursuit? A summons, a bogus appointment, and all would be over. It is well they don't have days of fog in the Latin countries - the countries of assassination."

-The Bruce-Partington Plans.

"When you follow two separate chains of thought, Watson, you will find some point of intersection which should approximate to the truth."

-The Disappearance of Lady Frances Carfax.

"A complex mind - all great criminals have that. My old friend Charlie Peace was a violin virtuoso. Wainwright was no mean artist."

-The Illustrious Client.

"I have been down to see friend Lestrade at the Yard. There may be an occasional want of imaginative intuition down there, but they lead the world for thoroughness and method".

The Three Garridebs.

"How often have I said to you that when you have eliminated the impossible, whatever remains, however improbable, must be the truth?"
-The Sign of Four.

"I never make exceptions. An exception disproves the rule."

-The Sign of Four.

"Like all other arts, the Science of Deduction and Analysis is one which can only be acquired by long and patient study, nor is life long enough to allow any mortal to attain the highest possible perfection in it."

-The Sign of Four.

"By a man's finger-nails, by his coat-sleeve, by his boots, by his trouser-legs, by the callosities of his forefinger and thumb, by his expression, by his shirt-cuffs.By each of these things a man's calling is plainly revealed."

-The Sign of Four.

"I am the last and highest court of appeal in detection."

-The Sign of Four.

"Detection is, or ought to be, an exact science, and should be treated in the same cold and unemotional manner. You have attempted to tinge it with romanticism, which produces much the same effect as if you worked a love-story or an elopement into the fifth proposition of Euclid".

-The Sign of Four.

"No doubt you think that you are complimenting me in comparing me to Dupin.. Now, in my opinion, Dupin was a very inferior fellow... he had some analytical genius, no doubt; but he was by no means such a phenomenon as Poe appeared to imagine."

-A Study in Scarlet.

"Lecoq was a miserable bungler-he had only one thing to recommend him, and that was his energy."

-A Study in Scarlet.

"There are no crimes and no criminals in these days. What is the use of having brains in our profession? I know well that I have it in me to make my name famous. No man lives or has ever lived who has brought the same amount of study and of natural talent to the detection of crime which I have done. And what is the result? There is no crime to detect, or at most, some bungling villainy with a motive so transparent that even a Scotland Yard official can see through it."

-A Study in Scarlet.

"They say that genius is an infinite capacity for taking pains. It's a very bad definition, but it does apply to my work."

- A Study in Scarlet.

"It is a mistake to confound strangeness with mystery. The most commonplace crime is often the most mysterious, because it presents no new or special features from which deductions may be drawn."

- A Study in Scarlet.

"The detection of types is one of the most elementary branches of knowledge to the special expert in crime, though I confess that once when I was very young I confused the Leeds Mercury with the Western Morning News."

- The Hound of the Baskervilles.

"There is nothing more stimulating than a case where everything goes against you."

-The Hound of the Baskervilles.

"My eyes have been trained to examine faces and not their trimmings. It is the first quality of a criminal investigator that he should see through a disguise."

- The Hound of the Baskervilles.

"There are seventy-five perfumes, which it is very necessary that a criminal expert should be able to distinguish from each other."

-The Hound of the Baskervilles.

"Surely our profession…would be a drab and sordid one if we did not sometimes set the scene so as to glorify our results. The blunt accusation, the brutal tap upon the shoulder-what can one make of such a denouement? But the quick inference, the subtle trap, the clever forecast of coming events, the triumphant vindication of bold theories - are these not the pride and the justification of our life's work?"

-The Valley of Fear.

"If criminals would always schedule their movements like railway trains it would certainly be more convenient for all of us."

-The Valley of Fear.

"You can tell an old master by the sweep of his brush. I can tell a Moriarty when l see one .... "

-The Valley of F¢ar.

Inspector Gregory: "ls there any other point to which you would wish to draw my attention?"
Holmes: "To the curious incident of the dog in the night-time."
Inspector Gregory: "The dog did nothing in the night-time."
Holmes: "That was the curious incident."

   -Silver Blaze.

Holmes: "I followed you."
 "l saw no one."
Holmes: "That is what you may expect to see when follow you."

   -The Devil's Foot.

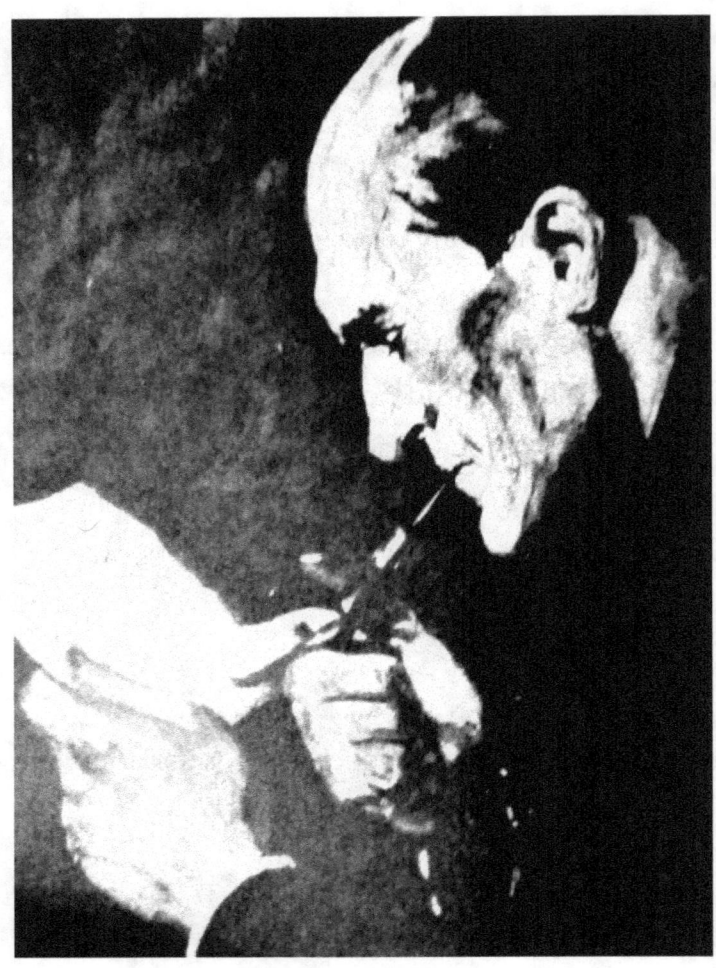

Fig. 68. Holmes examines a cryptogram in 'The Valley of Fear.' Illustration by Frank Wiles. From 'The Strand Magazine.'

The Criminal World of Sherlock Holmes, Volume 3.
List of and further comments on the illustrations.

1. Sherlock Holmes with the 'official police force,' i.e., the able detective, Inspector Bradstreet, in 'The Valley of Fear'' (first part), in 'The Strand Magazine' in 1914; illustrated by Frank Wyles. Title page.

2 Arthur Conan Doyle, who, in the 1880s, successfully reconstructed the popular short crime story. Public domain photograph, showing the newly successful crime author. Page 2.

3. Edgar Allan Poe, the Amercan genius and inventor of the detective story, who first defined its format, and which Conan Doyle was then able both to develop and refine. Public domain photo. Page 3.

4. Front jacket cover of 'A Study in Scarlet', no date. Author's collection, p.6.

5. Police quelling a political riot in 1866. Illustration from 'Mysteries of Police and Crime' by Arthur Griffiths 1904, volume 1. Page 9.

6. Detectives on trial at the Old Bailey London. From Arthur Griffiths' 'Mysteries of Police and Crime'. Page 11.

7. Courtroom drama in the trial of the fraudulent detectives from Griffiths' 'Mysteries of Police and Crime', Vol. 1. Page 12.

8. The two detectives who were given a prison sentence for their fraudulent activities, in the famous 'detectives on trial' episode; from Griffiths' 'Mysteries of Police and Crime,' Vol. 1. Page 13.

9. The old building of what used to be called 'New Scotland Yard', seen here in the 1880s; from Griffiths' 'Mysteries of Police and Crime.' Page 13.

10. The uncompromisimg Italian criminologist Cesare Lombroso. A public domain photograph. Page 15.

11. A photograph of an Italian criminal from the 1880s, from the book 'Criminal Man,' by Cesare Lombroso, the controversial Italian criminologist. Page 17

12. Portrait of an ear. Lombroso believed in the popular notion that a criminal could be identified by his ears. Page 20.

13. Rare French publication of a pamphlet by two late 19th century criminologists, influenced by Lombroso's theory about criminal 'types' and their physiogmony, describing the skulls of criminals and their identification; public domain photograph. Page 24.

14. Drawing of a naked man with tattoos. Lombroso claimed in his book that many male criminals tattooed their penises, in order to increase their criminal success rate, though he provided no convincing evidence for this assertion. An illustration from Cesare Lombroso's 'Criminal Man'. Page 29.

15. Front entrance of Cromer Hall in Cromer, Norfolk, taken in the 1880s and showing an uncanny resemblance to descriptions of Baskerville Hall. Courtesy of the Cabell family and their estate. Page 40.

16. Garrotters, shown here operating on an innocent citizen and using women, posing as prostitues, who have lured their unsuspecting victim into an alleyway. From a 'Punch' magazine illustration of the 1880s. Page 41.

17. Photograph of a Victorian cosh and the popular Webley Revolver, the tools of the Victorian garrotter. From Arthur Griffiths' book, 'Mysteries of Police and Crime'. Page 45.

18. Title page of the pioneering book on forensic crime methods, 'Criminal Investigation', published here in an English translation by Dr Hans Gross, but not until 1904; an indication of the lack of skill and expertise among British detectives, regarding scenes of crime and the handling and collation of criminal data. Page 48.

19. Public domain photograph of Arthur Conan Doyle which appeared in 'The Strand.' Like the great criminologist and contemporary of Sherlock Holmes, Hans Gross, Doyle had a library of works on criminology. He knew much about the process and empirical methods of crime investigation, and shared Dr Gross' opinion that an investigating detective should be 'possessed of a wide kowledge of poisons' and also that he should have 'a thorough knowledge of chemistry.' Page 51.

20 Late Victorian microscope of the type that Sherlock Holmes and Dr. Hans Gross undoubtedly would have used in the 1880s. Public domain image. Page 53.

21. A handwriting specimen from 'The Adventure of the Reigate Squire,' which, among additional factors, provided Sherlock Holmes with the solution to the crime. The story was published in 'The Strand Magazine' in June 1893, and is here illustrated by the popular artist, Sidney Paget, who based the profile of Holmes on his younger brother, Walter. It is also worth noting that, in his 1907 investigation into the real-life conspiracy against the Birmingham Parsee, George Edalji, arrested on the charge of horse maiming, the verdict subsequently concluded by a Birmingham magistrate was based almost exclusively on circumstantial evidence, provided by hate - mail letters. The prosecution claimed the accusations in these letters were true, regarding this young and unassuming victim of racial prejudice. Conan Doyle, like his immortal detective, Sherlock Holmes, based his own conclusions on a scientific analysis of handwriting specimens from the vitriolic letters sent to the police, and which were reluctantly provided to him by the team of Birmingham detectives who had constructed their case against the young lawyer. Thus, much to the embarrassment of the police force, Conan Doyle was able to prove without a shadow of a doubt, that the letters were unquestionably faked. Page 55.

22. Signatures of criminals taken from Cesare Lombroso's classic work on criminology, 'Criminal Man'. Page 56.

23. Unflattering picture of the young but already successful Austrian magistrate, Dr Hans Gross. Public domain photograph. Page 57.

24. Sherlock Holmes examines the curious figures in the message left to its newly wedded recipient in 'The Adventure of the Dancing Men,' shown here in 'The Strand Magazine' illustration by Sidney Paget. Page 59.

25. The pioneering German psychiatrist, Richard Krafft-Ebing, who first investigated what he then described as 'sexual perversions,' but which in modern psychiatry would now be defined as 'gender orientation'. Page 61.

26. Dr Hans Gross, seen here in his later years, and by then famous, both for his description of forensic investigation techniques and also much renowned for his teaching methods. Page 62.

27. A high precision magnifying lens of the type shown in the Holmes stories. This example is from 1888. The modern term, 'magnyfying glass' was not used in that time since it was regarded as a scientific instrument. Photo, courtesy of Debbie J. Jones. Page 63. [24]

28. Like his British colleague, Sherlock Holmes, Dr Hans Gross stressed the importance of footprints. Illustration to 'The Boscombe Valley Mystery,' published in 'The Strand Magazine.' and showing Sherlock Holmes examining footprints. Page 63.

29. Transvestite Victorian prostitute, here, posing in a burlesque type costume. Public domain photo. Page 64.

30. Mabel Gray a high-class prostitute, who had originally worked as a shop assistant in fashionable Regent Street, London. Public domain. Page 66.

31. The Canterbury Hall, a music hall, shown here in the 1880s. Music halls were most popular with the higher class of prostitute who attended performances on a regular basis. Page 67.

32. 'The Illustrated Police News' showing details of the 5th murder victim of Jack the Ripper and the crime scene in Berner Street where her body was discovere . Women like Kitty Winter suffered the threat of considerable danger during the Whitechapel murders. Page 69.

33. Mrs Ronder in 'The Adventure of the Veiled Lodger,' shown here wearing a veil to cover her disfigurement. Kitty Winter was one of several female victims of male corruption and violence in the Sherlock Holmes stories. Page 73.

---

[24] Also see note at end of this list of illustrations.

34. A vitriol throwing incident in Dudley in 1885, reported here in 'The Police News.' a case which Sherlock Holmes would certainly have known as if we are to believe Watson's comments regarding his companion's knowledge of sensational cases. Page 74.

35. Type of equipment used by the burglar Charlie Peace for smelting down gold and silver plate from his countless burglaries. Page 77.

36. A pamphlet concerning the escapades and burglaries of Charlie Peace who did more than any other criminal to popularise the art of burglary. Page 77.

37. Special ladders used by burglar Charles Peace. Page 78

38. A collection of dark lanterns used by Victorian burglars. Page 79.

39. A selection of burglars' tools, originally kept in the Black Museum. Photo from Griffith's Vol 2 of 'Mysteries of Police and Crime.' Page 80.

40. Phosphorous in a jar, used to illuminate areas of a property by burglars, p.81.

41. Selection of jemmies used by burglars. Page 82.

42 A ratchet and wedge, used by burglars to gain swift entance to properties. Page 84.

43. Cabmen were often thought to be in league with burglars. Page 85.

44. Set of burglars' pick lock tools. Page 86.

45 Small piece of button, left at a crime scene proved the identity of the murderer. Page 87.

46. Weapons salvaged from the Muaswell Hill and Hoxton burglaries. Page 89.

47. Victorian life preservers. Courtesy of The London Museum. Page 90.

48. A Billycock Hat found at a crime scene of the type worn by the commissionaire in BLUE. Page 91.

49. Charles Peace's essential burglary kit, Page 93.

50. Peace's smelting pot, Page 93.

51. Peace escapes custody Page 98.

52. The hanging of Charles Peace. From the chapbook published in the year of his death, 1879. Author's collection. Page 98.

53. The murder of General Trepoff by a Russian revolutionary. From Griffiths, vol 3. Page 99.

54. Novel by Joseph Conrad called 'The Secret Agent.' which helped spread public fear of the Russian revolutionaries. First edition. Author's collection, Page 104.

55. A drawing by an unknown artist, illustrating a French bomb outrage story by the French writer Eugene Moret in 'The Strand Magazine'. Page 104.

56. Diagram showing the whereabouts of Yoxley Old Place in Strood, in Kent. Page 106.

57. The High Street in Strood, Kent, near Rochester, the nearest town at which Holmes and Watson would have arrived to investigate the murder at Yoxley Old Place; from a rare postcard of 1886 in the author's collection, Page 106.

58. The Intrepid Colonel Majende, the Scotland Yard detective who undertook the quest to investigate the Fenian bombings in the late 1880s. In 'The Strand Magazine.' Page 108.

59. The Salisbury Infernal Machine, a large bomb used by Irish revolutionaries. Page 109.

60. Clockwork bomb mechanism devised by the Fenians. Page 111.

61. Scotland Yard, blown up by the Fenians. Page 112.

62. Photograph of Jean Leckie shown here on her wedding day. She represented to Conan Doyle the ideal of a desirable woman, exhibiting both intelligence and a simmering sexuality. Photograph: courtesy of Portsmouth Central Library, page 122.

63. A nightmarish illustration of the locked room tale by Edgar Allan Poe, 'The Murders in the Rue Morgue', drawn here by the artist Aubrey Beardsley in an edition of the Poe stories, printed in 1894. Page 136.

64. Handwriting example of a letter sent to the police by Jack the Ripper in 1888. Source: Griffiths. Page 233.

64. Drawing by Douglas Walters showing Sherlock Holmes examining footsteps, published in the book, 'Canadian Holmes: The first 25 years,' published by The Bootmakers of Toronto. Page 232.

65. Another fine example from Douglas Walters, here showing Sherlock Holmes applying theatrical makeup to his face. Source as above. Page 235.

66. The arrest of the murderer Wainwright who murdered his girlfriend and sealed her body parts into wooden barrels which he then placed in a Hansom Cab and which then left a trail of blood. Here he is shown demonstrating to police that was he was entirely innocent. Griffiths, Volume two. Page 239.

67. Professor Moriarty, seen here in the grip of his more powerful adversary, Sherlock Holmes as they fight at the edge of the awesome precipice of The Reichenbach Falls in Switzerland. Drawing by Sidney Paget from 'The Strand Magazine' publication of 'The Adventure of The Final Problem.' Page 242.

68. Frank Wiles illustration from 'The Valley of Fear', showing Holmes studying a cryptogram. Page 248.

NOTE RELATING TO ILLUSTRATION NO. 27, SHOWING A PRECISION-MADE HAND LENS.

The high precision magnifying lens from 1888, (the term 'magnifying glass', later to become the term still favoured, even today, by many toy manufacturers), was used rarely by Victorians, and certainly never once by Holmes, Watson, or their Scotland Yard associates. Such instruments, like this shown above, constructed of precision ground glass; mounted within in a hefty brass ferrule with an oak handle, and weighing about two lbs., was regarded as an essential piece of forensic equipment by a detective at a crime scene investigation, where it was employed in the detailed observation and recording of trace and contact elements.

We know that Sherlock Holmes possessed at least two of them, the second probably being smaller and pocket-sized. This elegant lens, hand-made in Norfolk, bears a striking resemblance to the lens in the Sherlock Holmes pub in Craven Street, London, and is similar to one displayed in The Sherlock Holmes Museum in Baker Street.

It is a family heirloom made by my wife Debbie's grandfather, Mr. Henry Billing. Mr Billing was a joiner by trade, but during the Holmes period, acted as the village blacksmith in Flitcham, a small village adjacent to the Royal Estate at Sandringham, Norfolk, where, he was required often to repair conveyances used by the Royal Family, When engaged on these repairs, he would frequently observe the comings and goings of Edward, the Prince of Wales, who would arrive by train each Christmas with a large retinue of expensively adorned, female visitors. (See index for other references to Edward, elsewhere in this book.). Photo, c. of D.J. Jones.

INDEX TO VOLUME THREE OF
'THE CRIMINAL WORLD OF SHERLOCK HOLMES'

www.ingramcontent.com/pod-product-compliance
Lightning Source LLC
Chambersburg PA
CBHW082358030726
47505CB00018B/2103